Praise for *The White Family*

'Tackles an unspeakable subject with quiet courage. Beautifully written, it tells the complex story of racism from the point of view of the perpetrators. The result is an astonishing examination of the changes, complexities and difficulties at the heart of a multi-ethnic suburban community.'
Big Issue

'*The White Family* is intensely touching, full of ironies, situational and verbal, [and] brilliantly connected with contemporary society.'
Financial Times

'*The White Family* is an audacious, groundbreaking condition-of-England novel [which] tilts expertly at a middle class fallacy that racism is something "out there", in the football terraces or the sink estates . . . Finely judged and compulsively readable.'
The Guardian

'A transcendent work, splitting open a family to bare the rough edges of prejudice, self-righteousness and petulant self-justification that we all recognise. The words of James Baldwin resonate throughout: "Books taught me that the things that tormented me the most were the things that connected me to everyone who was alive and who had ever been alive."'
Daily Telegraph

'Picking up where Toni Morrison leaves off, Gee . . . reminds us that racism not only devastates the lives of its victims, but also those of its perpetrators. Like Eugene O'Neill, Maggie Gee moves skilfully between compassion and disgust.'
TLS

'An unashamedly contemporary novel – a millennium novel – that embraces the ideological and emotional chaos of our times. It shows [Gee's] unusual ability to take contr‍‍‍‍‍‍ of a complex, many-layered narrative and make it as readable an‍‍‍‍‍‍ soap. A triumph of hope over desp‍‍‍‍

Also by the Author

MAGGIE GEE

THE WHITE FAMILY

Saqi Books

ACKNOWLEDGEMENTS

Thank you to those who made this book possible: above all, to Moris and Nina Farhi; to Mai Ghoussoub, André Gaspard, Hanna Sakyi, Barbara Goodwin and Nick Rankin.

Thank you to those who made it better: my editor Christine Casley, Mike Phillips, Colin Grant, Robert Taylor, Wesley Kerr, Michael Miller, Prabirranjan Ray, Norman Mitchell, Rita Patel, Roy Kerridge for lyrics from his beautiful book *The Storm is Passing Over: A Look at Black Churches in Britain* (Thames and Hudson), J R Shah, David Godwin and Sarah al-Hamad.

Thank you also to John Coldstream, Mark LeFanu, Peter Kemp and Jonathan Lloyd for their kindness. Thank you to Jonathan Warner who commissioned this book in another life, and did so much for so many writers. Lastly, thank you to Rosa for making me laugh; and to our local park keeper, whose devotion to duty and love of the park were an inspiration, though his character and personal life bear no resemblance to those of my own fictional park keeper.

None of the material in this book is based on real people, living or dead.

Cover photograph: *Closing*, by Robert Taylor (detail)

British Library Cataloguing-in-Publication Data
A catalogue record for this book is available from the
British Library

ISBN 0 86356 140 3

First published 2002 by Saqi Books
This edition published 2002

Saqi Books
26 Westbourne Grove
London W2 5RH
www.saqibooks.com

To Vic and Aileen

and for Hanna

THE BEGINNING

1 · Thomas

Albion Park on a fierce spring morning. A mad March day of ice and fire. Thomas's feet beat a tattoo on the path. Every hair, every bristle on his chin stands on end. He is a small star-ship of blazing neurons –

He is a librarian, on his way to work, half-blind with sun and cold and memory. He used to come here with Darren after school (were they six, or seven, when they first escaped their mums?) And Darren's dad, Alfred, was the Park Keeper –

Was, and still is. Still at his post. Something epic about it; nearly fifty years of service . . . Alfred White, who holds the fort.

Thomas hears raised voices, a little way away.

And glimpses Alfred beyond a row of plane trees, a small brisk figure in a military greatcoat. His familiar flat cap with its thin fringe of white hair, in the middle distance by the prize flower-beds. It's the only bit of grass where people aren't allowed to walk; one of Alfred's main jobs is shooing them off it.

Thomas sees that the woman he is talking to is black. There are two young children; she holds one by the arm.

'It's my job, lady. I'm doing my job –' The voice of authority, from Thomas's childhood.

"Ang on a minute. I'm tryin' to tell you –'

'Can you move off the grass, madam. I'm asking you nicely –'

'People like you don't never listen!'

'You don't have to shout, miss.'

'Look, I weren't shoutin' –'

'Next thing is, you'll be all over the tulips.'

Now the little girl begins to cry, a high-pitched sound that seems to come from a childish realm of pain and loss quite unconnected to the grown-ups' quarrel. She tries to yank her arm away. 'Mum, Mum, Mum, I can see it!'

'Shut it, Carly, I'm talkin' to the man!'

'Mum, Mum, I want to –'

'SHUT IT!'

From the woman's other side, Alfred presses his advantage. 'If everyone walked here, there'd be no grass left –'

Harried by both of them, she suddenly cracks. 'Fuck off! I'm tellin' you, you're OUT OF ORDER!'

A tall black man comes hurrying across, carrying a purple basket-ball, and stands close to Alfred, looming over him. He looks at least a foot taller than Alfred, and two feet wider across the shoulders. (Was he actually threatening? Thomas wondered later. Could you say he was threatening? No, just tall. And black, of course, that was part of it.)

'What's the problem?' the man asks, fairly politely.

'No ball-games here, sir, I'm afraid.'

'We're not playin' no ball-game. Why's Carly cryin?' he demands of his wife, who has subsided a little.

'He upset her, didn't he.' She indicates Alfred. 'She went and lost Dwayne's new plane, innit. So she gets it in her head that it's in the flower-bed.'

'So what's up with you man?' the father asks, frowning down on Alfred. 'What's your problem?'

The girl wails louder. Dwayne pokes her in the ear.

Alfred looks pale and old beside them. 'No mention was made of any lost plane,' he says, uncertainly, peering round him.

'This Park belongs to everyone,' the black man informs him.

'That's just it!' Now Alfred perks up. 'Same rules for everyone, as well. I'm just asking you lot to get off the grass.' He wags his finger vigorously.

The woman's face changes. Is it rage, or glee? '"You lot"!' she shrieks. 'That's racist, innit!'

A pause. The two men avoid each other's eyes. The word lies between them like an unexploded bomb. 'I've been doing this job for fifty years,' Alfred begins, but the rest is lost.

'JOHNNY!' she screams. 'Call the police on this bastard! Use your mobile! I'm tellin' you!'

But Johnny snickers, and turns away. 'You're windin' me up,' he says to his wife. 'Come on . . . An' leave it out,' he snaps at his children. 'Don't whine, Carly, do you hear me?' But he pauses a moment, staring back at Alfred, saying something with his eyes: this is our Park too.

Thomas feels it is time to announce his presence. 'Hi Alfred,' he calls, so Alfred knows he is there. For a moment the old man just stares at him, then raises his hand in a lame half-wave. He manages a smile, but his face is very red.

'The man is *ignorant*,' the black woman announces, beckoning her children in a queenly fashion. When the boy doesn't stir, she yells at him 'Dwayne! Get over here! Move it!' Cowed, Dwayne does as he is told.

They sweep away, a good-looking family, smartly dressed, young, glossy. The mother has righteous arms around her kids, who are still resisting, and pointing at the flower-bed.

'You see how it is?' Alfred asks, out of breath. There are bubbles of spit at the corner of his lips. 'Can't bloody win, whatever I do. And the language . . . The women are worse than the blokes. They'd turn the Park back into a jungle. There are notices. These people can't read.'

Now they are gone, he feels safe to say it. Thomas starts to protest, but nothing comes out. It's just a generation thing, he tells himself. The polite silence hasn't fallen, for them. 'Are you all right, Alfred? You don't look well.'

'Calling the police on me. Bloody cheek. They'd laugh in their faces, down at the station. I've got good mates there. Known me for years.' Alfred pauses, still breathing hard, and his pale blue eyes focus shrewdly on Thomas. 'I'm not against them, you know. Don't get me wrong –'

'I didn't think you were,' Thomas lies, feebly. This is a subject that cannot be spoken. He veers away. 'Have you heard from Darren?'

'They go on the grass. Always doing it. English people know not to go on the grass –'

'Alfred, shouldn't you sit down for a moment?' There is something very wrong about Alfred's pupils.

'I'm not a man of leisure, like you,' Alfred says. 'Things to do. Jobs on my list. Not least the toilets. It never stops.'

'You're upset.' Which is the wrong thing to say.

'I never let that lot get to me.'

'I'm not sure they intended –' Thomas tries.

But Alfred is off, with a bony smile, launching himself against the wind like a fighter. 'Bye, lad. Take care now.'

'See you, Alfred.'

Thomas watches him go, lickety-split, a white-haired soldier off at the double. Glancing back for an instant, his eye is held by a cross of scrap paper flickering on the red swathe of tulips ten metres away. As he stares, the cross becomes a child's toy plane, crazily poised on a crimson runway. He thinks of going to pick it up; rushing after the family, making everything right –

But as he turns to look for them, he sees Alfred collapse, fifty metres away, his cap coming off as he wheels and crumples, falling heavily backwards in his army greatcoat as if he has been shot in battle.

And Thomas begins to run, in slow motion, trying to run though his legs have stalled, to the spot where the Park Keeper lies felled, yelling 'Alfred, I'm coming . . .'

Darren's dad.

Alfred White, the Park Keeper.

2 · May

It's different in winter. Days are shorter. Alfred's locked up by half past four. So he's home in the evenings. We sit for hours. And I get used to him being there. Then when the days get longer, he's gone. Out all hours. And I'm alone. Never really alone, though. I know he'll be home. But spring is coming . . . spring is coming.

We're like the seasons, we ebb and flow. You take it for granted, after forty-odd years. His key turning. The voice saying 'May?' His familiar voice, which will always come, no matter how late, always the same.

I'm proud of him. The job he does. A big job for a little man. Looking after the Park. It's the best thing we've got. In summer I almost start to hate it, because I don't like his being out till ten, but I know the Park matters more than us.

It's something we can all share, isn't it? The place people go to be together. I think it's the heart of Hillesden, the Park. As London gets dirtier, and more frightening.

We don't talk a lot. But of course, I do love him.

And there he is. He forgot his sandwiches. I've kept them for him, and his tea in the thermos. The clink of the gate, then his feet on the path . . . Heavier than usual.

Why is he ringing?

Silly old thing, he's forgotten his key. We're getting older, both of us . . .

May opens the door, to smile, to chide. But it's Thomas, not Alfred. Black shapes behind him. A short policeman in a giant helmet. She furrows her brow, turning back to Thomas . . .

On his face, the dark, the cold.

THE HOSPITAL

3 · May

May read, as usual, before she went out.

First she got herself completely ready. Alfred's pyjamas, freshly laundered, neatly folded in a plastic bag inside another, larger plastic bag that held today's *Daily Mirror* and a quarter of extra strong mints, just in case he should be feeling a bit better, just in case he should fancy something. It was comforting, getting the bag together. It meant she could still look after Alfred, though she also experienced the usual sense of boredom; women spent their lives looking after men. And even that tiny skin-tag of irritation was comforting, because entirely familiar. The house was so much colder since he had gone.

She was completely ready, hat on, coat fastened, twenty minutes too early to leave for the hospital, even if she walked slowly, even if she dawdled, not that she would dawdle on a day like this, even if she stepped into the Park to have a quick look at the café and the flower-beds so she could report to Alfred later. Each day she had half-meant to do it; each day she had found herself unable to, because she couldn't bear to see the Park without Alfred. Without the hope of seeing Alfred . . .

Without the hope of seeing Alfred come hurrying down one of the distant paths, trim, narrow-shouldered in his old army greatcoat and the new check cap she had bought him for Christmas, eyes turned away from where he was going to follow the deeds of some child or dog. Then she might hear him shout or whistle to recall the wrong-doer to order. Not today. That piercing whistle. The Park Keeper's whistle which had sometimes pained her like the sound of chalk pulled the wrong way across a blackboard now seemed in its absence an arrow of light, a clear white line shooting out across the darkness.

Twenty minutes early. So she sat in her chair as she had done every day this week and began to read, clumsy in her coat, catching its heavy woollen sleeves on the pages.

And again she noticed a difference. It was normally evening time when she read and Alfred would be there, rustling his newspaper or clicking the cards as he laid out a game of patience, and he always said 'What are you reading?' in a grumpy, almost affronted way, as if he had failed to entertain her, as if she was rejecting him, and she always made herself answer cheerfully, she always ignored his tone of voice and said 'Auden, dear,' or 'Catherine Cookson, dear', though he had been doing it for nearly half a century. But now he had stopped, May found she missed it.

'Tennyson, dear,' she whispered in the silence, slipping inside the entirely familiar Victorian patterns in their long cool scrolls, the beloved rhythms of her other Alfred:

> He watches from his mountain walls,
> And like a thunderbolt he falls.

But she couldn't concentrate; *Alfred, Alfred.*

It was still too early, but she picked up her bag, checked its contents and the angle of her hat (for she wanted him to be proud of her; appearances mattered a lot to Alfred), slipped in her book as an afterthought although she knew she'd have no chance to read it, and let herself out into the chill March wind.

She always liked to have a book in her bag. In case she got stuck. In case she got lost. Or did she feel lost without her books? There wasn't any point, but she liked to have one with her, a gentle weight nudging her shoulder, keeping her company through the wind, making her more solid, more substantial, less likely to be blown away, less alone. More – a person.

Perhaps it was a little piece of the past, since her books all seemed to belong to the past, a far distant past when she was thin and romantic and in love with – what had she been in love with? Life, which seemed to mean happiness then, a word for the future, not the past. Not 'Life gets you down,' or 'That's life, I'm afraid,' but life, hope, poetry . . .

The harsh wind battered her hands and face, pummelling her ears with great noisy blows, and she felt she would never get in through the high red gate-posts of the hospital with their ugly array of cardboard notices, temporary things with clumsy writing . . . What was she but another piece of scrap, blown willy-nilly across the forecourt? Would the main entrance be closed again because of the endless building works? (They were building new bits all the time, but it never got finished, and the rest was falling down.) She tried to ask a nurse on her way home but the light was already beginning to fade and the wind blew hard between her teeth and turned her voice to a soundless whisper, so the woman passed by oblivious.

I don't exist. I no longer exist. When Alfred dies, I'll be nothing, nothing . . . I couldn't even read, today. The words were there, but they didn't help.

I love them still . . . *idyll*, *ambergris* . . . but maybe they're no more solid than us. Dirk only reads his computer magazines, Darren never liked poetry, Shirley reads mostly catalogues, so who'll have my books, after I'm gone?

> Twilight and evening bell,
> And after that the dark!
> And may there be no sadness of farewell,
> When I embark . . .

Onward, onward. Over the threshold. Into the frightening new place which was suddenly part of their life together . . .

Part of their new life apart. A place where he must go alone, a place where she could only visit.

But she shouldn't be frightened of this place. It must be one of the last good places. May told herself, this is here for us. We fought the last war for places like this. Hospitals and parks and schools. Not concentration camps, like the other lot had.

A hospital was a place to share. Where all could come in their hour of trouble. The light was harsh, but it shone for all. (Some of the bulbs were dead, she had noticed. Broken glass was replaced with hardboard.)

She stood for a moment, blinking, breathing.

She would get there first, because she loved him. Proud always to be the first. She stood by herself in the fluorescent sweep of the hospital foyer, taking off her hat, patting her hair, slipping off her old coat to show the blue dress, for blue was always his favourite colour . . . She saw herself reflected in the glass of the doors, astonishingly tiny, a little old lady, *but I'm not old, nor particularly small.*

Soon other figures would come out of the shadows, out of the dark with their bags and bundles, their flowers and sighs and shruggings-off of coats and scarves and hats and gloves. Nervous smiles, frowns, whispers, biting their lips, blind in the light. Newcomers. Latecomers.

May set off briskly, ahead of them.

She walked down the ward. It was becoming familiar. She no longer always took the wrong turning after passing the Hospital Volunteers' Shop. She no longer peered anxiously across into the nurses' room which guarded the ward, asking for permission and reassurance. The black sister gave her a smile (were there two of them? Did she muddle them up?) They saw she was not a time-waster; they had helped with the problem of Alfred's boots. They knew her now. She was almost a regular. Before she drew level with their open door she had already located the precise spot far down the long bright fallen ladder of the ward where

Alfred would be, if he hadn't died. And there he was: he had not died. A stern face propped on an enormous pillow, staring straight ahead of him, a king on a coin.

A rush of relief; he would always be there. Like the head on a sixpence, never wearing out . . . but growing smaller, somehow, as the world grew larger. A few more steps, and she saw he was asleep, upright as ever in his good blue pyjamas but his eyes closed, his mouth slightly open. She hoped he hadn't snored; Alfred was too proud to snore in front of other people. She would never let him, if she were with him. But they had been parted, after a lifetime.

I suppose that pride won't help us, now.

– How did my Alfred come to be here? Alfred of all people, who never was in hospital, Alfred who never took a day off work, Alfred White who was never ill.

But we all come here. I shall come here.

She shrugged the voice away, impatient.

The ward was getting ready for visiting time, combings of hair, straightenings of dressing-gowns, eyes turned longingly towards the entrance where faces from the other world might appear, younger, healthier, bearing gifts. Faces that once seemed ordinary, now brightly coloured, glowing, miraculous.

Why was he still sleeping? There was so much to do. In her bag there were documents for him to sign. Only now did she realise how foolish she had been, letting everything be in Alfred's name, the house, the pension book, the bank account.

Darren had got angry, on the phone. He rang so rarely, and it was gone eleven, the middle of the night, it seemed to May, and she was so drowsy and confused that she'd spilled out all her worries, and cried. And he'd made her feel a fool. 'What do you mean, you can't draw any money? You mean Dad always got the money? How could you be so bloody daft . . .?'

– But then, she had never really pleased her sons. Even the names she chose annoyed them. Darren and Dirk . . . They were film-star names that Alfred was unsure about, but he said 'That's your department, May. Women know better than men about names.' Their daughter was Shirley, after Shirley Temple. Then Dirk and Darren. She had done her best, though Dirk, the youngest, always complained. May had loved Dirk Bogarde with swooning intensity; his sideways smile, his dark deer's eyes, the narrow elegance of his body, and though he had mysteriously changed, become old and angry and homosexual, she still felt she had let him down, giving his name to someone who despised it.

Dirk was sulky, but Darren was rude. ' . . . You've never even had a banker's card? I can't believe it, it's unbelievable . . .' He shouldn't have talked to her like that. She had heard him be sharp with his wives and children – worse than sharp, worse than his father – but he had no right to be sharp with his mother. Why couldn't he be nice, like Thomas? Thomas was Darren's oldest friend, and he had always been kind to her. Thomas didn't make her feel old and stupid. (Yet he was quite successful too. As she'd once told her son, when he was rude about Thomas, Thomas was a real writer. And Darren had gone silent. She knew it hurt him.)

Of course Darren lived in a different world, where women had armfuls of credit cards, and wrote all the rules to suit themselves . . . . Whereas with Alfred, everything had been laid down. Rules that were lost in the mists of time, walls he built and cemented in till that red-brick labyrinth became her life.

Only now nothing seemed quite safe any more. The walls were shifting. The sea was rising.

May stared at the chart at the foot of his bed. The marks were mean and small, as usual, and she squinted at them, but they told her nothing.

There were languages you weren't meant to read. Medical people had their secret language. May's mother had felt that about all books, that they were meant for other people, better people, richer people with drawling voices, the ladies who sometimes peered in through the window of her father's workshop where he sat mending shoes, only coming in doubtfully, little mouths pursed, holding their skirts as if they might get dirty. Her father read books, history, politics, not books for women, he told her impatiently, books for men, serious books. But May knew different; both parents were wrong.

Because books were meant for everyone.

Of course there were writers she couldn't understand. Some she could like without understanding, but some she was affronted by because she felt they didn't want her to understand. If so, she could do without them. There were plenty of writers who spoke her thoughts.

Did doctors want people to understand? Probably not. It was probably less trouble. That way, they didn't have to get into arguments. But it didn't matter, she told herself. They were professionals. She trusted them. They were a bit like priests, in their clean white coats, and the nurses were like women tending a temple . . . She wished she could pray. She wasn't really religious, but Alfred looked so little, so lonely.

There must be a prayer. Shirley would know it. May found herself praying, in a kind of dream, praying to the past, or the future, or the doctors, and the words came slowly, refused to come . . .

Do what you like to him, but get him out . . . Send him back to me. He wants to be out . . . he needs to be outside, in the light. Please, if there's Anyone . . . or Anything . . . we've done our best . . . You know we tried . . . family was everything to us . . . There's the kids to think about . . . especially Dirk . . . he's no more than a baby . . . he needs his dad . . . Do what You like to him, but send him home.

4 · Dirk

I'll die before I get to the hospital, thought Dirk. Die of a fucking heart attack. They're killing me. All of them. Fucking killing me.

He rested his head against the window of the bus, leaning away from the fat cow in a sari who was taking up three-quarters of the seat. The thud of the engine beat a sickening rhythm through the bones of his head, so he jerked upright again. No fucking rest for the fucking weary.

His heart was full of furious dread. Dad would be lying there, looking . . . different. Horribly different. Everything changed. And Mum by his side, little, miserable, that fluttery, stupid, awful look she had had since Dad had his fall or whatever. She'd stopped cooking, hadn't she? She was never much cop at it but last night she'd done something disgusting with tuna and the rice was burnt black like mouse droppings. As if Dirk wasn't busy all day and didn't need his tea when he got home . . . Now his parents had to go and let him down.

And the bus had kept him waiting for half an hour. Three bloody buses went sailing past while he was ringing up the till in the shop. Then as soon as he got out to the bus-stop, sod all. It was freezing cold, with a bitter wind. So then he'd gone in the pub for a drink. First you felt warmer. Then colder than ever. And he had to go back to the bus-stop and shiver. He could have walked but his trainers hurt him, pressing on his corns, savage, spiteful. They were cheap, weren't they. Because he was poor. Going by bus was for poor people too.

Which was why they fucking mucked you around when you tried to pay with a five pound note (it wasn't like a twenty, or even a ten).

The driver had looked at Dirk as if he was rubbish. 'What's this?' he had said. 'I don't want this. Haven't you read the notices? Can you read? It says "Tender exact money please." In plain English.'

And so on and so on, blah blah blah, while Dirk tore his pockets searching for change, and there wasn't any, not even ten pee, and the whole bus was glaring and muttering as if it was Dirk's fault the driver was a tosser.

They're all in it together, of course. Look around this bus and you can see it. Ninety per cent coloureds. Well, fifty, at least. And the driver's coloured, so they're on his side. And he has the fucking cheek to talk about English. As if they owned it. Our speech. Our language. (*Tender exact money* . . . that's not proper English. Does a normal bloke use a word like 'tender'?)

The trouble is, they do own most things. They've taken over the buses, and the trains. And the bloody streets. You can't get away from them.

Not down our pub, mind. They know what's good for them.

The woman next to Dirk was very old and very fat, perched awkwardly upon the seat. A man's overcoat half-covered her sari. Indian people smelled of funny food. As the bus rounded a corner, she suddenly flung out one great fat arm upon Dirk's lap. 'Do you mind?' he asked her, stiff, outraged, but he didn't want to touch the arm to move it away. She smiled and nodded, not understanding, muttering some mumbo-jumbo at him. He turned away, furious, disgusted, but there was no way to escape her body, brown, gigantic, pressing upon him, old people, he hated them, and now his dad was suddenly old.

He felt beneath his jacket for the thing he kept there that always comforted him, always helped him. His fingers found it, pressed it –

pressed – pressed until there was no more blood in his fingers, pressed until all the life was gone, and when the pressure reached the point of pain he released it again, and breathed a bit easier, for he could simply cut them up, if he had to, slice off their limbs, their eyes, their hair . . .

Women and coloureds. They were everywhere.

He'd never liked women. Except his sister, till she went funny, till she went mad. And now he hated her worse than the others. Because Shirley had once been something of his own, she used to make him feel he was a bit special, but then she'd turned against her own flesh and blood.

He hated his family now. Except Dad.

Flesh and blood. It was meat. It was nothing.

5 · Thomas

Thomas was back in his high flat, writing. Or staring at the manuscript he should be writing. He was trying to write about the Death of Meaning, but would it mean anything to anyone else? He had a page by Mikhail Epstein open in front of him, which last week had seemed to explain the world. 'Post-postmodernism witnesses the re-birth of utopia after its own death . . .'

He scratched his head. Was he growing more stupid? Less modern, perhaps? Less post-post-modern? Thomas's mind began to drift.

Sex snapped on to it, like a magnet.

Could he hear Melissa above his head? Four o'clock. She would still be in school. Mornings and evenings were the hopeful times when he might hear her sweet feet padding on his ceiling.

Melissa. The first Melissa I've known. The name is cat-like and swift, like her. Honey-tongued, delicate, purring, golden . . .

Very groomed, was Melissa, in the early mornings, when he chanced to meet her on the stairs. Stumbling back upwards with his milk and his *Guardian* and his pyjamas under his clothes, he sometimes heard her come tip-tipping downwards in her brisk black booties with their sexy eyelets –

Six slick eyelets, slim pale ankles. She smelled of cinnamon, apples, musk, and soap and cornflakes and cleanliness. He probably smelled of old beer and bad breath but she still favoured him with her celestial smile, always slightly surprised, as if she thought she was on the moon and had just discovered that someone else lived there. 'Oh, hello. You're up early.' As if she wasn't always up early. Her job was so hard he shuddered to think of it, teaching hordes of savage young children. How could they ever appreciate her?

I could protect her. I could look after her . . .

Actually of course he had little to offer. A bad track record with relationships, a three-bed flat in a seedy part of London, a day job as senior librarian, one novel, written eight years ago (influenced by Proust and Woolf and relativity theory, though no one noticed – *The Wave, the Bridge and the Garden*, a title he now agreed was too long), a middling income he overspent, a guilty slither of credit cards, a second-hand car, a gift with words, his amazing penis, currently unused, needing tenderness, loving, licking . . .

Melissa does like me. It isn't an illusion.

But her eyes were bright, unkindly young, seeming to pierce beneath his skin.

Am I any good? Is there any point to me? What shall I leave behind on this planet?

Books. Words. The English language. I try to serve it. (And other languages. We have to now. Three hundred-odd languages are spoken in London, and people expect us to have books in all of them. Which is fair enough . . . Or maybe too fair. Sometimes I feel it's all gone too far. But I'm not allowed to think things like that. Librarians are servants of the people.)

He was writing his second book, very slowly. He'd been writing it for five years, to be honest. *Postmodernism and the Death of Meaning*.

Perhaps non-fiction was harder than fiction. He hadn't exactly got a publisher, though he'd sent a synopsis out to nine or ten editors, and one of them responded very encouragingly, wishing him the best of luck with finishing it, but begging him not to send the manuscript in case it should get lost in the post. Thomas still blushed with indignant shame, remembering what his ex-wife had said: 'It's twaddle, isn't it, you great lummox. Is this all you learned at university?' (Could she be right? Was he wasting his time?)

It was Thursday, the library's half-closing day, the day when his book should be sprinting along. Pull yourself together, he told himself. Forget about the book and set off for the hospital. See how Alfred's getting on.

It didn't seem believable that he was in hospital. Alfred who was never ill . . . A man of iron, Darren's Dad. They'd kept him in for a week already.

Thomas had decided to go and visit now, at once, in case Alfred died. Not that he often went round to the house (every few years? twice a decade?) – but he liked to know Alfred was *there*. Somewhere. The family he had always known. Safer than his. More stable than his parents, who had broken up, hopelessly, three years before they died, in different hospitals, still rowing by proxy. May wasn't a good cook, but she'd always made him welcome.

Darren must be forty, if I am. Darren White the Golden Boy. He's a journalist. Doing very nicely. The twenty-first century belongs to them, the e-mail he-men, the four-a.m.-faxers. Darren's just married for the third time. Must have found someone younger, glossier.

Will he come back, now his father's ill?

He always treated his family like dirt. Even his mum, who was nice to all of us hungry boys, piling in for tea after a football match. Alfred could be a bit sharp at times, but May was a darling, with her slow sweet smile and her dry sense of humour and passion for reading. I thought May did Darren's English homework, but I was probably wrong.

He had a knack with words. We both loved writing, in our different ways . . .

Melissa knows about Egyptian writing. She's teaching her kids to write hieroglyphics, though quite a few of them still can't write English. But Egypt's on the National Curriculum. (She had blue-green eyes, like Egyptian stones. Goldy brown hair, and small golden freckles . . .)

He told himself to forget about her. He had things to do, he had grown-up worries.

Thomas shaved too fast, cutting himself. He'd given up his beard twelve months ago. Melissa said it made him look younger. Yet he felt quite old as he emerged, blinking, into the thin late sun of wintry London.

As he walked, his thoughts returned to the library. Something faintly disturbing had happened that morning. A young black man had approached the Inquiry Desk. 'W. King', he had written his name. It was a face Thomas had seen before, he knew, though there were so many black students in the library. He sometimes thought the readers were mostly black, until he made himself count, one day. Funny how your mind played tricks on you. He guessed at the Christian name: Wesley? Wayne?

The young man's face was memorable, high-cheek-boned, fine-featured. His eyes were peculiarly intimate, golden-brown with a steady gaze. Often Thomas didn't meet people's eyes – it got very tiring, dealing with the public – but this young man demanded to be looked at. 'I left my name. I forgot some stuff. The man on the desk said he wasn't a librarian.' The punters always got puzzled by this, when the staff doing obviously librarian-like things, putting books on shelves, sitting at the Inquiry Desk, denied they were librarians – but it was the truth; most of them weren't, because it cost more to have qualified staff.

As the young man gazed into his eyes, Thomas remembered why his name was familiar. It was written on those fanatical notes Suneeta had found the day before. 'For the past four hundred years, the white man has been pumping his blood and genes into the blacks, has been diluting the blood and genes of the blacks . . . Many black homosexuals acquiesce in this racial death-wish.' Obsessionally neat italic writing. And then he began to feel vaguely threatened, for W. King, having reclaimed his notes, proceeded to eyeball Thomas closely as he read him a wish-list of titles, including two books by Eldridge Cleaver, and *One Hundred Years of Lynchings*. As the boy pronounced the titles, he had given a curious half-smile, half-laugh, at Thomas, and Thomas was aware of the boy's height, and youth, and his long strong fingers, playing with a pen.

Frowning, he walked on into the cold, taking the road that passed the Park.

W. King. He must live round here. He found himself peering at passing black youths with more than usual attention, then told himself to forget all about it. Libraries were always full of nutters. Parks, libraries . . . where else could they go?

It was hard to imagine the Park without Alfred. He was always in there, keeping an eye, guarding the flowers, bullying the kids when they tried to chase balls over the newly-bedded primulas, shouting at dogs, unblocking the drinking-fountain, forming little friendships with menopausal ladies, touching his cap to older ones, looking out for vandals in the toilets . . .

I don't want anything to happen to Alfred.

Instead of going straight to the hospital, Thomas turned in through the gates of the Park, magnificent tottering fairy-tale things, Victorian curlicues of iron-work.

Inside, the council asserted itself with a new municipal notice-board. No Littering, No Soiling, No Golfing: No Motor-cycles, No Camping, No Caravans. Were they afraid of Hell's Angels and gypsies?

This was England. If in doubt, keep them out.

6 · May

You weren't allowed to sit on the bed.

It was the only regulation she knew, from long ago when she gave birth to Dirk. May didn't like to break the rules, but the armchair was stuck right up by the bed-head where Alfred would get a crick in his neck from talking. She sank down on his bed with a sigh of content.

Rules and regulations. There were always rules. Their life at home was a mosaic of rules, mostly made by Alfred, but at least she knew them . . . Now they were on unfamiliar ground.

His body slipped very slightly askew as her weight changed the camber of the bed. He looked frail enough for a movement of the bedclothes to snuff him out, but she knew he was not. His bony strength would endure for ever. Come rain, come shine he had gone to the Park and done his day's work. Dawn till dusk. Summer and winter. Uncomplaining.

And many's the time he should have complained, for they let him down often enough. But we didn't complain. Not our generation.

Now Darren railed and complained for a living, writing pieces for the papers about 'injustice' and 'corruption'. The real world seemed to astonish her son, which May could never understand. Of course life was unjust. Of course people were corrupt. She had known that ever since she was six and her teacher made a pet of a school governor's daughter, although poor Elspeth was sour and plain. Of course the poor suffered and the rich flourished.

In any case, Darren was rich himself . . . but perhaps he wasn't really indignant; perhaps he pretended, to make his articles more exciting. In which case it hadn't worked, for her, for she no longer bothered to read the cuttings which arrived in bundles from all over the world. Alfred did, though. He read them, faithfully, and told Darren so in the curly-scrolled postscripts he added to her letters. His pride in their elder son was almost painful.

She gazed at his cheeks, which had sunken in as his jaw dropped with sleep, or was he getting thinner, was it happening already, the thing she dreaded? His beloved, angular, big-bridged nose on which he had perched his gold-rimmed glasses. Gently and fondly, she slipped them off, as she did at home when he dozed off in his chair. He couldn't have meant to fall asleep, it must have sneaked up on him unawares . . .

All of it catches us unawares. What if he never wrote letters again, sitting in his waistcoat underneath the bright light in the living-room after tea and his nap, reading aloud the few short phrases he had written and asking her anxiously 'Is that all right, May? Will it do?' 'Of course it's all right. Put what you want to.' Why did he need her reassurance so much? Men pretended to be strong, but really they were babies.

'Mrs Um . . .'

'Sorry?'

The nurse was freckled, pink, red-haired. 'You might be more comfortable in this chair.'

'I shouldn't be sitting on the bed.' May was mortified; told off by a teenager.

'Oh no, it doesn't matter, but the chairs are meant for visitors.' The girl dragged the great heavy thing across, with a long squeal of chair-legs on polished lino.

'Thank you.' May felt her deep, hot blush, but the nurse skipped away with the sweetest of smiles.

How did they keep it up, with all these to look after? How did they manage to be so kind?

The armchair was a disaster, though. Its brown plastic seat didn't yield at all, and its back was completely straight, tipping her chin forward, straining her neck. The unpadded wood hurt her elbows and wrists.

She felt a wave of longing for her normal comforts. Buttering the bread with the radio on, getting the tea-things out of the cupboard . . . But home wasn't home with just her and Dirk. The boy hadn't really talked to her for years.

All the same, she knew her youngest cared. He'd noticed last night that she wasn't eating. 'Mum. You haven't touched your food.'

'No . . . I suppose I'm not hungry.'

'I'm not surprised. This tuna is disgusting. I never liked tuna. Cat food, isn't it?'

May had been touched. He was a good boy. Alfred had always been hard on Dirk, but she saw his good side. She was his mother. Mothers were naturally soft on sons.

Whereas fathers weren't always easy on daughters. Of course Alfred had doted on Shirley as a baby. And she was a darling, sweet-natured and biddable, with yellow curls and a smiling mouth; people always smiled back at her in the street, and then approvingly up at May, as if she'd done well, to produce such a paragon. Shirley, in her way, was a good girl still, a girl in her thirties now, of course, a thing that May could scarcely believe.

But Alfred had had no time for his daughter ever since she'd taken up with Kojo.

'My own daughter. Taking up with a black man.'

'She's still your daughter,' May had said, after Shirley for the first time brought Kojo to visit and Alfred had sat at the head of the table ignoring them, mouth compressed. He had avoided shaking Kojo's hand, when they left, and shouted at their backs as they went down the passageway 'You watch out for yourself, Shirley. You be careful.' And

Kojo had turned round with that gleaming smile and said, 'It's all right, Mr White, I'll take care of her,' and Alfred had been gobsmacked, speechless. Then when he got inside, 'Cheeky black bastard! I know what he's after. Why can't she find herself a normal fellow?' May was a bit upset herself, but Kojo had such lovely manners. 'Well you can't really say he's not normal, can you?' she tried, but tentatively, not wanting to annoy. 'You bloody women,' he'd raged at her, Alfred who hardly ever swore. 'First performing monkey turns up in a suit, you're practically begging him to take our daughter –' 'No,' she had said. 'But I liked his suit. I always did like men in suits.' 'I've never been good enough for you, have I . . .?'

He went to their wedding because May said she would never forgive him if he didn't, and sat in a corner, he and Dirk, only talking to each other, morosely drunk. He never visited when Kojo got ill; she went alone even when Kojo was dying. Alfred only cheered up when he found out about the will, and she'd thought that then he would acknowledge at last that Kojo was responsible, a good provider, but he just said, 'Well that explains it, doesn't it. That's why Shirley married him.' And he'd softened to his daughter, briefly. And then she had taken up with Elroy, and May knew Shirley would never be forgiven.

But I'm her mother, and there's nothing to forgive. I've read James Baldwin, and Martin Luther King . . .

I loved Kojo. And I like Elroy. They're not so different, when you get to know them. I don't care what colour people are, thought May, looking at the glorious red of some enormous daisy-like flowers on a bedside table far down the ward. Flown in from unimaginably far away. Some beautiful, amazing part of the world I never knew existed then, when I was young, when Alfred was courting. He would have felt embarrassed, bringing flowers.

Though he did have nice manners. Which she liked, in a man.

She had tried to teach her sons nice manners.

7 · Dirk

Dirk stared out of the window of the bus at the windows of the big houses by the Park, very nice houses owned by people with money, white people, nearly all of them, though a few Paki twockers had wormed their way in . . . One day he, Dirk, would make money.

He would raise himself. He would better himself. He would prove to his father that he had backbone. He would be . . . someone . . . a gentleman . . . like some of the officers were in the war, though Dad said most of them were donkeys . . . he would make his father proud of him. One day he would own a house like that. The sunset light on the window-panes winked back at him, encouraging him.

He would go far. Farther than the others. Then he could do something for the family. First he'd make Darren and Shirley look small. Then he'd be kind to them. Give 'em a leg-up. *Maybe* he would, if she changed her ways.

He would be . . . an international businessman. The net was the answer. He would do it that way. And buy a mansion for his father and mother. And they would be grateful. Fucking grateful. And Mum would have to be nice to him, not laughing at him because of his crewcut, not sneering at him because of his friends. Head in a book, what did she know? Did she notice anything about what was going on? Did she know that a battle was being fought, on the streets of London, Liverpool, et cetera? – Bristol. That was the other one. The other spot where they'd gone in force. According to *Spearhead*. (Dirk had never been to Bristol.)

One day he'd travel. He'd like to travel. To parts of the world where things were still all right. Not that there were so many of them left. South Africa had fallen. Had been sold out. It was a black day for whites, when they sold out. It used to be paradise. He'd read about it. He tried to imagine it. Fucking paradise. He closed his eyes. Lions, tigers. Sort of pink blossoms, lots of them. Boogie-something. Boogie blossoms. And – swimming pools. And strong white men. Muscular. Toned. Working out in the sunlight. Short haircuts and – brick-hard buttocks. Press-ups flipping over into sit-ups, and fuck, they all had enormous hard-ons, and most of the men round the pool were black . . .

He jerked awake in a sudden panic to find he had been carried past his stop, tried to get up before the bus moved again, and was blocked by the old woman beside him, gasping and moaning in her scarecrow get-up, muttering in some horrible lingo, wailing as if he had hurt her foot when he only trod on the side of it, and only because she was in his way – He shoved her, hard, and was out in the gangway, pushing his way to the front of the bus, and the driver must have heard him coming, he closed the doors and began to drive off.

'Oi!' shouted Dirk. 'I want to get off!'

'Next stop Hillesden Turn,' said the driver.

'OPEN THE DOORS! FUCKING LET ME OFF!'

The driver stopped the bus, with a hiss of the brakes. Dirk felt good about that. So they still obeyed orders. Then the driver got up, and Dirk saw with a start that he was eight feet tall. A fucking giant. A great woolly-haired coloured bloke eight feet tall. And there were all the others on the bus to help him. Dirk wasn't a coward, but the odds were hopeless.

The driver got Dirk by the sleeve of his jean jacket. 'You are bothering me,' he said, smiling. 'I say when this bus stops and when it doesn't.'

The doors swung open, Dirk fell out and skidded on his bum on the slimy pavement. It felt very cold; the damp soaked through.

Fuck

Fuck

Fucking coloureds

Dad always told us. Always warned us.

8 · Thomas

In dirty Hillesden, the Park seemed miraculous. Just past the notice-boards, life came back.

The sky poured in through the gap in the roof-tops. Thousands of miles of cloud and sunlight, tethered to the neat square mile of grass. Pale paths gently traced the contours of the small hillside and rounded the lake. There were only a few figures walking today, a mother with a baby, a mother with a child, a man in a tracksuit with a giant poodle, a teenager (a truant?) on rollerblades doing showy arabesques at the foot of the hill, and there by the aviary surely Alfred – wasn't that Alfred, back where he should be? – Thomas's spirits leapt up for a moment before he saw it was an older man, bending stiffly to peer at the birds inside.

You would never catch Alfred doing that. Thomas had bumped into him one day near the dark wood hut with its chicken-wire windows, in which some dishevelled looking, startlingly yellow foreign birds had just appeared. 'Aren't these wonderful?' Thomas had asked him, more for something to say than from real enthusiasm. 'Matter of opinion,' Alfred said. 'Lots of us think it's a mistake.' 'But you always had an aviary here.' 'Ah yes, but before, we had British birds. Normal birds. Birds that would be happy.' 'I can't remember what you had before.' 'Budgerigars. Pheasants. British birds.' 'Actually, I'm not sure that budgerigars are British.' And Alfred replied, quite patiently, 'Of course they're British. They've always been here. My mum and dad kept budgerigars. It's natural, having budgerigars. Whereas foreign birds – It's not going to suit them. First touch of frost, this lot'll be goners.'

Now Thomas went to see if Alfred had been right, but the birds were still there, perhaps more than before, shivering at the back of the wooden hut, their tail-feathers long saffron flashes of satin that flickered against the drab colours of the background. The old man was trying to talk to them. 'Pretty birds, pretty birds,' he said. 'Pretty boy, pretty boy,' but they ignored him. Inside his brown coat was tucked a mauve silk scarf, surprising, beautiful, feminine.

The flower-beds, so bright in summer, were drabber now, flowers-in-waiting, wallflowers, polyanthus, winter pansies, each species set in its separate bed, with a few fierce blazes of tulips and daffodils, straight as soldiers, guarding the path. Thomas walked up to the top of the hill. Reaching the crown, he saw the children's playground, raw reds and yellows, against the far fence, and next to it brown hills of leaf-mould dwarfing the figure of a stooped Asian woman loading something into a child's push-chair (loading compost . . . why was that?), then beyond the Park, the cemetery, stretching away like a petrified forest, acres of quiet white and cream, then behind it the gleaming ranks of roofs, tiling the earth to the smudged horizon, greying to nothing, becoming invisible, dimming away into a pall of fumes.

He drew a deep breath, and the sun came out, very low and golden, tinged with red, skimming across the rows of houses, the factory roofs, the city windows, gilding, illuminating, planting shadows, burnishing cars and panes of glass, giving depth and life to the distant city.

The wind knocked him, spun him round, and the Park was suddenly a thing of glory, radiant in the last of the sunshine, a green field lifted towards the sky, the black branches of the cherry-trees waving thick soft flurries of pale pink petals, the weeping willows whipping threaded beads of gold against the coming evening, the boy on rollerblades swooping like an angel, arms uplifted, down the hill, the poodle rocketing, mad with joy, after a lolloping yellow cocker-spaniel . . . All shall be well, a voice told Thomas. His flesh prickled with icy pleasure.

Albion Park. It was a hundred years old, built in the spate of philanthropy that heralded the end of the nineteenth century, when the local hospital was built, and the library, both of them by the same local builder, who had a deft hand with stone and red brick and a love of detail; pediments, cornices. The drinking-fountain was a marvel, a spired, four-sided, stone creation modelled like a miniature Gothic cathedral. It was the focal point to which all paths led. Not far away the Park Keeper's lodge was a solidly impressive Victorian pile, two-storey, detached, with fine large windows.

I wonder why Alfred never lived there? I'm sure he'd have jumped at it, given the chance. Sold off, probably. Some shoddy deal. In the same way they tried to sell off the Rise's branch libraries. But people wouldn't have it. The public said 'No'.

They'd sell the Park too, given the chance. Build it all over with shops and offices. Then none of us would be able to breathe.

Alfred had stood here most of his life. Or marched like the soldier he had once been, left-right, left-right, patrolling his fiefdom. Every so often he would pause for a second to gaze across the flower-beds at some offender.

Here he had stood, and here he fell. 'They get abusive when he catches them at it.' That was May, grey-lipped, as she sat and cried, though Thomas said the black family weren't to blame. 'You have no idea what he puts up with,' she insisted. At any rate, the row had done for Alfred. Thomas briefly saw him stretched flat on the ground. His cap had come off. It was horrible. Thin hanks of white hair flapping back from his bald patch . . . helpless, naked, pink with hurt life..

Thomas had come to the Park since he was a child. He put out his hand and touched the drinking-fountain, the rough pores of the weathered white stone. It had stood there through rain and frost and pollution and been ready every summer to give water to the kids, some of them too small to reach the basins unaided, clutching their lollies, balls, sweets, clinging to the arms of their brothers or sisters.

Thomas was glad to see a gardener stooping dutifully over the bed by the fountain, trowel glinting in the sun as he dug. *She* dug, he corrected himself; a middle-aged woman in a navy mack he had mistaken for overalls, digging the crescent-shaped bed which was already a riot of tulips and daffodils.

'Cold, isn't it?' he greeted her, passing close by, a semi-automatic courtesy, one human being acknowledging another, together in the struggle against dark and disorder.

She whirled round instantly, craned anxiously upwards. He saw she held a bulb in her trowel. It had already sprouted a tight pink bud and a trailing beard of root-hairs, black with earth. 'Sorry,' he said, 'did I startle you?' Three others lay on the path beside her. 'Are you just putting those in? Isn't it rather late?'

'Yes,' she said, in a strange, throttled voice. Her cheeks were netted with purple veins, but her eyes were vacant, large, frightened.

'I don't mean to criticize,' he said.

There was a silence. She stayed crouched, frozen. Thomas couldn't fathom how he had upset her.

'I'm just going to visit Alfred,' he said. 'The Park Keeper. Did you know he's ill?'

'Yes,' she said, and to his horror the tears began trickling down her cheeks. 'Don't tell him.' she sobbed, 'please don't tell him . . .'

And then he realized. She wasn't a gardener. She was just a woman stealing flowers. She was digging them up, not planting them. An oil-cloth bag was waiting to be loaded, an old woman's bag, a poor person's bag. And then he remembered the Asian woman, loading compost into her push-chair. They were all at it, with Alfred away.

'I won't tell him,' he muttered. 'But do you think – should you be doing that?' He left her kneeling there, as if praying.

Alfred, of course, would have sorted her out. He probably knew her, and her habits. He would have done it quietly, with no fuss. He might have taken her round to his shed at the back of the toilets for a cup of tea. Or perhaps he wouldn't; she seemed slightly barmy. But he would have known. This is his patch. Like he knew the drinkers and the meths addicts. But he isn't here, and there's no one to help her, or to protect her from herself.

The sun had slipped behind the crest of the hill, and the Park dipped slowly down towards night. Thomas sat on the bench, with his back to the pond where Asian wedding photos were taken in summer. He thought about Alfred as the light lessened, the wonderful afterglow of lemon-gold light pouring up from the horizon, drenching half the sky, imperceptibly thinning to early evening blue. Which is how it is with us, he thought. In the afterglow of the last century, when the money from the empire was used for public works . . . But the ideals are fading. And the cash is nearly gone.

A large white van hove in through the gates. What was it doing? Cars were banned from the Park. A stranger waved peremptorily from the window. 'Hoy there, you. Closing time.' 'All right,' said Thomas, slightly affronted. 'I didn't hear the whistle blow.' 'There wasn't a whistle,' said the man, in a take-it-or-leave-it way. 'So no-one's standing in for Alfred,' said Thomas, partly to let the man know he was a regular, a man to be trusted, with powerful friends.

'Alfred . . .? Oh yes,' the man muttered. 'No.'

'What if he can't come back for a bit?'

'What if he never comes back at all?' Thomas couldn't see the man's face in the gathering twilight, but his voice was almost mocking. 'Costs a lot of money, a full-time Park Keeper.'

Thomas said nothing. He felt cold dread.

'Best get on home,' the man shouted, officious, and the ugly van snouted off across the Park.

Thomas walked towards the gate. That was quick, he thought. It doesn't take long for things to disappear. I'll ring the council tomorrow and find out what's going on, I'll write a letter to the local paper –

Or I'll be too busy, and do nothing at all.

Besides, I'm over-reacting. Nothing will happen. Alfred's too popular around here.

The path snaked past the public toilets, with their faded sign, The Premises Are Under Police Surveillance. Bollocks they are, he thought. The only surveillance they got was from Alfred. As he passed, he caught a flicker of movement in the corner of his eye, and turned. A man in a leather jacket was standing in the shadows. Then he spotted another, with a brutal crewcut. The van had driven straight by without seeing them.

Up to no good, said a voice in his head. I think that those two were up to no good.

Nonsense, he thought, you're turning into your mother. That loo is probably used for cottaging. Nothing wrong with cottaging.

But Alfred would know. And know what to do. As he knew where the meths drinkers hid their bottles, behind which bushes in which flower-beds, so they could climb back in after closing time . . .

Thomas glanced at the big notice-board as he left the Park:'Open From 8 a.m. Till Dusk'.

He remembered vanished evenings in the Park in summer, when he'd been engaged to Jeanie, so long ago. There were a few perfect weeks of late, scented light, dizzy with roses and tobacco-flowers. Alfred would be there every single night, doing his rounds, checking the bushes, making sure the lovers didn't get out of hand and offend the old ladies walking their dachshunds.

He can never have got home till nearly eleven. And in summer, the Park gate opens at six. He's spent nine-tenths of his life in here.

Of course he will have to retire one day. He must be past retirement age. But I want someone to hold the fort. Alfred's a father figure for me.

(I wonder if he knows I once kissed his daughter? Gorgeous Shirley. Darren's sister.

Was it over ten years since Thomas had seen her?)

9 · May

'Mum –' said the voice. Quieter than usual. Chastened by the hospital.

And Shirley was there, big, florid, beautifully dressed, all whites and vanillas and an armful of lilies and a smart pale handbag and a goldy creamy enormous box of chocolates, and she smelled of something foreign, delicious.

'Don't get up. Is Dad all right?'

'Yes. I'll wake him –'

'Don't, if he's sleeping.'

'You smell good enough to eat.'

'I'm sorry about the lilies. Not *Dad*, really, are they? Selfridges.'

'Did you come all the way from Oxford Street?'

'Yes. I was shopping.' Shirley was always shopping. May thought, she should have a degree in shopping. 'They hadn't got anything more colourful. Pale colours are supposed to be smart.'

She had a purring voice. A bit like mine, thought May, only – richer. Sort of glossier. 'I like your flowers, dear,' she told her daughter, and she did, as well; so ivory-elegant. 'I love your flowers.' Because she wanted to be sure Shirley didn't confuse her thoughts with Alfred's. May had a brain, not that Alfred didn't, but he was sometimes too set in his ways to use it.

And Alfred hasn't behaved right to her.

'You look lovely, Shirley.' May touched her daughter's wrist where a little ribbon of bare skin showed, between the camel coat and her gold watch-bracelet. Plump and cool and very soft. 'You're a good girl. You always make an effort.' They stayed like that for a moment, close.

Then May saw Elroy, hovering, back in the shadows near the entrance of the ward.

'You haven't brought Elroy here!' She was half on her feet, staring accusingly at her daughter. 'Why has he come? Why did you bring him –?'

But Shirley's face was uncomprehending, staring at May as if she was crazy, and briefly May wanted to kill her daughter. Did she have to upset him now when he was dying? (*dying* – my God, what was she thinking of? Why did that word flash up and stab her? Of course he wasn't dying, she was going mad.)

And she was going mad. Shirley's face said it. May looked again at the tall figure in the shadows in the small pool of darkness where the ward began, and as she looked, Elroy's face dissolved into another's, someone heavier, sadder, older than Elroy, and he walked down the ward to another bed where a young black woman lay and stared into space beside that flaring crown of red flowers.

'It isn't Elroy,' Shirley snapped.

'I'm sorry, love, I was just thinking of your father –'

'You don't half put your foot in it.'

May pleaded mutely to be forgiven. Shirley was so big, so fleshy, so . . . peachy. She had been lucky; love, money . . . Despite the awful things that have happened, she looks like a cat that's had all the cream. Can't she forgive me for being old and stupid?

Shirley was tugging off her beautiful coat, pale camel wool with a big shawl collar. She folded it, lining outermost, and tucked it at May's feet, in the lee of the bed. She was a good girl still; clean, careful.

Shirley sank down gingerly on Alfred's bed. She was heavier than

May. (Should she tell Shirley not to sit on the bed? She didn't want to annoy her further.) The metal frame creaked, and the two women stared at Alfred anxiously.

'Is he going to wake up?'

'Well I hope so. I've got all kinds of forms and doings for him to sort out.'

'Why are we whispering then?' asked Shirley.

'I don't know,' said May. (They had always whispered, when the men were around. Trying not to disturb them. Not to upset them. Not to let them know what they were getting up to. But now they didn't have to whisper any more. It was too late for whispering. He hadn't time to sleep.)

'Alfred,' May whispered, then made an effort. 'Alfred,' louder. 'Alfred, wake up.'

Sleeping like that, he was unprotected, naked as a baby despite his blue pyjamas, the fragile bony bridge of his nose, so near the skin, such taut red skin, the strands of white hair lying neatly as always like hanks of bleached rope across his naked crown.

She loved him completely for making an effort. Alfred would never let her down. He was probably ready hours ago, hair combed, clean pyjamas, shipshape bedclothes . . .

'Your Dad is wonderful,' she said to her daughter, as Alfred stirred, and coughed. Her heart swelled with love; Alfred, alive. Still there for them. Husband, father.

'Hmm,' said Shirley, half-rising, then sitting again, nervous, as ever, of being in the wrong, in the wrong place (which she was, of course, and her father would certainly let her know it) with the wrong clothes and the wrong boyfriend.

'Why's Dad so wonderful all of a sudden?' she asked, and it came out louder than she meant.

May frowned at her. 'Well he's shaved,' she said. 'In his condition. All combed and shaved.'

'Oh yes,' said Shirley blankly. 'Good for him.'

When they least expected it, one of his eyes opened, surprising as the eye of a waking elephant, liquid and glistening in its helmet of leather, large, war-like, shot with blood.

'Not a rest-camp,' he said, indistinctly. 'Not a bloomin' rest-camp, is it?'

'Well there's a café if you want something,' gasped May, who had been getting deafer for years, on her feet in an instant, taking his hand. 'It's not exactly a restaurant, but it will do. Shirley'll go for you. She's young.'

Now he was fully awake, stretching up, irascible, grasping the aluminium frame of the bed, finding he couldn't do it squarely and turning away from May and Shirley to pull himself up from the right-hand side, clutching the metal with stiff red knuckles that whitened with the effort, panting, straining, and surely his hands were too thin, like claws, his giant beak like a wounded eagle –

> He clasps the crag with crooked hands
> Close to the sun in lonely lands . . .

'I said, it's not a rest-camp here,' he repeated, looking accusingly at the two women. 'My daughter doesn't seem to know that.'

'She's come all the way from the West End,' May rushed in, nervous, protective. 'She's brought you some chocolates from Selfridges.'

'Well,' he said, more forgivingly. 'All the same, she's got to get off the bed. These beds are meant for ill people.'

'She's come all this way,' May repeated, stubbornly. 'It's a long way. She's a good girl.'

His pale blue eyes, watery, sharp, the eyeballs caught in a net of red veins, veered briefly across to the neighbouring bed before he said, as if nothing had happened, 'Aren't you going to kiss your old father, then?'

Perhaps he sensed heads turning towards her from other, lonelier beds alongside, drawn to the full-blown, sheeny glamour of the daughter who was mysteriously, definitely his – a delicate version of his eyes, his mouth – though none of the rest of the family was like her. She bent towards him; waves of perfume.

She's squashing him, May thought, distressed. There was so much of her. Fleshy. Wealthy. They'll overwhelm us, these giant children. Growing larger as we grow smaller.

I haven't had a chance to kiss him properly myself. Once we were lovers. He was my love . . .

But he had disappeared under the billows of their daughter.

> O love, we two shall go no longer
> To lands of summer across the sea

Once we were young and took the ferry to France and we stood on the sunny deck and held hands and he told me, 'Don't be frightened, silly, the Channel ferry will never go down,' and I said, 'I love you no matter what' but I never knew if he had heard me, the wind blew everything away –

May clutched the thin shoulder of her book for comfort.

Can Shirley be ours? Did she come from us? Why is she here, so tall, so pretty, smelling of countries where we've never been, flowers we couldn't even imagine, men her father can't stand the sight of – He must be drowning in her smell. How do they bear it, today's young men? I suppose I've always been a modest woman.

Then it was over. 'Good girl,' he grunted. 'Now pop down there and ask the nurses for a chair.' And off she sailed; surging, gleaming, a glossy galleon down a narrow channel. May saw he was happy to be released. He smiled a sheepish smile at her.

Left alone, they were suddenly intimate, restored to the state where they spent most of their lives.

'Has she put on weight?' asked Alfred, eyes darting after her, blue, suspicious, and he stretched out his hand to hold May's plump white one, tucking them together on the hard brown blanket.

'Pity they don't have eiderdowns or anything,' May said, touching the bare fibres doubtfully.

'I shan't be here long enough to miss that,' said Alfred. 'Are the peonies out yet ? They make a good show.'

'Too early,' said May. 'And it's been chilly. You're well off in here. Cosy in here.'

She was thinking, his hand is thinner than mine. It's bigger than mine, of course it is, he's always been half a head taller than me, but it somehow feels smaller. Colder.

A moment of fear as their eyes met. They hadn't practised being here. Then he smiled at her, her cheery Alfred. 'I'll be out in time for Easter, May. They'll fix me up so I'm as good as new.' But his voice was gruff, a little uncertain, and her answering smile was uncertain too. In this hospital ward they were helpless strangers –

But not to each other. She clung to his hand, feeling its pulse, which was fast but steady, the comforting knot of flesh and blood.

'I've got forms for you to sign,' she said, shyly. 'So I can get money from the bank.'

'Oh yes?' he said, at once suspicious. '*I* always get the money, May.'

'But you're in here.'

'I'll be out in a day or two. Still if you can't wait . . .' And he took the forms, hardly read them, signed.

She felt a stab of guilt. Was she giving up on him, acting as if he was nearly dead? Wasn't it as good as killing him? And she loved him so.

Alfred, Alfred.

'Can you believe she's our daughter?' May whispered, watching Shirley return with the extra chair. She had walked two paces, in her honey-coloured wool, a woman large enough to make the chair look small, her movements graceful, indolent, when a middle-aged man in a group around a bed broke away from his family and touched her arm, 'May I help you?', and as Shirley's face flashed into a charming smile he took the chair from her with a flourish, preparing her way like a courtier. 'She's got . . . an air, hasn't she? She's . . . somebody.'

'Queen of Sheba,' Alfred hissed at the last moment, but he winked as he said it, and May knew he was happy.

'Now we're all right,' said Shirley. 'Do you want to have a look at your chocolates, Dad?'

'I'd better get a vase for those lilies,' said May, stirring.

'The nurses'll do that,' said Alfred, sharply. 'Don't you move. That's what they're paid for.'

This was plainly untrue, but May realized that Alfred didn't want to be left alone with his daughter.

'I'll go,' said Shirley, getting up again.

'Just everyone sit still for a moment,' he snapped. 'You've only just come in, and you can't wait to leave.'

They sat in silence, suddenly uneasy, the bundle of lilies in their gilt-stamped paper becoming bigger, less comfortable, louder, rustling every time Shirley breathed, and May thought suddenly of arum lilies, flowers for a wreath, flowers for a funeral.

She only just got here, and she can't wait to leave. Life's like that, all rush, and then over.

'Isn't anyone going to ask how I am?' he demanded, grimacing his lips over his teeth where they sometimes slipped and made him look foolish.

'You were asleep. She did ask me,' said May, humbly, *don't be cross with me.*

'How are you, Dad?' asked Shirley, brightly.

'Can't complain. I don't really think there's much wrong with me.'

'Was it a heart attack?' Shirley pressed, and May wanted to shush her, for it wasn't right to talk of such things in loud voices.

'They keep calling it an *event*,' he said, with a certain amount of satisfaction.

'I think that's a stroke,' said Shirley.

'It was an *event*,' he said, displeased. 'They think I might have another one.'

'It's your circulation,' said May. 'That's nothing new. That was always bad.' She didn't want some alarming new game.

'Well it is new,' he said, staring hard at her, one huge white eyebrow twitching upwards like the feathers of the ostrich in the zoo where they'd gone with the two older ones, thirty years ago. 'Being found out cold on my back is new.'

'So are they going to give you drugs, or what?'

May frowned at her daughter, who didn't notice. (Why did she keep on bothering her father? If he wanted to tell them, he would tell them. If he knew, that is, if the doctors had told him, and she hoped they wouldn't tell him things to frighten him. It was she who should know. May would ask the doctors.)

'I'm rattling with pills already,' said Alfred.

'Stop questioning your father,' said May.

'I don't mind people taking an interest. They're doing a test on my brain,' he said, once more unable to suppress a note of pride. Medicine had ignored him for seventy-odd years; now important doctors were testing his brain.

'Must have been a stroke then,' said Shirley, satisfied. 'I mean, I'm afraid it must have been a stroke,' catching her mother's indignant glare. 'But lots of people get better from strokes.'

'How do you know so much about medicine all of a sudden?' May asked her.

'I don't,' she said. And then, foolishly 'Well Elroy does work in a hospital, so I suppose I have picked up a bit from him –'

'You've picked it up from bloody Elroy, have you?' her father demanded, stung into life, cranking up his head several inches from the pillow. 'This is medicine according to Elroy, is it? Well thank you very much, I want English medicine, English medicine from English doctors.'

'Elroy is English,' said Shirley. 'Well – British. Elroy is as British as me or you.'

'Oh yes?' said Alfred, now alarmingly red, blue eyes alight, clawing at the bedclothes. 'He's about as British as bananas, is Elroy.'

Shirley was trying very hard to keep calm. 'He is British, but I'm not going to argue. Thing is, you should know what's the matter with you. You have a right. All patients do.'

'He's not bloody British!' Veins bulged in his neck and his head poked forward like a tortoise.

'He was born in Peckham!' Now they were both shouting.

'Will you leave it?' said May. 'People are looking at us.' This wasn't true, but it had an effect. 'Can you stop upsetting your father?'

'Thinks she knows it all,' said Alfred, subsiding, suddenly tired, smaller, paler.

Shirley sat and stared at the floor. 'I'll fetch a vase, then I have to be going,' she said, standing up, not looking at them, flouncing down the pale clinging hem of her skirt.

They watched her swaying down the ward again. Now most of the beds had collected visitors, clustered round the bed-heads, helpless, eager. Amateurs at this, all of them.

May and Alfred looked at each other. Neither had meant to quarrel with Shirley. They needed them now, their large, strong children, now they were growing older, weaker. 'You didn't have to go and upset her – ' he muttered.

'You're the one who riled her. Saying Elroy isn't British.'

'I don't intend to waste time talking about Elroy.'

'You've only got one daughter,' said May.

Her mild voice sparked him off again. 'I know that. Do you think I don't know that? Do you think I don't want to see my grandchildren? No chance of that, till she settles down.'

Alfred was deluding himself, as usual. All through Shirley's marriage he had pretended that Kojo was a temporary fling. May had never told him about Shirley's miscarriages, had begged her daughter not to talk about them. Partly to protect him from pain. Partly to protect herself from his reaction, for May had longed for Shirley and Kojo to have children, no matter if they were black or white or striped, she knew she would love her daughter's children and hoped that Alfred would have loved them too, it would have mended everything, brought them all together . . . But the babies had died. Two in a row. In Shirley's well-fed, healthy body.

Shirley reappeared with a fountain of white lilies that turned her into a goddess from May's childhood encyclopedia . . . *Newnes' Encyclopedia*, was that it? Straight out of one of those shiny pictures where all the gods were blond and tall. Shirley was a goddess of fruit and flowers – Ceres? Or was that fertility? Goddess of spring, Proserpina. How could they not be proud of her, and yet she still wouldn't meet their eyes, lowering the shining lilies down on the grey Formica of his bedside table among the dim clutter of water, clock, glasses –

> Now droops the milk-white peacock like a ghost
> And like a ghost she glimmers on to me . . .
> Now folds the lily all her sweetness up
> And slips into the bosom of the lake . . .

May gazed at her, half-hypnotized.

'Help her, then,' said Alfred, testily. 'Can't you see she can't do it on her own?' May heaved herself round in the chair. 'You could get up,' he harried his wife. 'You could do something. I can't get up.'

'It's all right, Dad.' Shirley couldn't bear them arguing. 'I've got to go, in any case. Enjoy the chocs.'

'You shouldn't spend your money on me.'

'I like to spend money on my parents.'

'You don't want to go short.' He always worried.

'Dad, I'm all right. I – was left well looked after.'

He knew she was avoiding saying Kojo's name. 'You're a good girl, coming to see me.'

'Don't give the nurses a hard time.'

'Me?' He winked, looking suddenly youthful. 'I'm the perfect patient. You ask sister.'

'I'll come and see you again tomorrow.'

'Darren might have got here by tomorrow –'

'Well . . . I'll believe it when I see it.'

'Of course he's coming,' said Alfred. 'He's been talking about coming for over a year . . . It's his work. The pressure. Pressure of work.'

'But now you're ill –' said May.

'Now I've had this spot of trouble, he'll come.'

Shirley took pity. 'Of course he'll come.' She touched May's hand, bent heavily to pick up her coat (and May suddenly saw she was middle-aged, that stately slowness as she stooped, then wrapped herself round in the pale wool as if she were hurt, as if she were damaged, and blew a grand stage kiss at them, a kiss for onlookers to see, and was gone, sailing off down the ward again, wind in her sails, unstoppable. At the end she turned and raised her hand, a flag of truce, a flag of forgiveness.)

She's middle-aged, our Shirley Temple.

May stared after her, uncomprehending. One final flash of her curls in the light. Our golden girl. Our pretty baby. Soon she'll be too old to have children . . . But how can our children be too old for anything?

I haven't been a good mother to her. I didn't stand up for her enough over Kojo. I didn't tell Alfred he was being a fool.

But why has she turned out so different from us? Why does she want such different things? And Darren – he lives in hotels and planes, and has *huttuttupp* thingies, and *dotcoms*, and divorces – (Shirley had a point. Darren did let them down. Those last-minute phonecalls, to say he wasn't coming, when she'd cleaned the house from top to bottom and his dad had turned the mattress in the spare room. He'd be off to Hawaii, or Bali, or Greenland. Of course he couldn't come, but all the same they felt it. 'Enjoy yourself, lad,' was all Alfred ever said.)

But where does it all come from? Lap-tops, jacuzzis? Out of the future. The glittering future. And we two are slipping back into the past.

I shall go with him, if Alfred goes.

That thought brought May a queer kind of comfort. The new things were probably not meant for them. It would be too much, too fast, too loud.

Probably it's rich people live long lives.

10 · Shirley

Shirley was halfway down the corridor, a glaze of smile still fixing her features, before she remembered to stop trying to please.

I hate my family. Ignorant bigots. Mum thinks she's broad-minded, but she's bad as him, she almost fainted when she thought she saw Elroy.

Why do I have to put up with their nonsense? I'm thirty-seven years old, I've been married and widowed – They've never been anywhere. They don't know anything. All Mum knows she gets from books. She's only been with one man all her life. She can't see what a – *pig* Dad is, she dotes on him, he's the world to her.

Ignorant. Pig ignorant. That's what I say to Elroy; take no notice.

The truth was, Elroy got less angry than she did. Or showed less anger, which wasn't the same thing. Sometimes she thought he bottled up his feelings because it was so humiliating, admitting other people thought you were dirt. Better to say nothing, to ignore the pain. And he had low expectations, of course. To him, that was just the way white people were.

Kojo, older, richer, more confident, had found them comic, and slightly pathetic. 'It's because they have no education,' he said. 'They're afraid of us because they know nothing about us. I'll ask them out to Ghana as my guests, and then they will see another world.' 'I can't imagine it, though.' And of course it never happened.

The two men coped in their different ways, while Shirley was left mortified, speechless, furious. She sometimes wanted to kill her parents. Because they were hers. In case she was like them. To prove all white people weren't the same.

But Shirley's anger was playing itself out as she walked down the echoing yellow stairs. The lift had been broken for the last two weeks . . . Peeling paint, a smell of damp. She would have liked to get going on this hospital. Shirley had always been good at mending, painting, polishing, making good. I need a job, she thought, as so often. I could do something. I've got lots to offer.

But Elroy preferred her not to work, and Kojo had expected her to be a mother, as she had expected to be a mother.

She wasn't a mother. She would never be a mother. Unless there was a miracle. Very soon.

Maybe mothering Dirk when he was little is the nearest I'll ever get to it.

Just then she saw him, one flight down, that completely unmistakable pale stubble which filled her, at that moment, with fear and loathing, for Dirk was even worse than her dad.

But he caught it from Dad. Ranting on about 'the coloureds'.

I can't see him. I can't bear it.

She walked silently down the ward that opened to her right, and skulked by some curtains till his boots had gone by, clicking fast upstairs.

11 · May

'I wonder if Dirk will ever leave home?'

They held hands again, now Shirley was gone, and with her any tension between them. It was always the kids who made trouble; together they were comfortable.

'He's not very old,' observed Alfred, judiciously. Which seemed to prove he himself wasn't old.

'Twenty-five is quite old enough to leave home,' said May, mildly. 'He could get a little room. We don't want to baby him.'

'What he gets from George wouldn't pay for much.' Dirk had a 'little job' at the local newsagent, fixed up as a favour by Alfred's oldest friend. 'He can't leave home till he gets a real job. I mean, it was different in our day. I'd been working ten years already, at his age. But that's not his fault. Is it?'

'He still goes for interviews, you know. Even if he doesn't tell us any more. I find the papers from the Job Centre. Do you think he'd have more chance if his hair was different?'

Alfred had never thought about Dirk's hair. It was Darren who'd been trouble in that department, growing it long, looking namby-pamby.

'Are you saying it's old-fashioned?' he asked, doubtfully. 'I suppose he looks a bit like a GI –'

'Skinhead,' May corrected him briefly. 'They look like Nazis, but I suppose they're not . . . It is in fashion, with some people.'

'On the other hand, it's clean, it's tidy. He's quite a good boy, in some ways. He's good company for his old dad.'

'You mean, he goes down the pub with you.'

'Why are you being so hard on the boy? It's not like you. My duck, my darling.' He squeezed her hand, gentle, affectionate.

She knew Alfred was trying to tell her he loved her, and also asking her to spare him home truths, but she had to get it off her chest. 'He gets on my nerves, with you not there.'

'Maybe he could go and live with his sister.'

'The last place he could go is Shirley's.'

'In my day family looked out for each other. Do you think they'll look out for him, after we're gone? Darren hardly knows Dirk, does he?'

'They'll get to know each other while Darren's here.' May tried her best to sound confident. Would Darren like Dirk, if he got to know him? Her youngest son was hard to like. And he wasn't bright like Darren was. He wasn't interested in anything except computers. Well, and his peculiar new friends.

'I'm so glad Darren is coming home,' said Alfred, and a real smile, a smile of tenderness, lit up his face, making it seem less bony, younger, and she thought, he'll live, and things will go right, Alfred will get better, we'll all love each other . . . *Alfred will never be angry again.*

And Alfred Tennyson was ready, as always:

> Beat, happy stars, timing with things below,
> Beat with my heart more blest than heart can tell,
> Blest, but for some dark undercurrent woe
> That seems to draw – but it shall not be so:
> Let all be well, be well.

They sat in silence for a while, contented, as the life of the ward washed round them. Draggles of people spilled out from the bedheads and blocked the central channel down the ward, until nurses came, smiling but firm, and shepherded the overflow away. 'It's really only supposed to be two visitors per patient –'

One Asian family arrived in strength; around twenty people, from pensioners to babies. The old and the young both wore brilliant colours, the grandmother's white head wrapped in a marigold-orange headscarf, the little girls in frilly western party frocks, the middle-aged conventionally smart, men in pin-striped suits, women in chic tailored dresses.

'Lovely family,' May whispered to herself, quieting the tiny voice that said, *they're doing very well for themselves*.

'Too many of 'em,' said Alfred.

She didn't have to listen to what he said. It was just his noise, the stutter of an engine far away across the bay. 'Lovely family,' she repeated, contented. Families ought to be like that, all coming round when there was trouble.

She wished the boys were here tonight. In fact, they had hardly been boys together, for Darren was fifteen years older than Dirk . . . Dirk had always needed looking after. Darren was successful, Dirk was not.

Though Alfred wasn't the gentlest of men, she knew he felt sorry for their youngest son. And in his way, he'd been a very good father (but had he? she wondered, suddenly unsure). He'd tried to teach Dirk football, rugger, cricket – Dirk was useless at all of them. He'd tried to teach Dirk right from wrong. He was a man of principle. A man with backbone. Sometimes he talked too much about backbone, and he never thought Dirk had much of it.

Dirk was so much slower than the other two kids. Not tall like Darren, nor good-looking like Shirley. He was skinny, painfully so. And he'd inherited Alfred's great beak of a nose – a nose of pride, of character, May tried to tell Dirk when he was thirteen and she caught him crying in his bedroom mirror – together with a bony jaw that had suddenly grown heavier in his late teens. Between the two outcrops, his mouth seemed to shrink.

For years they told themselves there was a temporary blockage. They had flashes of hope; he could add up in a trice, could price a load of shopping before she reached the till. But his English essays were short and abysmal. 'No imagination,' the teacher had said. 'His basic trouble is no imagination.' She hoped he was wrong. Dirk just lacked words. But there came a time when you had to give up.

He did have nice hair. Unusual hair. Hair like May's when she was a girl. (May had been grey for thirty years, though until she was sixty she always dyed it, and Alfred, bless him, never knew. Even in marriage, there had to be secrets.)

Mr Punch. That was her youngest son. She made herself face it, finally. Overshot, underhung. And that shining blond head made folks look at him, which wasn't a kindness when you weren't a film star.

Shirley had always been kind to Dirk, and he had hero-worshipped his sister, saved his pocket-money to buy her sweets, which he ate himself, but the thought was there.

It was over now. They weren't close any more.

He just couldn't stomach her marrying Kojo.

'She can't love him. You've seen him, haven't you. I mean, he's not half-caste, or something like that. He's black as black. He's a fucking gorilla.'

'I saw him,' said May, coolly, calmly. 'He's a human being like anyone else. I talked to him. And I quite liked him.'

'You crept around him,' said Dirk, disgusted. 'You acted like he was the bee's knees.'

May wouldn't let him get away with that. 'I'm polite to everyone who comes to this house,' she said, turning to look him in the eye, putting down her tea-cloth, drawing herself up. 'You mind your manners with your sister's friends, while you're still living under our roof.'

She rarely spoke to him like that. She was the angrier because he had expressed her own feelings, the ones she had almost completely suppressed – why did Shirley have to go the whole hog? *Did she have to choose one as black as that?*

Dirk never discussed it with Shirley. Instead, he withdrew from her altogether. The women retreated to a knot in the kitchen whenever they wanted to talk about the wedding, planning the guest list, dreaming of the cake.

'We can pay up to two thousand pounds,' May had said, hot with fear as she spoke the words. Spinning noughts, whirling, disappearing . . . It was her own money, a savings plan she had put aside for over twenty years, cheating on the housekeeping, stinting herself.

But Shirley said, 'Don't be silly. Kojo wouldn't dream of accepting any money. His family were paramount chiefs, in Ghana. He's going to pay for everything, including a new outfit for you, if you want one. You could do with one. You know you could.'

On the day Dirk turned up at the very last moment, wearing a dark jacket he had borrowed from someone, not the sort of jacket that teenagers wore, and a bright pink tie, entirely surprising. He looked almost handsome, with his yellow-white hair, but he spoke to no one, stood open-eyed and furious throughout the ceremony, never kneeling down to pray, then afterwards retreated to a corner of the beautiful apricot hotel lounge and sat with his father, backs to the wall, drinking beer, not wine, and refusing to eat. They wove away together at the very end, self-righteous and sullen, looking neither left nor right, as if they alone had behaved irreproachably, as if they had won a great victory, between them.

Yet only a year after the wedding, Dirk had started going round to Shirley and Kojo's house. When Shirley told her mother, May couldn't believe it. 'He's not coming round to make trouble, is he? His dad's put some strange ideas in his head.'

'He said he missed me,' Shirley told her. 'I don't mind. Forgive and forget. He's found out Kojo likes football too.'

And so they had seemed to get over it, and be close again, like when they were children. Dirk didn't know what to say to Kojo after they had totted up the football scores, so he told him the plot of television films he'd seen, and Kojo sat and nodded, patiently, though he hardly ever watched TV.

Then Kojo got ill with lung cancer and Dirk was nearly as upset as May. He had kept his sister company when things were bad. He visited right up to the end. The night Kojo died and the phone call came he sat in May's kitchen, shaking his head, and after the funeral he went home with Shirley.

But eighteen months later she took up with Elroy, and to May's astonishment they started again, Dirk and his father, as if they'd learned nothing.

'Kojo was different,' Dirk insisted. 'Kojo wasn't like the others. You know he wasn't. You liked him too.'

'Yes,' said May. 'But –'

'I don't want to talk about it,' Dirk said, head down. His new blond crewcut stared her in the face.

And that was that. May had tried to make sense of it. People kept things in their brains in tight little boxes . . . Because Dirk liked Kojo, Kojo stopped being black. But her son still hated all the other coloured people.

Dirk wouldn't talk to Shirley, either. 'I can't understand him,' Shirley said. He hadn't talked to her, except to say 'Hello', for years. Which was a sadness to May and Alfred, who had always liked the two kids being close, and hoped it might last them all their lives, so the family wouldn't end with the parents.

But things didn't last. Why hadn't she realized? The years like water washed them away, the things of beauty, the things you loved, dipping and glinting away into the distance. The only constants were bills, and getting older, and the pain in her knees, and the ache in her neck.

And the house, the bloomin' house where they'd lived for ever. With its creaks, and its knockings, and its leaky gutters –

And its whitewashed front in the morning sun. And the smell of apples from the fruit-bowl in the living-room. And that dot of gold dancing about off the mirror. He would catch it on one finger, on his free afternoon, and point at her like a magician. His chair, her chair. With Shirley's cushions, easing their bones as they sank down. Their little house, with its steamy kitchen, smelling of washing and hot Ribena. Its warmth, its sheen, its – familiarness. Was that the word? Their family home.

Alfred, pet.

She would take him home.

12 · Dirk

'Here's Dirk,' said Alfred abruptly. 'Look.'

You couldn't miss him. That ash-white hair, and something jerky about his walk, as if he was head-butting a low brick wall. As if this habit had injured his brain . . . Dirk hadn't had an easy time in life.

'I wonder if he met his sister on the stairs.'

As he got nearer, you could see the boy was small. His head slightly bowed, he nodded on forward, blinking and grinning, glad to see his father.

May thought, he almost worships his father.

'Is that your boy?' It was a woman's voice. May turned to look at her, surprised. The body in the next bed was female. She was sixty-ish – maybe seventy-ish – with a plump red face, powdered in patches, and a swatch of red hair pulled back in a bun. *Alfred must have been encouraging her*. May didn't approve of these mixed wards.

Alfred had pulled himself virtually erect (he's certainly thinner – they aren't feeding him) and was grinning at the woman, a mask on a stick – if he knew what he looked like he wouldn't do it. 'No, this is Dirk.'

The woman smiled and nodded.

Dirk stood there, doggedly ignoring her. 'Dad,' he said. 'How goes it, then?'

Dirk had always lacked social graces. Once May had worried about his shyness because she thought it would stop him getting on with girls. But as Dirk grew up, there never were any girls, and sometimes she thought that he hated women. Then she'd started wondering if he liked boys, because May had read Oscar Wilde, and Thom Gunn. Once she'd found a strange magazine in his room, with photographs of black men without any clothes, but he got very cross, and said it was disgusting, he'd just brought it home to get rid of it. There were no other signs that he liked anyone at all.

'This is Dirk,' said May, to the painted woman. She used the most educated voice she had. 'I am his mother. I didn't catch your name.'

'I think Alfred has forgotten it,' the woman chirped, raising one eyebrow at him. 'He hasn't got much memory for names.'

May looked at her resentfully. *Why is she gazing at my husband?*

'This is Pamela,' Alfred said rather gruffly, with the hint of a smirk. 'Dirk, say hallo to Pamela.'

'So this is the famous journalist.' Her smile was smarmy, lipsticky.

'Oh no,' Alfred corrected her, dismayed. 'This is Dirk, the other one. I probably didn't mention him . . . Darren's flying in from Spain today.'

'Lovely,' said Pamela, vaguely, grandly *(but she's not a lady, with that dyed hair)*. 'We had a château in Spain you know. We always wintered in Andalusia. Olives, oranges, wonderful light . . . it was almost like a religion, with us.'

'Why did you come back then?' May asked coolly.

'That is a very long story, my dear. One I may well tell Alfred one day.' The woman winked, elaborately. May stared open-mouthed at her turquoise eyelids.

'He probably won't be here,' she said. 'We don't expect him to be here very long.'

'Really?' Pamela said, her voice almost pitying, then turned away in her bed, and read, and May wanted to say, I'm a reader too, I read the works of Alfred Tennyson, but she knew the woman thought she was stupid.

Alfred was looking very put out. Perhaps the family had let him down. Dirk wore scruffy denims and a studded leather jacket and his face was reddened by the wind. It somehow made his nose look bigger.

'Why do you keep on talking to *her*?' Alfred hissed at May, furious. 'Can't you see she's trying to read?'

Ignore the injustice, May told herself. Don't argue with him. He's not a well man. 'Dirk, your father's feeling much better –'

'I never said I was feeling better.'

'What did you say then?' She wanted to weep.

'Dad, I brought you some treacle toffees –' Dirk stood there, clumsy, at the foot of the bed, left out of the quarrel as he usually was. They both turned to stare. The boy was giving them a present!

'Thank you, son.' said Alfred, startled. 'I appreciate that. I hope you didn't nick them –' But Dirk's hurt face was an annoyance when it was Darren he wanted to see. 'Sit down, sit down, you're blocking the light.'

Dirk sat down swiftly, patting at his hair, though bristles like that could never be untidy. May realized that he felt in the wrong. He was patting at himself to put himself right. It's the parents' fault if they feel like that. Yet May felt nothing could ever have been different. Do your best, she had told herself day after day, struggling to deal with her growing kids, but her best had never been good enough, and now they had come to this strange place, one by one, to be inspected.

'How's work?' asked Alfred.

'Same as usual,' said Dirk. And that was the trouble, his mother thought. The newsagent he worked in was on Hillesden Gardens, only two hundred yards away from home. Their friend George Millington, the owner, was an asthmatic smoker with gammy legs. He had taken Dirk on for 'work experience' nine years ago, when Dirk was sixteen, when it wasn't yet completely impossible to hope that he'd scrape enough GCSEs to go to college. May had stopped hoping before Alfred did.

'How's St George?' Alfred asked. It was a very old joke.

'All right. He had a turn today.'

'You're a good boy to look after him,' May said quickly, comfortingly.

'It's disgusting,' said Dirk. 'He goes this horrible colour. Like he was dying, or something.'

'You're a good boy.'

'He's too old to work.'

'He's my age,' said Alfred, affronted.

'It's different,' said Dirk. 'You're not dying, are you.' There was an uncertain silence, then he carried on. 'I'm worried he's going to peg out in my arms.'

'George has been good to you, young man.'

'Has he, Dad?' Dirk went white around the nostrils. 'You don't know what it's like in that shop. He smokes non-stop. I mean *non-stop*. I come out of there, I stink of smoke. Every time he coughs, he starts sticking up his guts. And when he's not smoking, he's bloody wheezing. He doesn't do a shagging stroke –'

'Language,' said May. 'George is fond of you,' she added, suddenly afraid that Pamela was listening. 'He must have got fond of you, I'm sure. Not having any sons of his own.' (She dreamed that George would leave Dirk the shop, and he'd be all right for the rest of his life. Plus Dirk could afford to leave home, at last. They'd be left in peace, her and Alfred – Not that she wanted to get rid of him, of course.)

'He hates me,' said Dirk, simply. 'He couldn't manage without me, that's all. I do all the work. He gets all the money.'

'Of course he doesn't hate you,' said Alfred sternly. 'Course he doesn't. He's my oldest friend.'

'Have you managed to get rid of the Christmas stock?' May was determined to turn the conversation.

'The charity ones were rubbish, this year. No one round our way wants fancy things with otters on, they look at them and think they're rats –'

'Well *I'm* quite ecological,' May interrupted him, indignant. 'I bought two boxes of otters, dear.'

'We still got lumbered with twenty-three boxes. Chocolates were quite good this year though. No thanks to George. He can't think beyond Cadbury's –'

'Cadbury's were always good enough for us,' said Alfred.

'Point I'm making is, people want Belgian.'

'Good English chocolates. That's what you want.'

'What are you doing with these, then?' asked Dirk, triumphant, pointing to the giant white-and-gold box that Shirley had left on the bedside table. "Best Belgian Chocolates", it says, look, there.'

'That's Shirley, that is,' said Alfred. 'I can't stop her wasting her money.'

'She was looking very smart. She always does.' May couldn't resist a glance at Dirk's dirty jeans.

'These are my work clothes,' he said, flushing. 'I had to come here straight from work. We have to stay open late because the frigging Pakis do.'

'Will you shush,' May hissed, one eye on Pamela. 'Shirley asked after you. She always does.' (Then she thought about it, and realized she didn't.)

Alfred's voice got that preachy sound. 'You always used to be so close to your sister.'

Dirk glowered at him. 'You know what happened. It was you that said it, we had to make a stand.'

In a small clear voice that seemed to come from a dream in which she was someone stronger and braver, May said, 'I liked Kojo. And I like Elroy. And Kojo was very good to you. You forget how many times you got your tea round at their house.' She ran out of steam, surprised at herself.

'I never denied I got my tea.'

'She'll meet someone soon, and settle down,' said Alfred. 'Everything's going to turn out for the best.'

May thought, let all be well, be well . . . Tennyson was hopeful rather than certain:

> Oh yet we trust that somehow good
> Will be the final goal of ill
> To pangs of nature, sins of will,
> Defects of doubt, and taints of blood . . .

And what did he mean by 'taints of blood'?

13 · The White Family

Seeing Dirk had shaken Shirley. The hospital foyer was huge and cold.

I used to love him. I adored that boy. But what's he turned into? A thug. A – fascist. Worse than Dad, without Dad's excuses.

She wasn't quite ready to go out into the dark and struggle through the wind across the wild black car park. She sank down on to an empty seat, picked up a magazine and stared at it blindly.

When her focus returned, she was looking at furs. Two pages of red and blond winter furs. 'There are the whingers and the whiners, yes. There are the dowdies, the dated, the dull . . . And there's you. Daring to be a babe. Ready for fun. Purring for fur . . . You, babelicious in the new seal-skin . . .' The heart-shaped face of the journalist looked all of seventeen years old, and brainless.

Still the furs were pretty, thought Shirley. Soft. Elroy might like to see me in furs . . . But she knew it was just a fantasy.

No one wore furs. It just wasn't done. No one, that is, except rich foreign women you saw getting out of cabs with dark glasses and fussy expensive designer handbags. Arab men's women, she thought, contemptuously, then caught herself thinking it and was ashamed.

So she was a bigot like the rest of her family.

We all like to think we're better than someone.

She knew what people said about her. 'Shirley White goes with black men.' They never got over their excitement about it, though she'd been married to Kojo for nearly eight years. As if a marriage was just about sex.

I liked being married. I liked the comfort.

Her parents had been married for over forty years. What would her mother do if Dad died? Shirley remembered all too clearly the blank exhaustion when Kojo was dying. The sense that part of her body was missing.

But they've been lucky. They've had nearly half a century.

She slapped the magazine shut with a sigh.

As she focused on the big automatic doors that would let her out into the night again, they opened, as if by the power of thought. A man came in and blinked at the light.

Suddenly familiar. White, thickset, with golden skin and dark wavy hair. Handsome in a rugged, crumpled sort of way. Heavy eyebrows, frowning towards her.

'Isn't it – Shirley? It's Thomas Lovell.'

'Do you remember me . . .?' It was Darren's friend. 'Have you come to see Dad? That's very kind. I saw you on the television, you know. When your book came out. Some time ago.' Of course, it was Thomas who saw Dad fall. Used to be a writer. Then he became – What? – something sensible. Yes, a librarian.

'It must be ten years since we met.'

'Probably Darren's second wedding.'

'Yes.'

Simultaneously, they both remembered that they had got drunk and flirted with each other. They had possibly kissed. They had certainly danced. Shirley's spirits began to rise.

'He's on his third marriage by now, you know. None of us got invited to the last one. They ran off to Bali. Very glamorous . . . You didn't come to my wedding, did you? I can't remember if I asked you.'

'No,' he said. 'But didn't I hear –?'

'My husband died three years ago. Cancer.'

'I'm so sorry.' He really looked sorry.

'My little brother's just gone up to the ward.'

'I'd better give them some time together.'

On impulse Shirley said, 'Good idea. Come and have a cup of tea in the café.'

Two bored black women were standing by the till, which was full of ravenous young doctors in white coats, furiously feeding haunted faces. It was a banqueting hall for ghosts. The tables and chairs were of royal blue plastic, which made chill reflections on their skin.

'Hot meal arl finish,' one of the black women told them. There remained some cupcakes, two squashed jam-tarts, some ginger biscuits and some cling-wrapped salads, half-decomposed, like overcooked spinach.

'Just tea, I think,' said Thomas. 'Can't say I fancy anything else.'

They sat down at the only table free of white-coated inmates stripping their plates. 'They're like a plague of locusts,' she said.

'Stress,' he said. 'Exhaustion. They've probably been working twenty hours already.'

'I suppose you just expect them to have good manners. Seeing as they're professionals.' She saw on his face a kind of disappointment.

'Professionals are the rudest of all. In fact, they have qualifications in rudeness.'

'I haven't got any qualifications.' (Why did I have to tell him that?)

'I've got lots but I don't really use them.'

'I'd have thought you'd need them, to look after books. And to write a book, like you did.'

'Oh, any fool can be a writer.'

'Lots of people would love to be in your shoes,' she said. 'People admire writers.'

'Do they, still?'

'Well our house is crammed wall to wall with books' – (Kojo's books, if she was honest. Why was she trying to impress him? But Shirley herself had once been a reader, when she was young, doing teacher training.)

Thomas was looking inside her coat, his eyes slipping down the cream silk of her blouse. His kind of woman would be thin and sharp.

'Is Darren coming home?' he asked.

'Well he doesn't exactly keep in touch with me. Of course he doesn't, with his high-powered life-style.' She made herself smile, to cover her chagrin.

'I never hear from him, either.'

On the other side of the canteen, there was something going on. The voice of one of the attendants was becoming steadily shriller. 'Because it gone six o'clock already and dis kitchen not doin' any more cookin' –'

A man with his back to them was making a scene. 'You're supposed to serve cooked meals between five and seven. Which means there should be an hour to go –' A slim blonde woman dressed in pink was plucking ineffectually at his shoulder.

The black woman jabbed the air with her finger. 'I can't help what nonsense de notice say. The doctors come eat the lot. And that's that.'

It struck Shirley and Thomas at the same moment, and their eyes met, briefly, apprehensive, as the man snatched up his bleak tray in disgust and turned, with a little flounce of anger and tiredness – *It was Darren, of course*. Darren's tanned face, which gaped and grew pinker the moment he saw them. He had come after all, the prodigal son. 'Darren White, Voice of the Left, Man of the People', as the papers called him. A jet-lagged man with an American twang, making a mean little scene in a café.

He swept up to them in a gale of tension, handsome from a distance, gaunt close up. His hair had subtly changed colour, Shirley realized; the grey in his curls had disappeared. His face underneath was tighter, older, the lines set hard in a mask of tan. 'Hello,' he said. 'Hi everyone,' as if there were too many of them to manage individually. 'I'm just trying to get some *morsel* of sustenance out of the bloody NHS.' His wife hovered behind him, pretty, uncertain, her pink suit fitting like an elegant glove, her hair hanging bobbed, healthy, expensive. 'This is Susie,' he said, gesturing angrily. 'My new wife. She couldn't eat a thing on the plane.

Of course neither of us eats red meat, and the veggie stuff was drowning in saturated fat. We made a special effort to get here today – I had an interview to do in Madrid. Mum sounded so damn frightened last time we spoke. Then two minutes after we get to the bedside the consultant turfs us out –' He was plainly trying to get a grip on himself. 'Sit down,' he ordered his wife over his shoulder. 'This is Shirley, my sister. And Thomas Lovell. I'd forgotten you two knew each other.'

'Shirley,' said the woman with an enormous smile that revealed big teeth and polished pink gums. She took both Shirley's hands in hers, and squeezed them hard, meaningfully. 'I know this is a difficult time for you. And Thomas. I've heard so much about you, Tom.'

'*Thomas*,' Darren corrected her, swiftly, annoyed.

'You're not American,' Shirley said. She smiled at Susie, wanting to help her.

'I've lived there fifteen years,' Susie said. 'My mother thinks I sound completely American.'

'Where are the children?' Shirley asked. Darren had two children by each of his first two marriages. Susie's face registered it as a reproach. 'I had – I mean, we had – the kids last weekend. Both lots actually. They're great. But kids aren't good in hospitals.'

'I didn't mean . . .' Shirley trickled away. 'I've never met them, believe it or not.'

'Darren,' said Thomas. 'Long time no see.' He had got to his feet to greet his friend. They were almost the same height, two tall, dark men. After an awkward pause, they shook hands vigorously, like two boxers not exhausted by their fight.

'Darren always said you two were like brothers,' Susie remarked, encouragingly.

But a voice cut in from behind their backs, a new voice, thin, resentful, nasal. 'I'm his brother,' Dirk complained. 'I'm his brother. He hasn't introduced me.'

Shirley couldn't escape him. He butted in, anxious, albino under the angry fluorescent.

'Dirk,' said Darren, switching instantly into a social smile, his tan creasing. 'It's great to see you. You disappeared. This is my little brother, Susie. You were by the bed, but you suddenly vanished –'

'Had to go to the toilet,' Dirk said, simply. 'I thought you'd have waited. Hello, Shirley.'

And then they were all there, the whole family.

'How long is it since we were all together?' Shirley asked, but nobody answered, busy finding chairs, stowing coats and bags, glad of the respite from each other.

All of us are here. Me, my two brothers. We were never all together. We don't know how to do it.

The café was quietening down at last. The locusts had eaten, and were flocking away, muttering ferociously, back down the corridors, a flapping of jaws and creased white wings. The Whites were left at their table in the window, lost in a desert of royal blue plastic, Darren still too wound up to sit down, Susie perched gingerly, an acid-pink flamingo, on a chair she appeared to fear was dirty, Shirley feeling like a giant by comparison, clumsy, creamy, too heavy to move, Thomas disappearing to fetch a pot of tea, and Dirk sidling grimly round the table to escape the women and be near his brother, his brother who was taller, richer, browner, Darren who was more of a man than him.

'So that's a full house,' Shirley repeated brightly. 'All the family together at last.'

Not true, of course, she realized at once. The next generation wasn't there. None of them had met Darren's children. Shirley herself didn't have any. *And if, by a miracle, I manage it with Elroy, I doubt if this family will ever accept them – And Dirk – is Dirk. Impossible.*

Without any children they were curiously stranded, middle-aged people who were children themselves.

And where were the parents? No Dad. No Mum. It foreshadowed the future, when they would be gone. So who was meant to look after them?

Thomas put the teapot in front of her.

'I'll be mother,' said Shirley, gratefully.

THE SHOP

14 · Thomas

'One Stop Shop!' It still struck Thomas as strange to see the large yellow notice on the front of the library, though it had been there for two years now. A library, after all, was not a shop. That was the point of it; you borrowed, then returned, and the things you borrowed belonged to everyone. The ethos of shops was opposed to libraries . . . As he'd tried to explain to the councillor who unveiled the plan for the One Stop Shop, in one of the long Monday morning meetings that left them scratchy with frustration and boredom. 'It's a question of perceived social need,' said the man, who had already used the phrase a dozen times. 'We have to react to social need. We don't want to get too hung up on books.'

So the One Stop Shop, the public face of the council, had simply come to perch, inelegantly, just inside the front doors of the library, where previously there were book displays. The librarians had resisted the loss of territory, but now they were almost used to it. Thomas reflected that the notice chimed well with one Suneeta had installed on the stairs: 'Customers may expect to be serviced rapidly and politely by library staff.' Visions of swift and silent sex performed by librarians on special tables.

In Thomas's lifetime, the official term had changed from 'readers', to 'borrowers, to 'users' , and now to 'customers', which somehow meant less. Not that it mattered. They were 'punters' to the staff.

Did he like the public? – Occasionally. At any rate, he believed in them. But thank God you only had to be on the Inquiry Desk one hour in two, on a rota. You couldn't hide, sitting out at the front, though having the computers did help them to look busy. There was a combination lock on the librarians' office, where they worked and chatted out of public view, put on it after one of the alcoholics burst in with a can of meths and a lighter, in the eighties . . . Thomas wasn't a coward, he had never been a coward, but libraries did attract people with grievances. That young man King, the other day, with his long list of inflammatory titles. The old man who came up to the desk this morning and hissed, full of spittle, 'How do you spell "action"?' When Thomas told him, he stared in disbelief, then shouted in a fury, 'But where's the s? Where's the bloody s?'

And then there was what they called the Irish Question, which arose every morning with the daily papers. The *South Irish Recorder* was so popular that it had to be kept at the Inquiry Desk, and issued only in exchange for a deposit. The arguments, sometimes actual tussles, arose when two punters asked to read it at the same time, or when someone was late returning it, or when the object offered as a deposit cost less than the price of the paper . . . Thomas had been handed, in the past two weeks: one glasses case, mended with sellotape; one pack of tooth-picks, three-quarters empty; one handkerchief, soiled with recognizable fluids; a bag of boiled sweets; one wrinkled green pepper. When he objected to this last item, the woman who offered it got in a rage. 'It's . . . unsuitable,' he said, firmly. 'Well what *is* suitable?' she asked, red-faced. But he merely knew he'd reached the end of some line. 'Not greengrocery. Sorry, madam.'

Fortunately Thomas was the stock librarian, so he spent much of his time at the back, at his desk, in the pleasant shared office, out of public view, leafing in a warm leisurely daze through the approval lists for possible acquisitions. His budget was small, but he still enjoyed spending it. He had to balance whim with service to the public, so he dutifully checked on past issue figures. He needed guaranteed crowd-pleasers to disguise the odd book on post-modernist theory . . . Because the accountants did have a point – they had to keep the usage figures up. And the usage figures were going down, slowly but surely, year by year.

Suneeta Patel was fifty, easily, broad and soft, though she sometimes talked and acted like a hippy teenager. He liked her sibilant, caressive whisper, and her round golden arms, indeed most of her, though she teased him for being a 'book-man', which meant, in new library parlance, 'dinosaur'. She had worked here since the eighties, though she wasn't a qualified librarian, but she knew more than anyone else about the information side of things, the whereabouts of nursery schools, doctors' surgeries, Job Shops, yoga classes, sports centres, aromatherapy . . . All the touching hopes for self-betterment that the public brought to the library. She came and perched distractingly on his desk, which pushed out the rounded curve of her flank. (He hadn't had sex for . . . months? years? His thoughts slipped fleetingly across to Melissa. He usually saw her several times a week, either in the street or on the stairs, but for some reason this week had been a desert.)

'Thomas. Did that crazy come in for his notes? The one who wrote all that heavy stuff about race?'

'Oh. Yes. W King. He was young. Good-looking. Bit scary, to be honest. He's ordered all this stuff about lynchings.'

She widened her eyes, in a parody of fear, and squeezed his hand, which he found stirring, despite the pain as her rings dug in. 'Watch yourself, Sweet Pea,' she purred. 'Just call Suneeta. Suneeta will protect you . . . By the way, how's your friend who had the thingy?'

After a pause, he realized whom she meant. 'Alfred? Went to see him yesterday,' he answered. 'In hospital. He didn't seem too bad. The family all came.'

'That's very good,' she said, nodding approvingly. 'Family just has to be there for you.' Her almond eyes were elongated with an upflick of jet black eyeliner that looked as if you could peel it off whole; her lips were crimson, cushiony, with little soft lines of tiredness at the edges. 'My daughters,' she continued, 'are education-mad. We wanted them to be graduates, yes. But they forget what matters in life: family, innit?'

'I suppose you're right.' He didn't know what to answer. He was an only child, and his parents were dead.

'Too right I'm right. Have a peppermint.' And she sashayed away, smiling seductively over her cushiony shoulder.

Sighing, for Suneeta had been married for three decades, had seven children, and would never be for him, Thomas trudged downstairs to look at the shelves in the History Section, which were getting tight. Triage was part of Stocks as well, and he sorted titles, to go for disposal almost automatically, thinking of the Whites.

It wasn't exactly happy families, last night. Darren White, the People's Friend, blowing his top at that poor woman on the counter, and snapping at his wife as if she was a servant. Poor little Dirk, with his four sugars . . .

Shirley had changed for the better, though. So – *bien dans sa peau*. So confident. And glossy, and pretty, and prosperous. She seemed so – calm. When all the others were nervous. I felt I wanted her to – be my friend (oh be honest, I wanted to sleep with her).

Her breasts were nice. Her cheeks were nice. Her skin was soft and nice like May's, nice, nice, the niceness of women . . . Later, May's face, looking down on Alfred. The shine of a woman who loves a man.

I would like that. I've never quite had that. I had a wife, but she didn't light up.

By the time he had finally reached Alfred's bedside, the ward had been closing down towards night, and a nurse came round with a chinking trolley. 'Do you want something to help you sleep?'

May had said, 'Horlicks. He always likes Horlicks.'

The nurse ignored her. 'Mr White, Alfred, would you like something?'

'He doesn't like *pills*, if that's what you mean. Alfred never has sleeping pills.'

'Hang on,' said Alfred, eyes suddenly wide open. 'I will have something. I did last night.'

'Alfred,' May protested. 'You could never stand pills.'

'He moans,' said Alfred, pointing down the ward. 'Every hour or so, he starts this moaning. And there's a woman who wanders about. You wouldn't get a wink of sleep in here.'

May said nothing as nameless pills rattled into a tiny plastic beaker, but when Alfred took them, she caught Thomas's eye, mouthed 'Tranquillizers', as someone might say 'Heroin', and winked, to comfort them both. 'You're looking tired, Thomas. Working too hard with the books, I suppose.'

It was gratifying *someone* knew libraries meant work. Wonderful May. She was often at the library. And she had quite a collection of her own books, too. Once she had showed him her Tennyson. The bookplate said 'May Hill, IVA. For Promising Work. Form English Prize.'

May's smile. 'Your mother would be proud of you. Alfred is pleased you've come to see him. He's just a bit sleepy. Exciting day.'

Alfred opened his eyes, frowned, concentrated. 'I'm not asleep. I'm not tired . . .'

'Thomas, dear,' whispered May. 'I think I'll pop and have a word with the doctors.'

'Not tired,' Alfred muttered, doggedly, but furred with sleep, slurring slightly. 'Ni', Darren. Good boy . . .' His eyelids sagged.

'Thomas,' he had gently corrected him, but May frowned, *shush*. Then she bent over and kissed Alfred's hand, very lightly, as if it were precious. 'Wait here a mo',' she said suddenly to Thomas, and darted off after a passing doctor.

But Alfred, Thomas saw, was asleep, so he went to fill the water-jug. In the kitchen, though, he got trapped in conversation with a little man with an infected hip who was desperate to talk about the Queen Mother. 'She was up and walking the very next day. They get a different quality of care, you know.'

Thomas was half-jogging down the corridor, eager to get out into the clean night air, when he bumped into a body, someone soft, in the shadows, someone he realized was quietly weeping –

It was May, with her hands covering her face. May, with the tears streaming down between her fingers.

Thomas wanted her to stop, very much, very badly. There was a smell of disinfectant, and the sluice room gurgled, gurgled in the distance.

'I just saw his doctor,' she said, when she could speak. 'I don't think the news is very good. Don't say anything. Don't tell the children.'

Oh euphemism, oh sad non-speech.

'May, can I walk home with you?'

'I don't want to be a nuisance, but Dirk's already gone.'

They walked through the wind not saying very much. Thomas took May's arm, feeling she might blow away in the darkness . . . But he knew that no one could make things right, no one could lift the terrible weight that had swooped in one awful second, landed.

May had said goodbye at the clanking gate outside the little terraced house in the thirties street, the mean street, where they had lived for most of their lives. It was not unlike his parents' street, though the latter had been gentrified; loft extensions, magnolia-trees, obsession with restoring the original details, whereas May and Alfred's street was still tearing them out. Little brilliant florets of thirties' stained glass, sweet-shop red, sweet-shop green, still shone in May and Alfred's hall window, but the front door had been replaced by an aluminium horror with two dazzling slabs of glass. May stood in its glare and turned grey-white.

'Thank you, Thomas. Now you get off home.'

'Shall I come in and make you a cup of tea?'

'I don't want to be a trouble to anyone.'

That was always their fear, that they'd be a trouble. 'No trouble,' Thomas said, and followed her in.

It was very warm, and smelled of washing, which was spread across all the radiators, burnt toast, and polish, and age, and damp, and other hints; fruit drops? Earth? It smelled of old people, to Thomas.

'Coo-ee,' she called, 'anyone home?'

He appeared before them at the top of the stairs, hands spread out in mock benediction, bright blond bristles catching the light, a thuggish Christ waving a bottle of beer. Completely different from the sullen child Thomas saw behind the counter in the newsagent's. He didn't look wimpish. He looked – what? – vicious. Thomas felt, I mustn't leave her with him. Which was ridiculous, of course.

He remembered Dirk vaguely as a whiney baby whom Shirley carried around like a doll. (Was there another memory? Something unpleasant.)

'Dirk, dear,' said May. 'You're home.'

'Yeah . . . jus' got back.' He was out of breath. His tiny mouth panted.

'I'll make us cocoa,' she said to him. Thomas suddenly sensed it was her son she wanted. The sorrow, the secret of the sorrow, was for him. It was family business. They would draw the curtains –

She drew the curtains. Thomas slipped into the dark.

'Death is part of life, my darling,' Suneeta said, when he complained about having to get rid of books. It was always tempting to send them to Purgatory – the 'Reserve Stacks', three dingy portakabins somewhere north of Utterley Road – rather than direct to the fires of hell, sealed in a black plastic rubbish bag. 'Death is part of life,' he silently assured the small sad faces of the banished authors. Once the shelves got tight, of course there had to be disposals. All the same, today it seemed – barbarous. *History of the Empire. Part One: Expansion . . . Ethics in Post-War British Business . . . Into the Future With Hope: The Welfare State in Post-War Britain.* Thomas felt shifty and shamefaced, carrying the heavy bag through the library. Was he a barbarian, like those he dreaded?

He had felt afraid, on the streets last night, startled not far from Alfred's gate by a mob of white skinheads in leather and chains, jostling, giggling, surging onwards like a knot of oiled seals diving over and under, looking for someone, blaring with laughter, barking for someone, he hoped not him – past the phone-boxes with the smashed glass walls still lying in tiny chunks of ice on the pavement, past the Methodist church whose strip-lit notice-board was covered with black hieroglyphic graffiti, yelling on down towards the Park, a pack in full cry, baying for blood, boys who didn't know the rules, vandals who tore up the rules . . . Yobs, but they roared like murderers.

Thomas hefted the bag right out of the library, though normally he'd leave it for the cleaners to dispose of. Doing my own dirty work, he thought. I'm not a bad person. I do contribute. He dropped the heavy weight in the skip. Some kind of animal scuffled in the shadows. Cats, rats –

(*That was it. Mice.* The thing about Dirk he had tried to forget. Dirk was eight or nine, May had asked Thomas to lunch. Alfred was at work, as usual. She was showing him her seedlings in their dark shed. Then they spotted two tiny pink blobs on the floor. They glistened faintly in the light from the door. 'Is that nestlings?' she asked, frowning, stooping. 'Poor little things, has a cat got them?' But it was two mice with their skins half-removed. Dirk had found them in her mouse-traps, and cut them with a penknife. 'He's just a child,' she had said to Thomas. 'You won't say anything to his father? Alfred can be a bit strict with him. Boys will be boys.' But her eyes looked frightened.)

15 · Dirk

Head hurts. Head hurts. Hangover. Sod. Sod. Sod the mornings. Nothing good, for ever and ever. Nothing gets better. Nothing any good. Dad, Dad. She wouldn't say, but there's something bad. Something – worse.

I don't believe it. The water's cold. What has she done, the stupid woman? She's gone and switched it off, that's what. Old and muddly. Old and mad. She cried, last night. Just sat there crying. Wouldn't explain, just sat and cried. Saying over and over 'Your dad – Your dad –'

She talks to me like I'm a little kid.

I hate it when my mother cries.

I might have – given her a hug or whatever. But she hasn't liked it, since I've been big. (Did she like it when I was small? Dunno.) She sort of shrinks when I try to touch her. That's women, isn't it? They don't like men.

I hate living with old people. Why should someone young and strong like me have to live with old people? My Mum was ancient when she had me. Forty-seven years old, which is disgusting, still doing that at nearly fifty. I heard her tell Ruby Millington that I was a mistake, which made me mad. One day they'll die and I'll be happy . . .

Oh sod, I'm crying, oh shit, oh shit, Dad can't die, not possible.

Half past five is the shit-work time. The hour when shit-workers start work, and everyone else lies snoring. Pigging themselves with pigging sleep. Two to a bed, pigs in a trough.

I pass their windows every morning, knowing they lie asleep inside. Hundreds of smug curtained windows. And I'm out here in the pouring rain, with water running down inside my collar and water bubbling up through my shoes. I want to throw stones and smash in their windows, and they'd see me standing there, pointing and jeering, it's me, it's me, I'm here every morning, but none of you know I fucking exist –

But I know them. I think about them. Nobody notices, no one ever did, but I'm sensitive, a thinker. A – philosopher. Even Mum and Dad never knew I was smart, but I am, I am. And now I've got friends.

My brother's a thinker. They're proud of him. He's famous for thinking, and sounding off. I could do that. I've got my opinions.

I'm proud of him too. He's my claim to fame. I told him that in the hospital yesterday. 'Darren, you're my claim to fame.' 'Oh I'm not famous, not *really* famous . . .' He is, of course. He's on TV, and in the papers every other day. I told him so. 'You're a famous writer.' He liked that a lot. He got a funny look . . . What I would call an eager look. So I said it again. 'You are, Darren. You are quite famous.' 'Do you read my pieces?' He was pricking up his ears, keen as anything. 'I see your picture, and your name.' – I couldn't actually say I'd read them. And that wanker was listening, Thomas Lovell, and he smiled a funny kind of smile. Which Darren noticed, and his face fell.

'I saw you on *Newsnight,*' I told him. 'You were good. You stood up to Paxman. He's a ponce.'

'Which time was that? Was it recently? The piece about American abortion clinics?'

'Something about some women,' I said. 'But, you know, it was good. And your suit was cool. You walked rings around Paxo, in that suit.' That is the very phrase I used. It just came to me. I was pleased with it. And he was smiling. I'd said the right thing.

I'll be frigging soaked through before I get to the shop, it just keeps coming, like a tidal wave. I used to wish for a tidal wave, to wash us away. The house and everything. Mum and Dad, and Shirley and me, especially after Shirley went funny . . .

But now Dad's ill, I feel different about it. I want things back the way they were. Now it's as if my whole life might change before I've had a chance to think about it. When you're the youngest, you never get asked. The wave is coming, we'll be swept away . . .

Mum's cracking up. She's not herself. She's a different person when Dad's not there. I thought last night, she's going mental. My own mother, cracking up. She wanted me to sit with her. I mean, I never sit with her. And I couldn't, could I? I was upset.

She'd had a talk to one of the doctors. For some reason she'd talked to a woman, but perhaps the senior doctors were busy. 'What if he never goes back to work,' she kept on muttering to herself. The tears were streaming down her cheeks, I didn't know what to do with myself. 'If he never goes back to work it'll kill him.'

'Course he'll go back to work, stupid. He told me himself he's feeling much better.'

'That's not what this doctor said.'

'Talk to his proper doctor tomorrow. She was probably just a woman, panicking.'

Mum told me off for 'funny ideas'. She said this doctor was his real doctor. She said that women were real doctors.

But Dad's like me. We have the same ideas. They're men's ideas, of course they are. Men and women are different, aren't they? That's probably why Darren keeps getting divorced. Like coloured people are different from whites, only Shirley's too thick to notice it.

We go down the pub and talk about them. Unless George is there, in which case they ignore me, Dad and him treating me like a kid, going on and on about the past, what Hillesden was like when they were boys. Which was before coloured people came, of course. Which happens to be of interest to me, but they leave me out of it, as if I'm too young to understand.

But I do understand. The blacks are taking over.

The row of shops is completely dark. Sodding hell, George hasn't sodding got there. Left me locked out in the sodding rain. The sodding frigging soaking rain. Like a dog or cat left out to drown. My head gets cold now my hair's so short –

Mum's not keen on my hair being short. 'It's your good point, your hair-colour,' she says. As though it was my only one. 'That horrible crewcut makes you look bald. There's enough men have to be bald. You don't.'

My dad was actually there when she said that. Mum's always on at me not to be rude, but how about that from Mrs Manners? My dad's going bald as a cricket ball.

Seems to me women think men don't have feelings. They get together and go on about us and laugh and try to make us feel small . . . Mum and Shirley, out in the kitchen. It was always like that: Us and Them.

Come on George, you frigging bastard. I'm *dying* out here in the rain on my own. I haven't even had a cup of coffee. While bloody old George is on his first two fags, hacking and puking in the back of the car as his ugly fat bitch of a wife drives him over.

George keeps on about visiting Dad. 'Just say the word, and Ruby'll bring me. We're waiting for the word, my boy.'

'You're not allowed to smoke, in a hospital.'

'Do you think I'm unacquainted with hospitals?'

He talks like someone from a book. I don't know what he's going on about, half the time. He's keen on books, or the idea of books. He actually thought we could sell some here! They ended in a bin, marked '3 for 20p', and we still couldn't sodding get rid of them. And these were great writers – Dick Francis, Jackie Collins! There aren't a lot of book readers, round here.

He's past it, really, a long way past it, but he won't give up, he leans on me. I carry that man. I carry his shop. And I still can't frigging get in in the mornings.

Ah, there he is. St Fucking George. Half-falling out of the car, good, bumping his great fat knee on the door. Then the rest of his body, a sack of lard. 'It's wet, in case you haven't noticed.'

'Sorry, sorry. We had an attack. We soldier on, but –' The rest of what he said was drowned in a horrible sickbag of coughing and gasping.

What I put up with. I'm a hero, really. Never mind George, *I* deserve a saintdom. I am a saint already. St Dirk.

Silly bloody name that woman gave me.

Something's up. Maybe George is dying. He's definitely being funny with me. Less rude than usual. Almost pleasant. As long as he's managed to do his will . . .

Mum thinks he's going to leave me the shop. It belongs to him, not rented or anything. George's parents lived over the shop. Now they rent out upstairs for good money, which is handy because the shop doesn't make a lot. (It could do. Would do. If I was boss.) They live with Ruby's mother, who's ancient. She's going to be a hundred next year.

I want my dad to live to a hundred. I want my dad to go on and on. I used to pop into the Park on my lunch-break and eat my sandwiches with him. It felt good, being with the Park Keeper. Being with the man in charge . . .

Dad is my other claim to fame. As well as my brother, who's more – *world*-famous. Different kind of fame, isn't it, really? They'd never think of having Dad on the telly, but everyone round here knows Dad. And I'm his son. And Darren's brother. We've got a lot of go, in my family. And I shall be someone. I'll make my mark. I shall get into the history books. Carve my name. Carve my name with – whatever. I'm good with words, but sometimes they escape me.

I'd like Mum to be proud of me. And Shirley (then she would be sorry). *I* could be *their* claim to fame. 'White, the millionaire businessman.'

Mum must be right that I'll get the shop. George hates me, but he hates the Pakis worse. The Pakis will never get this shop. They try it on, and he just says 'No'. He doesn't even like them coming in to buy papers. When they did, he talked about them under his breath. Swearing till even I got embarrassed.

Now I'd never do that, personally. Doesn't make sense. You want their money, so shut up about them until they're out of earshot. As customers, they aren't that bad. At least they've got money, which the blacks rarely do. Not that you see them spending it here.

Just the businessmen in pin-striped suits, funny little brown men with thick hair in long haircuts, grinning at me and asking for George, and they go behind the counter with their brief-cases and shut themselves up in the room at the back which I couldn't stay in for more than ten seconds without throwing up because it stinks of George, of sweat and sweets and Players' Navy Cuts, and after twenty minutes or so George starts shouting, George starts swearing and shouting a bit and they all pile out, still very smooth, the Pakis, smiling at him, smiling at me. Grinning, grinning as if they were winning. But I know he hates them. I know he won't sell.

'I'm playing a little game with them,' he explained to me, the week before last. 'I'm having a little game with our friends. Our coloured friends. It's an amusement.'

'How do you mean, amusement?' I asked. 'I thought you couldn't stand them in your shop. Now they're always round here. Oiling and mincing. They stink of aftershave. They're poofs. They are, all Paki men are poofs.'

Just once in a while we have a laugh, and I think old George is not so bad.

Not that I'm joking. Pakis *are* poofs.

I hate him most first thing in the morning. Like now. When George is just sitting there smoking and choking and I'm shitting bricks getting everything done. And he always has to criticize, doesn't he. 'You're not going to put those there, are you? Are you?' Yet he does nothing. I mean *nothing*. Doesn't even serve the customers now, the early ones who come in while I'm busy. He says he's too slow to get to the till. Too fat, he means. Too idle, he means. So he's sitting there putting all his effort into breathing. In, out, like a very slow saw. While I'm cutting the bundles of papers undone. And getting the van-drivers to take the returns. And checking to see the numbers are right. And seeing the supplements are in. And putting the papers out on the shelf, upside down because the mean old bugger is terrified of people reading headlines for free. And pulling out *Hello!* and *Take a Break!* and *Woman* to sit in our premier selling slots. And sorting out papers for the smelly little wanker who goes round shutting his fingers in letter-boxes. Harry Rutter, the paper-boy. And giving him a hard time if he's late. (That was me, wasn't it, for years and years? So maybe things are on the up, after all. Maybe Dirk White is on his way.)

But George is still sitting there, lighting up another.

Careful, fat-face. Don't tire your wrist. Why not just stuff the whole pack down your throat, then chuck a lighted match down after it?

George will snuff it, and I'll inherit. And get the shop the way I want. Bring the shop into the twenty-first century.

Which is going to be big for paper-shops, believe me. Forward-looking paper-shops. Shops that have got a bit of go. Ours hasn't, at the moment, but that's down to George.

Think videos.

Think Lottery.

Think Fax and Internet.

Especially the net. The Thing of the Future (We'll advertise. Think money. Think big!) Because lots of people won't have their own computer. And that's where we'll come in. With ours. Laughing. They'll put money in the slot for quarter of an hour or however long they need to get what they want. A line of computers, a line of chairs. I can see it clearly. Smart . . . *red* chairs. And coffee. And snacks. As long as Mum doesn't make them.

The doorbell goes and a girl comes in. One of the regulars. Posh little cow. Big eyes, skinny. George has always been a dirty old man. He's sweet on this one. Always has been.

'All right George? You look a bit tired.' She's got one of those voices. Pretend caring. I bet she's hard as nails, really.

'Melissa, dear. How very nice to see you.' Cough, cough, spraying the counter. 'The old chest is playing up this morning . . . What can I do you for today?'

I've heard that line so often I could puke.

'I'm just wondering if you keep aspirin. I've got a bit of a headache . . . I really miss our chemist, you know. It was so nice to have a local chemist.'

The chemist closed six months ago. And the lav shop will close. Windsor Drainage next door. It stands to reason that's got to go. Who's going to shop for lavs down here? This shop won't close though. People like tat.

'That'll be one pound thirty-five. Yes, pity about the chemist. Betting-shop's doing nicely though.'

'Huge now, isn't it?'

'Shows some people have money to spend.'

'If they had, why on earth would they be living here?' And she gives a big grin, like she's really smart, like she really knows something about this area, and then Ms Melissa is off with her aspirin.

They come and live here. People like her. Middle-class people, who fancy themselves. They go down the end where the slums used to be. They ponce around in jeeps and things, I see them, couples, laughing together, talking in loud stupid voices, and fucking queers, fucking arse-bandits – I know they look down their noses at us. They're only here till they can afford to get out.

I shan't do that. I'll stay here and – prosper. That *is* the word. Be prosperous.

I had a bit of a talk with Darren, last night. Of course, I didn't give everything away. But he is my brother. And he gave me respect. Together we set the world to rights, though he didn't agree with me about the Jews –

But he thinks I've got lots of bright ideas. He thinks I'm on the right lines, with the shop. He says he's shafted without his computer.

He even came up with some names for the business. I mean words are his manor, selling is mine. MediaNet was one suggestion.

'Proprietor D. White, Esquire.'

They do sometimes write that underneath, I've seen it.

16 · May

May walked furtively past the paper-shop. It was bad enough being at home with the boy. She had done her best to – tell him, last night – he had a right to know, he was their son – but he hadn't seemed to take anything in. She supposed he couldn't help it, but it made her feel worse. As if she would always be alone, from now on. In any case, she usually made a point of not going in when Dirk was working. It annoyed the boy, and she felt ashamed to see him lounging in a fug of smoke. He thought he worked hard, but there was nothing much to do, because even she could see the shop was failing. Alfred denied it, but that meant nothing. Being a woman, she faced facts.

Besides, she preferred the shop down the road, which had a much better choice of magazines and cards. Perhaps Dirk could get himself a job down there, though the staff all seemed to be busy young Asians – The wrapping paper was infinitely better, not that thin shiny stuff that wouldn't fold. They made a feature of presents, there. May had bought a dozen sheets at Christmas, then hidden it, so Dirk wouldn't see. Alfred accused her of disloyalty, but that was men; unrealistic. May liked to think she was a realist.

When it was wet, May's bags seemed to shrink, and her pockets got twisted, so nothing fitted, nothing went in, nothing came out. Her knuckles grew bigger, her hands clumsier. As she walked, she was trying to pull on her gloves, put away her keys, check she had her purse. List. She had a list, or ought to have a list. She tugged it out at last from the depths of her handbag and watched as the rain sent it spidery, illegible, struggling to fold it and shove it back in. And her keys got caught in the wool of her glove, came clanking out and fell on the floor. May bent, sighing, and picked them up. The rain on the pavements was black and sour. Did no one clean the pavements any more?

She ached inside. She ached for Alfred. Without Alfred, she was older, more stupid. Alfred was a lump where her heart should be.

But she heard him talk to her. *This won't do. Buck up, May. This isn't like you.*

She straightened her coat and walked on more briskly. She didn't want the neighbours to think she was defeated. The curtains would twitch, and they'd say 'There she goes. Looks to me as if he isn't going to get better.'

Well whatever the doctors said, they were wrong. May made herself smile, like a wife, not a widow; made herself think about him coming home, for she wouldn't let them keep him in hospital. She knew her husband better than they did.

Even if it came to the unspeakable thing. He couldn't die there. She wouldn't allow it. Alfred could always depend on her. She had brought back his boots, when he asked her to. Had shoved them in his cupboard with the blooming greatcoat. And sister had turned a blind eye, bless her, whatever the rules and regulations . . . He felt a lot better once his boots were there.

And thinking of that, she felt cheerful again, for she had a purpose, she had a use. She would be his rock; if need be, his soldier. The things that he had been to her.

She was going to the off-licence first. Was there a hospital rule against alcohol? No one had mentioned it, if there was. She found herself grinning like a schoolgirl. He loved his beer, always had done. At a time like this, he should have his comforts. She wouldn't take in great clinking bottles of beer, but miniature whiskies might do the trick. He could tuck them away in his bedside cupboard.

The girl in the off-licence seemed half-asleep, pallid and bored, disinclined to chat. She looked too young to be working there, but May smiled at her, and thanked her nicely, which made the girl's lips twist into a sort of sneer. As she bent towards May with the change, May smelled her breath. Some kind of spirit, which was sad. She had read about it in the papers, how all the young women liked to drink these days, but that poor girl should have been in school.

At least we've still *got* an off-licence. Not that we use it much, normally, but . . . Things should be there, in case you need them. That's how it used to be, round here. That's how it was until – when did it start dying?

We used to have everything here, she thought. Hillesden Rise was like a village. We used to have a bank; that went in ninety-four. And a building society. That vanished soon after. And the chemist – that went six months ago. She'd seen it coming; Mr Frost had been depressed, especially since the incident last year when two drug addicts beat him with the butt of a gun. She wouldn't say it to Shirley, but both of them were black . . . The most innocent remarks offended her daughter. Two flower-shops; both of them had gone under. Served them right for charging too much, though she missed the great lilies and the golden chrysanthemums waving at her behind the glass. Two shoe-shops; gone. Where she bought the kids' shoes. Their first tiny sandals, their sensible school-shoes. Now there was just a man who did repairs, an Indian, a gruff old thing who reminded her of her own father, sitting in the dark all day, hammering and sticking, helped by shrill-voiced women who were daughters or grand daughters. (You wouldn't catch an English family doing that, these days, though I helped my father, when I was a kid.)

Once we had a bakery-cum-cake-shop. She used to buy gingerbread men for the kids, and a sponge on Saturdays, since hers always sagged. It was – an ornament to the high street, the cake-shop, a sign of the prosperity that came with the fifties. May used to like sniffing the air outside: eggs, sugar, butter, vanilla. But the shop changed hands some time in the eighties; they brought in rubbish baked in Kilburn. By the time they folded, no one much cared . . . There was a solicitor's where May and Alfred had made their wills twenty years ago, when it seemed like a joke that they would ever need them. That only survived the bank by a year. Electrical Goods; went in ninety-six. Hardware store; ditto. Jewellers; late eighties. May missed the jewellers; it was romantic, looking in at the second-hand rings and lockets and lucky charms, gleaming on the velvet. She had liked old Hymie, who also mended watches, and never minded getting things out of the window even though he knew May was only looking. (He was . . . partial to her, when she was younger, when they were both young; a lifetime ago.) But he got too nervous, after three or four break-ins, the last one with him present, in broad daylight. He didn't resist, but they still broke his jaw. 'My wife says, "Hymie, it's just not worth it."'

We had two or three butchers – three, after the war. They used to dress up properly, in blue striped aprons. Then later with little white trilby hats. Then the windows started to look a bit patchy, because butchers needed to have lovely full windows, gleaming chops and ribs and legs, not grey lumps eked out with plastic parsley. Last November the one surviving butcher closed. 'We had hoped to keep going till Christmas, Mrs White. I don't like to let the customers down.' His face had been pallid as the chicken-legs. 'Don't worry, we'll go down to Gigamart,' said a stringy young woman with a bright yellow crewcut, dragging her toddler out of the shop. May wanted to kick her, but she did have a point. If they'd had a car, she would have done the same. May had been keen to drive, at one stage, when Ruby and George had got their first motor, but Alfred was always too busy to learn, and he thought he'd look silly being driven by a woman. And now I'll be stranded, she thought resentfully, then realized that meant if Alfred dies . . .

There used to be a fish-monger's with marble slabs on which beautiful blue and pink bodies gleamed. She used to buy roes, and do them on toast . . .

When we were first married. It was Alfred's favourite. His eyes were so blue when he smiled at me. And kippers, for breakfast. And the odd bit of plaice. He thought fish was healthy, though the smell was awful, and I bought it regularly, twice a week, but what good did it do him, what good, what good?

May stopped, found her hanky, pulled herself together. She couldn't go crying in the street at her age.

She passed the betting-shop. She rarely looked in through the plate-glass windows with their crude graphics. It seemed like catching men at something shameful; they went in looking furtive, came out looking sad. In the past ten years it had doubled in size, to three times the size of a normal shop. May had bet twice in her life, both times on the Derby, both times when the names of the horses seemed lucky, 'Early Sherbet', which reminded her of Shirley, and 'King Alfred', which of course – of course. And she lost the money, naturally. It was a sort of sink, soaking up people's money. But all sorts of betting was popular, these days. The paper-shop she favoured did the Lottery. A huge yellow sign beckoned from the window. Whereas George had turned down the chance to have the Lottery. 'Ruby says it's taking people's money for nothing. They don't have a lot to spare, round here.'

They did. She saw them. A tenner at a time, and the poorest people were the worst of the lot. A tenner on Saturday and 'instants' on week days. Betting and boozing, as other things dwindled. Till all that was left would be the pub and the betting-shop. Nowhere for people like May to go.

The shop keepers all used to know my name . . . They knew our kids. Looked out for them. Shirley never went out without being given toffees. And the mothers all used to meet up in the shops. We stood there talking and blocking up the gangways till the shopkeepers started giving us looks. But it wasn't bad for business, not really. The local shops were like a club. If you asked, they would get things in just for you. They even cashed cheques when the bank was closed. It was like a dream now, all that bustle and variety, people who smiled and knew your name . . . In Gigamart, the staff all looked like robots. Stacking shelves by numbers, in nylon uniforms.

It was all going faster than May had realized. Almost trotting down the street, her blue coat clutched around her, she saw that more than half the shops were boarded up, or had their fronts covered with aluminium shutters, which rattled coldly in the winter winds. 'To Let', the boards said, hopefully, but no one new came except charity shops, and they already had three, full of wrong-coloured garments. So the boards got battered, and looked grimy, guilty, each one a confession of failure and emptiness. It was over, Hillesden Rise was over, over, and May found the tears welling up again, and realized she was crying for herself and Alfred and the silly young couple they had once been.

We liked it here. It was our – El Dorado. Once upon a time, it had all we needed.

17 · Dirk

His mother and father. He would never escape them. He was nothing at all, except their son.

Until he made his millions with MediaNet. Then he'd have his own place. In Brighton, maybe. Those pier thingies . . . So white in the sunlight. He and the lads had gone down one day, and before they'd got blasted, he'd seen the sea, very far away, blue and unfrightening behind all the pebbles, and the piers like – big white palaces. Two of them. Long. With lots of bits. He would have one, his family the other.

'So how's your father? I'm talking to you.'

Dirk wished he'd belt up. He enjoyed his own thoughts. In the quiet moments. The quiet minutes. The quiet half-hours, because today was quiet. Weekends were quiet. Well, weekdays were quiet. It was always quiet, except for George coughing.

'I said, how's your dad.'

'Uh . . . All right.'

'So. How about yours truly popping up to see him? Tomorrow would be good. For the wife and self.'

Dirk didn't want him coughing over his father. George's breath was lethal at twenty paces. 'Like I said, it's like, just family, at present. My brother's just come back from abroad. From – overseas.' That gift with words. Whatever the sodding teachers said, always comparing him to Darren and Shirley.

(Though Mum seemed to think he was pathetic at English. 'Not your best subject. Never mind.' 'What is my best subject then?' he'd asked. A long silence while she gawped at him.)

'That would be – Darren?'

'Yes.'

'Brilliant boy. Outstanding. Went down the brain drain, didn't he?'

Dirk felt like hitting his great ugly mug. How dare he say Darren had gone down the drain? 'You're going peculiar in your old age. He's famous, Darren. Everyone knows him.'

'Do they? Get on!' George was bloody laughing.

'He's Darren White, the People's Friend. He's a household name, my brother is. He has a column in *The Mail* every week. He e-mails it from the USA.'

That shut him up for a moment. George wouldn't even have a photocopier here, because he was frightened of machines. And Dirk did most of the addition in his head, because George said he was better than a calculator. It was true that numbers were easy for him. But he had refused to do maths GCSE. It was boring. He knew it, so why write it down?

'I'd be very happy to see your brother,' George said in a sickly, syrupy voice. 'Household name, is he, now? I remember him when he was four years old. Lovely little lad, curly brown hair. Apple of his father's eye.'

It was a pool of mush. Spreading out towards him. Darren wouldn't give him the time of day.

'So I'll pop along tomorrow. Have a word with Alfred. Like to have a word. Just show my face.'

Why couldn't he wait till Dad comes out? They saw each other twice a week. There's something up, I know there is.

Maybe he's going to retire, at last. Maybe he wants to tell my dad it's time for him to hand things over to me. Sound him out. See if it's OK, like. See if there's any hope of me accepting.

Look who it is. It's not my day. Wanker-in-Chief, King of the Wristers. Thomas Lovell the Librarian. Grinning away like a Cheddar Cat.

'Good morning, Dirk,' he says to me. That's out of order, saying my name! Just because he saw me in the hospital doesn't suddenly make us best of friends.

'Ah, Thomas,' says George. 'How's the book racket?' Rubbing his great fat hands together as if he was squashing a pack of butter.

'George. Morning. All right, thank you. Well, more cuts, that sort of thing. I've just popped home to let in the plumber.'

'Drains?'

'No . . .'

'Pipes?'

'No . . .'

'Is it your lav then?' says Nosey Parker. 'Windsor Drainage, next door. They'll fix you up.'

'Tap,' says Lovey, and he goes a bit red. Wanker can't even fix his own frigging washer! '*Guardian*, please', he says, very quick.

'Dirk. Fetch Thomas a *Guardian*.'

'They're on the shelf,' I say, outraged.

'Not to worry, of course I'll get my own . . . No news of your father, this morning, I suppose?' And Lovey looks at me as if we're best friends.

'No.' (*Guardian*-reader! Gobbler! Pansy! I hate the voices of people like him. Loving themselves. Too bloody loud. Totally . . . self-competent.)

'Regards to your family,' Lovey says to me. 'I'll probably pop in to the hospital again tomorrow.'

'Uhn,' I grunt, not looking at him.

'Regards to your sister. I didn't say goodbye.'

'She wouldn't have noticed.' One up to me.

And now he's gone, he's gone, thank God.

'I thought you said only family was visiting?' George's eyes are like the eyes of a spaniel. Big, brown, bloodshot and bloody miserable.

'Yes, but some people always push in.'

'Your dad's my oldest friend,' said George suddenly. 'My oldest . . . surviving friend, you know. Your mum knows that. She wouldn't mind. We go back a long way, me and Alfred. Before you were thought about, young man.'

And the coughing swells, a great gale of it, as if he will burst, as if he's exploding, as if what's been hiding has to get out, as if he's been holding it in too long, and now he will cough till there's nothing left and the shop is covered with blood and phlegm.

Maybe it's now. Maybe it's time.

And I'll sit and watch and do nothing to save him.

But no. Getting quieter. Calming down. Now I can hear the rain again, the hiss of rain as the cars go past. None of them stop. Roaring past us. Off to the shops that rake in the money. Doling their acash out at frigging Gigamart. Largeing it down the sodding West End. Putting on the dog in bloody Bond Street, flashing their cards for the wops and the Jews . . .

This is an English shop. What have they got against us?

18 · Shirley

Whenever it rained Shirley thought about Kojo. He said English rain was quiet, like tears.

He meant Shirley's tears. She was his 'quiet woman'. Quieter than his African loves. *He had many women before he met me but it was me he married, me he loved.*

Shirley dressed herself with elaborate care, though she was only going shopping. Leaving the house to escape the pain. Silks and wools of milk and honey that made her skin glisten rose and pearl . . . *Oh Kojo once called me his pink pearl, and his pale pearl, and his –*

Stop, stop.

Purse. Hanky. Cards. Umbrella?

It was the second time she had dressed that day. Jeans and jumper for breakfast with Elroy. He'd made her tea, then she made him breakfast. He left for the hospital at 8 a.m.

He never leaves without telling me he loves me. He isn't a talker, but he always says he loves me –

I don't know what to say to him.

Last Sunday I cooked him his favourite fried chicken and we sat together in the kitchen and talked. I said I could never marry again. (Once you've loved someone so completely . . .) But Elroy's desperate to marry me. 'We are living in sin,' he says, quite straight. He's twenty years behind the times – the Pentecostal church does that to you. I love Jesus as much as him, but I don't think God minds about marriage. Love is patient, love is kind . . . He's the God of Love, and He loves us all.

When it rained on Saturdays, we stayed in bed, Kojo and I, we loved to be naked, can that have been me, can life have been so good? Naked, in a nest of sheets, his beautiful warm slender body, curled round mine, stroking, playing, and then inside me, he spent hours inside me . . . Usually he'd worked till three in the morning, straining his eyes at that glaring screen, his big brown eyes always slightly bloodshot, then up at seven, racing, chasing – But at weekends he loved to lie in. I'd bring up our breakfast, we'd eat together, slowly, ravenously, playing around, jazz on the radio, rain on the window, the smoke from his fags curling up in the light, I liked the smell, it was part of the music, the smell of Kojo and our life together, how many cigarettes did I light for him? The curve of his lips with the tip between them, smiling at me, staring at me . . . His beautiful lips. So full, so firm, not tight and thin like English lips. He used to eat me with his eyes, he used to eat me till I came, I hardly knew my body before I met him. They say that black men won't go down on you, that they just like pumping away all night, jump on top and get on with it, but it isn't true of all of them, no more than any of these things are true, though Kojo could make love all night – (Elroy has never gone down on me, but Elroy is younger, less confident. He will, one day. When he loves me more. I go down on him, and it blows his mind.) But Kojo was an artist. Kojo loved me. Kojo found me. He found my joy, what was the word, the long French word, my *jouissance,* the word he used in his books for coming, the word he taught me, as he taught me to come.

No, I never came before I met Kojo. I never told him, but I never came. When we started, it seemed too big an admission, I didn't want to give him so much power. But now I wish I had told him, thanked him. Thank you Kojo. Dear love, dear heart.

(Are you somewhere? Anywhere? Listening?)

My lovely love. My African love. Maybe he's with his ancestors . . . He was westernised, he dismissed all that, but I think that part of him still believed it. He said he was a Marxist, but these things go deep. If he could be a Marxist and a Christian, he could be a Christian and believe in spirits, though he laughed when we went to visit his second cousin and found queer rubber balls in every room, and afterwards I asked him if Kwame had children, and he told me each ball stood for a different spirit, the spirits of the air and the wind and the forest. I thought it was a beautiful idea, but he claimed to think it ridiculous. 'I left all that nonsense behind in Ghana.'

I hope he is with his ancestors. I can't believe he is entirely lost.

Forgive me, Jesus, for thinking these thoughts. No one who sleeps in You can be lost.

We didn't have children. He was sure we would. It fell slowly upon us, the heaviest sorrow. If I had his children, he would still be with me. I did conceive. Twice. Two boys. One lost at ten weeks, one at twelve. In the first years of marriage. Afterwards, nothing.

I knew nothing about Africa when I met him, I thought all black people were Africans. My dad hated black people, of course, and he called them 'coloured', so I did too, though whatever Dad hated I was ready to like, and I never knew 'coloured' was insulting till I went with Kojo and he told me not to say it. I asked him the difference between 'coloured' and 'black' and he said, 'Right now you are blushing, Shirley. When you're upset, you turn every kind of colour. Don't you think white skins colour more than ours?' It was another world, with another way of thinking.

Elroy's family is Jamaican, though he was born in south London. That's partly why Elroy is jealous of Kojo, because he was African, and so highly educated. West Indians don't like Africans much and I always think it's jealousy. Africans have their own names, after all. West Indians don't. White people stole them. I felt so ashamed when Kojo told me West Indian names are all slave names. Slave owners stamping their names for ever . . . and then there are the Africans who don't like West Indians, 'slave babies.' The worst insult.

It isn't easy, being Caribbean. What they feel about Africans isn't simple. They think that Africans are backward and strange, as well as saying they're perpetual students. Which some of the Africans over here are –

But Kojo made it, he got his D Phil and became a lecturer, a Reader, in fact, which is next to Professor – A Reader in Comparative Literature. But his success makes Elroy feel small (because Elroy will never be as clever as Kojo). Though Elroy's done very well, in fact, at least he has a steady job, unlike most black men of his generation.

I used to feel so proud when I went to see Kojo. DR KOJO ASANTE on the door of his office. I loved being married to a doctor. I did, I admit it, I was sinfully proud, and perhaps that's why God took him away from me – No, nonsense, God isn't vengeful.

Today I got up at half-seven with Elroy. He always leaves at eight a.m. When you're up at half-seven, the mornings are long. I'd made the bed and washed the breakfast things and polished the table and watered the house-plants and done the dusting and a load of washing and ironed another by quarter past ten.

And looked out of the window. The garden I made. The garden I made to enjoy with Kojo. Long green tails of bulbs flicking up. The apple-tree where we used to picnic. And it's still raining, always raining . . .

Elroy's lighter than Kojo. He had one white grandmother. Kojo was black, dark, dark, beautiful black, a black with the sheen of coal or grapes, I loved his skin, I licked his skin. His blue-black shining West African skin. The skin of princes, emperors. Giving back light. Black full of light. I loved him so much I wanted to eat him.

When the cancer came, it did seem to eat him. At first he was slimmer. Then much too thin. And his skin lost its shine. It had a greyish tinge. It was me who insisted he went to the doctor, although I was as afraid as him, and he found so many reasons for delaying. Until he couldn't delay any longer. In constant pain, always coughing.

And then there were things he had to do. Practical things, legal things, things which took time he did not have, but he sat with the lawyer, coughing, gasping, as words like 'domicile' and 'future intention' and 'nationality' droned through the air, and I brought them black coffee, but they hardly looked up. Kojo had been given a great deal of wealth by his mother's brother, an international diplomat, descended, as Kojo did, from paramount chiefs and ultimately from Ashanti kings. We'd never had to worry about money . . . (So hard to get used to, being married, being rich, being loved by someone I loved in return. So hard to get used to, so hard to lose.) The Ashanti tribe believes all wealth must stay within the family, handed down through the female line, so Kojo knew that on his death they would expect his possessions to come back. He had given and given, all the time we were together, to his sisters and his sisters' children, his cousins and his cousins' children, but it wasn't enough, they would expect his estate. They weren't greedy, it was simply the custom. I knew that most of them had never accepted that I was his wife, though it was nothing personal, indeed they were warm and friendly to me, they were simply waiting for Kojo to come home and take his legitimate, Ashanti wife – I didn't mind if they had his money.

But Kojo minded. He wanted it for me, since he couldn't stay alive and protect me. In the end nearly all of it came to me, but I still send money to all his dependents. It makes me feel better, doing that. It somehow proves I was his wife, I am his widow, and part of his family, part of Kojo, Mrs Shirley Asante . . .

Now he is dead, I believe they accept me. His sister Abena brings her children over from Ghana to stay. To begin with, we were shy with each other. The little girls stared at me, deep into my eyes, touched my hair, tried to plait it, sat on my lap and stroked my face. At first my whiteness hypnotized them. Their mother seemed frightened or hostile on arrival, but she was grudgingly impressed when I cooked them dinner, jolof rice with chicken and corned beef and plantain on the side, great steaming platefuls, palm soup and peanut soup, so many choices. 'Not bad for an *obroni*,' she said. 'But you need more ginger. Didn't Kojo tell you?'

I said to her, firmly, 'He loved my food.' I had prepared a feast, enough for ten people, to show them they were welcome, to show them I could do it, I so much wanted to be part of their family.

But she still hadn't got over the dispute about the will. She smiled at me, but her eyes didn't smile. She said, 'No *obroni* could cook *fufu,* or *banku.*'

I put them on the table: *fufu, banku.* The consistency exactly right. Stodgy, starchy, but not too heavy.

By the time we had finished the meal we were friends. When she went up to bed she came and hugged me, close to her chest. 'Oh Shirley – I love you, Shirley.' So African! So very un-English! Over the next few days she wept with me, wept and laughed, held my hand. We swopped our memories of Kojo –

But only memories. I am a widow.

Such a bleak poor word. Widow, widow, wailing and sad, on two dull notes. All I wanted to be was wife and mother, Kojo's wife for the rest of my life, mother of his healthy children.

Despite the sorrows (my family, number one, and the morons who said cruel things on the street) – against all the odds, we were blissfully happy. And yet there were sorrows and differences. Ashanti men may not enter the kitchen! I told him that modern British men all did, but I happily cooked for him, cared for him, loved him, and he cared for me, he cared for me . . . And then there was his cousin who came and made trouble. She stayed with us; I made her welcome. On the second day, when Kojo went out, she asked me why I hadn't given him a baby. I couldn't speak; the hurt stole my breath. Then she laughed, and said he already had children, didn't I know? So it didn't matter. Soon he would leave me, and go back to Ghana. 'We are waiting for him, we know he will come.' When Kojo came home he could see I'd been crying. I said 'You're not going to leave me, Kojo?' and he stormed next door and shouted at his cousin. It was all in Tri. There was a long argument. She left, with her cases, hardly speaking to me. He came back into the house looking almost frightened. 'I shall never ask you, Kojo,' I said. And whatever the truth, he stayed with me.

We left our families to be together, we had to be all in all to each other. Beneath us, the Everlasting Arms. We thought there would be so many years.

Stupid tears. They never run dry.

Stop. Wipe. I have to go out.

Purse, make-up, cheque-book, coat.

How many times have I walked to this bus-stop?

Oxford Street is a vision of hell. The bus goes nosing down like a barge, crushing the struggling souls beneath. From the top deck, waves of them seem to disappear, sucked slowly under the metal prow, going under the wheels, silently under.

But I'm sitting pretty on the very front seat, which I took when two screaming kids got off, how can I like them when I've none of my own? (Elroy would like to have kids with me, Elroy is sure we shall be lucky. He says if we marry God will surely bless us, that it's to God's glory if we bear much fruit, for He is the Vine, and we are the branches. Elroy already has a child, seven or eight years old, a boy, Dwayne. He never sees the mother; he claims she hates him. He wants to start again, with me.)

I was sitting behind them. Sisters, I think. Nine or ten years old, I'm not a good judge. Arms round each other, giggling and screaming . . .

(I wish I could make friends with Elroy's sisters. If I had a baby, I think it would help. Elroy's brother Winston is sweet to me, because he is sweet to everybody, the younger brother, the pride of the family, a student at London University. He has big soft eyes like a baby deer, and he's always smiling, or laughing, as if he knows some secret joke about life. And he's clever; so clever I could listen for ever, though I wouldn't want to make Elroy jealous. The two of us are going to a film on Saturday about the life of James Baldwin, the writer. Winston suddenly invited the family to come but none of the others was interested, and Elroy said, 'Wasn't he a battyboy, Winston? We did him at school. Waste of a Saturday. Why don't you come down the club with me?' But I said, 'My mother's got one of his novels. I'll go with you, Winston, if you want me to.' The sisters are different – one shy, one prickly. I feel so awkward with Delorice and Viola. Delorice who always has the baby in her arms and only ever talks to her, and Viola, so lean and muscular and pretty, the older sister, the driving one, managing a boutique in Kilburn and planning on partnership and then expansion. Such a fast talker, so glamorous, working out in the gym every day. With her I feel meek and flabby and stupid. I'd like her to like me, but I don't think she does. I'd like to be part of their family.)

If Elroy and I had a family, I often think it would all be easy.

Warm and dry in the revolving door, sweeping me into sweet-smelling heaven.

The department stores: my second home. Mum says they never shopped like us, in her day. The big stores weren't for people like her. I think it frightens her, my shopping, even though I tell her I have plenty of money, even though it doesn't do any harm. 'We only shopped when we had to, dear. Too much to do, and we didn't have the money.' I do have the money. Kojo's money.

They make me welcome. I feel I fit in. I don't feel lonely or sad, when I'm shopping.

Besides, a lot of shops know me, by now. The Hosiery department, in DH Evans. Ladies' Fashion in Selfridges. I like to specialize, you see. That way, they start to take an interest. In the Perfume department in John Lewis, they know my face, they know my taste. They look at me and think Givenchy. Imagine that. A family of scents. A beautiful family, a Parisian family, worn on smooth skin all over the world, worn with lace, worn with pearls –

They look at me, and think 'Paris, Europe,' not Shirley White as I used to be, one of the family from Hillesden Junction, who've lived in Hillesden since time began. And with that thought, they set me free.

All my life till I was twenty-eight and married Kojo, I was Shirley White. Alfred and May's unmarried daughter. The one who somehow messed up her life. In the mean streets of Hillesden they thought they knew me.

Kojo saved me. Kojo re-named me. Kojo saw what I could become.

And then he bloody went and left me. Then he died, and let me down. Then he got ill from the wretched fags, the bloody awful lethal fags, the hateful stinking sticks of poison, drawers full of cartons from the duty-free.

Then he died and abandoned me. And I was dragged back to my family.

What if Dad starts shrinking like Kojo did? Before my eyes, inch by inch. I tempted him with all his favourite dishes, palm soup with *fufu,* spinach and okra stew, but he ate less and less, though he wanted to please me. I begged him to eat, one steamy hot day, and he lost his temper, Kojo *never lost his temper* but he shouted at the wall, the window, the garden, the little garden so unlike Ghana, 'Nothing tastes right . . . How can I eat it?' Then he muttered something angry about *obroni.*

I think he meant he was missing Ghana, perhaps he wanted to die in Ghana. After he shouted, I began to cry. I started to clear the plates away. And he said, very quietly, himself again, 'But I love you, my *Obroni Yaa.*' It meant, 'White Person Born on Thursday'. I went and hugged him. He was skin and bone. 'I don't want to leave you.' 'You're not

going to leave me.' *Thursday's child has far to go* . . . I would have
followed him anywhere, but I couldn't die, though I lay beside his body
and begged Jesus to take me.

But Dad won't die. Of course he won't. People get better from strokes
all the time. I should worry about Mum. She'll wait on him even more
than usual, hand and foot –

I don't think I shall be able to help her. I'll do my best, but I don't
think I can bear it. I don't want to look after his body, however old it's
become, and weak.

Because when he was strong, he frightened us.

The boys worse than me, but he hit me too. When I was too little to
protect myself. I took it for granted for years and years, and then I realized
he had no right. That *I* had a right to mind, to be angry. And I was
angry. *I am angry.* More for the fear, I think, than the bruises. No bruises
to speak of. Only the fear.

I like the café I'm going to. One of the nicest of the big store cafés. I
look good in the mirrors: blond, confident, surging upwards on the
escalator. Past Children's Clothes, which I never look at, searching for
the pale pink sign for heaven: *Café Claire.* Waitress Service.

I like to sit where I can see the view. Right across the roofs of London.
I once tried counting all the windows you could see. Windows where
people might be sitting and dreaming or getting better from illnesses.
Windows where lovers might lie in bed. I stopped when I got near two
hundred.

I don't want to think. Turn up the Muzak. Well-dressed women,
mostly older than me, blond-streaked helmets, their heads held high.
They have had husbands, sorrows, triumphs, they lift their chins, they
put on a good show. (And children. Most of them must have had
children.)

Mum had three children. I have none.

19 · May

May butted on down the dark road in the rain. Every part of her felt uncomfortable. The fingers of her gloves were cold and soggy. There seemed to be nobody around to chat to, though there would be a queue in the post office.

She liked the postmaster, Mr Varsani, a meticulous man who had come to England after the war and brought up his family in Hillesden Rise. They were the first in their street to modernize their house, the first with an extension, the first to concrete over the little front garden. They kept the plane-tree, which others had not. Two cars shone side by side on the concrete, cleaned and polished every weekend. He chatted to May when the counter wasn't busy. She liked his smooth tan skin, his sharp intelligence, though Alfred picked it up and got jealous and accused him of cheating with the change. 'See what they're like. You can't trust them.' That was her husband. Men did get jealous.

Now May was depending on Nimit Varsani to sort out her problem with the pension book. Thank heavens for the post office, she thought. Where would the old people be without that? She herself wasn't old, but there were so many people who could hardly walk, and wouldn't make it to Kilburn. And the young mothers, trailing crowds of kids. They didn't all have cars. They didn't all have husbands. The post office was the heart of Hillesden Rise.

The young ones seemed to view it as a cash dispenser, going in to collect their weekly wage, though all they were doing to earn it was breeding – May caught herself back. She disapproved of envy. But she and Alfred had always worked for their money, and she had cleaned floors when the kids were little, taking them with her, which was miserable in houses where they weren't allowed to make a noise. She didn't wish hardship on other people. But she sometimes wondered how Nimit felt, handing out thousands of the government's money, seeing the same faces year after year, when he, as he had once told her proudly, had 'tried to take nothing from this country' – he paid for the children to be born in private hospitals, sent them to expensive private schools. He put a lot in and took nothing out. Nimit served the community, didn't he, as she had once pointed out to Alfred. 'I know you don't like him, but he's just like you. Both of you serve the community, Alfred.'

Which was why May was glad that for once today she was paying something in before she drew their money. They had a little giro account at Nimit's, and she meant to pay in the thick wad of crisp notes that Darren had handed her last night. 'Take it – don't fuss. Picked it up at the airport. My God, you are my mother, after all. I'm not having you short of money.' Susie was watching, which May didn't like. It made them look poor, in front of strangers, which was what Susie was, though she was Darren's wife. 'I'm not short,' May said. 'It's just – a technicality. To do with signatures. You know your father.'

'It's a Stone Age marriage. Dad signs everything,' said Darren to Susie, with a superior smile.

'Well at least it's lasted,' May flashed back, shoving the notes crossly into her bag. Unlike yours, Mr Bighead, she thought to herself.

Later, much later, she counted them and marvelled. Could he hand out three hundred pounds just like that? Even if he could, she wasn't going to spend it. Maybe when Alfred was better, they could take a little break . . . Nearing the red sign, she was suddenly uncertain, patting vaguely at her bag in the whipping rain. It didn't feel fat enough to hold the money. Had she gone and forgotten it? Old, stupid.

Ignoring the rain, which was dripping down her neck, she shoved her gloved hand inside the bag's hard jaws. But her big metal comb hooked on to the wool, and she shook her hand, irritably, to get the damn thing off and suddenly everything was clattering downwards, all caught together in some ghastly muddle, purse, notebook, mirror, change – and finally, just too fast for her, the bundle of notes went spinning downwards, and as she gasped and reached out desperately to catch it, May herself went sprawling, foot turning and slipping on the greasy pavement, and as she fell, she dropped her whisky. The crash of the glass sounded very final.

First she registered she wasn't much hurt.

Winded, stung. But she could move her ankle.

Then she began to scrabble for her things.

But someone was coming, two feet in Nike trainers, big black and white trainers moving quiet and fast, and she looked up to see an enormous black man looming out of the rain, panting, gasping, his golden eyes boring into hers, and she shrank back, covering the money with her skirt, as the pantherish face swooped down towards her.

'Help,' she cried feebly, still out of breath, and then 'Help', louder, but no one would hear her, and she thought, in that instant, knowing she would die, please God take care of Alfred and the kids.

20 · Shirley

We were nearly always well behaved, as children, well-mannered, hard-working, not answering back. Darren, being the oldest, had tried it on. He staged his rebellion and had it crushed, brutally, wrestling hand to hand with Dad, because Dad was tough, he was small but tough, he was very fit from his life outside. The women stood in the kitchen sobbing, me and Mum, with our arms round each other. 'Call the police,' I begged her, as they shoved and grunted. 'He'll kill my brother. Call the police.' 'He won't kill him,' she said, but she didn't sound sure. There were horrible sounds of fist on flesh, bone on wood, thumping, yielding, sounds I have never been able to forget. 'I'll break you,' I heard Dad shout, insanely. All of a sudden, they stopped exhausted. Darren knelt on the floor, wiping dribble from his mouth, sobbing, 'Stop it, stop it, stop it, I'm sorry.' Then he ran from the house. I ran after him because I thought he would never come back, because I thought he would kill himself: 'Darren, Darren!' I couldn't catch him. I could never run fast and I had the wrong shoes and no coat in winter and people looked at me as though I was crazy. I probably was crazy, with fear and grief.

How did we ever get over that? How do families ever recover? And go on to seem normal. A lovely family. People congratulated Dad on his family . . .

'Madam?'

'Sorry, I was dreaming. A cappuccino. And if you could bring some cakes?'

'Certainly, madam. With grated chocolate?'

'Oh plenty of grated chocolate, thanks.'

When Mum had another baby late in life I wanted to protect him, the little blond scrap, his thin pale face and his frightened mouth, from what had happened to the rest of us. Poor little Dirk. Is that why I loved him?

'Leave him alone!' It was suddenly easy to stand up to Dad on Dirk's behalf. So perhaps that was the gift Dirk gave me. Perhaps it wasn't all one way.

He had spilled Dad's beer. An accident. It was his second beer, it was Sunday lunch. That second beer had often spelled trouble. I stood up to Dad. My heart was bursting –

'Coffee, madam. Excuse me.'

I hadn't heard the waitress. She stands there smiling.

'Your cakes are on their way.'

'Yes. Thank you.' – Nearly twenty years later, my voice is still shaking.

My father hit me in the mouth. 'You mind your own business, how dare you,' he yelled, beside himself, insane with temper.

Then Dirk was crying and begging him. 'Please don't hit Shirley, please don't hit Shirley, it's my fault, Daddy, I'm sorry, I'm sorry –' Lying on the floor. Submission posture. Trying to make his father less angry. I had learned about that in psychology, I was studying then, I was different then, I thought I was going to be a teacher, before things went wrong, before my life went wrong, but perhaps it had already all gone wrong, being brought up in that house of torture.

And Mum in the kitchen, her low frightened voice. 'Don't, Alfred.

Please don't, Alfred. She's only nineteen. He's only seven.' But very quiet. Too scared to speak up. Too scared to come into the living-room and help us.

Later she crept upstairs after me and stood on the landing outside the bathroom. Dirk had been sent to bed for making trouble. Dad had slammed out of the house for a walk, off to the Park where he always went after there was a row, as if *he* couldn't bear it – But it was all his doing, wasn't it? He made the rows, didn't he? It was his fault. If he didn't enjoy it, couldn't he have stopped it? This time he left in the middle of things, so the horror wasn't over, the lump in the throat, the lead weight in the belly, the fear of worse to come. Mum hissed at me through the rickety door. 'Shirley. Darling. Are you all right?'

I didn't answer. I was sponging my face, pressing cold water against the bone, where I felt so bruised, where I felt so hurt, for he'd never before hit me in the face. It was too personal; it almost felt sexual –

'Shirley. Please.'

'Just go away.'

'Shirley, dear. I have to see.'

'Come in and see then.' I flung the door open. There was a little cut, from his watch, I think, and a red-blue mark was steadily deepening. 'I hate him, Mum. I'll have to kill him. How dare he hit me. I'm *nineteen*, I'm grown up!'

'I'm sorry, darling.' She took the flannel and gently pressed it against my skin.

'It hurts.'

'I know. You shouldn't get involved.'

'Oh great.' I turned and pushed her away. 'So I let him hurt my brother, do I? That's your policy, never get involved.'

'It is his house. You might be better away.'

'Then who would stand up for my little brother? Not you. You're . . . disgusting. You're hopeless. You're a coward.' I spat it at her, tears bursting, flowing. At that moment I hated her as much as him.

And then of course Mum started crying. She sat beside me on the edge of the bath, and I pushed her away, but she held my hand, held on to it grimly as I tried to shake her off, and then I gave up, and we sat there crying.

'I think you could cover it with make-up.'

'Yes.' Cover things up; we always did.

'I'm sorry, Shirley. I feel afraid.'

'It's all right, Mum.' I was sorry for her. Sorry for her, for Dirk, for all of us.

We went together to peep at Dirk. 'Do you want some milk before your father gets back?'

He was under the blankets, curled up in a ball, his blond hair sticking out on the pillow, and then he uncurled, we saw his red blurred face, streaming with snot, a baby's face, the face of a boy turned back into a baby by having his courage beaten out of him – (I would never hit a child; never, never. Perhaps it's as well that I've never had one. They say you always pass it on.)

'I'll kill him,' he sobbed. 'I hate him. When I'm bigger, you wait, I'll *smash* him' – but that was my father talking, you see. Those were Dad's words, when he got mad. Dad liked to think he could smash people. People were things when they got in his way.

And he had turned Dirk into a kind of thing, all smeared and swollen and unlike himself.

In fact, Dad met his friend George on the walk and went back to George and Ruby's for tea. By the time he came home, he was over it. He was almost shamefaced, though he never said sorry, but he came and talked to me, unnaturally friendly, asking about my work at college, something he didn't know anything about, and he watched TV with Dirk on his lap, stroking his hair, which made me want to throw up.

And Dirk went along with it. Dirk was grateful. That was the most sickening part of it. Dirk always idolized our father.

(And he's never grown up. I think he still does.)

The row was over, but I couldn't stay at home. I had to get out of the house that evening. I went to a party at Alison Green's, a party I never meant to go to, at the house of someone I didn't like, though she was in the same group at college as me. (She kept her hair in a fat French pleat, and wore very short skirts, though she claimed to be religious, with a crucifix and a polo-necked sweater that showed two decks of bosom and bra. I can see her so clearly; her plump pink lips, her enthusiastic questions in lectures, her grey eyes gleaming with real passion, for she was so eager to be a teacher, to go to Africa, like her parents, and then come home and 'teach the underprivileged'. I thought, my family is underprivileged, but save me Lord from Alison Green.)

I wanted to teach then with my whole heart. But it didn't happen. I messed things up. I had my chance and messed things up. People from our class don't get two chances.

Alison's parents were some kind of missionaries ('Taking the faith to the savages in Kenya', but I never even noticed the way they talked.) And they were both abroad that spring, and it was her birthday, in their strait-laced house with its fussy rugs and dried-flower arrangements and pelmets and flounces and Roman Catholic pictures. I arrived early. It looked utterly grim. But I helped her switch off most of the lights, and put red crêpe paper over the others, and hide the worst of the holy pictures 'in case people spill their drinks on them'. She had laid in plenty of bread and cheese and a great many bottles of cider. We all clubbed together to buy some wine, *six bottles* of a warmish white that I thought delicious, and impressively French – *vin de table*, probably, mere *vin de table,* but the vowels on the label looked strange and sweet and a world away from the bottles of beer on which my father became obnoxious –

'An *éclair*, madam?' the waitress asked, her pale peach apron tightly wrapped around an unreasonably tiny waist. 'A *millefeuille*, perhaps? Or the *tarte tatin?*'

'I'll have the éclair.' These days it means nothing, French or English, we're European –

There were several boys that I didn't know. Two of them were friends of a cousin of Alison who looked confusingly like her, but more so, with bigger bosoms and more prominent teeth and a shorter skirt and higher heels . . . however, Kate didn't wear a crucifix. And the boys she was with were very attractive, both of them tall, with well-fitting jeans and coloured shirts and narrow ties. Alison had told me they were all students. Classy students, not people like us. Trainee teachers couldn't hope to be classy. Whereas these were *university students*.

'I'm not religious,' Kate announced to me, pouring the wine with impressive freedom. 'My family are. I think they're cracked. Alison is. Do you know her well?' 'Not very well.' I felt disloyal, but repressed it. I wasn't particularly Christian then, and Alison was not a close friend. I wanted to be glamorous and fun, like them. I wanted something I had never known. I wanted to be taken away from my family, away from littleness, away from rules. The boys were tall and slim and dangerous. One of them was swaying his hips as he danced, narrow and definite and sexual. My cheeks felt hot. I wanted him. My eye still throbbed where my father had hit me, how dare he hit me, I'd never forgive him –

His name was Ivo. Imagine! *Ivo*. Not Ivor, as I first thought, which is just Welsh, but Ivo. Unbearably aristocratic. I soon found out that the other boy was Kate's. He's mine, I thought. Ivo is mine. I had the haziest idea of what to do with him, but I started by dancing with him, decorously, watching him closely, which was easy enough as he liked to dance with his eyes half-closed, immensely cool, looking at the floor, making strange little sallies to left and right which at the time seemed like the acme of dancing. I wasn't really sure he was dancing with me, but when the music slowed down he took hold of me, and started massaging the tops of my arms, my trembling shoulders, my neck, my hair –

'Watch him, Shirley,' shrieked Alison, in passing, over David Bowie's 'Aladdin Sane'. 'Oh, I'm all right,' I told her, airily, trying to be airy and failing, failing, because his hands had found the toggle of my zip, because he was gently kissing my eyebrows, and no one had kissed my eyebrows before.

Soon I was swimming. We were swimming together, through shoals of limbs and warm wine and music. Breathing was hard. Swimming through space, and someone had put on 'Ziggy Stardust', flying out further, too far to come back, 'Ground Control to Major Tom . . . Ground Control to Major Tom' . . . and now I was drifting with Major Tom, out across a Milky Way of pleasure, shivering stars of electric feeling as his fingers brushed the smooth ridge of my spine, going lower, lower as I flew higher, above the crowd, above the voices of my mother and father saying, *not too far, don't go too far,* and Ground Control was getting fainter and fainter . . .

There was an ugly screech like a demented bird as Alison stopped the record-player 'It's too slow,' she yelled above a chorus of complaint. 'I want to have fun. I want to – rock!' It sounded as if she'd read it in a book, but she meant it from the bottom of her heart; her eyes gleamed frantically behind her glasses, her dress had slipped down low on her chest, a film of sweat lit up her breasts. I thought that Ivo would notice them, but he was burrowing into my neck, breathing hard, one hand down my back, caressing the last few points of my spine. The silence was odd; I heard his heart beating, or my heart beating, or both our hearts, and his embarrassingly heavy breathing. 'Upstairs,' he said, as Alison's favourite Rod Stewart record roared into life behind us and everyone started to jump like monkeys. 'Let's go upstairs. I can feel you want to.'

I don't think I did want anything much except to go on in this dream for ever, being stroked and held and dissolved by him, being carried so far away from home, so far away from pain and anger. I wanted more wine. He fetched more wine.

But dreams don't last. We went upstairs. I can't imagine how I got upstairs. I have lived this evening over and over and I still can't remember going upstairs, I still can't remember deciding to go. That's more important, if I ever decided.

I hope I did it for some kind of purpose. I hope I wasn't just another stupid girl who slept with a man because she was tipsy. I hope I wasn't just a stupid cow. I hope my life had some pattern, some point.

Because that evening changed it for ever. He pulled off my dress and stroked my back and held my breasts one by one in his hands, and told me I was beautiful, and I thought, yes, he is mine, this is bliss, we shall be together forever like this. Then he pulled down my pants. I know I protested, partly because I wasn't sure I was clean, or clean enough for whatever he intended. I think I felt sad I could no longer hear the music or be with the other young people dancing, young people, not grim old parents with their rules and habits and desperation, young people in the world we would make, all of us free and unfrightened and happy.

'Let's make love,' he said, and kissed me. Just 'Let's make love,' but at least he asked. I don't think I heard that as sexual intercourse, although my pants were round my ankles, although his penis stood up like a candle. I heard it as love, and as a request. I heard it as tender, and infinitely hopeful. And I did have a choice, and I did say 'Yes'. I did make a choice, even late in the day, I did make a choice, even if it was the wrong one. I didn't just – let people do things to me.

And with that choice, I changed my life. Because I got pregnant, with that first sexual act. It seems amazing now, impossible now, it seems bitterly, unfairly *enviable* now. It lasted three minutes, and he didn't walk me home, and I lied to my mother that the party was boring, and I waited five weeks or so for him to phone, and I waited three months for my period to come.

And then I went to the doctor in terror, and he was definite, and grim.

I saw Alison in the Refectory next day. It was September; the party had been in June. 'Have you heard from Kate, at all, since the party? You haven't heard from Ivo, have you?' 'I hate my cousin now,' she said. 'It was Ivo and his friend who were smoking cigars and made burn marks on our carpets. You haven't fallen for him, have you?'

When I told her the problem she went very pale and her long ugly jaw wobbled in horror. 'But you'd only just met him,' she complained. 'And you must have seen they were different from us. Kate's an atheist. She told me so. And Ivo wouldn't help with the washing-up . . . Besides, they're modern linguists. They've all gone away to France for a year.'

Total despair. I can feel it still. He had gone away, he had gone to France. I was nineteen years old and I'd never been abroad, and if I had a baby I knew I never would –

'May I offer you more cakes, madam? Perhaps the *religieuse?*'

'No more thank you. I'd like the bill.'

I make mistakes, then pay for them.

Alison put her arm round me, I remember. It felt heavy, and out of place. 'Oh Shirley,' she said, 'what shall we do?' But I didn't want her pity. And we weren't the same. I couldn't bear her thinking that we were the same. I wanted to be the same as Ivo, tall and slim and sexy and selfish. I wanted not to be Shirley White, the sort of silly booby who'd get herself pregnant.

I tried to be mature. I went back to the doctor. I said I had discussed things with the father-to-be. Neither of us was ready to make the commitment. I wanted an abortion. He looked at me.

'Do you know what it means, a late abortion? You'll go through labour, with a dead baby.'

Oh God, I thought, I've got a Catholic. 'It isn't a baby, not to me.' But for some reason then I burst out crying. I couldn't bear the sound of the words, 'dead baby', I don't know why not, it was stupid of me, and only encouraged him to give me a lecture.

He talked about adoption, and I laughed in his face. I didn't know that one day I'd try to adopt, that one day I would be accepted to adopt. Kojo and I had just been accepted when he started to get ill, and the dream collapsed.

'I can't have this baby. I'm at college. I'm studying.'

I suddenly saw in a sickening flash that I'd have this baby, there was no escape, I had started to walk down a long straight tunnel that led to a room full of absolute pain, and after that I could see only darkness.

What happened was messier, more tortuous. My doctor reluctantly agreed to a termination, but there was muddle and delay until somehow I was already four months pregnant. I rejected all knowledge of the life inside me, but whatever was growing refused to be rejected. One day I had woken to feel it stirring, a gentle tickling, a gentle stroking. I didn't care. I went ahead.

I took a taxi to the hospital. I went with a friend, who sat and cried. Lynn was a true friend – (indeed she still is, we try to meet twice a year to go shopping) – and funny, and kind, and not prim like Alison, but she was very fond of me, and scared of blood, and scared of me dying, so she wasn't happy. By then I don't think I'd have minded dying. To be taken away from all the horror. She kept saying 'Are you sure? Are you totally sure?' and staring at me with big frightened eyes.

We sat side by side in the waiting-room on rock-hard chairs that made me long to go to the toilet. She held my hand, and both of us were sweating. 'I hate the smell of hospitals,' she whispered. Suddenly she took her other hand off her handbag and laid it on the lump of my belly, my swelling belly underneath my dress, it was warm late spring, I was young and pregnant – 'Shirley,' she said, in absolute horror. 'I felt it move. I felt it kick.'

'I know,' I said. 'I know. I've felt it.' I wouldn't look at her. I made my voice hard. *Against You only have I sinned.*

'It's alive,' she said. 'It's really alive. It's already alive. I know you know that –' The tears were pouring down her face. You would have thought it was her who was having the abortion, and me the friend who was holding her hand. I was trying hard not to hear what she said except with a mechanical part of my brain.

'I know she's alive, I know she's alive –' It wasn't what I had meant to say.

'*You know the sex.*' She was calm this time, almost beyond shock, but she dropped my hand. She sat there watching me as if I was an alien.

'I don't know why I said that. I feel it's a girl.' I got up off the seat, walked to the window with its view of a garden, a neglected, walled-in hospital garden, just scrub, really, in the gap between buildings. I stared out across the dark bushes to the sky, which was blue with wild clouds sprinting across, and I thought, this baby will never see it, this baby will never get out alive . . .

She. She. Will never do it.

And I couldn't go ahead. Of course I couldn't. I never had a chance, once she started moving.

So I had to tell Mum. 'I knew,' she said. 'I've been watching you. I hoped I was wrong.' She went grey, I remember. She slumped by the sink, then sank on to a stool to stop herself falling. 'He'll go mad. Mad. You should have thought about your father.'

'I don't care about Dad.' But I did, I did. 'Will you tell him, Mum? Will you do that for me?'

She looked at me. She twisted her rings. She twisted her rings as if to torture herself. 'Don't ask me,' she whispered, like a little girl. 'I'd do anything for you. Anything else.'

So I waited till Dad came home from the Park, practising my lines, stroking my stomach. And he came home in a benevolent mood, and told me I looked pretty, and I *was* looking pretty, because pregnant women look pink and pretty.

Mum brought him some tea. He put his feet up.

I told him. He was remarkably calm. He sometimes was calm about big things; it was little things that annoyed him most. Or perhaps he hadn't quite taken it in.

'Who's the father?' he asked.

I remember feeling blank. What on earth did he mean? *He* was the father, he would always be the father.

'Oh, no one you know.' It came out wrong, as if I were saying, he's too good for you.

'I suppose *you* know him, do you? You knew him a bit before you let him get you pregnant?'

'He's a university student,' I said.

For a moment he was cheered. Only a moment. 'And when is he going to put in an appearance?' I didn't say anything. 'Oh, I see. It's like that, is it. We'll see about that. If he thinks he can just muck about with my daughter . . .'

'He's gone abroad. He doesn't know.'

'What do you mean, he's gone abroad? What do you mean, he doesn't know?'

I didn't speak; didn't know where to begin; and besides, his voice had begun to rise, and the lump was rising in my throat.

But another part of myself was calm. I was different now. I was a pregnant woman. That made me a woman, for the first time.

'What is this man? Some foreigner? Answer your father. What's his name?'

'He isn't foreign.'

'What's his name?'

'None of your business.' It just came out, and I knew as I said it that he would kill me, and then I thought about the baby, and I saw him coming across the room, red in the face, his arm lifted –

'Don't you hit me.' I backed away. 'His name is Ivo.'

And then he hit me. 'Ibo! What kind of bloody name is that? He's a bloody darkie, isn't he? *Isn't he?*' He hit me on the shoulder and upper arm, the usual places he would hit me, but I was afraid he would hurt the baby, I couldn't stand there and take my medicine.

So I went on backwards, and he kept on coming, head down, fists up, as if he had to hit me but couldn't bear to look at me. I suddenly thought, no more of this. I shan't have any more of this. And I stepped aside, so he bumped into the mantelpiece, and waited for him to come round again, and hit him as hard as I could in the face, full in the face, across his huge red nose, and I winced as I did it, I winced for his pain, but I screamed from a place that knew how to scream, 'I'll kill you if you hit me again. I'll bloody kill you. Are you listening? *The child isn't coloured.* Not that it matters.'

And then my mother came in from the kitchen and my father said in a muffled voice, 'I'm bleeding. Do something, May. I'm bleeding. I think Shirley has broken my nose.'

Then Dirk ran in, eyes wild, frightened. He had a cricket bat in his hand; he'd been out in the yard, batting at the wall. He saw Dad bleeding and began to cry. 'Dad, you're bleeding. What happened? What's happening?' I remember the blood splashing red on Dad's shirt and a few drops going on Dirk's new jeans, I was sorry the blood went on Dirk's new jeans –

And Dad said, 'I bumped into the mantelpiece. Bent down to pick something up, judged it wrong. Mummy is bringing me some sticking plaster. Hurry up May, for goodness sake.' And he didn't look in my direction. I think I knew it was over then, and he wouldn't dare to hit me again.

It was just a habit, really, like smoking. People need help with breaking them. She helped me, didn't she, my vanished daughter?

By now she must be eighteen years old. If nothing bad has happened to her . . .

She was eighteen on the twelfth of December. I thought of nothing else all day. I tried to keep my thoughts happy and hopeful. I have something to be proud of, after all. I kept her alive. I didn't kill her. I hope she's happy and beautiful. I hope her family is happier than mine – and yet my family will always be hers.

I told myself adoption was the best thing to do. The doctors were helpful; almost too helpful. So many couples waiting, they assured me, for babies like yours (I suppose they meant white ones), you'll make some childless couple very happy, so the whole thing should have been perfectly happy.

I did what I was told. I had a caesarean because she was presenting upside down. I was full of drugs, but I held her, briefly, and tried not to see that she looked like me, *she looked like me*, not at all like Ivo. She looked like me; weeping, weeping, screaming as if she was being abandoned.

I did as they told me and took some pills that made me feel sick but suppressed the milk. My breasts hurt horribly. They sang and cried. They throbbed and yearned and I ignored the pain, and when it subsided, when my breasts lay down, I began to give up, I began to accept it, I gave her to the nurse to bottle-feed. 'I can't do it. She's not really mine.'

The rest disappears into a mist of terror. They took her away and I went back to college and two weeks later had a total breakdown. I left Winthrop College, never to return. Yet I'd given her up to protect my studies. If I had been older, richer, more confident, I would have done everything to get her back, because I knew without doubt that I wanted her back, that without her my life could never be complete.

21 • May

May closed her eyes and prayed very hard, her whole being cringing away from pain. *Save me God oh save me God.* Waiting for his shoe to crush her soft stomach, waiting for bone to smash into her face, waiting for her money to be torn away. He was shouting something, but she was deaf. He crouched down over her, almost on top of her, and his big black hands closed over her shoulders, perhaps he was going to strangle her . . . She opened her eyes and stared into his, big yellow eyes, cat-like, inhuman, veined with red, she couldn't breathe – 'Don't touch me,' she gasped, but hardly any sound came. 'Help,' and then louder, 'Help! Help!'

Curiously little was going on.

No pain came, except the ache in her ankle. He smelled of unfamiliar aftershave, surprisingly sweet, almost floral. She began to wrestle her shoulder away.

Then she heard what his voice was saying. 'I've got your money, don't worry. Is your leg all right? Can you get up?'

Then she realized he was trying to help her. He was peering at her anxiously, clutching her bundle of notes in one hand, trying to help her up with the other.

Then she felt shocked, and ashamed. And the base of her spine hurt horribly.

'Oh,' she wailed. 'I'm such a fool.'

'It can happen to anyone,' he said. 'It's slippy.'

'My bag came open,' she babbled. 'Then everything fell out. I'm sorry, young man. I'm very sorry –'

'No problem.'

Perhaps he hadn't noticed she was afraid? But just in case he had, May plunged onwards, talking without stopping as she straightened her coat, tried her ankle, pulled down her hem. 'My husband's in hospital, I'm in such a state, I've got all the money to sort out, my son's come back from America and he's given me this but it's got to last us, I was just off to the post office, do you know Mr Varsani, he's a lovely man, my daughter lives with a West Indian . . .'

'Steady on,' he said. 'Slow down.' He was smiling at her in a different way, amused, now, and slightly ironic, she saw it was an intelligent face, a humorous face, not frightening at all. And he wasn't very old. Sixteen? Eighteen? Nineteen at most. Younger than Dirk. 'I think you've had a bit of a shock.'

She began to haul herself back to her feet. 'I don't want to be a trouble to you.' He was picking up her things from the ground, wiping off the black water with his handkerchief.

Relief and shame washed over her in hot waves, and her voice rushed on. 'Are you local? I've lived here all my life. It's not what it was, Hillesden Rise. I don't mean because of the foreigners. I'm not saying you're a foreigner –'

'I'm not a foreigner. Now, are you OK?' He was putting her brush back into her handbag, and her mirror, and her shamefully hair-clotted comb. 'Where shall I put this money?'

She took it from him, humbly, and thrust it back to the very bottom of her ancient bag. 'You're very kind. *Very* kind. I don't know how to say thank you –'

'That's all right. Have you got everything?'

Six feet away she suddenly saw the carrier-bag from the off-licence. When she picked it up it clinked suspiciously. Peeping inside, she saw golden liquid and pieces of glass. 'My bottles have broken.'

'That's a pity.'

She realized at once he would think she was a drinker, and had fallen through drink, so she started again: 'They're for my husband, not for me, it's to cheer him up in hospital . . .'

'I've got to be off, now.'

'What's your name?' she said, suddenly. 'My name is May. I'm very grateful.' And then, impelled by an obscure impulse, but also because she felt it was true, 'My husband would be very grateful to you. For looking after me. He would.'

'Winston,' he said. His smile was self-mocking. 'That's not a foreigner's name, is it?' But he looked as though it embarrassed him. She thought about Dirk, suddenly. *Maybe kids never like the names we give them.*

'No,' she said, so as not to be rude, but inside she reflected that it was. No English people called their sons Winston, though Winnie himself was English, of course. It was only Americans, and blacks. Why were they more patriotic than us? 'Thank you, Winston. I'll remember you. I'll tell my daughter about you.'

'You say "Hello" to her for me.'

There was something very boyish in his manner, his dancing smile, his soft intonations. 'I will,' said May. She didn't know what to say. She was almost two feet smaller than him, but she realized, now, that he was very slender, and his eyes were gentle, rather shy. He looked exotic, and faintly out of place, outlined against the grim metal grille where Freddie's Flowers had once flourished. It was cold, in Britain, and hard, and grey. 'Take care,' she said, rather foolishly, for it was she who was falling about, she who was breaking and losing things and imagining muggers and talking rubbish. She frowned up, trying to take him in, wondering why she had only just seen him. And then he was gone. 'Take care, Winston.'

22 · Shirley

Shirley felt happy, gliding down on the escalator. God-like, swooping down over the world, a world that was made entirely good, light years away from the world of her childhood.

She hoped she wasn't being blasphemous. Shirley rendered to God and rendered to Mammon. She put the notes in the plate every Sunday, sometimes brown ones, usually blue ones. She didn't do as well as Elroy, of course. Elroy paid tithes to Paddington Temple, one-tenth of his income, before tax, not after, which she thought was too much, and told him so, quite early on in their relationship.

'It's better to give than receive,' he'd said to her. 'I'm surprised at you, Shirley.'

'My church feels you should give as you want. Your way is like income tax.'

'But my way means they get a lot more money.'

'I know. But Elroy, you're not rich.'

'God will bless me. I got enough, woman. I try to give to you, but you say you don't need it —'

She went and put her arms around him. He was a proud man, easily hurt, and he wasn't comfortable with her having money, especially since it came from Kojo. 'You're very good to me. I just worry . . . It's as if they're too interested in your money.'

'Maybe you don't like my church,' he said. 'Maybe you don't like black people's church.'

'But I've said I'll go with you every other week – I'm sorry. Let's not argue about it.' And they did go together on alternate Sundays, to Paddington Temple and St John's in Piccadilly, where she had worshipped for sixteen years, since she lost her baby and had her breakdown.

She'd tried very hard to respect his church, although it was so different from what she was used to. But only last month May had come to tea and made the subject of church more fraught.

Shirley was out in the kitchen, getting out the cake-plates, and Elroy was taking off his coat in the hall. He had just come in, tired from work. May was pleased to see Shirley's 'new young man'; she had only met him half-a-dozen times. Elroy was pleased to see her, as well, though he remained wary; did she really like him? 'Mum does like you,' Shirley had told him, 'because you are young and nice-looking. And not being Dad, you can't boss her about.'

May picked up a booklet, *Paddington Temple: Impacting the City*, which Elroy had left lying on the dining-room table. '*Impacting the City*. What does that mean? Sounds like a bomb. Or a wisdom tooth.'

Shirley didn't always listen to her mother, and Elroy was complaining about his hospital, which had all gone downhill since it became a Trust. 'Seems like everything is rule by money . . . Last year the cleaning is privatize, this month they put the catering out to tender, and our people lose it because their bid is two thousand pound higher than the other . . . Two thousand lousy pound! In a budget of millions! And now they're telling me this new lot is saying they can feed a man for seven pound a week. OK, right, if they feed them rubbish –'

'That's terrible,' Shirley said. She knew he was upset. When he was upset he sounded more Jamaican. She was trying to listen, as she opened the oven.

But her mother was waffling unstoppably on. 'This isn't English. It's American. *Discipling the Church to Impact the City.* Disciple is a noun, not a verb. Shirley never did care enough about English. Kingdom Economics? What is that?'

Elroy was suddenly listening to her. 'It's about giving, Mrs White,' he said. Shirley knew she must shut her mother up, but she was trying to lift the sponge from the cake-tin without leaving half of it behind, and her face was too hot, and the gas was roaring.

'This bit is a scream,' Mum was saying. '*Question.* Do I have to tithe on my gross or net income? *Answer.* That depends on whether you want to be blessed on your gross or net income.' Surely you don't believe that, Shirley? Are you listening, dear? I'm talking to you. I mean, God isn't an accountant, is he, sitting up there working out how much to bless you?'

'*Mum.* That's Elroy's. Don't be rude.'

Elroy was bright, but not quick with words. He sat there pretending he didn't mind. 'Never mind Shirley. Just leave it.'

'Oh dear, Elroy. Have I put my foot in it?' Mum blushed red; she was quite crestfallen.

'Yes,' Shirley said. 'You have. Well done.'

He drove her to the underground, and when he came back he said no more about it, but the next Sunday – two Sundays ago – the day before Dad had his *event* – they got up as usual to go to church, and it was his church's turn, they were going to Paddington Temple, but Elroy suddenly said, as he put on his tie, 'We better go each to our own.'

'What do you mean?'

'We don't have to worship together.'

'I know we don't. But you like us to.'

'Your mother thought our church was a joke.'

'Oh Mum. What does she know? It was just the booklet. She's always been like that. She laughs at things.'

'The fear of the Lord is the beginning of wisdom.'

'Oh lay off, Elroy. My mother is my mother – God would understand her.'

'I don't want no one to mock my faith.' It was said with a wealth of bitterness, it was not about her, or Mum, or now, it was about all the times that Elroy had been mocked, because he was black, or because they were poor.

'Elroy, I'd never laugh at your faith.'

'Your mother did.'

'No – she was laughing at *me*. She thought it was my booklet.'

'She was laughing at the Word of God.'

'No, she was laughing at the English in that booklet.'

'You people think you own the language –'

Elroy sounded more of a Londoner than her, unless he was excited or half-asleep. He didn't come on like a Caribbean, unlike his mother and his older sister, and he usually insisted that there wasn't an issue, so when he said *You people,* Shirley listened.

'Elroy, I'm not white people, I'm me. Of course I won't come, if you don't want me.'

But afterwards he came back upset and said his mother had asked after her, and please would she go next week instead?

So tomorrow we both go to both churches, which is a bit over the top, in one day.

But I do love Jesus. Because He forgave me – *He heard my voice, He heard my cry. The cords of death entangled me . . .*

I do love God, because He saved me. I do love God, who made all things good . . . Jesus, who did not let me fall.

Shirley went gliding on down into the basement.

Here they kept China, Crystal, and Lighting, a cave of wonders next to food. As she moved, rainbows shot and glinted. An elderly man was shielding his eyes, while his wife blinked, startled, at a chandelier. Odd, all this brilliance, deep underground . . .

I tried to kill myself on the underground. Seventeen years ago. There was nothing left to live for. I had given up my daughter, given up college, given up hope of getting better. I remember wanting to sink so deep. Deeper and deeper and never come up.

My father was surprisingly good at first. He said something I've never forgotten. When I hate him most, I remember it. Because God is love. God is love . . .

I had the ironing-board in the front room. It was only a few days after I'd come home. I had felt too bad to get dressed in the morning, and I came down in my nightie, which was simply not done, we were never allowed to walk around in our night-clothes. I must have been slightly mad, at the time. And I went and put up the ironing-board, in the front room, not the kitchen, which again was very odd, the front room wasn't for working in. And I got all the washing. There was a huge pile, and I'd brought some home from the hospital.

(They brought her to me to say goodbye. She had too many clothes; I couldn't feel her body. I crushed her to me. 'Don't wake her,' said the nurse, eyes on the baby. Flushed face, tiny hands lost in mittens. In a few seconds, she took her away. I stood there, frozen, then I followed them, slip-slop after them in stupid slippers, too late to get to them before the swing-doors. The nurse was taking her away downstairs. Her thin cruel back hid the baby from view, but I glimpsed a small crown with a whorl of pale hair, and one small hand, opening, closing.)

It must have been a Sunday. Dad had had his breakfast. I think Mum had gone to the allotment. He came in with his *Sunday Express*, sat in his armchair and began to read. As if he hadn't seen me, but he must have done. I'd begun with the underwear – most of it was mine. All of it went into a neat flat pile. Then I did his shirts, which I've never found easy. Thank God Kojo never made a fuss about his shirts. Then I got to the sheets. They went on and on. It made my arms hurt, stretching them out, and the bits you'd already ironed got crumpled again. And I was upset because the stain was still there, the stain on the sheets where I had my show, the little rose of blood that meant she was coming. My mum must have bleached it, but it was still there. I wept and ironed, ironed and wept.

I realized Dad was watching me. Down at his paper, then up at me, then just staring at me, kind of helplessly. And then he got up and came towards me, raised his arm and I flinched away, because I knew I was doing the wrong thing, in the wrong place, at the wrong time. 'Shirley,' he said, but he couldn't speak. Then he took the iron from my hand. 'You'll tire yourself out. Your dad'll have a go. Come on, give it here. You have a sit down.'

'You don't know how to do it,' I protested, but I did sit down, I think I would have fainted. He sized up the job, slowly, methodically, re-folded the sheet, began to work. He didn't have a clue, but he did the job. 'I was a soldier, girl. We looked after our kit.' He ironed in silence, frowning, smiling. I sat and watched him. It was like a dream. Just before he finished, he spoke to me. Staring at the iron running over the cotton, his eyes never lifting, his voice breaking. 'You're a good girl, Shirley. I know you are. You know what they say? It's the good girls get pregnant. *The good girls get pregnant*. So don't take on.'

He did love me. And I must love him. Somewhere underneath all the anger and resentment, somewhere where all of us might have been different. A lost place, somewhere, I don't know . . . I think Dad wished that he could have been different.

He couldn't keep up the kindness, of course. Quite soon he thought I ought to pull myself together. Actually I think he was afraid that if I drifted on like that I would end up in a loony bin. Nothing like this had ever happened in our family, or so they kept on telling me (of course it must have done. Shamed into silence.)

They were very upset when I didn't go back to college. Dad, of course, could only express it through anger. First a great roaring, when I made up my mind, then endless rumblings of discontent. 'I hope you don't think *I* can keep you . . . You had a great chance . . . You're wasting your life . . . Pull yourself together! Haven't you got any backbone? . . . Look at you, Shirley. You've let yourself go.'

It was true, I had. Even my mother noticed, my mother who never noticed people's clothes. 'I could wash that cardigan,' she offered. 'You could wear something else.' 'Leave me alone.' She arranged an appointment at the hairdresser, but I didn't go, and she was annoyed, Mum who rarely got annoyed. 'You're a pretty girl, Shirley, it's a shame.'

My shame was deeper than anyone knew. I had let my daughter go deep underground, to a place from which there was no return.

One day I got up before nine o'clock, which pleased my mother. 'Shirley, dear. You must be feeling better.' 'Yes,' I said, but I ate no breakfast. 'I'm going for a walk.' 'Comb your hair.' I stared at her. She lived far away, behind the glass, breathing different air.

I walked down the road with my hair uncombed. I'm not sure I knew where I was going, but I remember walking quickly through the rain to the underground station, where I didn't buy a ticket, because I didn't know where I was going. I stood and shivered by the queue for tickets.

And then I knew there was nowhere to go. I went down to the platform of the north-bound trains. Going down the steps I met Ruby Millington, just coming back from her morning job, I think she was a lollipop lady at the school. Mum pitied her because they didn't have children. (Perhaps that's why she and George got so huge.) 'Shirley,' she said, 'are you all right?' 'Fine,' I told her. 'You're soaked,' she said. 'You haven't got a coat.' 'Oh, I like rain.' Her mouth opened again, but I pressed on down through the unfamiliar bodies, people who didn't know my name, people who wouldn't call me back from the special place where I was going.

I stood on the platform in a veil of rain. I looked into the tunnel. Which train would it be? Yellow eyes. They have yellow eyes. Thundering out of the underworld, thundering back down into the dark. It would be easy, a falling, an ending, gliding down where I could sink no further.

There would be the moment of impact. I flinched. But then, I already knew about that, the moment when something very hard and heavy crashes into something breakable, and once it has happened it will happen again, it will never stop happening till the smash-up is final. I wanted it over, I wanted to go. I heard the echo of the train approaching, the first small tremors, then the gathering roar. I looked it in the eyes. I walked to the edge. My mind was perfectly blank and final. At last I should be released from myself, just a little step forward, it was coming, it was here –

Then something lunged at me, from the side, grabbed me, winding me, knocked me over, I felt myself fall and was suddenly praying: please God, no, I'm not ready . . . Jesus, save me. Jesus, save –

A big face was staring down at me, upside down, frantic, familiar. I was lying on the platform, bruised, shocked, with Ruby Millington hovering above me, saying, 'Shirley, Shirley, are you all right? I didn't mean to knock you over, but what were you doing? *Shirley, love.* You were right on the edge. I saw you, I saw you.'

Everyone else had got on to the train, and the train was moving out of the station. If they saw the two of us, they thought I had fainted, but I think that no one but Ruby saw me. No one but Ruby would ever have seen me.

I didn't try to deny what she'd seen. I was too grateful, because as I fell I had finally found out I didn't want to die.

We sat on a bench and wept together. She kept her big fat arm around me. We had never been close, but she was Mum's friend, and she had known me since I was a baby. She smelled of sweat. Of warmth, and kindness.

'Oh Shirley,' she said, 'you're much too young. I know you've been in trouble, dear. Your mother told me. It's all right, I don't judge you.'

I had turned into a helpless baby again. 'No one loves me. No one wants me. I'm no good to anyone. I've been driving Mum and Dad crazy . . .'

She held my head against her shoulder. Then she said slowly, '*I* want you. *We* want you. George and I. Come and stay with us. Just till things get easier.'

'I couldn't.'

'Why not? Of course you could. We've no kids of our own. We'd love to have you. Besides. I understand. I felt like you. A few years ago, I tried to do what you did, I took half a bottle of sleeping pills. It must have been fate, my meeting you. I saw it in your eyes, what you were going to do.'

It wasn't fate, though. Jesus saved me. He sees each sparrow as it falls.

I sobbed like a baby, and Ruby listened, and took me home, and let me weep, and didn't tell me to pull myself together. I think some part of her liked me weeping. Because of the tears locked up inside her, because I could cry for both of us, and then she could mother me, comfort me.

Jesus saw me. Not a sparrow falls . . .

I know that God sent Ruby to save me.

23 · May

Though her ankle was sore, and one palm was grazed, May found that her fall had left her in good spirits, so far as she could be, with Alfred ill. That nice young man had cheered her up, and Mr Varsani was concern itself, finding her a plaster behind his counter, and giving her new forms to fill in for the pension. Now the money, thank God, was safe in his till, though she'd kept twenty pounds, on a sudden impulse, to buy a few bits and pieces on the Rise. Very concerned about Alfred, he was. Though Alfred never had a good word for him.

That's what we're here for, to help each other. I'm not a good Christian, but I do think that. And that's what that young man was doing. I blame the light, for the misunderstanding. My eyes aren't good, but I'm not prejudiced. I never have been. Unlike poor Alfred.

What goes around, comes around, Darren likes to say. Maybe one day I shall return the favour. Do something good for one of *his* people. May found she had forgotten the young man's name.

She daydreamed, wandering on down the high street, further south than she ever went, about saving a pretty black toddler from a river . . . But she couldn't swim, so it wasn't very likely. She changed it, plunging in front of a car to snatch a black infant from the jaws of death. The mother wept and hung round her neck. 'Thank you, thank you.' May smiled to herself.

The sun was coming out, flickering, steadying, coming in lances through the dull grey cloud, and as it came out, life came back. The red brick bloomed, and even the road had a sheen of bluey-purple petrol. A red-and-white, feathery, luxurious cat came delicately picking its way across it. May shook the water off her sleeves.

She was looking for the other off-licence which used to exist near the end of the high street. She couldn't face going back to the one with the bored young girl who smelled of whisky. *She'd think that I was no better than she is.*

What she found, below the traffic lights, was a whole new world coming into existence. As upper Hillesden had been decaying, lower Hillesden was on its way up. She nearly walked into a chair on the pavement, and thought, confusedly, was it a junk-shop? But then she saw another one, two, three, and a half-caste youth setting up small tables, it was a café, for goodness sake, a pavement café like they had in Paris. She peered at the menu; it was all in French. She thought the young man was looking at her oddly, so she said, with a smile, trying to be friendly, 'My daughter would like this. She likes French things', but he gawped at her as if she was crazy.

Suddenly there were more people around. May took her time, enjoying it. Something new to tell Alfred about. Young people lived in lower Hillesden, girls with crewcuts and boys with dark glasses, their hair all the colours of the rainbow, carrying computers in little flat cases like the one Darren had when he last came home. Some of them had frayed flared trousers and tangled hair and looked like beggars, but some of them had that glossy look, and the confident voices that meant they had money. There were cars, too, frivolous cars, a yellow one shaped like a cigar and a silver one like a shiny beetle. Brand-new cars, parked carelessly.

And she dimly recalled what Shirley had told her, which May refused to credit, at the time, that young people liked Victorian houses and turned up their noses at modern ones. Which explained why lower Hillesden's slummy little houses, where May and Alfred would have blushed to live, funny red terraces with fussy patterned windows, were suddenly sprouting 'For Sale' signs, and some of them, she saw, when she looked more closely, had already grown expensive lace curtains, not the old grey nets they used to have, and window-boxes, and fancy knockers.

This off-licence was not like the other one. Instead of the bored girl, there were two smart young men, chattering and laughing in caressing voices. They had shelves of red wine costing more than ten pounds, and the fridge cabinet was full of champagne, not beer and white wine, like the other shop. When she asked for whisky, they pointed to a section with kinds of whisky she had never heard of, all of it from places with choking names that sounded like Dirk being sick after the pub, but really they belonged to tiny islands in Scotland. She chose three miniatures, judiciously. Something different; he might like that, though the price they rang up nearly made her faint.

She walked back up the road in the strengthening sunlight. There was a Sushi Bar – imagine it! – with narrow windows and queer blue light, and a girl peering out had half-moon eyes but the boy she was with was very black. There were three Indian restaurants, side by side, which made you wonder how they could survive. The Star of the East, just fancy, in Hillesden! There were two shops advertising 'Cheap International Phone Calls', and another one selling those uncomfortable beds with wooden bases and thin flat mattresses. But lovely colours: bright blue, bright green, and as life and hope ran through May's veins she thought, If only Alfred were here, if only Alfred was home again. We'd come for a stroll, the two of us. May patted the bag with his whiskies for comfort.

Hillesden isn't dying. It's coming up.

24 · Shirley

Shirley was still in China and Crystal, looking for a present for her father.

Something nice. He won't be here for ever. (Or else Dad will beat around our hearts for ever. Maybe the Africans are right about that, God forgive me for thinking it.)

It isn't easy, buying presents for fathers. Particularly *my* father.

Something English would be a good present (but what is there that's English, these days?)

'Can I help you, Madam, or are you just looking?' The salesman was young, with an insinuating manner. 'Some people find it a bit overwhelming.'

'I don't,' said Shirley, giving him a look.

His smile faltered, and then recovered. 'Are you buying a gift?'

'Yes.'

'I thought as much.' He looked pleased with himself.

'For my father.' As she said it, her eye fell on a defiant little figure of John Bull with a squat glass bulldog beside him. The man's face was a cross between a baby's and a butcher's, made rounder by his low flat topper, his waistcoat an engraved Union Jack, straining across a sturdy pot-belly. 'That's quite nice.' It wasn't, to her, but it was small enough for a bedside table.

'Would you like a closer look, madam?'

The thing had a small square pedestal, engraved at the front with 'Land of Hope And Glory' and at the back 'John Bull Esq'. Although Dad looked nothing like him, of course, there was something about the way John Bull stood, braced to the world, feet splayed, shoulders back, jaw pushed out towards the foreigners – Shirley had seen Alfred stand like that, back to the flower-beds, arms sternly folded, glaring across at some Asian children wondering whether to play ball on the grass.

'How much?' she asked the salesman, rather curtly.

'Just seventy-five pounds,' he grinned, bold as brass. 'It's a very fine piece. The Americans like them. It reminds them of the war, and Winston Churchill.'

Shirley hated to admit something cost too much. It mattered to her that people knew she could afford things.

'It's made in Britain, of course?'

'Without a doubt.' But he sounded shifty.

'I'll take it,' she said, hardly missing a beat, flicking out her quiver of credit cards, signing.

Turned, and someone was beaming at her. A keenly smiling face, narrow, shining, with wide red lips, pulled right back over large white teeth.

'Sorry, I don't know –'

'Susie Flinders.'

She couldn't link the name to the beaming face.

'We met yesterday! Darren's wife!'

'Of course. Forgive me.' Shirley thought, do I kiss her? She's my brother's wife, but I hardly know her.

'So wonderful to meet you!' Susie was all animation, yet her cheeks were gaunt, and her eyes did not look happy. 'I'm just hunting down a few things for Darren. The food department next door is so great. They've got gluten-free, vegan, macrobiotic, and all the special English things . . . Darren, poor darling, is exhausted today.'

'Travelling –?'

'Oh no, he lives his life on planes. The emotional shock, you know. Your father.'

'We knew Dad was bad a week ago.'

'The shock of seeing him like that.'

Well Darren didn't break a leg getting here. Shirley found it hard to look her in the eyes. Her fizz, her loudness, her overload of scent; Giorgio, was it? The American choice.

'So what are you shopping for, Shirley?'

Shirley made an effort. 'A present for Dad.'

'You've been a great daughter, Darren says. It all falls on the ones who stay behind, doesn't it?'

Shirley thought, I'm a doormat, to her. 'I've hardly been a model daughter. I married a black man, which outraged my father.'

'Darren says he tried to give you support.'

Shirley felt her smile go even stiffer. 'Did he? Well . . . at a distance.' (So Darren thought he was noble, did he, coming to the wedding and then Kojo's funeral?)

But Susie beamed on, not noticing the chill. 'So. I've got my Earl Grey tea-bags and my Thick Cut marmalade and my Gentleman's Relish and my Bath Olivers . . . Darren has a passion for things from home. The only thing I miss is the NHS.'

'There's not a lot of it to miss, any more.'

'You've got to fight for it. It's unique, isn't it?'

'You're preaching to the converted.'

'Have you seen any of the pieces Darren's done about what's happening to the NHS?'

'I don't need to read Darren's pieces. I know about it first-hand, thanks. I live here. And my boyfriend's a Patient Care Officer.'

'Sorry, I didn't mean it that way –' There was an awkward pause, then Susie grinned again. 'I do hope we can all get together some time.'

Shirley managed to meet her eyes, and smile back. 'His name is Elroy. He can't come to the hospital. Dad would have a fit. He's black.'

'Your dad really has a problem with that?'

'Is the Pope a Catholic?'

'Shirley, I'm so sorry.' Susie touched Shirley's arm.

(Everything she did was frenetic, overdone, as if she was an actress from a faster film. Shirley sensed she was already bored, already halfway out of the door – And yet there was something sympathetic about her. At least she tried. You could feel the effort.)

'I'd love to talk further with you, Shirley, but I left my umbrella in Quarantino's –'

'Quarantino's . . . that's posh, isn't it? At least, I've read about it in the papers.'

'Probably because it's a journalists' watering-hole. We tend to eat there when we come to London.'

When we come to London. As if they often do. Perhaps they did, and never got in touch. It felt like a small sharp kick in the stomach. 'Do you always travel with Darren, then?'

'Oh no. You know, I have my own assignments.'

'Assignments? Aren't you a therapist?'

'I trained as a therapist. But I'm a journalist also. It pays better!'

That curious mixture of English and American . . . All those *-ists*. She could pick and choose. If you had an education, you could pick and choose. But Shirley refused to be jealous of her. 'Maybe you and Darren could come for a meal. I guess you're going to be around for a bit.'

An awkward silence. 'In fact – Darren's planning on flying back tomorrow night. Your father seems to be doing OK –'

'So this is the classic flying visit.' It sounded more bitter than Shirley meant.

'Darren has a lot of problems with your father. It isn't easy for him, coming home.'

'None of us finds my dad very easy.'

'Darren's holding on to a lot of anger. He has to work through it. Work with it. I've told him frankly I think we should stay.'

There were two furrows of tension in Susie's wide brow, as if she felt guilty, as if she worried – But what was all this about Darren's anger? Poor old Dad, thought Shirley, suddenly. He loved Darren so; Darren was his favourite. 'It's just that Dad really likes to see him,' said Shirley, but she didn't want to rub it in. She continued, 'In any case, he's seen him, hasn't he? So that's OK.' (Why must she always be nice?)

'Shirley, it's been great meeting with you. I hope we can talk again properly. Really.' Susie was already tapping her feet, waisted heels as sharp as knives, shiny black shoes, almost blue-black, curving sheerly into her instep. Shoes for a quick neat getaway – She bent like a dancer, kissed Shirley's cheek, giving her no time to return the gesture.

She was gone, with a shake and a stroke of her hair, her shiny, healthy, American hair, narrow hips whipping through the flashing displays, turning for a last swift wave of her hand, white light on her teeth as she mouthed 'Bye'.

Leaving Shirley standing there wondering. How could Susie be so different from her? Faster, slicker, brighter, sharper. Therapist, journalist, talker, world traveller . . .

But maybe I would have been like her. If I had finished my education. Is that what makes women lean and quick? Instead I stand here. Solid. Slow.

She's a fly-by-night. I suppose I'm a stayer.

Upstairs, Shirley found the sun had come out, sweeping across through the glass swing-doors and catching the jewellery in its nets, flashing and glinting from gilded counters, the middle-aged customers warmly lit, floating along through deep golden valleys where sun-warmed scents of rose and vanilla, oranges, musk, peaches, lemons, wafted on balmy winds from Perfumes.

All of us here are in paradise, she told herself as the sun embraced her. Everyone's walking, everyone's well. This is heaven, compared to the hospital.

All shall be well . . . Let all be well . . . Make all our family well, she prayed.

25 · Dirk

Dirk was sitting thinking of the final reckoning. The glorious day when it would all come right, when the goats and black sheep would really get sorted.

Then George said 'You'd better go and get a bit of lunch.' Just like that. As if it was normal.

'What?' – Dirk never, ever got a lunch break, because George couldn't manage on his own. 'I'll nip out and get some sandwiches, then.'

'I'll hold the fort. Go on, take your time. They say the new Burger Bar's quite good. There's a Sushi Bar opened, if you're feeling ambitious.' George laughed, nervously. 'Not really your scene.'

Dirk stared at him blankly. 'What, *eat out?* Not come back to the shop with it? – I can't afford it, in any case.' Perhaps the asthma was affecting his brain.

George's eyes had a funny kind of glint. 'Feeling a bit guilty about this morning. Making you wait outside in the rain. You're a good lad. I couldn't have managed without you.'

And then Dirk got it.

He thinks he's going to die. That's why he's talking about himself in the past. He really *is* thinking of giving up the shop. He probably *is* going to leave it to me.

What followed was even more amazing. 'Here's a fiver. Towards your lunch.'

'Thanks George.' Dirk felt himself going red. He was really pleased. *George was giving him a present.* Maybe he wasn't such a bad old bugger. He had never done that before, not once, not in nine years of working for him. 'Are you sure you can manage?' Dirk knew he couldn't.

'If I can't manage, I'll shut up shop.'

Dirk wished he had asked him for a tenner, since a fiver didn't go far these days, but it was good to hear the shop door ring behind him and step out into the rain with a fiver in his pocket. In the middle of the day. A free man.

I've never really felt that. Free, or a man.

So maybe soon I'll have the keys to the shop. MediaNet. And I'll expand next door. Buy up Windsor Drainage before it goes bust.

I'd like that, buying up the lav shop. And I'll drive those other buggers out of business, the poncing Patels with their gifts and their greeting cards and more computer magazines than us. (They opened their shop, on purpose, less than a hundred yards down the road from us. Our shop's been there since the beginning of time, then the Pakis try and blow us away.)

Not actually, of course. They don't use force. I wish they would. We could fight to the finish. They can't fight, Pakis, they're soft and weak. I remember them at school; swots, pansies. We could crush them like flies. We'd break their legs . . .

The other blacks are different, of course. Very very violent people, blacks.

We could still smash them, even if the blacks joined the Pakis (which isn't likely, they hate each other's guts) – we could still win through. Because we're – *motivated*. I read that in *Spearhead* and I agreed. We could still break them, because *our cause is just. To free our streets of crime and fear.* That's the way they put it in *Spearhead.*

And they are *our* streets. They always were. When George and my dad were little boys, these streets were safe for kids to play in. My dad always talks about it down the pub. How all the kids were normal then. Normal white. And there wasn't any crime. Not everyone beating the shit out of each other. Not everyone hating everyone else. There was brotherhood then. We were all English.

Hillesden was a village, in those days. I sometimes think I was born out of my time. It's just my luck to be born now, with no opportunities for native English. And prejudice against us just because we're white.

'Ozzie! Ozzie!' My mate Ozzie. 'Oi, Ozzie, are you going in here?'

'Going down the pub.'

'I'm supposed to be working –'

'Buy us a beer.'

'All right, just one.'

I really meant it to be just one. But three's not many. Not for me. I can hold my liquor. So Dad always says. I got some peanuts and half a ham sandwich. I'd have got something hot, but it was frigging curry. Even down the pub. My local pub. I wanted something English like spag bol or a burger, but all that was on offer was frigging beef curry.

I was back on time, give or take a few minutes.

There was a sort of atmosphere when I got back. I'm sensitive. I can feel an atmosphere. As if I had come back too soon. As if George didn't want me here. And there was – this man, messing around.

He's still in here, by the magazines. I say a man, I mean a Paki man. I'm not that good at telling them apart – can anyone really tell them apart? – but he looks familiar, he looks like one of the oily geezers who tried to buy the shop. The geezers George was amusing himself with. I try winking at George and pointing to the man but George looks funny, as if he'd gone blind. Normally he hates people messing about. He hates people standing there fingering the goods . . . I suppose this moron can't read English, because there are signs all over the shop, handwritten signs George did himself, a bit faded now but in nice big letters, Please Do Not Touch The Goods, and by the papers, two different versions of No Reading Allowed, one in ink, one in red biro. Now the Paki's picking up a dirty magazine, he's got a wank mag off the top shelf, grinning all over his ugly mug, he's got down a *Big Ones International* (which is very popular round here, at three pounds fifty, thank you very much), and he's laughing at it, trying to look all superior, but enjoying it too, getting his rocks off, he thinks he can get his rocks off for free, you'd think he bloody owned the place –

'George,' I hiss, to attract his attention, he'd sort of sunk down into himself, he's normally so quick on things like that. 'George, that man.'

'What?' he says, lifeless, quiet, not George at all, not the George I knew, not the George of old, not George and the dragon, George who got lively at times like this. The only time, really, that George got lively.

'That man's got *Big Ones International.*'

'Well he's not doing any harm.'

It must be softening of the brain. And he's whispering, too, as if he's afraid, as if he doesn't want the Paki to hear him.

It's over to me, then. All down to me. My dad is in hospital, and George is dying. The older generation is on its way out. Up to us lot now to keep the torch burning. Up to us lot now to – what was the phrase? The very good phrase they used in *Spearhead,* the phrase that made me think of my dad – up to us now to *hold the pass*. Up to us to *dam the flood*.

'Excuse me, Sunshine,' I say to him. 'Can't you read English? Can't you see this sign?'

'Yes. I recommend removing it.'

'You what?' I say, not believing my ears. 'You bloody what? Did you hear that, George?'

'It's giving a bad impression,' the man says, smiling as he says it, cool as anything.

'I'll give you a bad impression,' I say. 'I'll give you a very bad impression! I'll thank you to vacate this shop.' It's not coming out quite right, I realize, perhaps the third pint was a bad idea, but I go right up to him and stare him in the face, his little brown face, his ugly face, in case he's in any doubt of what I meant.

'George,' he goes, 'will you introduce me? I'm very interested to meet this young man.'

And that was the point when everything changed. That was the point when my heart began to thump. I thought, he's mad. He has to be. But I swung round to George, and he had this funny look, sort of beaten, shamed, like a wheezy old dog that had pissed its bed, and I started to realize, I started to see, and I thought, if it's that, I'll kill you, George, but of course it can't be, come on George –

'Er, yes,' he said. 'This is Dirk White. He's been giving me a hand. Just for a bit. Sort of work experience.' The greasy little man held out his hand, he smiled and held out his hand to me, his pin-striped suit, white shirt, gold cuff-links, laughing at me, looking down on me . . . Laughing with George behind my back.

What did George say? *Giving me a hand . . . Just for a bit . . . Work experience . . .*

He said, 'This is Dinesh. Mr Patel.'

It was all so sudden, I wasn't ready – and before I knew what, I had taken his hand, just because he was sticking it under my nose, and his other paw still clutching *Big Ones International*. I wanted to break his frigging fingers, but because I couldn't decide what to do I stood there right next to him *holding his hand,* we were holding hands like a couple of pansies!!

George was still talking, but it didn't make sense. 'He's going to buy the shop, you see. Mr Patel is – going to be buying the shop. It's my health, as you know. You've always known I couldn't go on like this for ever . . .'

'Buying the shop? Are you winding me up?' I finally managed to drop his hand, which had stuck to mine as if with glue, but I swear I never actually shook it. I suppose there was a moment when we joggled up and down because he was trying so hard to shake mine, but I never shook his. I'd rather die. Or kill him. Kill them. *Kill them all*.

George was shitting himself. He was scared of me. I realized then he was scared of me. He looked like an old red wrinkled balloon, slowly going down, shrinking, disgusting. He was trying to get out another cigarette, but his hand was shaking so much he dropped it. 'It's the truth, Dirk,' he said. 'I meant to tell you. I was going to tell your dad tomorrow.'

Everything was falling around my ears. My dreams of the future. My ... *expectations*. My own *legitimate expectations*. That's what *Spearhead* says; *we are losing our birthright*, and suddenly it was all happening to me, beneath my very ears, in broad daylight.

The words that came out weren't right at all. 'But I like this shop. I love this shop.' It felt like pepper at the back of my nose, it felt as if I had been punched in the stomach, it felt as if I was going to – break down, but I'd do the breaking, I'd do the punching –

'Well if you have a strong commitment to this shop. We could probably come to some arrangement. At least in short-term, see how things work out. See if we can rub together, and so forth.' The Paki was talking like a radio.

'What?' I said, looking at him, so he knew what I meant, just looking at him as hard as nails.

'I might be needing a manager.'

I didn't bother to answer him. It was George that I was talking to. 'You make me sick. You disgusting old man. You disgusting old pimp. You fucking old queer. You –'

The Paki butted in. 'I think you are saying things you regret, young man.'

George was trying to say something. 'Dirk,' he managed, but wheezing so much it sounded like 'Ergh', it sounded as though he was having an attack, and then he was right in the middle of it, rising to his feet, one hand in the air, one hand straight up as if he wanted to wave or give me the salute, the old Heil Hitler, but really he was reaching for his inhaler, I knew where he kept it, on a shelf at the back, I had fetched it for him so many times over the years, I had wanted to vomit through so many attacks, and that I suppose was my *giving a hand, just for a bit,* my *work experience* . . . Everything seemed to slow down, for a second. He was very red, sort of roaring, roaring, and then the roars had long gaps in between, and then all the red has gone from his face and he goes all white, and not roaring, not wheezing, not breathing at all, just sort of frozen, clutching his throat with one great fat hand and sort of clawing away with the other one, and horribly quiet, the quiet was horrible, clawing at me or the inhaler or both, and then I see his lips going blue, all round his mouth this awful blue colour.

I always wanted him to die. I've imagined it for years, George dying in front of me.

But in the end, I couldn't do it. Thing is, he's been around all my life, I knew him when I was a toddler –

I got his inhaler down from the shelf. I pulled him down on to his stool, I pushed his chest forward on to the counter, I touched his head, his greasy bald head, and laid it on its side on a pile of *Sun*s, a great thick pile of unsold *Sun*s, I put him in the correct position and shoved his inhaler into his hand. 'Use it, you bastard,' I said to him. 'I'm fucking saving your fucking life. USE THE INHALER OR I'LL FUCKING KILL YOU!!'

I would have been justified. I had a right. But sometimes things just don't work out.

I couldn't kill him. I just wasn't ready. It probably takes practice, killing someone.

Maybe each time you get a little bit closer. You can lose a battle and still win the war.

We shan't lose the war. It's too important. The future of England depends on us. Never forget what *Spearhead* says . . . *We are many, and our reach is long.*

THE PARK

26 · Thomas

Thomas worked every other Saturday. Today he was working on two hours' sleep, but he felt amazing, he felt fantastic . . .

Until he awoke with his head on the keyboard, and looked around hastily, to see if he'd been spotted. He'd been asleep for forty minutes, but everyone was busy with their own machines. The air in the office was hot and torpid, but Thomas was instantly awake, and buzzing –

It wasn't a dream. It had really happened.

After the grim evening at the hospital, Melissa had descended, in the middle of the night, like a sensual angel, all ruffled feathers, and stood on his doormat, and asked to come in.

Around three a.m. Thomas was still glued to *Postmodernism and the Death of Meaning*. How on earth could he refute Fred Burnett's point in his review of Kevin J. Vanhoozer: 'I remain unconvinced that either speech-act theory or Trinitarianism is the way to spiral out of the (postmodern) hermeneutical circle . . .' Thomas felt trapped, with Fred and Kevin, in the coils of a hermeneutic hell.

Then it had begun. The familiar pattern. It sounded like next door, on the same level. First they would quarrel, rumbling on for hours, like an earth tremor passing from one room to another. Thomas almost managed not to notice it. But last night the man had started to shout, then the woman screamed, then the child started crying . . . Then it had died down for a minute or two. Then erupted again, only slightly quieter.

He was just wishing he could kill them – they were so fucking violent – when screaming broke out in terrible earnest.

There was a padding of feet on the stairs above. Someone was standing outside his door. A long pause. Then someone knocked.

Straightening his dressing-gown in case it was a woman, drawing himself up in case it was a man, he had gone to the door and flung it open.

Melissa was standing on the doormat. 'Can I come in?'

'Come in, Melissa.'

Night-time Melissa. A vision of wonder. She had been lying on her hair, which was flat to her head in some places, floating up in others, a strange little blond mouse's nest, and two bright eyes, red from sleeplessness, or rubbing, and she wore pyjamas – *Melissa in pyjamas, and in my flat!* – the sweetest pyjamas he had ever seen, white cotton, rumpled, with small red ships, and bright red piping around the neck. A curved white neck. And she had breasts. Little round hills that softened the cotton.

'Excuse the pyjamas, they're ghastly,' she said. 'A Christmas present from my mother.' She sounded normal, but she looked very pale. 'Do you think we should call the police, Thomas?'

'No, I think she's quietening down. You wouldn't like a cup of tea?'

'Were you working?'

'Oh, it's just this, um, book thingy . . .'

He wanted to offer her a drink, but didn't, because *drink* would sound like *sex*, which took up disproportionate space in his mind, looking at crumpled, half-naked Melissa.

'I don't suppose you've got a whisky?' she said.

'*Yes* –'

'Is it true all writers drink whisky?'

Before he could answer, a single scream, more piercing than any of the others, tore through the walls, and they both stopped dead.

'Oh God. We'd better go. Oh God.'

Then silence. The silence was very loud. In sudden panic, he had pulled his shoes on, grabbed a greatcoat to go over his dressing-gown.

'Pour yourself a whisky. Call the police. Don't come.'

Her jaw was determined. 'I'm going to come.'

They suddenly heard a different sound, an animal roar, what horror would follow? Then Melissa, who had been standing by the door, slim shoulders hunched, straining to hear, suddenly relaxed, and sank into an armchair.

'Oh can't you hear, Thomas. They're laughing. I swear they are.'

It was true. Now they were both screaming with laughter.

'Bloody people,' he said. And then, 'Well, good.'

'They must be drunks,' she said. 'That explains it.'

'I'll drink to that . . . Will you still have a whisky?'

The miracle continued. Melissa said 'Yes.'

She was not a bit like he had thought. Softer, less glamorous, funnier. The pyjamas helped. And his dressing-gown. With the safety pin holding the tear together. You can't help feeling friendly, in pyjamas.

I hardly touched her, but we had such fun. I poured her, at first, a most modest whisky, a whisky that said my designs were modest, a whisky that said I respected her. Except that she failed to read it right. 'Are you afraid I'll get drunk?' she asked, holding the eighth-of-an-inch up to the light.

'Of course not, of course not,' I stuttered, muttered, swilling in another three-quarters of an inch.

'I don't often drink, so I might as well enjoy it.' She smiled at me, a wonderful smile, the smile of a twenty-five-year-old woman expecting mostly good things from life.

What did we talk about? Everything; nothing. She was born in Sussex, on the south coast . . . Naturally Melissa was born in Sussex. She loved her job. 'I love the kids, they break your heart, they're just so sweet –' Yes, I thought, you do, you are. But she gets so tired by the end of the day, she sometimes comes back and falls asleep, still with her coat on, on the bed. (That they should tire her is a disgrace, I told her I would write letters to the council – I think perhaps I overdid my attempt to prove I wasn't mean when I sloshed our second glass.)

There was one of those moments when two people are quiet, two people who have never been so close before, and the membrane between them could almost be broken, I heard her breathing, she heard me breathing –

And then there was a great cry from next door. 'Oh no,' said Melissa, half-laughing, half-frightened, and the tension, the moment of silence was broken, we moved apart, we both stopped and listened – what followed was utterly electrifying. For the woman was crying in orgasm, running up the scale, getting faster and higher, a final yelp of excitement and then a purring release, small peaceful mewlings. Neither of us dared to look at each other. We listened in silence from first to last.

And then Melissa began to giggle, sipping her whisky and giggling happily. 'I don't think she needed us after all,' she said, and laughed, and choked on her whisky, and coughed until she was red in the face, and even red in the face she was pretty.

At half-past four, she was falling asleep, curled up in my chair, her eyelashes drooping, fair, unmascara-ed against her pink cheek. I saw her upstairs, Mr Responsible.

'Oh dear,' she said, stumbling a little, 'I've had too much whisky. I've stayed too long. I've been having such a lovely time . . .'

She was having such a lovely time! She was having a lovely time with me!

I was King of Hillesden as I took her hand, her small firm hand which clutched her keys, and helped her direct them into the keyhole.

'Goodnight, Melissa.'

'Oh Thomas. Thanks. I'm awfully sorry to have stopped you sleeping. I promise not to disturb you again.'

On impulse, I reached up and kissed her cheek. 'Melissa,' I said, 'Disturb me again.' The smile I got in return was brilliant.

Some time this morning, between six and seven, I lay in bed, remembering Melissa, imagining unbuttoning her cotton pyjamas, running my finger along the red piping, so easy to imagine her kissing me, liking me, and yet there are women who make you feel that everything about you is hateful, too big, too loud, too rough, too rude, and your cock a monster, put it away, back to the kennel, you slobbering brute, slink away like a beaten dog to tug all night at your chains in the yard . . . Jean, you cow, you threw me out, I stayed in the cold for years and years . . .

Innocent, really, how I thought of Melissa, the little games we played together, I stroked her breasts, she let me suck them, two puppy-noses, pink and damp, we lay on the bed in each other's arms.

But when it was time to come at last or I should never go to sleep, someone slipped in through another door, someone kind, someone sturdy, someone who knew just what a man likes, at first I didn't see her face though her flesh was firm and warm in my hands, her heavy breasts, her comfortable belly, a woman moving on top of me, then she was slipping down my body, oh bliss, to take my cock in her mouth, the warm wetness of that special place where Jeanie never in a decade put me, opening, opening to take me in, taking me, oh loving me, a woman loved me and I came at once – and just as I came I opened my eyes and saw her face, and saw it was Shirley. Shirley White! Thank you, Shirley.

Half an hour later I woke again. Spring was coming, because, because . . .

I remembered it in a rush of joy. Melissa appeared in the middle of the night. Melissa had asked for help, for comfort. Melissa had almost suggested a date.

I walked to the bathroom patting myself.

Oh, but Shirley . . . I'm rather shocked. Shirley, Alfred White's daughter, a respectable widow, a hospital visitor –

Melissa, darling, there's no competition, honestly, dearest, you are the one.. The name that's singing in my brain, Melissa, Melissa, over and over. For yesterday we came so far, we came from nowhere at all to somewhere.

And something else. Something very exciting.

Melissa has borrowed my book from the library.

Shirley White, the Wankers' Friend. What did she do to deserve my sperm? I suppose she's just desirable. Of course completely wrong for me, but the sort of woman who – knows what's what.

I almost felt she fancied me, when we sat in the café, before the others came. And perhaps it's not impossible. Perhaps I'm more of a man than Jean thought. Thank you, Shirley.

Sorry, Shirley.

Bloody hell, what would Darren say?

He doesn't even know I once kissed his sister. . .

Thomas forced himself to awaken his computer, which had sunk into tell-tale blank screen mode. He stole a quick glance round the librarians' room, but no one had noticed he wasn't working. I work a lot harder than bloody Darren, he told himself. And for less money. Saturdays too. Screw you Darren.

27 · Thomas and Darren

We hadn't really talked in over two decades. All I'd had to go on were appearances. He smiled a lot more, looked more successful . . . no longer kept in touch with me. He'd made some kind of effort at the hospital, said we must 'hang out' while he was here, even pretended he might come and see me – as if he would bother, after all this time.

In the first few years he had mailed me his cuttings. Perhaps I didn't praise them enough. We had started primary school together; learned to swim by nearly drowning each other; fallen in love with the same blond plaits; had our first kiss at the same party, though I was the first to get my tongue inside; started a school magazine called *Tall* . . . I was the editor, Darren was features. I got to write the editorial, which was grand, scornful, and very short. Darren wrote most of the rest of the contents, but I, as the editor, edited him.

(But Darren always came top in exams. And he was good at sport, whereas I was lazy. Now he had outstripped me at life, as well. Not that it mattered; Melissa liked me.)

By twelve midday I was flagging again as I called up book titles on the library system. I went across the road to the Italian café.

We call it Italian, because of the owner, Mario, who comes from Milan – he fell in love with an English girl and got stuck here long ago. Actually it couldn't be more English, with its salty, fatty, stewed-tea smell. I'm never quite certain where I come from (with a rugby team of genes on my father's side – Jewish, Scottish, Italian, Spanish? There was even a rumoured great-grandma from Barbados) but walking in here I know I'm British.

Stale cigarette smoke, Formica-covered tables, eggs and beans and Nescafé. I ordered double fried eggs on toast, and sat by the window, away from the kitchen. There I could watch the cars go by, and the women doing their Saturday shopping, women too poor to drive to Quicksave, their push-chairs hung about with carrier-bags. Shouting children; sun and wind. Perhaps I could drive Melissa to Tesco's –

My father never shopped in his life. A teacher's son with pretensions to more who at one point was quite a successful bookie, until he gambled the money away. Mum feared his gambling and hated his drinking. In the end they had moved into a rented flat, and my mother sat staring at the radio. I longed for parents like May and Alfred. Alfred-and-May. May-and-Alfred. But Darren didn't seem to have learned much from it –

I looked up from my second mouthful of toast to see a madman tear across my field of vision, almost knocking down a woman with a paper bag of plantains, her orange African head-dress swivelling to watch him, talking to himself, mouthing, grimacing – There was something about the shape of his head.

'Darren!' I shouted, through the deaf plate-glass, and ran out after him, and tapped him on the shoulder. To my surprise, he turned straight towards me, like a drowning man, flung his arms around me.

'Darren. Well met!'

'Thomas. Thank God. I was looking for you. They said you were in the Italian café. I couldn't bloody see any Italian café.' His voice was thick, emotional. I pulled back a few inches and looked at his face. He was ten years older now, by daylight, than the rugged film-star I'd seen in the hospital. His eyes were bloodshot, his features blurred.

'Are you all right?'

'Yes. No.'

I smelled his breath. Whisky, in the morning. Maybe it meant we could cut the crap. (Did I want to be friends? – He *was* my friend. After thirty years there was no going back.)

'Come and keep me company?' He was dragging me away. I don't think he had much clue where he was going. 'Drink,' he insisted. 'Let's go have a drink.'

'Well – actually I haven't finished my lunch. Come back and have some lunch with me. They aren't licensed, I'm afraid.'

'Do I want to drink coffee? Maybe I should.' He made an effort to sound sober. 'I had a few drinks already this morning. Just had a tremendous row with my wife. Marriage – why the fuck do I keep doing it!'

I ordered him All Day Breakfast. Darren sat in the window, chewing his nails. 'It stinks of smoke in here. That's so English.' (I prayed that Mario just heard the last bit, but Darren was shouting, deaf with drink.) 'I fucking miss it. Susie made me give up. Wouldn't bloody live with me until I did. I smoked like a chimney. Sixty a day . . . Helps when you're in a hotel on your own.'

Perhaps smoking explained the lines. He looked older than me, or I hoped he did (but better dressed. The suit, the trench-coat. The quiet, definite print of money.)

'Susie seemed, well, very nice,' I said. Tactfully. Or nosily. 'And she's a therapist, is she?'

'Fucking therapists,' said Darren, furious. 'She drives me fucking mad. Always trying to understand. Usually things she knows nothing about. D'ya know any therapists? So fucking arrogant.'

'Didn't seem arrogant.'

'They're all bloody experts at other people's pain. Though she has her own problems. Abused, bulimic. Everyone's fucking abused these days.' He tried to get a grip on himself. 'I mustn't tell you all Susie's problems. They're only therapists because they have problems. She thinks

I should fucking *confront* my father. She doesn't know my father! She should try it! You know Dad, what a bastard he is –'

My jaw dropped open. Alfred? A bastard? 'How do you mean, confront your father? Sorry, not with you. What about?'

'About the way he wrecked my life. And Shirley's life. And Dirk's probably. I know sod all about Dirk's life, except that he's a little fascist . . . and all his opinions come from Dad. Dad terrified us. Appalling temper. It's taken me years to admit it. *Years*. I used to be in awe of him. Working-class hero, and all that crap.'

I strained to see it from his point of view. 'I suppose he did get stroppy, sometimes . . . My dad was never around to get cross. At least you knew where you stood, with yours.'

Darren shook his head, vigorous, dismissive, waving his hands, short jerky movements. Mario plumped down the breakfast in front of him, flinching away from Darren's flying arms. 'Wan brea'fast,' he said, with his usual huge smile, inviting the customer to wonder at the marvel, but Darren didn't seem to see him. He seized the knife and fork and plunged in, wordlessly hacking at a very large sausage.

'We were always on tenterhooks, when he came home. We had to be quiet. Things had to be just right. It affected the men, their time in the forces. If anyone touched his kit, he went mad.'

'My father was unfit for National Service –' Or feigned unfitness, my mother had hinted.

Darren's thin furious mouth was working. 'Don't you remember what happened that time I borrowed his army knife without asking, when we went to scout camp, in Storrington? That bayonet thing we boys were so thrilled with? He was waiting on the doorstep when they brought us back. Half-crazed with rage. He boxed my ears, and kept on shouting it was *dangerous*. But *he* was dangerous, *he* was the dangerous one, living with Dad was *fucking* dangerous!! He even hit Shirley – He even hit Mum. Well once, I remember. At least once.'

'I had no idea –' A few memories came back of Alfred being crotchety when I went round. Exploding when we didn't put back the lid on the dubbin tin, after doing our football boots. We were eleven or twelve. He had told us off. Then later on he walked me home. 'Always finish a job,' he said. 'If a job's worth doing, it's worth doing properly.' My father, of course, never finished a job. He would start the lawn, which was postage-stamp-size, shave a small strip of green, then collapse in a deck-chair, sighing, despondent, a beer in his hand. 'Maybe I idealize your dad.'

'Everyone thinks he's wonderful. It makes me puke.'

His coffee came. He swigged it down in one. It was boiling hot. As he registered the pain he started blowing like a whale, then spreading his lips in a tragic mask. Very white teeth; I had neglected mine. 'Aach! Ounnnhhh! Bloody burnt myself!'

'I like your dad,' I said, feebly. 'I like your dad, I liked your wife.'

'I feel like shit,' he said. 'Sorry. I am a shit. Life is shit.'

Part of me wanted him to crawl a bit more, but another part needed him back on his feet. 'Come on, Darren. You're not a shit. Your dad being ill – it's very upsetting. But I mean, you're – great. You're basically fine.'

'I'm not bloody fine!'

'You've made it, Darren. You've got money and fame and wives and kids and all the other things we should have by our age –'

'Wives? Ex-wives. That isn't such a triumph. I'll probably soon have another ex-wife.'

I tried to suppress a twinge of pleasure. 'You only just got married, didn't you? I did like Susie. The little bit we talked. She's . . . attractive, obviously.' (But less so than Melissa.) 'She seemed, you know, well, very – direct.'

'Oh she's that all right. She's fucking direct.'

'Well that's something, isn't it. My wife was a liar. And *she* left *me*.'

He looked at me astonished. (I saw the boy. A flash of his face when he was a boy.) 'What do you mean? Rose and Katy both walked out.'

'I thought – I assumed –' And I had assumed. 'I always thought it was you trading up.'

He shook his head, three times, over-vehement. 'No, I would never have left my kids. It hurts like hell. It's a fucking disaster.'

I avoided his eyes. His tie was expensive, but bore a trail of tomato seeds, drying. 'Might you – will you – have kids with Susie?'

'That bitch.' A pause; he seemed to hear himself. 'She's not really a bitch. I've had too much to drink. But she says we're not ready for them yet, as a couple. Whatever that's fucking supposed to mean.'

'What does it mean?'

'We fight a lot. She thinks it wouldn't be good for the child . . .' There was a long pause. He stared at his nails, or the bare fingertips where his nails should have been. He had bitten the flesh, little blackened pink wounds. 'She's right in a way. It was hell for my kids . . . Do you know what it means to feel you've fucked up?'

'Well can't you stop?'

'Look, it's all handed down. They dole it out, we pass it on. The bloody therapists are right about that much. My fucking father's got a lot to answer for –' He broke off with a gesture of despair. 'You don't believe me. I can see it in your face. You're so bloody English. Can't you handle anger?'

It was so American, 'handling anger'. 'Look, you're my mate. My old mate. It's just, I was sitting here, half-asleep – It's a shock to see you. I'm just – catching up. And I am quite fond of your old man.'

'He's a cunt,' he said, but he didn't sound convinced. I think his energy was wearing down. He'd eaten the bacon, fat and all; so much for his elaborate diets.

'But he and your mum are happy. Aren't they?'

'She was always blind to Dad's weak points. And he's fond of her, I can't deny it. Though he could be bloody rude to her as well. If the food was wrong. And she was not a great cook . . . I've never expected my wives to cook. I take them out, or we get food in, so I've managed to escape that part of the pattern.' He seemed to sit up a bit straighter, briefly. 'Look, as a father – Dad was, well, hell. Expected too much. Nothing was good enough. Why do you think I went halfway round the world? I still hear his voice, in the back of my head.'

'But can't you forget him, now you're so far away?'

He looked at me with a kind of desperation. 'Will you listen to me? I have to tell someone. I hate my life. *I hate my life.* Never at home, no time at home. Which is partly why it took me so long, to realize the problem with my father. My last wife tried to tell me, and I thought she was mad. Then Susie said it and it started to make sense.'

Aha, I thought. So it was all still new. Darren is embracing hate like a convert.

'My life might look good from the outside. But my wives walk out. Because of my temper. I *can't* control it. Any more than Dad could.'

'You've got a beautiful wife. You're rich –'

Darren reached across the table and took me by the shoulder, and when he spoke he was almost choking, he'd gone red in the face, and the words burst out – 'Can you please stop telling me how lucky I am?' Slowly his hand loosed its grip on my shoulder, and his colour faded back towards normal. 'We had breakfast in Covent Garden today. We started going over the same old ground. It drives me crazy. Susie can't leave things alone. She keeps on saying I should tell my father that he made us suffer. Then I'll be less angry . . . Apparently. I don't see why. He could never say sorry. Never. *Never.*'

I myself had never managed to tell my father about the million ways he failed us. But one day, when he was getting weak but before they started on the morphine, he said to me, out of the blue, 'I should have given you a wedding present. You and Jeanie. I'm sorry, Thomas. I've never been able to keep hold of money.'

He'd made his speech absurdly late; Jean had left me a few months earlier. Maybe he wanted to say sorry for something more than the missing present. I muttered, stupidly, 'It doesn't matter.'

It mattered, though, that he tried to say sorry.

'I lost my temper in the restaurant,' said Darren. 'Shouted my head off. Which Susie hates. Everyone stared. I came over here . . . I don't know why. I wanted to see you.'

'I'm glad you did. I'm very glad –' I cast around for something to say. 'Look Susie might be right, you know. You could give your dad a chance to say sorry.'

'*Dad?* You're joking! He's always right. And he is, about some things. He sticks to his guns. His opinions are shit, but he's brave, by his lights. Maybe I'm afraid he's a better man than me. I mean, I'm soft. I like the good life –'

'I knew there was a reason why you left Hillesden.' We smiled at each other. The mood lightened.

He boasted a bit. I encouraged him. The Ritz, the Plaza, trips to Tibet, regular slots for the *Washington Post*, Susie's income, his children's brilliance . . . Just when I was starting to flag a bit, he looked at me, with his reddened blue eyes.

'But you know I always wanted to write a book. And a book is the one thing I have not written.. I hate being tethered up with my thoughts.'

'It's hard,' I said, though I like my own thoughts. Which were, in that instant, I'm happier than you. Less successful, but less unhappy.

After a refill of coffee, he stood up to go. I wondered if he would pay his bill.

'I'll have to go back to the hotel and find Susie . . . I talked too much –'

'Not at all. It was good.'

He cleared his throat, and looked embarrassed. 'Um, I do love Susie, actually. Although I give her a hard time. She's – the best woman I've ever been with.'

I looked at the table. This was new. Darren and I had never talked about love. Women, yes, but not about love. 'Good,' I said. It was all I could manage.

'Will you come and stay in the flat in New York?'

'Yes, if you like. If you really mean it.'

'Don't wait too long. We're all getting older. That's what Susie says; what if Dad dies?'

'I'll walk with you to the underground.'

He didn't pay. Perhaps he hadn't got much sterling. Mario was listening to opera very quietly, smiling and nodding at his radio, and he winked as I paid the bill for two, with a tiny nod in Darren's direction that perhaps meant Mario thought he was a loony. 'Nice to see you, John.' He always called me John. After seven or eight years, it was too late to correct him.

Darren and I said goodbye by the Catholic church with its grill of ornate painted iron-work, towering above us, the patterns repeating, up and up into the cold blue sky, then sunlit thunderheads, one above another . . . He turned to walk down the steps to the tube, then without a word came back and embraced me.

It wasn't comfortable. He had a brief-case, and I was clutching a newspaper. But we held each other, awkwardly. Sons, brothers. 'See you at the hospital later, maybe.'

'You're good to visit him,' said Darren.

'It's easy for me. I'm not his son.'

28 · Alfred

Alfred lay shivering slightly in bed. Sister had opened a lot of windows. Someone had died five beds down the ward. Bad news travelled fast, in hospitals . . .

At least it's not me. But is it coming closer?

Alfred knew he was too young to die. Too young to be lying in hospital.

I never expected to be here.

And his arm moved restlessly towards his cupboard. Were his boots and greatcoat still safe in there?

Funny, isn't it, how life turns out. Hospitals were always for other people. Other people got ill and died. Other people took time off work. I never did. I never would. I suppose I despised people who got ill. Except for May when she had her babies. She was a good woman, and she nearly died.

The courage women show in childbirth . . . there's a lot of courage around, in life. They don't put it in books or films any more, but I'm sure it's still there. Ordinary courage.

I never had to think about my body. It always did everything I asked of it. No problems in the romantic department, not right up until I was sixty-five. No problems with the waterworks. And on my feet, day after day, all day and every day, in all weathers. Yet I never got coughs or colds or flu.

And my feet are pretty miraculous. No call for Dr Scholl's or the chiropodist. May's got corns and an ingrown toe-nail. Probably because they wear daft shoes. Women always wear daft shoes, bless them. I've always kept as close as I could to the boots I wore for National Service. They carried me through the deserts of Palestine, they'll carry me through whatever life brings –

I'll put them on again, of course. My boots will carry me out of here. Shuffling about in slippers, well, it's not my style, though I'm not complaining.

I mustn't complain. Life's been good to me.

But I'm only seventy-one. That's not old, is it? Not old for nowadays, at least. And I'm still in harness. Still a hundred per cent. They've extended my contract because I deserve it. I'm over-age by my birth certificate, but they know I do the work of six men . . .

I'm only seventy-one. Too young to die. I thought I could manage another ten.

It doesn't seem right, when I've always been fit, always eaten healthy, and kept on my feet. A drink or two, in the past a smoke –

Nothing that could explain getting cancer. I thought unhealthy people got cancer. It can't be cancer, they've made a mistake.

But when the consultant had come round this morning, what he said seemed to leave no room for doubt. Except the great window of unbelief where Alfred knew he would live for ever, patrol the Park for ever more, tipping his cap to white-haired ladies who would always, somehow, be older then him. Of course he'd keep going. He always had, ever since he finished his National Service –

But the doctor stood there, tall and thin, a gentleman with a thin kind voice, a bit of a weed, Alfred might have thought once. And as he spoke, the whole world shifted. A cold weight of fear Alfred hadn't felt since he was first shot at in Palestine and suddenly knew he wasn't immortal, landed on his belly, and he started praying. *Please Lord no may it not be true oh please Lord no may it not be true* –

'Mr White? Do you understand me?'

But Alfred hadn't heard a word he said after the first few deadening sentences.

'The results of the tests have come back now.' He had paused, and looked up at Alfred over his glasses, seeing if Alfred was *compos mentis*; or just making sure he was listening.

'Were they OK then?' Alfred sounded too breezy, he knew it before the words had left his lips.

'We-ell,' said the consultant, carefully. 'They were not entirely what we had expected.'

Which meant death.

But Alfred had dismissed the thought as quickly as it fell through the air.

'We had assumed your problems were circulatory – That is to say, we thought you'd had a stroke.'

'Didn't I, then? Is that good news?' But he already knew it was not good news.

There was a pause. The thin man had looked at the nurse, as if her face would give him strength. 'I'm afraid we have discovered some obstructions in the tissues of the brain. We shall therefore pursue a different course of treatment.'

That sounded all right; but it wasn't all right. Alfred waited, but nothing was forthcoming.

'Do you have any questions you'd like to ask, Mr . . . Er?' He had already forgotten Alfred's name.

'Well I'm not going to die, am I?' Alfred laughed, making a joke of it, as you must. It was serious, yes, but as long as it wasn't fatal –

'We shall do our very best for you,' the doctor replied, not meeting his eyes.

'I don't mind being operated on,' said Alfred, hearing his voice sounding hoarse, desperate, not his voice at all, a frightened voice.

(But he refused to be frightened. Even of the knife. He had had his appendix out after the war. Nothing to it, really. He had woken up singing an army song, which was the effect of the gas. He'd been good as new, after that. And the surgeons were wonderful, nowadays.)

'We don't think an operation would be helpful.'

Another punch of cold ice in his stomach.

'You'd better tell me what's going on. The full whack. Go on, I can take it.'

And the thin cold voice, perhaps trying to be kind, awkward, scientific, reluctant, told him what was the matter with him. But Alfred couldn't listen. After 'a number of small tumours' he heard no more.

Until the consultant talked himself to a standstill.

Then Alfred swallowed, and fixed him with his eye. The doctor was looking at the lino. 'So it's cancer, you're saying. And you can't operate.'

'We don't think an operation would be helpful.' He repeated himself, politely, firmly. Alfred said nothing. 'At your age, you see . . .'

'So I'm a goner because of my age. You're going to throw me on the scrap-heap, are you?' A brief spurt of temper made Alfred feel better.

The doctor and nurse both looked embarrassed. 'Not at all, Mr White, I do assure you. We'll do everything we can to make you comfortable.'

'So it's hemlock, is it?' Alfred crowed at them. At least he was in control of them now.

'I don't quite follow,' said the doctor, wearily.

'I know about history. I went to school. I think you understand me, doctor.'

But suddenly all his energy left him, and the cold fluid began to leak through him, filling his veins with icy fear, and he had to lie back on the pillow, exhausted, which the doctor took as a sign to depart, saying 'I'll be back before long if you have any more questions.'

He'll be back before long my arse, thought Alfred. He'll be back if we're lucky in two days' time, and then he'll be telling some other poor sod they're not worth saving, same as me.

Shirley had brought him flowers, yesterday. A huge great boat-ful of snowy-white flowers. The only thing was, they stood on the table between him and Pamela, so he couldn't see her properly without straining round. It had been quite pleasant, having a chat, just now and then, when he felt like it, or when she felt like it, because she was chatty. Bit forward, maybe, though that hadn't struck him till May came in and started looking daggers. (But May was just jealous, of course. Why shouldn't a woman try to look her best?)

Women always liked me, he thought to himself. I always had a bit of charm.

All in the past, the cold voice said, the chilly liquid that coursed through his veins.

White as snow; white as clouds. They were a beautiful bunch. Must have cost a packet. No one could ever say his daughter was mean. She was a good girl in lots of respects, though they hadn't always seen eye to eye . . .

It'll break May's heart. How shall I tell her? Perhaps I'll ask the doctor to have a word.

They do their best. They're professional men. I don't suppose it's an easy job. Perhaps I was a bit short with him. Lucky no one was listening. I didn't really show myself to advantage. That's what my mother always used to say: 'Try and show yourself to advantage, Alfred.' And she was right. That's what we're put here for. I always said to the kids: 'Just do your best. Fear no man, and do your best.'

The trouble is, I was – afraid. I don't remember being so afraid, since I was young, in Palestine. You need time, to be brave. And I wasn't ready. When the big battle comes, I want to be ready. I shan't be short with anyone, then.

I was short with Shirley yesterday too. If I have a fault, it's a touch of temper. A man gets tired, a man with a job, a man who is doing a difficult job. With the various pressures that job entails. May understood. She's a good woman. May knew a man has to let off steam.

I wasn't the easiest man at home. I tried to be fair, I was hard but fair – I hope I was fair. I did my best. Things happened I'm not entirely proud of, now. Still a father has to take the lead. And boys get cocky, and their heads get swelled. Need to be taken down a peg or two. It was all quickly over. Over and done with. None of our family ever bore a grudge.

But I think I was remiss in hitting Shirley. Never hurt her, of course. But hitting a girl . . .

I never lost my rag in the Park, all the same. In the Park I had to be calm as Job. (I think it was Job. May would know.)

Those flowers. Shirley thought I wouldn't like the whiteness. I remember the Park, covered with snow. The perfect place. Suddenly perfect. Everything clean and shining bright. Not a mark on it, first thing in the morning. And the café turned into a magic palace.

Kids think they know you. When they don't at all. They can't get to know you, because they're bored. They think they know the answers, so they don't ask questions. They go deaf if you talk about anything that matters to you . . . They're afraid you'll go on about it, you see. They're afraid that you'll embarrass them. (Though Dirk was a bit different. That boy could listen.)

The flowers in the Park were always a joy. Very bright, of course, all the colours of the rainbow. We didn't go in for white, in the Park. You have to make a show, it's a different thing. That's probably what Shirley was thinking of. As if the Park was me, which it isn't.

(Funny thing is, that's been said to me. And I do confess to a certain pride. More than once, by a member of the public. 'You *are* the Park, Alfred. Can't imagine it without you.' But I know the truth. I'm not irreplaceable. Any good man could hold the fort. That's what they need. When all's said and done. They could train someone up alongside me. I'd be happy with that. Life goes on. I'm already over age. It stands to reason . . . And it'd be nice to have company. Like the old days when we went out in pairs. You had someone to have a chat and a laugh with. They're good men, in the Parks Service. Better than average. The cream of the crop. Probably because it's a job to be proud of. Serving the public, maddening as they are. Even if they're coloured, even if they're barmy, even if they're like the unfortunate woman who came and sat in my hut for a chat and the next thing I knew she had taken her blouse off – I had to cover her up double-quick. It takes a good man to cope with things like that.)

The flowers in the Park are a little bit special. Lovely reds and pinks and blues, tulips, geraniums, hyacinths . . . And yellow primroses and golden polyanthus and hundreds of daffodils in February. 'Yellow Gold'. That was one of May's poems. She was shy about them, but it was one of her best. It was after she'd seen the daffs in the Park. I'd forgotten my flask, and she brought it in, and when she saw the lines of daffodils, she just said, 'Ooh. Ooh, that's lovely.' And went away and wrote her poem.

I found it that evening on the Basildon Bond. She liked to have a nice pad to write on. I always told her she should publish them, but she laughed at me, and said I knew nothing about it. Which wasn't very nice; I can have my opinion. But she always thought herself better than me, better than all of us I suppose, with her books and her reading and her poetry.

I suppose I'll see the daffs next year. A sudden uprush of choking fear.   But of course I'm going back to work. That's the good thing about them not operating. I ought to get back to work a lot sooner.

I might have years. People have years. People go on for years with cancer.

Most things turn out all right in the end. We won the war, coming from behind. I got the job I always wanted. May married me, which I thought she never would. We had three kids, all of them healthy. Shirley got over her childhood asthma. I've always been fit. It'll help me now. If anyone's got a good chance, it's me.

Besides, I'm – needed. The Park needs me. Until they've trained up another man. There used to be six of us. Unbelievable. They cut the jobs down one by one. Now there's just me. And if I go – I've sometimes wondered if they'd ever replace me.

They'd soon find out. What every Park Keeper knows. Given half a chance, it goes back to jungle. Fences get broken. Flowers get picked. Disgusting things get dumped in the shrubbery. Girls get frightened. Windows get smashed. People can be nice, they can be very nice, but give them an inch and they'll take a mile. There's good and there's bad, but the bad will win if men like me don't keep a look out.

To say any different is lazy rubbish.

You have to be tough. You have to be strong. That's how the British got their empire. And maybe we've lost it by going soft. Just like the fall of the Roman Empire. The best of the Romans died at their posts. Died fighting for what they believed in. Too few Romans, there were by then, and great dark hordes pouring over the walls . . .

They've kept cutting down, the council have, they've gone on weakening us, year by year. The new idea is, authority is bad. The new idea is all *softly softly*. 'For fear of upsetting people,' they say. For fear of upsetting the *coloured* people. That's who they mean; call a spade a spade. That's why they took the dogs away. The whole of the building at the back of our yard used to be kennels for the Alsatians. We used to patrol the Park in pairs, and each pair had an Alsatian with them. But no, they said people were getting upset, they said people felt we looked like policemen. They meant coloured people were getting upset. It's coloured people who don't like policemen, and ask yourself why? Why don't they like policemen? If you don't like the police, you 've got something to hide.

The bloody coloureds, that's all they care about, down at the town hall these days. It's because of them they took our uniforms away. We had proper uniforms, till a few years ago, uniforms you would call uniforms, nice black serge, very warm in winter, with silver buttons and a decent peaked cap and the badge of the Parks Service on the front. Those uniforms were a godsend to us. One look and people could see what was what. So they didn't argue the toss, did they?

The old days. The good old days.

There weren't any coloureds when I was a kid. It was just a normal part of London. We were all the same. We were all one. No one was rich. We stuck together . . .

May says I do too much looking back. But sometimes I don't like to think about the future.

Sometimes I think our world is ending. All the things we believed in, gone.

But it's me that's ending. Me that's going.

Nonsense. I'll be back in the Park next week. Make sure the gardeners haven't been slacking. Good boys, all of them. Decent boys. When I started in the Park, I was young, so young. Younger than these young boys I work with.

Alfred still felt as young as any of them. He still walked fast, you had to walk fast to keep the whole Park covered on your own (would he still walk fast when he got out of here? Of course he would; in his head he did; in his head he walked up and down the ward, keeping an eye on things, touching his cap). He still felt young, when there was no one around he would even have a little dance, in his hut, when the radio played one of the good old tunes – but he knew his children didn't think he was young. Parents were people who had never been young.

(I wish I'd had more time to play with the kids.

I wish I hadn't been so hard on them.)

I was young, and hopeful that the world would get better. We were sure there would be miracles, after the war. I thought we'd all walk into a golden future.

Where did it go? What happened to our future, the one so many people suffered and died for? There was something wonderful we all meant to share, after going through so much together. But it just . . . evaporated. That was it. The free orange juice, the milk, the ration-books, the things we had in the nineteen fifties. The National Health spectacles; they were free, little round wonky ones that sat on people's noses. Pale blue and pink ones for the kids. The National Health. It was for everybody. That was a miracle, we all thought so. Nit shampoo and aspirin when you needed them. And then they began to charge for prescriptions, pennies, at first, then just a few bob, and now they come asking for paper money, and most people just do without. And yet it's still here. Just about still there. The National Health Service, waiting for me. Even if I've left it a bit late to ask.

Was it to this ward that my life was pointing?

Alfred closed his eyes against the glare of the lights. Visiting time would soon be beginning. He mustn't drift off, he looked up again, but he couldn't lie staring at the bar of fluorescent, he turned on his side for a moment's respite, propping his eyelid on the slope of the pillow, closing the eye that faced the light, but the pillow was blinding, too soft, too white, he'd liked a flat pillow ever since the war when they'd slept on the concrete floor of the shelter, but that was all over, things had gone soft, softer, softness, sucking him down . . .

And Alfred slept, despite himself. Slept until a quiet coughing woke him.

He was rather put out to see Thomas Lovell. 'I thought you'd be May,' Alfred said. 'Are you early, lad? If visiting's started, May would be here.'

He didn't like the feeling of being looked down on. They all came gawping, once you were ill. And he wanted May. He wanted her badly. What the hell was she playing at, not being here? He craned his neck round to look at the doors. Typical woman, never there when you needed them. Though to be fair, she had always been there, ever since they were little more than kids together. When he lost his mum. When his brother got cancer. May nursed his brother until he died . . . But now, when Alfred needed her more than ever, she'd skipped off and left him. Damn her, damn her –

Just at that moment the doors flapped heavily and May hurried through, screwing up her eyes, looking for him, peering, anxious, breaking into a beam when she saw his face, and all his anger leaked away into relief. She was wearing her smart blue coat for once. Then he saw how pale and tired she was.

He hadn't any time to make her welcome. There was something vital to talk about. He couldn't leave it to the doctors to tell her. Why ever did he think he would? – In any case, he needed comfort. Only May could comfort him.

'Thomas is here,' he said fretfully, as if she couldn't see that for herself. 'I thought you'd get here early, May.' But they took each other's hands, like magnets, halves of a whole springing back together.

'I'll leave you for a moment,' said Thomas, after a pause. 'I'll take a stroll along the ward.'

'Thomas,' said May. 'You're a good boy.'

And he was gone; tall and young. Leaving the ward with that casual ease. How Alfred longed to follow him.

They looked at each other, and both guessed at once the other knew what there was to know.

'Have they told you, then –?'Alfred began, and May at the same moment stumbled through 'Did they say anything? Did the doctor come –?'

She sighed slightly with pain as she rotated her arm, the one which had the worst arthritis, to put it gently round his shoulders, and she stroked his head, she touched his bare scalp, she had never got used to the bareness of his scalp, how naked it felt, how intimate.

'They told me Thursday,' she said. 'On my way out. I haven't slept a wink since. Oh Alfred, love . . . I can't believe it.'

He lay there unable to speak for an instant. Their two skulls touched; they were one in grief. Their hands squeezed gentle and unconscious as a heartbeat. Somehow her love would keep him alive. But then he thought, nothing can keep me alive, if the doctors give up and say I'm a goner. She was sniffling, quietly, like a little dog, a heartbreaking sound like the puppy they had when they were first married, a black-and-white mongrel which got run over. He'd had to carry it into the house. He was the man. It was up to him.

I don't want to leave her, he thought, suddenly, it's nonsense, how ever could we say goodbye? But he brushed the thought away. He had to be strong.

'What are you crying for?' he asked her. 'People will look,' and from the corner of his eye, he saw Pamela clutching on to someone's armchair, concentrating on her balance, one stop on her long hard journey back. Not that he cared about Pamela. Liked her, yes, no more than that; but you had to keep up appearances. He didn't want May to let herself down.

'Oi up, my darling,' he said more kindly. 'We haven't got anything to cry about yet. I could go on for another ten years –'

But he saw from her face that she didn't think so. *Perhaps they told her more than me.* That thought injected a brief spurt of anger.

'It's just that I – I need you, Alfred . . . I don't want to be alone.'

Which moved him, because all their life together he'd known she longed to be alone. To get away from him and the kids and the housework and read her books and write her poems. But now in the end it seemed she didn't. Which softened his fear, unreasonable, real, that secretly people would, well, be glad. That the kids didn't like him, and nor did May. That he was somehow a burden to them.

'I'm not going to leave you, May, darling. You're . . .'

He struggled. Now words had to be said, for May loved words. She needed them. When things had gone wrong in their life over the years, she had sometimes looked at him – 'Say something, Alfred' – with the eyes of someone staring out at the desert, hoping against hope that something would come, but all too often he had left her thirsty, hating himself and pitying her. Then the only thing he could do was be angry – 'Talking won't mend it,' he would snap at her. So how was she to guess he would have loved to talk if the words hadn't locked themselves away? That was why she needed the other Alfred, he thought to himself, her secret lover – and he smiled at her with old affection, and gave up the thing he could never quite say.

'You should have been married to Alfred Tennyson. What good have I ever been to you? You deserve better, with your books and your poems.'

But it wasn't enough. She didn't smile back, and her big blue eyes were full of pain, not so different, he thought, from when she was a girl, their rounded lids, their funny pale lashes. A surge of emotion lifted him up. 'You're . . . a good wife, May. A lovely wife. No one could have been a better wife.'

He had never said such a thing before. To his slight alarm, she turned her face so it couldn't be seen from the ward around them, turned her face against his neck, and leaned against him, she was quite a weight, she felt bigger than he was, now he was brought low, and the tears ran down and soaked his pyjamas.

The fear left him, then. For she must really love him, a thing he had known for over forty years, but always needed to know again. He realized she would never leave him. He'd thought all their life that she might leave him, because he'd gone bald, because he wasn't handsome, because he had never got the Park Keeper's lodge where they'd dreamed of living when they first got married, because he lost his temper with the kids (and all right it sometimes went further than that, but he wasn't a brute, there were far worse than him), because she was pretty (though she wasn't vain and didn't often make the most of herself), because she was sensitive and a lady, not by birth but in every sense that mattered, because she was educated and refined, because he farted whenever she cooked cabbage, because she had to wash his underpants. And now he saw that she would not leave him, would never leave him, now, till he died, and with that knowledge a great fear was conquered, a fear as strong as the fear of death, and for a few brief moments he felt safe and warm, for a few brief moments they were both quite happy, each clutching the gift that the other had given.

I've been a good wife, after all.

If I die first, I shan't be alone.

After a few moments, May sat up and blew her nose, briskly, modestly, still turned away from the sight of the ward.

'We've been through a lot, together, Alfred,' she said, and her voice was firmer now, the old crisp May, putting strength into his bones, fire in his belly. 'We've been through a lot, and we'll come through this. Together we're . . . unbeatable.' Her voice went funny when she said 'unbeatable', but then she managed to smile at him, as if life was a joke, *it's all right, Alfred*, as if they could laugh at it together.

'That's right,' he said. 'That's right, my duck . . . .' He patted her hand. It would all pan out.

'Are you going to tell the children?' she asked. 'We don't want to upset them, do we?'

'Maybe not Dirk. Dirk's too young.'

'He's not as young as we think, you know. But I don't see the point of upsetting them yet. It might all come to nothing, Alfred.'

'Do you think the doctors are making it up?' He dropped her hand, suddenly annoyed. Sometimes her mouth was not connected to her brain. 'The children have a right to know. For instance, Darren might decide to stop home. He might even bring my grandsons to see me –'

'– not forgetting your granddaughter,' May put in, correcting him in the way he hated.

'Of course I haven't forgotten her. "Grandsons" obviously included Felicity.'

For a second he could see she was ready to bicker, but then her softer side prevailed. 'It would be nice to see them, wouldn't it? Better than photographs at Christmas.'

'He does his best,' Alfred said staunchly. 'The pressures of fame –'

'Extraordinary, isn't it?' May said, softly. 'That one of our children is actually famous.' Their hands sneaked across the blanket again and held each other, held and squeezed.

'When you think how poor we were. We didn't do badly with those kids. You were always a good manager.'

'I taught them to read,' May said, pleased. 'All three of them could read before they went to school, though I had the devil of a job with Dirk. I helped all three of them with their homework.'

'So did I,' said Alfred, untruthfully, and waited for her to contradict him, but she looked at him indulgently, said nothing, and so he was able to continue, ashamed, 'Although it was mostly you, I admit.'

'There's Thomas,' she hissed, 'coming back again. He's a good boy. Let him have a word.'

'We've had our chat,' Alfred said, briskly. 'I feel a lot better for it, duck.'

'Would you like a paper? I'll get you one. I'll go and have a cup of tea while you two talk.'

And things seemed almost normal again, hearing her comfortable, ordinary voice talking of comfortable, ordinary things, and the stone in his heart was manageable. Thank you, May, he said to himself, watching her familiar figure tack off down the ward like a brave little tug boat, her thick grey hair, her rounded back, her determined set against the tide of blue nurses, *thank you, God, for a wife like May*.

29 · May

May managed to keep the smile on her face until she was halfway down the stairs. If she showed her grief, the whole ward would know . . . Perhaps the rumour was already out. She knew how hospitals preyed on death. When she had gone for her hysterectomy after the problems that followed Dirk's birth, there was always whispering, when people were goners –

(*Alfred's a goner.* No, not possible.)

– the ones whose cancer had gone too far, the ones whose operations had gone badly –

(They won't even operate. He does deserve that. He deserves a chance, but he isn't going to get it. Because we're too old, so they think we're no good.)

Her face twitched and writhed with the urge to weep, but she forced the tears back, made herself smile.

(*Alfred is dying.* No, never.)

For May had always tried to be brave. She wasn't self-pitying, or self-indulgent . . . They made her wince still, the cruel long words her father had used against her mother, her father who had educated himself enough to use long words like wooden paddles . . . on Mum who had no learning at all. She washed for thirteen children by hand . . .

(*Alfred, Alfred. I'll be alone . . . Alfred, my darling. Alfred, duck.*)

I was the youngest. Then the only one left. How can they be gone, my big laughing sisters?

(*Just me and Alfred. Alfred and me. I suppose we thought we would go on forever.*)

(*Without Alfred I –* No, don't think it.)

I mustn't complain, I've been very lucky.

My father criticized. My clothes, my hair. 'You're a pretty girl. Why must you look so scruffy? Can't you make something of yourself?' I didn't know how to answer him. I suppose my mother never taught me to dress. She didn't give a moment's thought to her looks. How could she, poor woman, with thirteen children? And I've never known how to get myself up. I try for Alfred, but I never get it right. Except when Shirley buys me something.

(Will Shirley forgive him . . . when she knows he's dying? The final lap. The final slope.)

It was sinking in in a different way from the conversation May had had with the doctor. On her own, it had all seemed dream-like, wrong.

But as soon as I saw his face today. As soon as our eyes met, we knew. We shared it, didn't we? We shared the fear. And after that it will always be true –

May pushed it away. She could not bear it.

It didn't do to dwell on the bad things, did it?

My father was sometimes very sweet to me. Softer on me than all the others, my mother told me, when she was dying. I was the youngest, his baby girl, and he loved me helping him in the shop, and was proud of me for being clever at school, though it never occurred to him I could go further. Of course it didn't; he had raised thirteen, and he'd paid for the boys' apprenticeships, so the girls had to marry, and that was that, yet he wasn't happy about losing me to Alfred.

I hear him still. Angry, cold. He read all the papers, he had opinions, he'd hoped his daughter would find someone better. I cried when I told him. I knew Alfred wouldn't suit.

Yet he is a better man than my father.

May held her face on red alert, smile against sorrow, smile at the world, an effort of will all down the ward.

Halfway down the stairs, which were cold grey stone, she found that she had sunk to her knees, on the first-floor landing, clutching the wall, hands held flat against cracked cold plaster. Tears came flooding down her cheeks.

She didn't care what people thought. She – didn't give a curse about her father. Damn him, damn him, we hated him.

But I can't go and sit in the café like this. I can't go and sit there with everyone gawping –

So perhaps she did still care, a little. Scrubbing her handkerchief over her face. She had never worn make-up, and now she never would.

(Will anyone ever think me pretty again? No one could be as blind as Alfred. I asked him a few weeks ago if he thought that film-star Sharon Stone was pretty. We were watching her in a telly thing. He said, 'Not half so pretty as you. Any way, she's a bit past it, isn't she?' – Sharon Stone's thirty years younger than me!)

His kind of love. His kind of fondness. He was slow with words, but his eyes said it, and the way he patted me, and held my hand, and the way he looked when I wore the blue dress he likes so much, that matches my eyes . . . I never doubted that he loved me.

How many people can say as much?

It can't be over. Alfred, Alfred.

She had wandered down the steps to the corner of the corridor that would have taken her down to the café. She stood there, sniffing and trying to breathe normally, clutching her wet hanky in her hand so tight that by the time she noticed it her fingers were numb.

A glass door led out into a little wild garden in the middle of the block. It would be locked, of course; it was a rule of life that all doors were locked, the ones you wanted to go through, at any rate. She turned the handle; it grated, refused. She started to cry again with frustration. Oh all her life the doors had been locked, her mother was weeping, May could never not hear it, her father was storming, she couldn't get away, and then there was Alfred, shouting at table when she'd forced herself to make a nice lunch, and the children screaming when she tried to read, or Dirk, once, sobbing in that animal way because she had forgotten his birthday (but she'd had Asian flu, she'd been in bed, Dirk's grief wasn't reasonable, was it? No) –

She had never been able to slip out into the open, the quiet, clear space where happiness was. Not joy so much as an end to sorrow, a rest from anger and fear and resentment.

She pushed, a last angry, hopeful little push –

The door opened, and she was in the garden.

30 · Alfred

'I went in the Park a few days ago,' said Thomas. 'I wanted to tell you that everything was ship-shape. Bulbs looking good. Willow turning yellow.'

'Was the mesh cover over the pond?' Alfred asked, anxious, focusing.

'Oh yes,' said Thomas. 'That was all fine.' (He hadn't looked; he hadn't noticed, distracted by the woman stealing bulbs.)

'Otherwise it gets choked up with leaves . . . The teenagers. They take it off. If no one stops them. Then they throw things in the water.'

'No, it was fine, honestly.' (Darren had said: 'I'm not bloody fine.' And there had been the van with the chap from the council, the one who had spoken slightingly of Alfred.) 'Everything was fine. Don't worry.'

'That pond . . . It's a special place, that pond.'

Alfred saw it almost hourly still in the hospital, a picture window in the ward's dull paint. It was a water-lily pond, with fat Koi carp winding in and out of the lily roots, leaves like green plates, reflected clouds. Behind it a terraced rockery with bonsai trees and dwarf rhododendrons. Flanking the rockery, dark cypresses, a magnolia tree which was one of Alfred's favourites, and the trailing yellow of the tall weeping willow.

Once there had been two, but one was cracked apart in the great storm of 1987, and the head gardener had wanted to save it, but the council decreed it had to come down, Health and Safety, rules and regulations, it was simpler and cheaper to take it down, though it would take a hundred years to grow another one.

'I count the beginning of spring from that pond. Every March for the last ten years or so a pair of ducks have come and settled there. They only stay a couple of weeks but I always say to myself, spring's here. One year they raised a brood on the pond. I had to stop the children chasing the ducklings. Lovely little things. Like a picture in a book. Comic, really. Going too fast. Always falling over. Just like kids . . . You don't have children, do you Thomas?'

'No,' said Thomas. 'I'd like to, one day.'

'Don't leave it too late. But of course you've got your job. You've got your library to think about.' Alfred was afraid of having hurt Thomas's feelings. All men wanted children, didn't they? (And then once they'd got them, they longed to escape. From the mess and the fuss and the bickering.) So he added, 'You've got to keep the books coming, too. May looks forward to you writing another one.'

'That's very kind of her,' said Thomas. He blushed to think of May reading it. He'd tried to explain the title, once, but she'd patted his hand and said 'not to worry.' An old woman screamed, suddenly, painfully, far down the ward, too far to see, behind one of the drawn green curtains, and twenty heads looked up, nervous.

Pamela had made it back to her bed. She collapsed on to it, pulled herself up, then swung up her legs, one by one, an endless process of sighing effort, but once she was settled, hands clutching her bedhead, she turned on Alfred a glittering smile. Very brightly coloured – a touch on the puce side. She had taken a detour to do her make-up.

'Helloo there, Alfred. Is that the famous son?'

'Wrong again,' he said, and winked at her, surprising himself with this moment of gaiety. 'He is a writer though. Thomas, this is Pamela.'

'Hello, Thomas.' She waved a clawed hand. 'I could have been a writer, you know.'

'Oh really,' said Thomas, not sounding impressed. Then he tried again, politely: 'Really?'

'Novels, poems, I could do them all. My husband said I was a born writer.'

But Alfred had picked up Thomas's boredom. Women could be boring, it couldn't be denied. Always butting in when men were talking. When men were talking about serious things. 'You'll excuse me if I talk to my friend,' he said to the woman, with the bluff manner he'd used to get rid of people in the Park. 'Thomas and I are talking over old times.'

She gazed at him, indignant, then gave a short laugh like a dog barking, and sank back on her bed, where she rummaged noisily in her bag until she produced a radio and head-phones which she jammed on her head and turned up the volume until it was distantly, annoyingly audible.

'We never allowed transistors in the Park,' Alfred said quite loudly to Thomas, who smiled, but Alfred could see the noise annoyed him. That was writers for you. Sensitive. Perceptive.

'How many years have you been there, Alfred?' Thomas asked. 'Of course I remember you when I was a boy –'

'It was different then. There were six of us then. Six of us, with dogs and uniforms.'

'Why did you need dogs? Was there a lot of trouble?'

'There's never been a major crime in that Park.' Alfred had said it many times, and he said it now, heavily, proudly. 'No violence, except the odd ruck when the alcoholics fight over a bottle, or two kids have a go at one another. No rape. No murder. No . . . There's never been a death in the Park. It's a record to be proud of. And a lot of it is down to the Park Keepers. I mean the whole lot of us, over the years.' He could feel his strength coming back as he said it; he was proud of himself; he was Alfred, the Park Keeper.

'I've always had a thing about parks,' said Thomas. 'Places where everybody can go. And people usually look happy. Don't they? Probably because they're not working.'

'Too many people not working nowadays. But you're right, Thomas. It's a happy place. Did you know there was dancing, after the war?'

And Alfred began to talk to Thomas, seeing genuine interest in his eyes (he was a nice boy, though perhaps a touch soft), remembering things he hadn't thought of for years, talking as if there were no tomorrow.

'Did you know I was born twelve yards from the Park? So it really has been my life, in a way. Of course that house was bombed flat in the war.'

He told Thomas how he'd played in the Park as a boy, when all the shrubberies were ringed with railings and the Park Keepers seemed like gods to Alfred. 'P'raps I got an inkling even then that that was what I'd like to be. But they were so tall, like men from Mars.' The boys never bothered with the grown-ups' end, where the flower-beds were, where people sat on seats. You had to behave, up there, which was boring. Instead they made a den down the very far end, in the middle of the shrubbery, where there was a path that led along by the wall behind the railings to a wonderful-smelling tower of grass-clippings, it seemed like years of grass-clippings, hidden in the middle of the laurel-bushes where no one could see them if they didn't know (though of course they had to try not to laugh when the Park Keepers happened to patrol nearby, and once Alfred had wet his pants though he wasn't going to tell Thomas that). They had hollowed out a den like a mouse's nest. Deep down the clippings were warm, fermenting. 'The Park seemed like heaven to us in those days. You see the best of people in parks . . .'

And he was off again among happy memories. The cards and presents he got at Christmas. A ham, mince pies, the odd bottle of spirits which people probably imagined he took a nip of in his little hut, though he never touched a drop till he was off duty . . . (well hardly ever, he thought to himself.) Letters from America, Malaya, South Africa, wherever folk from Hillesden went. Scarves and gloves and cardigans, knitted by some of his married ladies, for he did have a following among the ladies, all perfectly innocent, he assured Thomas, perfectly innocent on his part at least.

'I've dreamed about the place, since I've been stuck in here. You'd think I'd be glad of a break, wouldn't you? I mean, it's not a cushy job. Cleaning out the aviary I never liked. I'd give that away, any day. It's not the little birds like the budgies, they're child's play, but the pheasants were always that bit aggressive, and I don't know what to make of the new foreign birds. Too bright, aren't they. Too bright for the Park. They don't look right in an English park –'

'I like them,' Thomas put in, mildly.

'– I don't trust 'em. They put their heads down and look at me and I think they're going to rush me. So now I always use my broom. I open the door of their shelter at the back and the little ones fly up into the enclosure and then I get my broom and bash on the door and the big ones scuttle out pretty quick. You have to show them who's boss,' said Alfred. 'With all these things. Show 'em who's boss.' Something about Thomas's face stopped him. He felt less certain. He thought about it. Why did he hate those big yellow birds? At first it was only because they were foreign. But now it was worse, somehow worse. *I hate them because they're afraid of me.*

'Tell me about the dancing,' said Thomas, swiftly. 'Was there really dancing in the Park?'

'It was where the kids all ride their bikes. The big ring of tarmac. We used to have a bandstand. A proper bandstand. Thatched, like the café. Lovely. But took an awful lot of maintenance. Any way, it started after the war. I loved dancing. Still like to watch it. Still jiggle my feet when they dance on the telly.

'But I was in Palestine, you see. I was out there doing my National Service. Nineteen forty-seven to forty-nine. I used to think about the Park. Out there in the desert. It was like a bloomin' oven. Nothing growing for miles and miles.'

(It looked white, in the heat, Alfred remembered. No colour at all. And the sky was so hot that was white as well. I used to remember the Park, and the dancing. I tried to imagine the colour green. You start to appreciate it then. It's better than anywhere, really, England, although I had a lot of fun in the army, they made a man of me, Dad said.)

'I'd met May, by then. I was sixteen when I met her. Nineteen forty-three, I think it was. She was just the girl who matched the shoes to the tickets in the shop where we took our shoes to be soled. She had just left school. She never looked at me. She just took the ticket, and her head went down. But she had big blue eyes. I expect you've noticed. And she wore blue ribbon in her hair. I took her dancing once before they called me up.' (We were shy with each other, Alfred remembered. I had the wrong shoes, she stared at them, and I thought, she'll want someone better than me, but the music was lovely, romantic, wonderful, and there was a moon behind the trees, and even though in the end it started to drizzle and the band gave up and we had to go home, the memory somehow lasted me, out in the desert, those two dry years.)

'The day I got demobbed, I was with Reggie, wasn't I. The two of us had travelled back together. We hadn't any English money on us, so we walked all the way home from Victoria Station to Hillesden, in the middle of the night. Knocked on the door and my mum stuck her head out of the bedroom window and started to cry. She got up and cooked me a gigantic fry-up which must have used every bit of food in the house, and I didn't sleep a wink all night, I felt crazy, and I couldn't get used to not being shot at, I couldn't sleep in a bed for months . . . We'd always had to sleep on the floor, you see.'

'PTSD,' Thomas nodded, sagely.

Then wished he hadn't.

'What did you say?'

'What they call post-traumatic stress disorder.'

'Nothing like that. I wasn't mental,' said Alfred, annoyed to be interrupted. There was a pause; he sucked his teeth. Mum, he thought. She was a good soul. I wonder if she's up there waiting for me. As long as Dad isn't waiting for me – Let's face it, Dad was a holy terror. Took a leather strap to all of us . . . I never did that; I would never do that. 'Am I boring you?' he asked. 'I'm talking too much.'

'No please go on, I'm enjoying it,' said Thomas, and he really was, despite the appalling discomfort of the chair which the National Health must have put there on purpose to stop any visitors staying too long. The lights were coming on in the ward.

This, he thought, is the real Alfred. Darren's just worked himself into a state. It's Susie's fault. Pure . . . psychobabble. He eased his legs; the chair farted.

'Next day I got up and it was English summer. I couldn't believe the noise of the birds. I had spent the night with my uniform on, and for some reason I got up, put my hat on, I suppose because I'd have felt naked without it, a great sombrero, it was, with a feather, a little cockade thing stuck on the side, not exactly the thing to wear in Hillesden . . . But I was in no state to realize. And I walked to the Park as if I was asleep. I didn't decide, I just found I was off there. Like a pigeon, I suppose. Homing. Homing. I hadn't had breakfast, not even a cuppa. And I walked up the hill –'

Alfred couldn't continue. Fifty years later he still wanted to weep.

(It was green, so green, and the smell of cut grass, and the shade of the oak trees, dappled shade, rippling over the hill in the breeze, and the wood pigeons billing, it was all like a dream . . . like the dreams I had dreamed in Palestine, but now it was real, the men had come home. But I lay on the hill, and I felt like a ghost. It was all the same, but I was not. No one knew me now. I was no longer Alfred, but a killer sent from another world, and if anything moved I should have to shoot it . . . The hill looks out over the burial ground. There seemed to be millions of graves in the sunlight, white and grey stones marching on for ever, blurring as I looked across the sweep of the graveyard, as if they'd seeded like weeds in the war years . . . How many bodies of boys I had known were lying under the ground somewhere, with nothing to mark them, far from home? – names I had known, lost, forgotten – and the peace and the sunshine had come too late. I felt – queer, I felt very alone, I felt guilty, although God knows I had done my bit. But soon as I lay down, I slept, and dozed and dreamed half the day away, waking sweaty and frightened, every so often, and being calmed by the sound of the birds. And the wind in the leaves, and walking feet, not crunching boots but peaceful feet, padding, strolling, human feet, British feet, English feet, those wonderful sounds said I had come home, now I could rest among my people, here in the grass I was safe to sleep.)

Thomas thought Alfred had nodded off, but after a second he began again.

'I slept all morning outside in the Park. When I finally woke I felt a lot better. Almost human. I could hear children. The school-kids must have just come out of school. The children in Palestine were different; they all looked alike, all brown with dark eyes, and they never really looked at you, and of course they spoke in their own language, a sort of screeching, jabbing noise. But this was the sound of English children –'

(I remember it as if it was yesterday. I thought quite clearly, I want a family. I'll never die, if I have a family. I want that girl, and I want a family. I saw in that moment that that was what I'd fought for. A world where the White family could live.)

'I went off up Hillesden High Road looking for May. I thought she might be in her father's shop –'

(The sun was in my eyes. I hadn't eaten since the night before. I hadn't shaved. I was at least half-barmy, I no longer knew how to walk, I marched . . . I was half in the desert, although I was in Hillesden. I'd probably have frightened her to death.)

'The great thing was, I never got there. I heard a crowd of beggars tagging behind me, beggar-kids, they always followed the soldiers, and I turned on my heel to scare them away and saw they were English children, not beggars, and I was in an English street. They were mad with excitement, shouting and laughing. "Cowboy!" They were shouting. "Look, here's a cowboy!" I'd forgotten I'd got my stetson on . . . I was a hero to them. Well, perhaps I *was* a hero. We took it for granted, but we all risked our lives.' He stopped for a moment, to steady his voice. 'After a bit, I realized I'd scare her to death, turning up in that kit like a lunatic. I turned round and marched home, took my hat and boots off and went out like a light on Mum's settee. They tell me I slept for three whole days, but I reckon it was one, at most.'

'I like that story,' said Thomas. 'Amazing. My generation's never seen things like that.'

'The war did pull us together, in a way. Something we all went through together. All shoulders to the wheel, as they say.'

'Are we the selfish generation?'

'You're not too bad,' said Alfred, kindly. But he thought to himself, the lad is right. Darren and Thomas are boys, not men. They've never had a chance to find out what matters. Never been tested. Had it too easy. Nothing was easy for me and May. We waited for years, saving up to be married. If a thing's worth having, it's worth waiting for. 'Things fell apart, after the war. We were very hopeful, in the fifties. I don't know what happened. People got greedy –'

'When was the coronation? 'Fifty-three?'

'Coronation year,' said Alfred. 'Lovely . . . I think they were still dancing, in fifty-three. Dancing in the Park. May and I were newly married . . . We could do what we liked, and we hadn't got kids. It seemed like we'd died and gone to heaven. Soon after, some idiot set a fire in the thatch of the bandstand, and that put a stop to it. Nice while it lasted.' He smiled. 'It does me good, remembering. They were great days. Tremendous days . . . You young ones think we didn't know how to have fun, but we did, you know.' And he winked at Thomas. 'May and I danced with the best of 'em.'

(She changed towards me when I came back. Probably because I had lived a bit. I went away a stupid boy who had never been further than Blackpool in summer. And she wanted something better than that. My May was a reader even then . . . I had something about me, when I came back, so she told me. I was tense as a watch-spring and trigger-happy and a stone too thin and burned practically black, but I'd been to the other side of the world. I'd seen the sun set over Jerusalem. I'd had – *glorious* times. We were like princes, sometimes, young and fit and fancy-free . . . I'd smoked *kif* and bumped about on a camel and heard the *muezzin* wailing their prayers, though it sounded like demons howling, to me. I'd seen men dying, and nearly died. I'd kept the peace; that was how May saw it. I'd lived in a desert that went on for ever. It was hell, of course, but not to May.)

'I took May dancing, my first weekend home. I'd borrowed a suit from my elder brother. Everyone put on the dog, in those days – you didn't go dancing in a leather jacket –'

(And the girls were so pretty in summer dresses that were really dresses, tiny waists, full skirts, like flowers, like poppies, whirling round and round in the summer dusk –

But I was with May. She was in my arms. May and I never left each other. She wore blue, I think, with a tiny print, forget-me-nots, was it? – and her eyes were so blue, and she gazed at me as if I was a film star, and whispered 'Alfred' into my shoulder, I shivered with disbelief to feel it, a woman's warm sweet breath on my skin, because while I was away she had turned into a woman, so white and rounded and serious and beautiful that I was afraid – till the tempo changed and the dance band let rip with 'In the Mood' and all of a sudden I was dancing like crazy, copying the spiv with the pin-striped jacket who was jitter-bugging with the girl next door, 'Come on May,' I shouted, 'Come on, we can do it,' and we did, although I'd never done it before, I whipped her around till she was flushed and laughing and fell into my arms when the music slowed down, and I silently swore I would love her for ever, cheek to cheek under the rustling plane-trees and the blue sky of evening we no longer had to fear, cheek to cheek under the same pale moon that had made me long for her in Palestine.

'We could be together,' I whispered to her.

'Not until I'm married,' she said, quite sharp, I remember she didn't understand, she thought I was suggesting something improper, which I'd never have dared to, with an English girl.

'I'll marry you, May,' I said, 'if you'll have me.'

'Well ask me then,' she said, but she was smiling, she was smiling at me with that slightly wicked dimple, and I realized with a sense of complete amazement that May Hill was going to say 'Yes', that she hadn't noticed I was poor and ugly, or how much better than me she was. Or perhaps she had, but she still said 'Yes'. In the middle of the dancers, a crowd of happy people, in the middle of the Park, under the evening sky, while the band played 'Bewitched, Bothered and Bewildered', my darling girl said 'Yes' to me.

(After that we always called it 'being together', it became our joke, our little secret.)

'– I proposed to her, that first weekend. But I was amazed when she accepted.'

'Very romantic,' said Thomas, smiling.

But his generation is so different, thought Alfred. Are they ever together, really, like we were? Do they stay together through thick and thin?

My children. Will they end up alone?

31 · May

May sat in the garden for half an hour. There was a blanched wooden seat minus one of its bars, and she sank down on to it gratefully. The bushes had grown wild in the absence of a gardener.

(If Alfred goes . . .

When Alfred goes . . .)

> The woods decay, the woods decay and fall . . .
> Man comes and tills the field and lies beneath
> And after many a summer dies the swan.

She sat and thought about their life together. His dependability, which made him sound boring, but really it was miraculous, to do the same job for fifty years, to love the same woman, to live in the same place. And always do it with a will. Faithful Alfred. Her loyal man. Even when the council let him down; even when they sold off the Park Keeper's lodge that he'd always expected to be his, he wouldn't complain: 'I expect they have their reasons.' That stubborn, closed look which Dirk had inherited. Alfred would never criticize.

They took away the uniforms; they took away the dogs; they took away the good men who worked with him. They left him there unprotected, on his own, they wouldn't even spend a few tenners on a mobile, and all he could do was walk a little faster, always hurrying, she'd seen him, these last few years, whenever she popped in for a chat, a driven man, you might call him, now, his white head sprinting along the pale paths that crossed the Park from corner to corner, for all of it was his territory, these days, the whole responsibility was his, his duties growing larger as he grew smaller, his drive growing stronger as he grew weaker – For now she could admit it, she knew he'd grown weaker. She had seen the effort, sometimes, when he pulled on his shoes, standing on one leg, as he always did, balancing pluckily on one leg and pulling on his work-boots with the opposite hand, rather red in the face, concentrating too intently where once the absurd procedure had been easy, once he'd balanced like a dancer, graceful, automatic.

But he never gave up.

He never slackened.

He never made life easy for himself.

She admired him with every bone in her body. His high standards, his fierceness . . .

There were holly-bushes here that had grown into great trees, nearly berry-less, now, in March, the red beads eaten by the birds, but the thickets of sharp leaves were glassy bright in the sun that caught them halfway up their height, so they were half black, half glittering. And beside the bench were the larger, longer-toothed, spiky leaves of a Mahonia, and now she identified the slow sweet smell that had come to her nose as she sat and wept: long yellow tassels of densely-set flowers, it was a Mahonia 'Charity', one of Alfred's favourites, though he wouldn't know the name –

I helped him with words, he helped me with things. We made a good pair, the two of us together. We're still a good pair. I'm strong. I can help him –

...Tho'
> We are not now that strength which in old days
> Moved earth and heaven; that which we are, we are.

She could feel the cold increasing as she sat, she saw the sun's slow retreat up the holly, but she breathed in the air that the trees made sweet.

His sweetness to me. And his fierceness.

He adored his kids, yet he made them wretched.

If they totted it up, how would he come out? I know he is a good man. I have no doubt. If there's any justice, God will let him in. God will tell St Peter to let him in. Because Peter's job is a bit like Alfred's, he was the man with the key to the Gates.

(But was there any justice? – May wasn't sure.)

Perhaps in heaven – if there was a heaven – but there must be a heaven – she hoped – she prayed . . . She hadn't prayed in a church for so long.

(Shirley, of course, was always on her knees, as if we had given her a lot to pray about.)

It felt so awkward. May squeezed her eyes shut.

Take care of Alfred, Lord, because he's tried . . . he has been a good man, haven't you noticed? . . . Stay near him now in his hour of need . . . Don't let him down, like the council did –

But it wasn't any good. She was arguing with God. Arguing against the contradictory voices,

> the little rift within the lute
> That by and by will make the music mute . . .

It couldn't be denied he was bad to Shirley.

He felt – mortally threatened, I know he did. He thought that Shirley chose Kojo to spite him. Perhaps she did, because *he* hurt us, when he lost his temper he hurt all of us, I try and forget it but I know it's true. Even me, one hot summer when the café in the Park had been broken into and he came home desperate, I accidentally cooked the wrong thing for supper and he got up and hit me across the mouth, and my denture broke, and my cheek swelled up, and I told myself I would never forgive him, and Dirk was crying, his little white face . . .

But it went away, when the children did. He hasn't hit anyone for years and years. And he can't say sorry. Lord, he can't. But I know he's sorry. I know he is.

Lord, forgive us, take care of us.

She sat there, shivering up at the sky, the rectangle of blue, growing deeper, more distant.

If only we could live with just the best in us. The best of Alfred was heroic, marvellous. No one was braver, no one more true. He would have died for me, for the Park, for the kids.

It must count more than the – unpleasantness.

32 · Dirk

Dirk had moved beyond unpleasantness. Dirk had moved beyond failure, or pain. Dirk had swigged down four cans of Special Brew in half an hour, and was off to the game. There was a match between Hillesden Wanderers and the Dublin Demons, and the lads were going, and so was Dirk, though he hadn't got a ticket. With the beer inside him, he knew he'd get in. When he'd had a few drinks, he was – invincible. He was more than himself. He was enough, at last.

(The trouble was, it always faded, leaving him worse, leaving him less.)

But today would be brilliant. Seeing off the Irish. Bloody Catholics, bloody bombers –

Dirk and the lads barrelled on to the train.

He wasn't as keen on football as his dad had once been. As a boy, he'd gone to matches with Dad and loved it, sitting there together and yelling for their team. Dad used to stick an Aero chocolate bar in his pocket, and Dirk tried to eat at the same pace as Dad, one section at a time, bursting the bubbles very slowly, but he always finished first, it was harder for a kid.

The other side of football wasn't nearly as much fun. Dad expected him to be a good footballer. On Sundays, he took him in the Park with a ball, when he was off-duty and his mates were on. 'This is my youngest. We've come in for a kick-about. His elder brother played for Middlesex Juniors.' On an average day it took Dad around thirty seconds to lose his temper. 'Look what you're doing! You kick it, you fool! Come on, Dirk. What's the matter with you?' Then he would dribble away on his own, dancing with the ball, showing off, Dirk would think. Or showing his work-mates that he wasn't like his son, that clumsiness didn't run in the family.

These little outings didn't last long. 'You're never going to be an athlete, are you?' Dad had said in the end, one bright winter day when he'd shouted more than usual, and Dirk had begged to be allowed to go home. 'Never mind, lad, we can't all be winners.' Although Dirk wanted it over, the weekly torment, it gave him a horrible, sickening feeling to hear that he would never be an athlete.

Failure left a shadow on the game. When Alfred next got tickets, he said, 'I suppose you can watch it even if you can't play it,' and Dirk said, 'No thanks, I'd rather watch TV.' But he didn't really mean it. He felt a bit better for at least ten minutes, but he missed standing there with his dad sucking chocolate, shoulder to shoulder, on the same side, howling at the enemy, yelling for their heroes.

As a teenager Dirk began to go with the lads. He didn't much care about the football but he liked the buzz. All for one, one for all. An army of men who accepted him. Then sometimes when they took an end. Taking an end was the best feeling, when they drove the fans from the other side out of their favourite end of the stand. Just shoving on through, all fists and elbows, giving a good kicking to anyone who fell. A knee in the groin and they usually fell. When they took an end, then Dirk was a king.

But he'd hardly been to football for the last three years. Frigging George had stopped him. Always frigging ill. The frigging shop. He'd been a frigging slave, he'd been a frigging fool, an idiot –

Now he was free. He was free at last.

(*He had nowhere to go. He was nothing, no one.*)

Darren was a winner, unlike him.

It makes it harder for me, Dirk thought. My brother was a very good footballer. (I have to take that on trust, because I've never seen him. Being fifteen years older than me, of course. By the time I was old enough to have noticed he'd got too smart for it, hadn't he? He was being very good at other things instead. But I heard about it. Oh, I heard about it. I've always heard about how good he is. When I went to secondary school there was a master who'd been stuck there for thirty years, he'd been there when it was a grammar school and Darren went there and won all the prizes and got a scholarship to sodding Oxford. All right, good for him, but a pain to me. Because old Plummer went on about Darren whenever he saw me. 'You'll never be the equal of your brother, White. Now there was a boy. Scholar, athlete.')

Scholar, athlete! What a wanker! Fuck off!

Which is not to knock my brother, of course. I'm proud of Darren. Course I am. And now he's come back, we can really be brothers. He'll stick around. We'll hang out together.

He doesn't want to. He doesn't like you. He thinks you're a pain, like everyone else . . . 'You'll never be the equal of your brother, White.'

You'll never be the equal of your father, Dirk.

Dirk took another swig from the can in his pocket to keep the hateful little voices away.

'Oi, Dirk,' yelled Ozzie. 'Give us some of that.'

'There y'are, mate.'

Ozzie was standing on the seat of the train, trying to freak out the girl sitting opposite, a stuck-up bitch in a tiny cream mini-skirt who'd hidden her twitchy little nose in a book.

He's a great guy, Ozzie. Everybody likes him.

Well, nobody likes him that much. But I do.

I think he's great. He's a real laugh, Ozzie. He comes from Australia.

He's got a broken nose. People pick on him because he's six feet four. He's got a good body. Muscly, hard. His family didn't want to know him, and so he came here to work in England. He worked for a removals firm until this midget started picking on him, calling him a racist, etcetera, etcetera, just 'cos Ozzie's got a bit of a crewcut and occasionally wears a Union Jack t-shirt. I mean everyone sometimes wears a Union Jack t-shirt.

If they've got one, granted. So a lot of people haven't, but thousands of people have got short hair. Why should it be racist to get a haircut? Why should it be racist to show the flag?

What's bloody wrong with being pro-British? You had to be pro-British, in the last war. Then it was OK to be patriotic.

When Dad got going on a subject like that, it was wonderful to hear him. Dad knew facts.

He has to get better. I'd be lost without him.

Ozzie is offering that blond bint my drink. Says she doesn't want it, does she, bitch? Not good enough for her. Well I bloody want it. *I* bloody want it, so don't give it to *that* –

'Ozzie, mate. I'd like that back. That tart doesn't need it. Give it over –'

And he chucks it, doesn't he. Joking, like. Just having a laugh, meaning no harm, but it sprays all over the slapper's skirt, which was made of pale leather, like a whatsit, pelmet, the silly little thing at the top of the curtains. And she starts screaming, though nobody touched her, God's my witness, we didn't even touch her!

So then this animal sitting behind us – and *nobody* had been talking to him, it was none of his business, but he wanted to make trouble – and he was old, which makes it worse, he was probably forty, with a suit and tie – gets up and comes and stands in front of Ozzie and tells him to apologize.

Ozzie was provoked. So he gets him by the tie.

Then suddenly all hell breaks loose, everyone is picking on Ozzie and me and Terry and Flick, all these barmy old guys, all ganging up with the one with the tie on and going at us as if we were making trouble! They got Flick on the floor before he had a chance to get his knife out, and at the next station they sort of rolled him out the door, then pushed us after him.

The injustice! We'd paid our fare! For once we had paid our fare in full! Six of them, there were, all on to us, and the women screaming rude names as well, it was like the whole carriage was against us! It took a bit of time for them to shove us out. I had got my fingers up one old guy's nostrils, and tears were streaming down his face, that served him right for treating us like dirt, my whole fucking life I've been treated like dirt . . .

(Dirt White that's who you are Dirt White.)

I was kneeling on the platform as the train went out. Shaking my fist at the people in our carriage.

You wouldn't believe the way they were going on. All sort of smiling and patting each other. I swear they'd never met each other before. Now they were thick as anything, through kicking us out!

We had to wait twenty minutes for the next one. So we got to the Gate late. It wasn't our fault. With a load of other stragglers who I must admit I might have had my doubts about, two of them coloured, but Hillesden supporters, so I didn't have a go at them –

The bastards wouldn't let us in. I had good money. I had fucking earned it, I earned it the hard way, but they wouldn't even look at it. 'No tickets, no admittance, that's the rule,' the bastard told me, smug as anything. 'You need a photocard and a pre-paid ticket. How long is it since you last went to a game?'

So here was yet another thing I couldn't get in to. Every fucking thing has been closed to us. Jobs, football games, everything that matters. Girls, women, they're closed to us. Not that I care, they stink of minge, but why should they think they're better than us? We need money or photocards or qualifications or pass-words that we can never learn. We need skills or languages or posh bloody accents or cars or computers or ties or suits –

Or a black face. The two niggers got in. They said they had tickets, but I don't believe it.

It didn't stop Ozzie and Flick and Terry. We went round the back, we were steaming mad, no way were we going to take this lying down.

'I know a good place,' Terry said. 'I've climbed over before. I know we can do it.'

And he got a leg-up on a wheely-bin, clung by his fingernails, inched his way over, tearing his coat on the barbed-wire at the top and disappearing with a dirty great yell that either meant he was hurt or happy. We were all well rotted. I don't think we cared.

But when it came to my turn, and they were all in, I couldn't get my fingers on the top of the wall. I was just too short. I tried jumping. It was hopeless. They shouted a few times. Then they forgot me. And they had gone. They had done it. They were in. And I was left outside, on a stinking rubbish bin. I was outside in the cold on my own –

(*Dirt White Dirt White just a dirty little dosser*)

I'm not a bloody wimp. I'm not a bloody woman. I knew I could get in there by will-power. *You can,* I told myself. *You can fucking do it.*

So I launched myself at the top of the wall, and caught with one hand but missed with the other, swung round hard and crashed my face on the brickwork, smash in the cheek on the cold wet brickwork, and lost my grip, and fell *whoomp* on the ground.

That was the end. Then I knew I had to kill them. It didn't matter who, I would have to fucking kill them.

Kill

Kill

Fuck

Fuck

Kill

33 · Darren and Susie

'Thank God I've got you,' said Darren, solemnly, lying beside her on the hotel coverlet they'd just anointed with a small dark stain. Their suite at the Inn on the Park was quite poky, just bedroom, sitting-room, jacuzzi-less bathroom, but it had the advantage of a king-size bed. 'I'd go mad, you know. If I were quite alone. My little brother's barking, I suddenly realized. Last night he was going on about the Jews –'

Susie lay naked, her small bright hip-bone catching the harsh light from the wall. 'He's just projecting,' she said, idly. 'Darren, darling. So glad you're back. Hate it so much when we fight.'

'I hate it too.' He stroked her thigh. He loved the hollow between her thighs, two shallow brackets that lithely enclosed him when they were happy, when he was home. 'Suze, let's never fight again.'

'Love you,' she said. 'What's the time, honey?'

'Oh, three, four, plenty of time.'

'We'd better check.' Her voice sharpened up. 'Oh sugar – three thirty – I guess we should leave.'

'Let me just hold you. Need to hold you.' But she had stiffened in his arms. 'Is oo my baby?' he asked, demanded. 'Does oo love me, Poopsie?'

'You're my baby,' she said, swiftly, and pressed him to her bony breast. 'But we have to get up.'

'We were silly again,' he said, in a little boy, a baby voice, and took her finger, and traced the dark stain.

'Hell, I forgot.' A sharp intake of breath. 'And I'm right in the middle of my fertile time.'

He began to kiss her, her cheek, her neck, her scooped-out collar-bones, her delicate ribs. 'Mummy,' he mumbled. 'Do you want to be Mummy? . . . Mmm, mmm . . . Poopsie could be Mummy . . .'

She was caught halfway between laughter and panic, struggling up and away from him. 'I'm not ready – we're not ready –'

Susie would be forty-one next month.

'Let's start again. Everything new. A new family. You'd be brilliant with babies.'

'I'm not so sure.' But she flushed with pleasure as she pulled on her sports bra, supple, elastic. 'I would love babies. You know I would.'

'So why –?' he said, faintly truculent, wandering over towards the bathroom. The hum of the fan disrupted his words. 'You want them. I want them. Let's do it.'

'We've already discussed it.'

She chose the neat-jacketed blue Chanel suit which made her look like an air-hostess, crisp, efficient – not a good sign. Not a good sign at all, thought Darren, glancing over his shoulder as he shaved. 'Is it still all this stuff about my family?'

'I hear your anger,' Susie said. 'I hear you, Darren. We've already discussed it.'

'I talked about it to Thomas,' he said. 'I gave him your spiel about confronting Dad. He didn't actually say so, but he thought it was shit. He dotes on my father, actually.'

She didn't rise to the bait, though she hated swear-words; it was one of the ways he could get to her. She looked at him steadily, coolly. 'It's your feelings that matter, not his.'

(She was always telling him about his feelings. Was it his feelings, or her feelings?) Darren sighed, and changed the subject. 'The trousers of this suit are tight.'

'Back to the gym as soon as we're home,' she said, and flashed him a brilliant smile. 'I like you slim. I love you slim.'

'Don't you love me any way?' he pleaded.

'You're my *husband*,' she said. 'You know I love you.'

'But not enough to have my babies.' (She was painting her lips, a wide slick of orange. She should talk less, and love him more.)

'We've been through it,' she said. 'Must I explain again?'

(As if she was a teacher, and he was a child.)

The silence between them was heavy with resentment and the steady burr of the bathroom fan, tirelessly working to clear the air, to remove the smell of age and pain, the alcohol in Darren's urine, the taint of Susie's seafood lunch, most of which she'd sicked up again. She wasn't ill; it was part of her diet.

If I got pregnant, she thought, I would stop.

'I'd like another drink,' he muttered to the glass, his face in the mirror, puffy, flushed.

If we had a baby, I know I'd cut down.

'You don't need one,' she said, very definite, clicking her heavy snake handbag shut. 'We've talked about this. You don't need to drink.'

'Fuck off,' he exploded, furious, and his cuff burst away from the Dior cuff-links she'd given him as an engagement present, which he'd always suspected of being a freebie from an advertorial she'd done on designer shirts. 'You don't know everything. You're not my keeper. I'm forty years old. I do what I like –'

'Is it me you're angry with? Or is it your father?'

'That's *it*,' he said. 'That's the last time. Get this into your head. Once and for all. I shall never, ever confront my father. I don't want to. Don't need to. It's some cock-and-bull notion you therapists have got, that everything is solved by *expressing our anger* . . . It's such bullshit. Such a load of crap. He's an old man. He's probably dying –'

'Precisely,' she said, with infuriating calm. 'If you're ever going to tell him, now is the time.'

'Leave it!' he shouted. Then heard himself shouting. And stopped, unnerved. She hated shouting. He hated it too. His father shouting. (The bloody old bastard. And he never said sorry.)

'Sorry,' said Darren, gruff, sheepish.

'Fine,' she said. It sounded like 'Die.'

There was a timid knock. They both froze, embarrassed. 'Who the fuck?' said Darren. But they had to answer it. 'Are you decent?' he asked, then shouted 'Come!'

It was the chambermaid. She was a small, pretty girl, perhaps South American, with golden skin and broad Indian features. She said something in a soft, singsong voice.

'Speak up,' said Susie. 'We can't hear a word.'

'Is everything OK with room?' she asked. 'OK I turn your bed down now?'

'You can see we're half-naked,' said Darren. 'Go away.'

The girl flushed, and backed out swiftly. 'Sorry sir, miss.'

'Why do they employ idiots?' he asked the air. Just before the door closed.

'Shush,' said Susie. 'Because they're cheap. But try to be polite, or she'll nick our stuff.'

They carried on dressing in grumpy silence. The mock carriage clock on the mantelpiece hummed. The heating laboured. The hotel was loud. Feet came and went, of happy families, hateful imaginary happy families. Somewhere the lift groaned and thudded. Susie started to whistle, then stopped abruptly.

'Look, let's not row,' he managed to say.

'I'm not rowing,' she hissed, crossly, then heard her own voice, and suddenly laughed. She came over and kissed him, once, twice, light and cool on his aching brow. 'All right, I shouldn't have mentioned your dad. Let's go. I'll put my mascara on.'

'At least we've got each other, darling.' He clung to her hand, so much smaller than his, smooth and brown in its hard bright rings, and one of them was his, the largest, the latest. *The last, I hope. Shall we stay together?* 'I couldn't manage without you, Suze.'

'I love you too.'

She sounded slightly reserved. Darren pressed her hand to his mouth, wincing slightly as his lips touched the point of her diamond. She was clutching her mascara wand. A small cool hand. 'Does oo love me, Poopsie?'

'Yes, Darren.'

'Does oo? *Does oo?*'

She sighed very faintly. 'Wuv oo, Flops,' she said in his ear, put down her mascara, clasped her arms around him, and hugged him, firmly. Then patted his shoulders to indicate an ending.

He gazed at her adoringly. 'You keep me sane, you wonderful woman.'

'This is sane?' she laughed, resuming her make-up.

'Do you ever wonder what the point of life is?'

She stopped poking at her eyelids and focused on him. 'Um – I used to think I'd be a doctor, in Africa. Don't laugh. Imagine me, in the jungle . . . I realized I wasn't cut out to be noble. I just do the best I can at things. I guess I'm a try-er. I'm not a bad person . . . You matter to me. My patients matter. What do you think the point of life is?'

'Shit, I don't know. Love. Money . . . Seriously, I'd have to say the kids. And you,' he said hastily, seeing her lips tighten. 'Kids are important, though. I'm not a bad father.' He prided himself on being a good father, though naturally a lot of things got done by e-mail.

'By the way, did you remember to ring Felicity this morning?' Susie had a soft spot for Darren's daughter.

'Was it important? – Shit. Her concert.' Women had diaries implanted in their brains, a genetic knack of remembering things – which came in useful, when you had kids. Whereas Darren's strong point was the bigger picture. 'I'll ring tomorrow.'

'I sent her flowers.'

'You're a genius. Did you charge it to the office?'

'Naturally.'

'Well done, darling.' He smiled at his reflection in the mirror, and hers, blond, shiny, attentive, in the background. A man of substance.

He suddenly felt happy. 'I was a bit sharp with the chambermaid, wasn't I?'

'Oh leave her a tip, if you feel guilty.'

'It gives life variety, having kids. My friend Thomas hasn't got any –'

'Does he regret it?'

'Haven't the faintest. He seems all right. Doesn't say much.'

'But isn't he a bit of a failure?' Susie asked, as they let themselves quietly out of their suite.

'What do you mean?' He felt annoyed. 'Thomas likes to do his own thing.'

'Writing one novel doesn't make you famous. Whereas everyone's heard of *you*, darling.' She cocked her head, and snuggled against him.

'Do you think so, Poopsie? Do you really?' Waiting for the cab, they pressed very close.

'Look maybe I'm wrong,' she said, suddenly. 'It's not for everyone, confronting their fathers. '

He stared at her amazed, then laughed, and kissed the lacquered strength of her hair. 'I thought you'd never stop banging on about it.'

'It was for you I wanted it, Flops, not me. In fact, I was kind of charmed by your dad. One day we'll come and bring the kids –'

'All five of them,' he whispered, slyly.

'Four, darling . . . Oh.' She fell silent, realizing.

Darren was blowing in her ear. 'Let's say six. We ought to have two. I don't believe in only children – It isn't right. Kids need playmates.' (Some modern parents were incredibly selfish. He was writing a piece about it at the moment.)

'Would we be good parents?' Susie mused, staring out of the window of the taxi at blank bright buildings rushing past. 'By the way, did you remember that tip?'

He didn't hear her, dreaming of the future. 'You'd have to stay home a bit more,' he said. 'Which I would like. I like you being home. We could get a Filipina nanny. The Websters' Filipina was brilliant . . . Couldn't do enough for them. Sweet little thing. And Poopsie would be a lovely Mummy. Wovely wovely Mummy, Poopsie.' He looked at her with a rush of love, her narrow shoulders, her teensy hips. 'I want a little girl just like you.'

'When I'm sure we're ready.' Her lips closed tight.

He smiled, remembering the stain on the coverlet.

34 · Thomas

Thomas had stayed longer than he meant to with Alfred. He hurried back to the library. It was warm for March; the wind had dropped.

It was quarter to three when he arrived, uncomfortably aware he'd had a very long lunch-break. A little crowd of people was milling about.

Saturday film, he realized. He was surprised to see Suneeta among them, with a tall Indian girl in jeans.

'Thomas. Are you coming to *The Price of the Ticket*?' (Yes, he remembered. James Baldwin. A biopic about the novelist.) 'It's supposed to be excellent,' she continued.

'I'm on duty –'

'So am I. But there's hardly anyone upstairs. Razia and Ingrid are on Inquiries. And film only lasts hour and a half.'

'I think it's a bit specialized for me,' said Thomas, steering away from her with a smile. 'What I really need is a large black coffee.'

'What do you mean?' she asked abruptly. He was suddenly aware of an atmosphere. 'What does this mean? Specialized?'

She managed to corner him, against the creche, so no one else could hear what they were saying. 'Baldwin is a wonderful writer. Have you read him?'

'I didn't know *you* had . . . Years ago.' He thought about it. Perhaps he hadn't. Though he'd definitely bought *Another Country*.

Her large brown eyes did not entirely believe him. 'You need, what do you call it, a refreshment.'

'Refresher,' he said, evading her, sliding around in the direction of the stairs.

'Thomas!' You didn't ignore Suneeta. He had seen her get angry once or twice in the ten years that he had known her. She was looking hard at him, slightly flushed. 'Come and meet my older daughter, Thomas.' She indicated the girl in jeans, who he now saw was a taller, thinner version of her mother.

Anita shook hands; she looked amused, patrician. Thomas began to feel smaller and less solid, just as he did when talking to Alfred. The girl was inspecting the exhibition of Turkish paintings along the walls.

'Anita is completing a doctorate in cultural studies at SOAS. Thomas is writing a book, Anita, something very clever, too clever for us all. Tell Anita why you will not go to the film.'

Her elegant profile swivelled towards him.

'Oh really, Suneeta, I don't know,' Thomas protested, embarrassed. 'I haven't decided. Perhaps I will.'

'Go and buy your ticket,' Suneeta said, pushing him gently towards the box office.

He found himself queueing for a ticket. (Bossy cow. It was a damn nuisance. He had a backlog of work to clear. This was one of the special cultural events the cinema ran in association with the library, and he and Errol had helped work out the programme, but surely this film was Errol's province. He could see Errol chatting and smiling by the door, his matt black curls now salted with grey.)

Turning round, Thomas was suddenly face to face with Shirley. A wonderful summery smell of vanilla. He breathed it in. Her neck was round and smooth. Her lips were moist and slightly parted.

'Shirley! What on earth are you doing here?'

'Waiting for someone,' she said, with a smile. She looked – stunning.

Creamy, glowing, and she smiled at him as if she was really glad to see him. 'I'm going to the film about James Baldwin.'

'Oh. Why?' he asked, without thinking.

She stared at him a moment. 'Because someone asked me. Writers are interesting, any way.'

'Of course they are,' he said hastily. He felt slightly jealous she was meeting someone.

'Film will begin,' called Suneeta, imperious.

'See you inside,' he said to Shirley.

He sat with Suneeta and her daughter. Anita started telling him about her doctorate. Her mother still seemed to be keeping one eye on him as if he might escape at the last minute.

As the lights went down he turned round and looked for Shirley, but she wasn't among the scattering of faces.

Then someone came in, and as the blue dark engulfed the cinema, his nerve-ends prickled. Tall, black, with those light strange eyes and an intense way of gazing across the room, as if he felt he had been chosen by fate – It was the worrying young man from the library. The one who had ordered *One Thousand Years of Lynchings.*

'Suneeta –' he tried to attract her attention, but she shushed him, staring ahead at the screen.

By the time the lights went up again he had forgotten his moment of fear. Baldwin's voice, caressive, teasing, rising to biblical peaks of anger but more often lucid and to the point, had seemed to be talking to him, Thomas. 'I went to the library at least three or four times a week and I read every single book in the library . . .'

Thomas had forgotten why libraries mattered. He'd almost forgotten that he loved books. Baldwin's clear intelligence made him feel embarrassed by the quotations on the file-cards stuffed in his pockets. 'A sign is interpreted into a different sign, an interpretant, which can be interpreted into a different sign, and so *ad infinitum* . . .' Was it just waffle, *The Death of Meaning*? Did the book he was writing express his own numbness?

What was the wonderful thing Baldwin said? 'Books taught me that the things that tormented me the most were the very things that connected me to everyone who was alive and who had ever been alive.'

Thomas had tried to forget his awful divorce. He'd tried to forget the hellish months when his parents were dying, in separate hospitals, on different sides of London, with him going between them. Avoiding pain, he had become cut off. Then Melissa had come to knock on his door . . . Perhaps he could rejoin the human race.

Watching the footage near the end of the film when Baldwin, huge-eyed, faun-faced, grey, thin as a blade of grass from cancer, flittered like a dying butterfly through his sun-flecked garden in the South of France, through bushes burning pink and gold for the camera – a few seconds from one last hot summer day – Thomas felt acutely, in his whole body, how precious life was. How bright, how short.

Whatever life offers, I shall take.

The audience sat quiet as the lights went up. Somewhere at the back, a few people clapped. After another minute, Thomas touched Suneeta's arm. 'Thank you, Suneeta. Magnificent.'

'*Specialist interest*,' she chaffed him. 'Ha!'

'Suneeta,' he said. 'I am sometimes stupid.'

She said something to her daughter in Gujarati, and they laughed at him, but without malice.

Then he remembered Shirley, and got up, quickly.

He was just in time to see her leave, her halo of bright blonde curls under the lights, through the exit on the other side of the cinema. Somebody was with her, his arm round her shoulder. He was black, Thomas saw first, and then, unbelieving, he realized it was the strange young man. With a short sharp intake of breath, he followed them.

35 · Shirley

Sitting by Winston in the half-empty cinema through that extraordinary film, Shirley was aware of his excitement. He hooted with laughter at a clip of Baldwin replying to a fat Irish critic: 'You are black, impoverished, homosexual – you must have said to yourself, Gee, how disadvantaged can I get?' 'No, I thought I'd hit the jackpot.' Winston laughed so loud that other people turned round. But later she was almost certain he was crying. Or perhaps he just had early hay fever.

At the end of the film, he put his arm round her shoulders. 'I loved it,' she said to him, before he could speak. 'You know I don't read. But I want to read him.'

'I'll lend you *Giovanni's Room*,' he said. 'Shirley, you're a special lady.'

He was half-bending over her under the light between the cinema exit and the foyer when Thomas Lovell bumped into them, obviously half-blinded from the dark inside, because he practically pushed between them.

'Hey, Thomas,' Shirley said. 'This is Winston – Thomas Lovell.'

'Hi,' said Winston. 'I know you, don't I?'

For some reason Thomas hardly smiled. Could he be jealous? Surely not. 'Yes,' he muttered. 'I see you in the library.' He was noticeably slow taking Winston's out-stretched hand.

'Winston and I were going to get a coffee. Would you like to –?'

'I've got work to do –' Then he seemed to change his mind, and stood there, frowning. 'So what did you think of the film?' he asked her.

'It made me cry,' Shirley said. 'I thought that Baldwin was – wonderful.'

(She knew she would never be able to explain it, but everything he'd said seemed to be about her. She couldn't remember it word for word, but something about the point of suffering. That the things that made you suffer most were the ones that linked you to other people. Connected you to everyone who'd ever been alive . . . So it wasn't for nothing, she suddenly thought. They weren't for nothing, her lost children.)

'I liked it too,' said Thomas, but he didn't seem to be listening. He had turned his body to exclude Winston. She glanced at Winston apologetically, and Thomas seemed to realize what he had done. 'Did you like it, uhm?' he threw in Winston's direction, but he had apparently forgotten his name.

'Baldwin's, like, an icon,' Winston said, and smiled his radiant smile at Thomas, the smile that usually made people like him, the smile that probably protected him (because Shirley sensed he was vulnerable).

But Thomas didn't respond to his charm. The conversation faltered and died; Thomas's coldness made things awkward. Winston suddenly remembered he had things to do. Shirley felt sorry; it had been a rare chance for her to be alone with him. She had been sure he wanted to talk. Now Thomas had put paid to that.

Shirley stared after Winston forlornly. She felt she had failed him in some important way. He had asked the family to come to the film; only she had come. And she'd let him down. She watched his elegant narrow head weaving away through the indifferent crowd. His shoulders looked rounded to her, defeated, as if he had lost an important battle. She told herself she was exaggerating. But later she would remember it.

'I'll drive you home,' Thomas said.

'You frightened him off. He's a very sweet boy.'

'I'm sure I didn't.' But he looked triumphant. 'Have you known him long?'

'Yes. Why?' She was aware she was snapping.

'Oh nothing.'

She could see there was something. It has to be jealousy, she thought, and found herself faintly stirred. Thomas was a big man. Clever. Attractive.

She knew she mustn't think like this. 'I'm not going home, as a matter of fact. I'm going to the hospital to see Dad.'

'I'll drive you there.'

'I thought I would walk. It's a lovely day.'

He was visibly relaxing. 'I actually saw your dad this morning . . . But I'd like to walk with you, if you don't mind.'

It was almost as if he wanted to protect her. They walked together to the hospital, talking about the Baldwin film. She warmed to him, finding he had liked it too.

'I thought he was amazing,' Thomas said, as they crossed the road, arms touching lightly. 'That bit when he said to the journalist, after the deaths of Malcolm X and Martin Luther King, "I have been trying to write, between assassinations".'

'Yes. Very witty. But terrible. But what got to me most was the simplest thing. He said something like, "They're killing my friends, and have been as long as I've been alive."'

'At least things have never been that bad in England. I watch a film like that, and get all fired up –' He was waving his hands, and walking faster.

'That's to your credit –' she said, eagerly. (Perhaps that was why he had been rude to Winston. Perhaps he had simply been upset –)

'– and I realize things are relatively OK here.'

She digested this. 'Mmm. Well, I was married to an African.'

'You don't agree?'

'Look, it's complicated.' But Shirley didn't want to argue.

So Thomas felt encouraged to go on. 'At the library, you know, it's all sorts – West Indian, Asian, Irish, a Swede – and nearly half the staff are black. But we all get on. It's just *not an issue*. Apparently the only time we didn't was the eighties, when the council got terribly p.c. and sent two race relations advisers in. Then everyone started to hate each other. Meanwhile these advisers ruined the stock, chucking out books that had the quotes, *wrong message* and spending the earth on, I don't know, huge glossy books on Portuguese slavery that cost forty quid and never went out . . . Hundreds of books on racism. But the public doesn't care about things like that. People aren't interested, is the bottom line.'

He obviously thought he was being daring. Shirley was used to people doing that, priding themselves on saying the unsayable. Though what they said was often predictable. 'Are you sure no one's interested?' she asked. They were turning in through the gates of the hospital. 'Surely a lot of the readers are black. Winston for example. My boyfriend's brother.'

There was a silence. His step checked slightly. 'Just now? *Was that man your boyfriend's brother?*'

Why did he seem so taken aback? Had he assumed her boyfriend was white? 'He's doing a thesis on James Baldwin.'

'What? . . . *Is he?*'

Thomas looked shell-shocked. Irritated, Shirley expanded.

'At University College London. Not just on James Baldwin. On another two writers who were friends of his as well.' She tried to remember. 'Norman Mailer. He's American too. And – Eldridge Cleaver. Who turned against Baldwin . . . He hated white people and, you know, homosexuals. Winston was telling me all about it. I think he's been taking notes in your library. So some of those books would have come in useful. What's the matter, Thomas? Your mouth is open.'

He looked briefly like her father remembering a name, slowly, unwillingly, with very great pain, when he needed it, and her mother was out.

36 · Winston

Winston walked quickly into the Park. He felt as if skeins of inky water were twisting and turning into one great river that poured, undeniable, through his head. He was exalted; he was cast down; he was electric with conviction, leaden with doubt. *The Price of the Ticket* – Baldwin paid the price. He would like to speak the truth like him, he would say it, speak it, sing it out – life would be simple, lived in the sunlight (life was detestable! he lived in prison . . .)

He'd come here regularly when he was thirteen and Elroy had bought him rollerblades. The Park meant ice-creams and heat and shade, under the trees where you lay and got your breath back. He admired his brother, and wanted to be like him.

But around fourteen, the other thing started. The sense that he was not like the others had begun to be stronger and more fixed than his vague yearnings for Elroy's friends. He could not let himself think what it meant, because what it meant was impossible. He was a normal boy, from a normal family. A normal, God-fearing family. His father was no longer around, of course, but his mother marched them to church every Sunday, and there they stayed for two or three hours, listening to the preachers shouting from the pulpit, hammering at him till his head ached, then the waves of song washing round like balm. Sex meant sin (but he knew it didn't, because Elroy and all the other big boys went looking for it, talked about it all the time, teased the younger ones about not getting it). Winston joined in with the foolery but he always felt he was missing something.

He fell in love with the new head teacher who came to his primary school when he was in Year 6. Mr Glover was tall and athletic – he demonstrated a sprint start on Sports Day – but best of all, he liked poetry and read them a poem every morning in assembly. When he noticed how gifted Winston was at English, he often asked him to read instead. Then Winston wrote a poem for homework so good that Mr Glover printed it in the School Newsletter. He called Winston's mother in to see him, but she refused to tell Winston what he had said.

'No good will come of it. I won't do it,' he heard her jabbering to his sisters. 'The fear of the Lord is the beginning of wisdom.' How tired Winston got of hearing that phrase.

Later, too late for him to do it, his elder sister let it out that Mr Glover had recommended he try for a scholarship to public school. 'Mum wasn't having it. And she right! You don't want to go to no battyboy school.'

So he didn't go to a battyboy school. But he still grew up clever. He still grew up different.

Unthinkable, impossible. But true, and real.

There was no one he could tell. He was completely alone. At first he thought that only white men were queer, because his brother said it was a white thing, that only white men were dirty perverts. At school, 'battyboy' was the worst insult, but they threw it around with perfect freedom, because they knew none of them was gay.

None of them was gay. So nor could he be.

(He sometimes found himself imagining, insanely, that his father would come home, and he could tell him everything. A father who was young, kind, all-understanding . . . In real life, Winston had a scanty memory of a tall grizzled man who had once been handsome with an overhanging belly and big gold chains. Elroy had once told him Dad had fifteen children. What would it be like to know your father?)

Winston had tried to go with girls. They often liked him, because he laughed a lot, and made them giggle. Because they felt safe with him, unlike his friends. Because he didn't hassle them for sex.

Of course he didn't. He didn't really want them. They were hot and shrieking and smelled like his sisters. He watched the boys doing weight training. Silent concentration; sweat, muscle. They must not notice him watching them.

And so his life became a net of secrets. He had to go with girls, or his family would suspect him, but after he'd had two or three girlfriends, and had sex with them adequately, but with little pleasure, he told his brother that he had decided to follow the teaching of the Church.

'Winston,' said Elroy, who was in his mid-twenties, still working, then, at the Leisure Centre, where his smile and his six-pack was a hit with the world-a-girls. 'I feel that way once a month as well. Lasts me ten minutes after the service.'

'I mean it,' said Winston, and he did. Though Elroy playfully beat him up.

Then Elroy had gone through his own bad times when his baby mother Desree got another man and said she never wanted to see him again, and Elroy changed completely, pining for his son, starting to retrain with the NHS, going to the Temple every other week.

Not that it had lasted, Winston thought. His brother might be crazy for Shirley now, his brother might even want to marry that girl, but he still went clubbing and saw the sistas. One or two sistas in particular. As far as he could see, Shirley knew nothing. And Elroy seemed almost to believe his own propaganda, reformed man, pillar of the Temple . . .

But now he'd started getting at Winston again, nudging him to come down the club with him, asking him things about his sex life. 'Why you so close, man?' he'd asked last week, running into Winston in the supermarket car-park. 'Reckon you running a baby mama somewhere.

Now you got to make a honest woman of her.' But underneath the jokes, was he on to something?

Winston knew his family could never accept him, never in a thousand years. So he had started to avoid them. But James Baldwin said, 'You don't ever leave home. You take your home with you.' Terrible but true. He stared at the pleasant green hill before him, crowned with its ring of waving trees.

He began to walk up the side of the hill, past a bed of red tulips blazing red in the sun, stiff as soldiers, with sooty black centres. Danger; anger. He had to be himself. But they'd never, ever let him be himself.

And Elroy thought *his* life was complicated . . .

Brother, brother. Winston needed a brother. But the brethren all hated battyboys. To think it was still actually illegal in Jamaica!

This Park had changed for ever one day. He was – fourteen? Fifteen? It was high summer. There had been a row in school that day. There was an Asian boy whose name he had forgotten, perhaps because he didn't want to remember – Ramesh, yes. The shame, the shame . . . He had been seen walking in the playing-fields at lunch-time with the R. E. teacher. The boys had suspicions of Mr Webster already. Someone had seen him buying food with a man. A dozen or so boys trapped Ramesh by the toilets after school and, with Winston watching, shoved him inside. At the last moment before he was dragged out of sight, his eyes seemed to meet Winston's in desperate appeal, saying, *please, Winston, are you like me?* – and Winston could neither deny what he telegrammed, nor find the courage to answer it. He stood fixed to the spot, sweating, wincing, till the screaming started and he ran home.

Later that evening he had come into the Park and sat alone on the seat near the gates. He was going to kill himself, that was clear. He'd felt better, he remembered, having made that decision. But a young white man in jeans and a black singlet came and sat beside him. They looked at each other. Then Winston got up and followed him.

It was a kind of pattern, for the next six years. Except it lacked the beauty of regularity. And Winston could never tell his family. So he had to travel on in the shadow of the lie. And part of him went on hoping he would change. He might fall in love with – *anybody*. He might suddenly find he was in love with a girl, and the cramped knot of falsehood would resolve, in an instant, everything would be free and easy –

But it never happened. He knew it never would.

So he had resolved they would have to know. They would have to know, or he'd never be free. Even if they rejected him (but his worst fear was simply of hurting his mother; of watching her sit and shake and cry). He felt pity for her, then burning rage, because why should he always feel pity for others? – why should he think about his family's feelings when they cared as little about his feelings as if he had just dropped down from the moon –?

He would tell them even if it killed him. He thought, in the end I would rather die –

His life for six years had been horribly lonely. Endless deceptions. Constant watchfulness. And he had grown weary. Too weary to bear it. They did not know him. So did not love him. They refused to know him, so could not love him. Lies, lies and loneliness.

He had tried with hints, small acts of daring. Choosing Baldwin, for example, for his third-year thesis. But his family were too ignorant to take the hint. What they did not want to see, they could not see.

So he'd asked them to the film last week. Surely Elroy or one of his sisters might come. They might see in a flash what he'd been trying to tell them. But only Shirley took up his invitation. He had still been hopeful. Would she understand? If so, maybe she would talk to his brother . . . He had nerved himself to tell her everything, although she was white, although she was a woman. There was something about her he almost trusted. As if she had been hurt, so would not hurt him.

Then that fule fule librarian had come along. And there was no more chance of saying anything.

He felt lonelier than ever, as he came up the hill with the low afternoon sunlight dazzling his eyes. He couldn't see where he was going; dogs barked, birds sang, he walked blindly onwards.

Up at the top, the view opened up. To the east was the graveyard, grey and final. He could hang himself by his belt from a tree. It would not be so terrible, maybe, up here, with the view of the city and the children's playground, and the golden light bathing everything in kindness. Then he turned west and looked over the roof-tops, their hard, unforgiving regularity, the way they marched on to the edge of vision . . .

The hills could crumble into the sea. The gardens could dry and become a desert. The rooks on the plane-trees could burn to ash. This cruel city could come to dust, the people of the city run gnashing and weeping, their children's children wither away –

But Winston's family would never accept him. Never accept that he was gay.

He could hate himself, hang himself, hang himself. He could punish his sin, as they would wish. He looked at the branches of the nearest tree, thick and strong, but salted with green, where the leaves were coming, slowly, unstoppably –

Would they grieve? They would come and grieve. He saw ghosts of flowers underneath the tree, bunches of bitter flowers, drying. He saw his mother with her thin frail arms, clutching the trunk, being pulled away –

He turned back, and saw in the middle distance two men idling near the aviary.

Life was better than death, he knew it.

Lying was better than endless nothingness.

Could he make use of his wound, like Baldwin? For the root of suffering, the dark smothered root, was also the root of everything that lived, reaching up shining and straight into the sunlight –

Making up his mind, he left the Park, but he knew before long he would be back.

37 · Shirley

Thomas came up to the ward with her. It felt comforting not to be alone as she searched nervously down the line of pale imprisoned faces for her father's familiar Roman nose. (All her life there'd been that pang in the pit of her stomach when she was expecting to see her dad. What would it be like not to fear your father?) She patted the bag with the glass figurine.

Dad was sitting up. He was chatting away to the painted woman in the bed next door. Where's Mum? thought Shirley. She won't like that. But Alfred was flushed and animated.

'Hello, Dad.'

'Hello, my duck.' – She rested her present on the bedside table. Had he ever had the slightest use for ornaments? But *duck* was his most tender endearment. 'What's Thomas doing here again? Not chasing my daughter, are you Thomas?' Thomas said nothing, for a second, looking big and bashful under the fluorescent.

'Don't be silly, Dad,' said Shirley, embarrassed, but the two men were grinning at each other.

Beside Thomas her father was so small and fierce. Red as a little bantam cock, with his thin white hair and his thin shiny skin. Whereas Thomas looked almost Mediterranean, with those corrugated waves of healthy black hair.

A thought, irrelevant, flew in through the window – *If we had children, they'd have really curly hair.*

(He's childless too. That failed marriage.)

I was always sure I would have three kids. We schoolgirls used to sit and talk about the future. Three seemed just right. Two boys and a girl, but close together, not like me and Dirk and Darren. They would run down the street, with me behind them, running into sun, with the light on their curls. Me calling them back, in case they got lost . . .

Shirley had had dreams of huge relief, where she hadn't forgotten, after all, to have children, they were there all along, all three of them. And maybe her childless life was the dream, and one day she would wake for ever in the brief night world where she felt so happy.

'She's gone all dreamy,' her father continued, winking – positively winking – at Thomas!

'*Dad!*'

'You missed something this morning,' said Thomas hastily, changing the subject. 'Your father was talking about the Park. About the old days.'

'Oh, she'd have been bored,' said Alfred, but cheerfully.

'No,' she protested, she wouldn't let him down in front of Thomas, and she bent to kiss his cheek. 'You look better, Dad.'

'That's down to your friend Thomas here. Coming to cheer an old man up. Your mother's gone off to look for Darren and whatsherface and get us both a cup of tea –'

'Susie,' said Shirley.

'Not much to look at. Skinny little thing. She's got herself a catch, with Darren.'

Thomas and Shirley exchanged glances, trying not to laugh. 'She's your daughter-in-law, Dad,' Shirley reproved him.

'I know. But she's the third one he's brought home.'

The cheery chappy, smiling and twinkling. Only the family saw his other side.

And yet, he loves us. It's us he loves best.

'I don't know how Darren finds time for it all,' said Thomas, looking almost laddish.

But Alfred had already lost interest. He was leaning back on his pillow again. 'It's all different now,' he remarked to himself. 'May and I have been married for over forty years. Your mother's never looked at another man.'

Then he turned to Shirley, with a sentimental nod, and the faintest hint that she could learn from them.

As if I was less faithful than Mum. Whereas I'd have followed Kojo to hell and back. She looked away. How come he could still hurt her? But she had to make an effort; he was old; he was ill. 'How are you?' she asked, frightened of the answer.

He shook his head slightly. 'Well not too bad.' He obviously didn't want to expand.

'I'd better be going,' Thomas said. 'Leave you two to talk to each other.'

'No rush,' said Alfred, and 'Don't go,' Shirley added.

Then Darren and Susie came striding down the ward, with May in their wake. She was walking very slowly, clutching two cups of tea.

The others seemed to come from a different planet. Darren looked like a man on an assignment, a successful man with things to do, shoulders back, trench-coat swinging, wielding a smart black shoulder-bag that might have looked better on a woman. Susie walked like someone twenty years younger trying to get a job at the Paris collections. Smiling at air, tossing her hair, pushing her narrow hips forward. And then came May, looking tired and old.

'I met them in the corridor,' May announced. 'Darren lost his handbag, and so they got late.' Did she give a little smile as she said the word 'handbag'?

'Darren,' said Shirley, getting up to greet them, and 'Susie – Did you finish your shopping?' She stared at Susie's long, thin dieter's face with its sideways slash of lipsticked smile, the ravenous teeth, the expanse of gum.

'Have I got *crème brûlée* on my nose?' said Susie.

'I was just admiring your suit,' Shirley lied.

'Freebie from *Bazaar*. With the cutest mink gilet –'

'Not something to boast about,' said Darren, irritated.

'It's just the way of the world, my darling.'

'Not in Hillesden,' Thomas interjected.

And May began to laugh, at the back of them, a peal of disrespectful, youthful laughter. At moments like this Shirley loved her mother.

There were too many people round the bed. 'Dad, I'm going to love you and leave you,' Shirley said. 'I've got a little present for you . . . Mum, come here and sit down in my chair.'

But she didn't. May hardly ever seemed to sit down, at least when the family were around, as if she had to stand there waiting to serve them.

There was no alternative to giving the glass John Bull in front of everybody, so Shirley went ahead. 'I shan't stay while you open it.' She laid it on the blanket by his weathered hand.

'We tell her not to waste money on us,' Alfred announced to all and sundry. She knew he liked to have a well-off daughter who chose to spend her money on them. He didn't open it, but left it lying there, even more impressive with the wrapping still on. 'Thank you, my duck,' he said graciously.

And that was two 'ducks' in only one day. Shirley thought, he's enjoying this, his family all round him, and he's on the mend – But was he? she wondered.

'I'm off,' she said. And then remembered that Susie and Darren were flying back. 'Am I going to see you two before you go?'

Darren's charming smile looked slightly evasive. 'We've got an early dinner-date with Christopher Ritchie.'

'I meant, before you leave the country.'

'They're not leaving the country,' said Alfred sharply.

So easy to forget people, when they're horizontal. The silence that followed was uncomfortable.

'They're flying back to New York tonight,' said a little voice from the back of the group. It was May, who always liked knowing things, Mum, who enjoyed knowing more than Dad.

'I don't want to go,' said Darren, sounding insincere, 'I – we don't want to leave you, when we've only just got here –'

'You've only just got here,' Alfred echoed, but flat, barely indignant, looking suddenly pale. 'I've hardly exchanged two words with you.'

'Still it's been a great relief to me to see you,' said Darren. 'When I got the phone call, I thought you were at death's door.' He laughed; it rang hollow. 'Now you're almost yourself again.'

Alfred looked at Darren levelly. 'The news isn't very good, in fact.'

The family went quiet. Was this something momentous? 'I wasn't going to tell you. Your mother didn't want it. But the tests aren't quite what they ought to be.'

'But you're doing very well for a man who's had a stroke,' Darren said, indignant.

And Alfred pulled himself up in bed. It was as if he wanted to savour the moment, a moment when he still had power over them. Perhaps he felt himself slipping away from the world of busy people who strode down the ward, or flew halfway round the world after dinner. 'I never said I had a stroke. It was an *event*, the doctors said. Apparently I had another one last night. A stroke's just something with your circulation. They can fix that –'

'– Of course they can fix it,' Darren affirmed, to no one in particular.

'– but that's not the problem. They've found some blockages. Lots of small blockages in my brain –'

'Blood-clots?' asked Darren, over-helpfully. He'd started to sound like an interviewer. Shirley thought, why can't he just shut up? She was frightened, suddenly. Sharply frightened.

'In plain English, they think I've got cancer. The so-called *events* are kind of fits. They look like strokes, but they're not.'

All Shirley could think was *he's going to die*. Dad was trying to tell them he was going to die. Poor Mum. Poor Dirk (and where was Dirk, any way? Poor Dirk, he always got left out) – *But it was impossible. It couldn't be true.* 'But Dad,' she burst out. 'I can't believe it. You've lived outdoors, you never smoked –'

'It's secondaries,' he said, with a certain relish. 'They don't know where the primary is.'

'He did smoke, actually,' May put in. 'He loved his smokes, when we were courting.' Shirley saw none of this was news to her. She looked grave, but not shocked, whereas the children were dumbstruck. 'You did smoke, dear, didn't you?'

'Oh never mind that,' cried Alfred, furious. 'That was years ago, woman. It's not to do with that.'

Now it was Darren's turn to put his foot in it. 'It's not exactly brain cancer, if it's secondaries. The primary might well be lung.'

'So you're all doctors, are you?' Dad fumed on his pillow. 'And it's my fault, is it, because I smoked?'

This scene was going terribly wrong. Shirley saw he was fighting with himself. He wanted to be brave, and dignified, but his wife and children weren't letting him.

She felt a surge of simple pity. For he was a brave man, in his way. If there were shouts in the street, he would always go out. She had watched him chasing yobs from the Park, louts who were six inches taller than him. 'You're a fighter, Dad,' she found herself saying. 'You won't be beaten. I know you won't.'

'Of course I shan't give up,' he snapped, but slightly appeased. He looked at her, suddenly, his pale blue eyes seeming to see her properly, as if they might be together in this. 'You're a good girl, Shirley . . . a good girl.' He pushed himself up again with one thin arm, and made an effort to smile at his family. 'I am a fighter. I've always been a fighter.'

(But that was the trouble with Dad, of course. Fighting made their lives miserable.)

'When are they operating?' asked Darren.

'He doesn't know,' said Mum disapprovingly, as if all this openness had gone too far. As if once they let death come into the room, it would stay with them always; no going back. No going back to their normal bickering.

(But Mum was always so afraid of change. She was a coward, really, though Shirley adored her. Because just possibly, Shirley felt then, if we knew Dad was dying, if everything was spoken, we could find something different. An openness. A new way of being together. A new way of being with my dad. As if fear and lying could finally end –

He might be sorry. We might be sorry. All of us might become less frightened.)

'They're not going to operate,' Alfred said. He stared at them, defiant. 'They say they can't operate.' This was his moment. He waited for what he had said to sink in.

'OK,' said Darren, stupidly smiling. Perhaps her brilliant brother was stupid. Susie had put her arm around him, her thin arm in its bright blue jacket, three gold cuff buttons, five red nails, but under it all she offered human comfort. Shirley wished that Elroy were here. She too needed an arm around her. Darren's mouth opened, and closed again. Then Thomas was beside him too, bearing him up.

'People are listening,' said May, very quietly. 'I don't want everyone to know our business.'

Shirley realized she meant the raddled red-head on the bed next door, who was listening avidly, not trying to pretend. She met Shirley's eye, and did not look away, her veined eyes glittering with terrible hunger. Shirley felt a kind of senseless horror, as if it was death, lying waiting for them, and told herself, *but she's just lonely. No one ever seems to come to see her.* She wriggled past Darren and Susie to her mother, and put her arm protectively around her shoulders (*I'm sure I never used to be so much taller*). 'Doesn't matter, Mum. Never mind . . .'

Shirley needed comfort, but gave it, instead.

'Do you have a prognosis, Mr White, Alfred?' said Susie. They all turned and looked, surprised by her daring.

'It's cancer, I told you,' said Alfred, but gently, more gently than he would have done if it was his children.

'That's not what prognosis means,' said May, unable to hold back, as usual. 'That's diagnosis, what you're talking about.'

Shirley let go of her mother and moved forward to the bed; it was time to intercede to prevent an argument. She ought to work for United Nations –

But Thomas, bless him, stepped in to help. 'Did they talk about the future, Alfred?'

The future, she thought. Such a brilliant choice of words.

And Dad turned towards him with a strange expression that Shirley slowly realized was gratitude. (Because sometimes families couldn't talk on their own. Sometimes they needed outsiders to help them.) 'They don't think I'm going to get better,' he said. 'So we'd better face up to it. I'm on my way out. But I'm going out fighting. I've got things to do. Lots of loose ends to tidy up at the Park.'

Somebody was sobbing. A woman, sobbing. The volume of noise became sensational, terrific . . .

'He has to ask the doctors if he wants to go back to work,' said May, to everyone and no one. 'He hasn't mentioned it. They might not agree. Dirk, dear, sorry, you've had a shock . . .'

The shuddering roars came from Dirk, not May. Dirk had come in while Alfred was speaking. Dirk had come in, and no one had noticed. He was standing with Mum, his face buried in her shoulder. All Shirley could see was his leather jacket, the pattern of studs heaving and shaking.

'You can't all stand there bawling,' said Alfred, with a hint of his old sardonic humour. Indeed he was back in control again, now he had seen his news take effect. 'Making a spectacle of yourself. Now you older ones had better move aside and let me have a word with Dirk. Not you, May,' (irritably). 'You stay.'

They wandered numbly back down the ward. 'I don't believe it,' muttered Darren. 'Of course we'll seek a second opinion. We'll find someone seriously good in the States.'

'Are you still flying back?' Shirley asked him.

'We have to, don't we,' he said, to Susie.

'I don't see why. We could just make a few phone calls.'

His face had a spasm of irritation. 'You're a therapist,' he said. 'You can't let your clients down –'

'But you're distressed. Your family's distressed.'

'Dad's aiming to go back to work. You heard him –'

'Your mother didn't sound too sure.'

Darren stopped on the stairs under an unshaded bulb and leaned against the wall, suddenly. He looked terrible; at least twenty years older. 'Are you all right, baby?' Susie asked. There was sweat on his forehead, and on his upper lip. 'Cancer. It can't be. Can it?' he muttered.

Shirley began to cry, quietly.

They were still standing frozen in the stairwell when Dirk came running down from above them.

'My God, what have you done to your face?' Shirley asked. He had great red bruises down his left cheek, and a small dark cut underneath his eye.

'Football match. Christ, it doesn't fucking matter.'

'Are you all right? Come to the café with us.' She was still his older sister. She always would be.

'Nah. Come down the pub with me.' Dirk gestured loosely at all of them. His eyes were not quite moving together.

'I'm sorry,' said Susie, sounding suddenly American, 'we have to go to a dinner party. And then, you see, we don't really drink.'

It was the first Shirley had heard of Darren not drinking. Dirk swayed towards her. Her back was to the wall. His blond stubble, she saw, had a thinning patch, and his face (so much coarser than when he was a boy) was red with grief and something else, for as he bent close, she could smell the beer. It was like walking into a brewery. 'Darling Shirl,' he said, and sprayed her with spittle. 'Come for a jar, go on, why not? Come for a drink with your little brother.'

'I think you've had a few already,' she said. 'Maybe we should go to Casualty. Your poor face. It looks awful.'

'Bollocks,' he said, but without malice, then 'Come on, Shirley, come on, Darren, when was the last time we were all together?'

There was a silence. They were never together. The White family found it hard to be together. The silence extended wretchedly.

'Too good for me, aren't you,' he flung at them all, 'Too bloody good for me, so you think. I lose my job and Dad is dying and my fucking family just don't want to know. That stupid fucking woman' (gesturing back towards the ward, presumably in May's direction) 'has the fucking cheek to tell me to go home and sober up. My dad's the only one I care about. My dad's the only one who cared about me. *He* wasn't too proud to drink with me –'

'I'm not too proud to drink with you.' Shirley tried to reach her arm out and touch him, but he wrenched away so strongly that he stumbled off the step. 'But I just have to stay and see Mum's all right. And then Elroy –' she realized her mistake. Mentioning Elroy wouldn't help matters. 'And then I'm being picked up and taken home.' (But what was that he'd said about losing his job? Surely George and Ruby would never sack him?)

'Fucking *Elroy*,' he yelled, half-mad by now, in a frenzy of grief and booze and pain, his face a mess, battered red and shiny. 'Fucking *nigger*,' he yelled. 'And you. You . . . nigger-lover . . . Dirty slag . . . Can't believe you're my sister . . . Dad made a stand about things like that. People like Dad –' (and now he was sobbing) – 'men like Dad –' (exploding with grief, snot bursting out of his nostrils in bubbles, reddened blue eyes streaming with tears) –

But he couldn't finish. He turned and ran. The light caught the studs on the back of his jacket, and they heard him blundering through the swing-doors, then clumsy feet pounding off into the darkness.

38 · Dirk

It isn't true Of course it isn't Can't be true No, no.

Anyone could see Dad was fit as a fiddle

He isn't old, is he? Not old *old* *Not bleeding old enough to die –*

Dirk ran down the road in the stupid moonlight, the stupid moon was laughing at him, its great round stupid gob, smiling. The cruel thoughts came with the beats of his feet, with each panting breath, he couldn't escape them.

I lost my job

I'm losing my dad

I lose everything I ever had

Dad was the only thing I cared about

And Mum, a bit, when she isn't gabbing. When she isn't going on at me.

That's why she got all weepy on Thursday.

She wasn't making sense, so I didn't get it. Didn't bother to explain, the stupid cow. Nobody thought that I was worth telling. They think I'm a nothing. A moron. A punk.

Everybody hates me

They always did
They always thought I was stupid and ugly
They can't even bear to have a drink with me.
So fucking what. I don't fucking need them.
I'll fucking show them. I will. They'll see.

He went to the pub, where his mates would be, but they weren't, the pub was full of strangers, full of *women*, in the first place, which looked all wrong, all over their boyfriends on Saturday night, giggling and shrieking and nuzzling and slurping. He watched them, gagging. Dirk hated women. They hated him, and he hated them. And foreigners. There were a lot of foreigners. Not actual blacks, of course, no, actual blacks didn't dare show their mugs in here, but Spanish or French or whatever they were, fucking Europeans, fucking dagoes, shooting their mouths off in foreign languages, hooting and tooting loud as lords –

And soon they'd be ruling over these isles. There wouldn't be a government, it wouldn't be Britain, they'd just be some piddling little county of Europe, *Englandshire*, or *Englandstein,* or whatever disgusting bit of lingo they chose, and everyone would lord it over us . . . They'll come to *Londonburg* for their hols!

Londonburg! He laughed aloud. It was a fucking good joke against the Krauts, but there was no one here to share it, and they looked at him funny, when he laughed on his own.

'Another pint, mate,' he called down the counter. The barman was deaf, he didn't hear what Dirk was saying, standing there chatting to someone else. 'Oi! Dosser! I'm dying of thirst!'

Everything's going. Everything's gone. There's nothing left for me round here. Nothing left of what I had. Even Dad won't be in the Park any more. No one will know us. We won't exist.

Darren's jetting off as though he doesn't give a sod.

Darren doesn't give a fuck about us.

When Dad is – *dead, actually dead*, Darren won't show his face again (he wouldn't bother, just for Mum. He'll send me one of his printed

Christmas cards, with some smart joke about America, and that's all
I'll hear from him till next Christmas. Not that I care. Couldn't care
less –)

'Dosser! Whasser matter, have you gone deaf? Can I get some service
round here, or what?'

'I think it's you that's gone blind, mate,' said the barman. 'Dosser's
not working here any more. My name is Paolo. What'll you have?'

Cool as anything. Snotty little git. Dosser was my mate, we could
have a laugh.

'*Pow-lo,*' said Dirk with elaborate irony. '*Pow-lo.* Now that's a funny
name.'

'What's your name then?' the barman asked.

There was a pause before he said, sulkily, 'Dirk.' He had never been
happy about his name. Some of his mates called him Dick, or Dicky. He
wasn't going to tell this wanker that.

'Well some people might say that's a funny name. Not me, mind.
I'm not a comedian. I never laugh at people's names.'

So what was he on about, laughing at mine? Dirk stared at him
amazed. He was fucking cheeky. He would have to get the lads to give
him a kicking. (But he found it hard to concentrate. The words weren't
coming out as clear as he wanted.) 'You're foreign, aren't you? *Pow-lo.*'
He belched. 'We used to have a *English* barman in here.'

'Born just round the corner, mate,' the barman said. 'Now what'll
you have? I've got to get on.'

'Heineken,' said Dirk, confused, disgusted. 'No, I'll have two bottles
of Holsten Pils.'

He drank them on his own, musing, brooding. The pub was getting
hotter, wilder, noisier, and everything was slurring, jumping, shifting.
Perhaps he didn't feel quite well. He put his head in his hands for a
second, but his elbow wasn't properly fixed on the table or else some
joker had pulled it away because the next thing he knew he was on the
floor, he had toppled sideways on to someone's lap and down to the
floor. It felt very greasy. He lay there, among the dog-ends and the crisp

packets. He felt very sick. He wanted to die. But he wanted to kill the arsehole who'd done it. His leg felt cold. He looked at it. He had spilled his Holsten Pils on his trousers.

The next moment people were helping him up and he felt very happy, though still rather sick. He felt good, he had friends, he would buy them all drinks. He staggered across to the bar again.

'*Pow-lo,*' he called, rather fuzzily, and then tried again, at the top of his voice. '*POW-LO! OI!*' This time everyone heard him. In fact, they all seemed to be looking at him. It was a good feeling. He was here among friends, he had all their attention, new friends, good friends. He wished he could think of things to say to them. They were waiting for a speech, but no words came. He reached out his hands towards them all, but in the distance he heard the crash of glass, and someone screamed, a bint was screaming. 'They shouldn't let them into pubs,' he said, smiling, smiling at them all, for they all understood him, he could say whatever he wanted to, he could speak freely, they were on his side. 'Fuckin' foreigners. Eh? An' fuckin' women.' He nodded at them; his head felt heavy.

'Two pints of Holshdepizh – thass for me,' he told Paolo, pointing at his chest, and it seemed very funny, this pointing at his chest, his hand got away, he was crossing himself, he'd be a fucking Christian, next, at this rate, which made him burst out laughing again, 'an –' Then he was stuck. His brain stalled, grinding. He knew he was buying for someone else, or everyone else, but what were they having?

'No more for you, mate. Sorry,' said Paolo.

From then on, his memory of things was uncertain. Someone was pushing him. He pushed them back. He didn't know why, but everything had changed, they were against him now, they had turned against him, and before he knew it he was out on the pavement, crouched on the pavement, throwing up.

He sat there a long time, his head spinning, telling himself to get a grip.

It got colder. Perhaps he slept . . .

Then he saw them coming. (When? He didn't know. He would never be able to answer that question. Someone had bitten great holes in his memory. But he saw them coming, like a happy ending.)

He saw them coming towards him at the double, running, shouting, his own true mates, Ozzie, Belter, Moke and Westy and all the lads, running like an army, hard and lean, tall and strong, and his spirits surged, they had come to save him, to back him up, for he'd lost a battle, though he couldn't remember where or why. But when he waved at them, they didn't seem to know him, then Ozzie spotted him and skidded to a halt shouting, 'D'ya see them, Dicky? Where did they go?'

Dirk didn't know who they were talking about. But then he got it. They were after someone. Chasing the enemy.

The hunt was on.

Dirk would never be able to explain the details.

Wasn't me that started it, so don't blame me. I only joined in because they were my mates. Once you have mates, you have to stick by them. Things just happen, then they blame it on you.

Someone yelled from the front, and we were off again. Usually I'm hard, I'm fast and hard, but I couldn't keep up, I was all over the place, I kept bumping into parked cars and lamp-posts, the lads were way ahead of me, and the animals we were chasing were only in view as they turned the corner, and I caught a glimpse –

They were black as night. Not Pakis, darkies. So black they must have thought they were safe, at night. But they're not, see. Not round our way they're not. Not when the lads are out, in force, together.

It didn't seem to hurt, when I bumped into things.

It didn't stop me. I kept on after them. I thought of my dad; he never gave up. Somehow we chased them down near the Park. They looked a lot bigger, when we got close.

Why did they decide to climb over the wall? That was disgusting. Showed no respect. *My father's the Park Keeper, remember.* The man who actually locks up, at nights. It was a personal insult, like, to Dad.

Dad would have killed them. But he couldn't, could he? He was in hospital, flat on his back. Dad couldn't stop them. It was down to me.

Who was it decided to go in after them?

Over the wall, all ten of the lads, shining over, swarming over, Dirk was the last, and he nearly didn't make it, *fool, failure,* out of breath, arms aching . . .

But he thought about what happened at the football match. No way would he let that happen again. And will power hauled him up over that wall.

After that there was another gap in his memory.

Fucking weird to be in the Park at night, he had never been in the Park at night. It seemed a whole lot bigger. Wilder. Blacker. He couldn't see a fucking thing, though the moon was out, and the sky was all silver, like the stupid fucking picture Mum had got in the kitchen, always staring at it instead of drying up . . . by *Atkinson Grimshaw.* (That *must* be made up! *Dirk* was bad enough, but *Atkinson Grimshaw*!)

He remembered worrying about Mum and Dad. Once he'd got into the Park, it just didn't feel right, he wasn't sure any more it was a good idea, he didn't feel happy they were all in there, in his father's place, in the middle of the night, not knowing what would happen, or where it would stop. In the darkness he couldn't even tell who was who . . .

They all looked the same, who was us, who was them?

They were quite near the edge, he knew that, at any rate, because you could see the lights of the houses. Then someone – he didn't even recognize the voice, it could have been Moke, it could have been Belter – started yelling blue murder, so the blacks were attacking him, the lads all charged towards the sound of his voice, but Dirk tripped over a bush, went flat on his face, and by the time he managed to get over there it was like everyone on earth was fighting and yelling.

We were howling for them. Coloureds, darkies. We were up for it. We wanted blood.

The only trouble was, Dirk couldn't actually see them, but he knew they were there, in the thick of it, so he just piled in, kicking, punching, he didn't feel fear, he didn't feel pain, he was like *invincible,* one of Dad's words, one of Dad's words for the British army, and he was a soldier, he was like Dad –

Until some crazy bint started screaming. Some woman started screaming, not very far off, *Police* and *Murder* and *Help* and everything, and then they knew the game was up, she was screaming as if her house was burning down, though they weren't hurting *her*, it was nothing to *her*, they could see this little figure in a lit-up window in one of the houses alongside the Park, screaming, 'What are you doing? Murder, murder!' Some crazy woman. Some trouble-maker. Sounded Paki, to Dirk, sort of singsong, foreign, so why was she bothering to stick up for niggers?

The screams were so loud. They like cut into his ears. She'd have everyone opening their windows and gawping. So they more or less stopped. One of his ribs felt broken, or else one of the bastards had winded him. (But at least he felt it. His feeling was back. He had a headache, but he wasn't so drunk.) Funny thing was, he never saw the buggers plainly, it was like they disappeared in a puff of smoke . . . It was almost like the lads had been fighting each another.

They were on their own. Panting in the darkness. Listening to this crazy woman screaming.

Dirk suddenly noticed he was shivering, shaking, although it was very warm for March.

So we legged it, didn't we. Course we did. We had defeated the blacks. We had given them a kicking. Now we had to run before the police car came –

But we heard it in the distance, they'd been fucking quick, we heard the sirens wailing, and we split.

39 · Shirley

Fate took a hand – did God take a hand? She had never felt Jesus was a puritan. *Because He's young, and we see His body* . . .

So many pictures of his naked body, although He was dying, his nakedness. Perhaps the Bible can't admit He had sex because it would be complicated if He had children. Then there would be grandsons and granddaughters of God. Neither wholly human nor wholly divine.

(Maybe that was the truth of life on earth. We do wrong things. We do terrible things. But we do have sparks, moments, of goodness. Maybe we're all God's grandchildren.

She would never dare say that to a priest.)

As they sat in the café, Shirley was paged; there was hideous crackling, a blare of howl-round, 'Mr Elroy King regrets he is prevented by work from picking up Mrs Shirley White.' And Thomas said, 'Then I'll walk you home.'

It had grown dark, while they stood round the bed. The air was still fresh from the morning's rain, but a warm wind, almost summery, completely wrong for the time of year, had blown most of the clouds away from the sky, and behind the silver edges of the last small cloudlets a calm white moon came into view, a moon that looked down on Shirley's hurt heart and said, *This is only one night among many, only one pain among so many, look at me, I am always here.*

She had always loved the moon. So did Kojo.

'Great moon,' said Thomas. 'I'm glad to be outside.'

'You helped with Dad,' she said to him, putting her hand upon his shoulder, which was rather broad, she couldn't help noticing (what precisely had they done at Darren's wedding? Danced, certainly. But kissed? – More?) 'Thank you.'

'I admire your dad.'

She wished he didn't; she was glad he did.

It was Saturday, she realized, listening. The roads around the hospital were quiet, but she could hear odd shrieks in the distance, the young enjoying themselves in the moonlight . . . At least, she hoped they were enjoying themselves. Despite her sorrow, she felt oddly content, walking down the road with a different man, slightly taller and broader than the one she was used to.

'Will Dirk be all right?' asked Thomas. 'He looked awful.'

'He lives at home, it's not much of a life.'

'I see him nearly every day, you know. When I buy my paper. Don't think he likes me.'

'I'm sure he does,' she cut in, firmly. She had a sudden urge to tell Thomas he was nice.

'I can't believe he's lost his job,' said Thomas. 'Nothing ever changes, in that shop. He must get very bored, poor kid.'

Shirley always tried not to think about Dirk. Sometimes he seemed comic, like a bad cartoon . . . But all that anger. All that pain. 'Yes, I think he's always been bored. It'll be worse than ever, if he loses his job.'

Talking in an easy, disjointed rhythm, as if they had known each other for ages (which they had, in a way, since they were both kids), they wandered on towards the Park.

They were about two streets away when they began to hear screams, which at first sounded like all the other Saturday night shouting. Playful shrieks that sounded like murder. Teenagers, off the leash, on the booze.

Shirley started to think the screams were getting louder.

But Thomas had just made her laugh, telling her something about the library, and she was telling him dribs and drabs of gossip about the end of Darren's second marriage.

Then there was a moment when neither of them was talking, there was just the companionable tramp of their feet, and they both heard it very clearly, a high-pitched screaming, going on and on, a woman's voice, surely, and a male voice, or voices. They stopped and listened, staring at each other, trying to read each other's faces, pale and tense in the light of the moon.

Then suddenly Thomas broke into a smile. 'Oh it's OK,' he said. 'I think I know what that is. It's just a couple rowing, I heard them last night –'

'Couples can still kill one another –'

'But then I heard them making love.'

He looked at Shirley; she looked at him. The thing he had said became very exciting.

'We're quite near my house, actually,' he said, gesturing past the moon-touched shadows, the glitter and dark of the roadside puddles, a cat that shot out and retreated again. Thomas's fingers brushed her shoulder.

But the screams went on. Shirley hated the sound. She wanted to muffle it in cloth. She wanted the comfort of his large warm body, but she knew she shouldn't be thinking like that.

He touched her again. 'Look would you like a coffee or a drink or something – before I take you home? You've had a ghastly day.'

'I don't want to put you to any trouble.' (That was the authentic voice of her parents.)

Then the world exploded. The night tore apart down a blinding line of fluorescent blue and red and white, there was a deafening noise of sirens blaring, two police cars came tearing down the road and straight at the corner where they were stood, they were going too fast to corner properly and suddenly one was coming straight for her, its white eyes blazing out of the black, she couldn't move, she was paralyzed . . .

Then she was on her knees, half-stunned, in the darkness, the blaze had gone, the noise was retreating, my God, they had hit her, she was bruised but alive, her heart lurched and thudded against her breastbone –

'Bastards! Bastards! You nearly killed me!'

'Shirley, Shirley, are you all right?'

'He drove straight at me –'

'I pulled you over –'

'You saved my life.'

'They were going so fast.'

Thomas held her tight. 'You're shivering.'

But he was too. 'Look, I will have a coffee.'

He helped her up. Her legs trembled. They walked the few hundred yards to his door with his arm lightly around her shoulders.

He turned the key, but the doorway was blocked by a couple standing with their arms around each other: a very pretty girl, rather red in the face, skinny and blonde like Michelle Pfeiffer, and her boyfriend, a biggish, greasy-haired type, who leered at Shirley, and said, 'Sorry – are we in your way? Just saying our goodnights.'

He somehow made the words suggestive. The girl looked annoyed or upset or nervous, but when Thomas said, 'You all right, Melissa?' she nodded and looked down at the ground.

Shirley and Thomas went upstairs. The skinny girl called up after him, 'I've started your book. I really like it!' But Thomas didn't answer her.

Shirley looked around while he did things in the kitchen. His flat was crammed floor to ceiling with books, and big jungly plants, and photographs. One of the moon in the night sky. Thomas must have a romantic streak.

She could see the real moon, slightly smaller, sailing above the trees through the window, silver-white against the black of the sky. A true full moon. *We nearly died* . . . She tried to thank God, but she couldn't pray.

She looked at his desk, which was covered in paper, and books propped open with envelopes and pencils. Thomas was a writer, of course he was. She peeked at something he had underlined, and 'mourning' caught her eye. Kojo, she thought.

'Derrida's contretemps of mourning – where the other's death is always first and constitutive of my most proper *Jemeinigkeit*; and where my 'own' death is never actually my own . . .' She stopped reading. It made no sense, it had nothing to do with actual mourning.

Then she saw something else. On the mantelpiece. A moon-faced figure, unmistakable, long trunk of a body, small hills of breasts – it was an Akua'ba, surely. A Ghanaian figure. But why was it here? Her flesh prickled, remembering the bitterest days with Kojo, when endless cousins seemed to come from Ghana.

All of them teased us about having babies, until they saw that something was wrong.

Then they began to offer advice. Most of it seemed to be aimed at Shirley, they always assumed that Kojo was fertile (and she sometimes wondered now, did they know he was? Did he really have children already at home, as his cousin Gifty had tried to tell her? – She would always love him. It didn't matter.) 'I could bring Shirley an Akua'ba doll. Never mind if it's old-fashioned, it works.' If childless women held the dolls, it was meant to help them to have their own babies. But Kojo refused, laughing angrily. 'She's a modern woman. She doesn't need witchcraft.'

Shirley had seen one in his second cousin's flat. Like babies, Akua'maa, little black babies, rounded necks, big eyes, high foreheads. Wooden dolls you could hold in your arms.

She picked up Thomas's Akua'ba.

Thomas came in with two mugs of cocoa 'to warm you up'. And a bottle of whisky.

She didn't drink whisky, she didn't drink spirits –

But she felt she could do anything, anything at all, because she had come so near to death.

She heard her heart. Still loud, still jumping. She felt very wild; her father was dying, the rigid pin at the centre of the world.

'You still look shaken,' Thomas said, glugging a whisky into a glass. 'Is that too much?'

'Yes . . . No – Thomas, where on earth did you get this?' (Cradling the Akua'ba.)

'My moon goddess? In Canada. Isn't she pretty? I just bought her in a shop.'

'She's Ghanaian . . .' Shirley shivered, remembering. She didn't want to explain it to Thomas.

'You're still trembling. Those maniacs.'

She tried to pull herself together. 'Mum always says they're just off for their tea.'

'They nearly killed you. We should complain.'

'And get nowhere. Well *you* might get somewhere, Thomas.' Because she felt they owned the world, people like him, with degrees, and good jobs.

'No one takes notice of librarians . . . Journalists are a different matter. Your brother, for example. We should tell him.'

Shirley took a deep draft of her drink. The fire ran straight to her throat, her cheeks. 'Darren'll soon be on his way back to New York, as soon as he's seen his trendy friends. He doesn't care about us in England. He writes his column, but he couldn't give a toss. He said that to me once, twenty years ago, when those American bombs were coming to England. Cruise missiles, weren't they. And Darren said, "I write pieces saying it's an outrage, but the truth is, no one in America cares. The British Isles are just so small. No one would care if they sank into the sea." Darren wouldn't care if we were blown to buggery.' Shirley swore rarely, but now she enjoyed it.

Thomas was watching her with odd intensity. 'We could both have been wiped out, just now. In one split second. Who would have cared? I wouldn't even get an obituary.'

Shirley thought, we're living on a different planet. Thomas wants his life to be written about. Whereas mine is so little. So ordinary.

And yet she liked him, all the same. He had a wistfulness she related to. As if the surface had been chipped away. She tried to remember about his marriage. The wife had red hair. Almost certainly left him.

They were sitting on his sofa, quite close together. 'But you're bleeding,' Thomas suddenly said. 'Look.' And he put his hand on the side of her knee, and she saw there was a big hole in her tights and a black patch of skin traced with lines of red. His hand was large and white against the blackness. She wasn't used to large white hands. His finger was tracing the edge of the nylon, the delicate edge where clothed became naked.

'You're still trembling,' he said. 'I'll bring a bowl. We ought to wash it.' His face was absolutely fixed on hers, stricken, tender, a kind of rawness as if they had been through fire together, and it seemed quite natural, inevitable for her to reach out and touch his cheek, his big man's cheek, which was warm and rough – Elroy shaved twice a day, religiously. All her nerve ends felt near the surface.

And after all, he had saved her life, God had sent him to save her life, she could never have moved, it came so quickly – it was Thomas who pushed her out of the way.

What happened next seemed equally natural, he took her hand that was stroking his cheek and pressed it to his mouth, kissed it, sucked it. Why did she think of a child feeding? He was older than her, but he needed comfort, they all needed comfort, hungry men. Men without sex. She could always tell. She felt his hunger; it excited her. And yet he was also comforting her, and she needed comfort, she was sore, she was bleeding, she had faced death two times that day. Now he was stroking her knee again, in a kind of wondering, hypnotized way.

He seemed like all men and all boys to Shirley. He was like the boys she had grown up with, his whiteness, the softness of his hair, but too big and too gentle to be her father, thank God she had never had men like her father, and she took him in her arms, he took her in his arms, they were holding each other and kissing, suddenly, trying to suck out each other's centres, trying to eat each other like fruit.

Taking their clothes off felt easy and simple, as if they had always been naked together.

They were very quick, as if it was essential, as if they had to steal what they wanted before death came and took it away, as if they were teenagers hiding from their parents instead of the middle-aged people they were. But they weren't shy, and they weren't guilty, though Thomas had a look of stunned delight as if he was half-afraid of waking up.

But his erection was real, and solid, his beautiful, smooth, heavy penis, the weight and swing of his big male body, she had always been moved by men's nakedness, by the way their passion shows so clearly, their huge hunger, their desire to come in.

And she wanted him. She needed him. She could hardly wait to pull him inside her, and they lay on the sofa, side by side, one of her legs between his two, and he pushed inside with a groan of pleasure, she held his hair, it was thick in her hands, she stroked the naked back of his neck, she moved her hips and they moved together and his face had an expression of bliss as if everything in the world was right. One of his hands was holding her breast, pulling gently on the nipple. 'Beautiful breasts,' he whispered to her, 'Your beautiful breasts, you're so lovely, Shirley, why didn't we do this years ago?' She put her finger upon his lips and soon they were moving in rhythm together, their breath getting faster, they were panting, moaning, she wanted him, oh she wanted him, she wanted this, it was racing through her, nothing could stop it, she came, she came – she came with a great deep moan of pleasure that seemed to go on and on around him, and then he changed rhythm and began to groan and came with a shuddering, shouting roar and then stopped moving, deep inside her.

They were exhausted. They lay as one.

Shirley realized she had been asleep, for Thomas was staring down at her, leaning on one elbow, his face anxious. 'Shirley,' he said. 'Are you all right? My God, Shirley. I don't know what happened . . . I didn't even think about contraception.'

She couldn't help smiling at his rueful face. 'Well you don't have to blaspheme about it.' She was half-joking, but he looked depressed.

'Are you religious? – I suppose you are. Sorry, sorry. *Sorry*.'

'Look I didn't think about it, either.' She still felt sleepy. She didn't want to talk. It was curiously peaceful, lying there, in this unfamiliar place, with his face gazing down.

'It's moon madness,' she said to him, running her finger along his collar-bone. To her he looked pale, compared to Elroy, but actually he was golden, olive, she remembered they called him *dago* at school, because he was part Italian (or Spanish).

So good to be close to another person. We're close to so few people, in the course of a life . . . She held the moment in her hands. She wanted him to be happy too. 'Don't worry about the contraception angle. I was trying to get pregnant for over six years.'

'Did I pressure you?' he asked. 'I probably did. I just – wanted you, Shirley. I mean, I don't go round doing things like that.'

She laughed out loud. 'You've got it all wrong. It's the woman who's supposed to say things like that. Just in case you don't respect me.'

'But I do respect you,' he said at once, earnestly, how young he looked with his curls all crooked, a kind of soft halo round that big face, so different from Elroy's lean, muscular head, which was beautiful as a panther was. *Elroy would kill her* – but he'd never know.

'Look it was very nice. It was lovely.' She nuzzled his arm and smiled at him. She wanted to lie a while naked together in the warmth of this unfamiliar room, this holiday from the rest of life. The time would be short, but that made it sweeter.

But Thomas ploughed on doggedly. 'I'm not having sex with anyone else.'

Shirley suddenly thought things were going wrong. Was he promising her fidelity? 'But you know I'm virtually married, don't you? I mentioned Elroy. I love him, actually –'

And that made her realize she did love Elroy. She had always held back, could never say it, because it was hard to love anyone but Kojo. But as she spoke she was perfectly sure.

'No,' Thomas said. 'I didn't mean that. I meant, I won't have infected you. But there is someone – there's a girl I like –'

And they smiled at each other: conspirators. Two people who had crossed the line. And no one knew. *No one knew.*

Then he went on. 'I haven't slept with anyone for some time. You probably noticed. That's why I was so quick – You could say I was celibate, in fact.'

'Well that's a waste,' she told him. 'You were very nice. Very nice indeed.'

'And so were you. It was . . . delicious.'

He sounded like a boy who had eaten the tuck shop. 'But you didn't eat me,' she said, to tease him, getting up off the sofa, stretching, yawning.

'May I kiss your breasts?' They had moved apart; he already had to ask her permission. 'Of course,' she said. 'Be my guest, Thomas.'

He kissed her breasts, tenderly, slowly, first one then the other, reverently, and then moved down and kissed her belly, nuzzling over the globe of her belly, round and white, her moon-belly. Then 'Thank you, Shirley,' he said. 'You're really beautiful. Thank you.'

She looked at her glass. All the ice-cubes had melted. The pale gold liquid winked in the light. 'What's the time?' she asked. 'You took my watch off.'

It was nearly eleven. She was suddenly business-like. 'Quick, get dressed and take me home. I've no idea when Elroy's back.'

And everything became ordinary; a married couple getting dressed in a hurry. She never did finish that glass of whisky.

Outside the house where Elroy might be waiting, she turned and kissed him, swift, light. 'Thank you for the lift, Thomas. Oh, and thank you, you know, for saving my life. And Mum's the word.'

'Yes . . . We'll never know where those police cars were going.'
Back inside, she hugged herself.

And twelve hours later she was still doing it, hugging her body and its
happy secret, the secret that helped her come that night when she woke
from sleep with Elroy inside her, home from work, tense, exhausted,
desperate to lose himself in her body. She came without him touching
her, rose to his penis like a fish to the rod, swimming up, up through the
waters of the night where she had been dreaming of sex with Thomas.
And deep inside, his sperm joined Thomas's.

All that life, deep deep inside her. Shirley loved life. If it could only
live.

40 · Thomas

He drove back home through a city of props. The houses were scenery, shadowy, shallow. White pools of street-light waited for the actors.

Shirley and he had made love in a dream; it had nothing to do with before or after. He laughed aloud. Nothing made sense. Something so delicious, so undeserved.

She didn't make me suffer, or beg, or wait. She didn't even make me use a condom.

Jeanie always made him use a condom, though later he discovered she was on the pill. On the pill because she was unfaithful, and her lover was too selfish to use condoms.

God knows what I'd do if Shirley did get pregnant.

Maybe nothing. Just – not worry.

Maybe human beings are laughable, sitting in our offices, planning and worrying.

He realized he had parked too near the corner for safety. What the hell, he thought, I'm invulnerable, nothing is going to hurt me tonight. It was quarter to eleven; the moon still hung, white and expansive, overhead, trailing a halo of pearly cloud which fell away, as he looked, like a twist of pale scarf, leaving the planet calm and radiant.

Slipping his key into the outside Yale, he remembered, with a jolt, the yob and Melissa, slouched against the door, interrupted in a kiss.

Perhaps that will make her jealous, he thought. Then, don't be ridiculous, I was the jealous one.

The yob had looked – rough. Young and brutish. What things could he be doing to the lovely Melissa?

And her husky young voice, floating after him. 'Oh by the way, I've started your book –' Did she say she liked it, or had he misheard? Such a sensitive girl, such a sensitive woman. And she hadn't looked happy (did the yob mistreat her? Thomas would kill him if Melissa asked.)

Bounding upstairs feeling pleasantly superior, Thomas remembered he'd just fucked another woman and felt momentarily sheepish, because of course the one he wanted was Melissa, Melissa with her respect for his book and imminent appreciation of his greatness, Melissa of the sexy voice and large green eyes and heart-shaped face, Melissa with her wispy blond hair softening the collar of her leather jacket, Melissa the jogger, rosy on the pavement.

Was she upstairs now? Her hot little feet. He had always imagined her, mouse-feet, ballet-feet, skipping so lightly upon his ceiling. She appealed to his brain, his imagination.

But his body was drumming to a different beat.

His body had flared one nostril at the wind and made towards Shirley like a hunting dog, sniffing, eager, drooling with hunger.

When he was writing his book he completely forgot he had fangs and powerful hind-quarters. But when he was with Shirley, he was a dog. Panting with doggy happiness.

Thomas bounced around his living-room. It was here that he had her, here in this room . . . The pile of books on his desk had got knocked; half of them were splayed across his carpet. He started to pick them up, and close them. 'The postmodern utterance of "I love" was masked by citationality . . .'

Suddenly it seemed like portentous nonsense. I love, thought Thomas, I love. *I love.*

41 · Alfred

Everyone heard. The whole ward heard.

(They had always been such a close family. And Darren was his pride and joy.)

Alfred had started it. Not meaning to! By saying that Darren's writing was changing. True, in his view. But should have said nothing –

I'm just an old fool. I don't understand.

What a day it had been. With the terrible news that Alfred had had to cope with already –

Darren didn't mean it. He couldn't have done.

But Alfred knew his son had meant it.

At first Alfred had been overjoyed to see him. Darren came back, when everyone had gone, just when Alfred was starting to feel a bit down. Then suddenly, as if in a dream, Darren marched back in, on his own. It was nearly nine o'clock, so he only just made it.

'You've come back to see me. What about your dinner?'

'We cancelled it.'

'What about your plane?'

'We're not going.'

Joy turned to worry. 'But you've got to go back. You'll be late for work.'

'My work's not like that.'

But Alfred still fretted. 'This bother of mine – it's messing you about. You've got your life in America. I hope you're not letting anyone down.' It was one of his rules: *never let people down*.

'You're more important. We've decided to stay. I mean, I've hardly talked to you.'

Alfred hoped Darren wouldn't talk about the cancer, which he'd put aside, mentally, for the day. It was one of his knacks. He'd learned to be strong. If things upset you, put them out of your mind.

'I've been meaning to say, I've been enjoying your clippings. I read every one of them. Every word. I'm proud of you, lad. Very proud of you.'

'Thanks.'

'I sit down and read them, one by one –'

'I appreciate it, Dad. I really do.'

(He was smiling too much. That was television. They always ended up smiling too much.) '– But recently, they seem a bit different. Not all of them. Some of them.'

'Different good?'

'Well I don't know. You're top of the tree, goes without saying. But it's like, you're being more – sarcastic. Not saying what you think. Making jokes of things, like. I liked the pieces where you gave them hell. Laid down the law about right and wrong.'

Alfred saw at once that Darren wasn't happy. He wished he hadn't said a word, because he wasn't an expert, he knew he wasn't.

'Journalists don't lay down the law,' said Darren. He looked as though he could smell a bad smell.

'You used to, though. You gave them what for.'

There was a funny pause. Darren was biting his nails. Childish habit, biting your nails.

'You don't want to bite your nails, Darren.'

'I'm forty years old!' He exploded at his father. *'How dare you tell me not to bite my nails!'*

It gave Alfred a shock. A horrible shock. His son had never shouted at him. Not since Darren was a little boy. Or quite a big boy. Alfred sorted him out. Kept him in his place, as fathers must. Alfred tried to laugh. Make a joke of it. 'I didn't mean anything,' Alfred said. 'Just thinking of your television shows. You have to look your best. Don't you, son?'

Something funny was happening. Darren's face was very red. 'How dare you tell me about my writing? Who the hell cares what you think, any way? What business is it of yours, what I write?'

'Darren, boy – Darren, lad –' Alfred made an attempt to pat his arm, but Darren was waving both arms about. His voice was rising. And a nurse was looking, paused in mid-step, you could see she was worried.

'It's you who always laid down the law. You were the one who thought you were God. If I did write like that, it was your bloody fault –'

'But I liked your writing! I'm praising it! I always said, "Darren'll be a writer!" – Mind you, I thought it would be books.' At the mention of *books* Darren clenched his fists, it was like the paddies he had when he was little, and Alfred added, hurriedly, 'But newspapers are very good as well.'

He was doing his best to calm things down. But Darren had forgotten where they were, it was as if he'd forgotten how old he was and slipped back in time to his teenage days (which weren't very easy, now Alfred thought about it. He was a difficult boy. Too full of himself. Had to dress him down for his own good.)

'Nothing I did was ever good enough. You always criticized. You never let up – *If a thing's worth doing, it's worth doing properly*. I hear those bloody words in my sleep –'

'No need to swear. In front of ladies.' For Pamela was listening. And the nurse. Alfred never saw the need for bad language. 'It's done you no harm. You're rich – you're famous –' Alfred tried to find something kind to say. 'George Millington came round after you lot left. He was saying how everyone's heard of you. Not as my son. As . . . *a household name*. That was the actual phrase he used. Me and your mother are proud of you.'

'*Who the hell cares about George Fucking Millington?*'

It wasn't working. Darren was getting worse. His voice was going up, he was practically squeaking, it sounded as if his voice hadn't broken, and Alfred suddenly remembered Darren's temper, how he couldn't control it, and Alfred had to hit him –

Had to. Had to. What was I to do? He was a big lad. How can you control them? And Alfred had a temper of his own, as well.

'I don't write for the Millingtons. I don't write for you. You tried to run everything. You wrecked my life.'

It came bursting out. Was he almost crying? It gave Alfred a shock, to see him like that. He felt his whole insides turning over. And he'd had enough shocks already that day. I wrecked his life . . . What on earth does he mean? It was cruel, saying that. Alfred loved his son.

(How can he attack me, when I'm so ill?)

'I'm not very well,' Alfred reminded him. 'I shouldn't have upset you. I spoke out of turn. I don't really know a great deal about writing.'

'Never mind upset me. You *terrorized* me. You terrorized all of us. Have you forgotten?'

Why couldn't he leave it? Dragging things up. Raking over things that were best forgotten – Does he think I enjoyed it, being a father, being the one who had to keep them in order?

'Do you know that Dirk is practically a fascist? And do you know where he got it from?'

'That's bloomin' stupid. Are you calling me a fascist? I lived through a bloomin' war against the fascists –'

Then Alfred remembered losing control. He remembered hitting Darren as he lay on the ground, he had just called his father a 'little Hitler', he didn't know what he was saying, of course, but Alfred couldn't listen to something like that, we spent so many years hating Hitler, and then my own son –

My own dear son. For he was crying, now Alfred saw it clearly, dreadful to see the tears running down, what would they think, the watching women – he hauled himself up, using all his strength, stretched out his hand and squeezed his shoulder. 'Darren, my duck. Darren, Darren –'

So all his efforts had led to this.

He'd got things wrong, then. Done it wrong. He'd done his best, but got it wrong –

I never meant to. Does anyone?

'Everything all right, Mr White?' It was Staff Nurse Akalawu. Very pleasant. Though coloured. She seemed to be keeping a weather eye.

'Darren here is a bit upset. If you could leave us alone for a minute . . .'

'Just one minute, then I'm afraid he'll have to go.'

Darren pulled himself together. He had snot on his nose. He looked like he used to when he was a boy.

So I wasn't a good father. Perhaps it was true. Of course Dirk's a bit odd, and Shirley's had her problems, but Darren – I thought we'd got that part right.

Alfred bit his lip. How could you ever know? You just had to get on with it, there wasn't a textbook, you did the things you thought fathers had to do. And May never criticized, May backed me up, if I was so wrong, you'd think she would have said – 'Mum and I only wanted the best for you.'

'My life is a mess. I hate my life.'

'You're upset, Darren. You'll feel better in the morning. Go and get some air. Have a word with –' What's her name? How can I remember, if he keeps on marrying? '– your wife. She seemed a sensible girl.'

'It's nothing to do with my *fucking wife*.'

Darren stared at Alfred, furious, his jaw stuck forwards, his fists half-raised, but pulling his coat-sleeves over his hands, a peculiar gesture, trying to hide.

Alfred thought, I suppose he's embarrassed himself. But his son was still angry. Would go away angry. Alfred couldn't help feeling he was at fault. *He wants something from me, but I don't know what.*

'It isn't any good my saying sorry.' Alfred knew it wasn't. He wasn't one for sorrys. Best not to do things, if you're going to feel sorry.

But Darren's response was not what he expected. 'Well you *could* say sorry. It would be something.'

There was a long pause. Alfred was annoyed. Had Darren thought about his illness, one bit? Making a scene. Demanding things. Wanting him to crawl, with so many people listening.

But then he remembered Darren's tearful face, so like his face as a teenage boy. Those years had been awful, if Alfred was truthful. *For me as well. It was miserable. I never enjoyed it, being the dictator . . .*

How Alfred had longed to get out of the house, away from Darren's cheek, his sulks, his anger. He'd almost started to hate the kids. You couldn't say a word without somebody rowing. There was never any time alone with May . . . And in the end, it was her who mattered.

I escaped to the Park whenever I could. And later I forgot. We got over it, didn't we?

It seemed they hadn't, after all.

'I'm sorry, then . . . I am, Darren.' Alfred didn't find it easy. It caught in his throat. But he did mean it. Of course he was sorry. If he had faults, they should be pointed out. (But it wasn't fair to talk about *fascist*.)

'You've left it rather late to say it.'

They were Darren's parting words, shot over his shoulder. He didn't said goodbye, not properly, and his soles made an angry sound on the floor so he couldn't hear Alfred trying to speak, he was old and hoarse, his voice didn't carry – 'But what can I do, lad? To make things right?'

So Alfred just lay there. All shook up. The doctors had told him he ought to keep calm.

He'd never get to sleep, if he thought about Darren . . .

Or Dirk and his friends. His queer new friends. With their leather jackets, and crewcuts, and chains.

Fascist –

Nonsense. Put it out of your mind.

He had taken his pills, which were nothing, really, just tiny little things, but if they offered them, well . . . If May didn't know, she wouldn't worry.

And he was desperate for sleep, after Darren. He couldn't bear to lie awake, thinking about what the lad had said, wondering if his brain would kick or jiggle or fit or whatever it was they called it. Wondering if he would have an *event*.

(It was a funny word. He had known great events, he had stood in the street on VE day after the news came over the wireless, his heart bursting with happiness, and watched all the people flooding out, they didn't clock off, they just got their hats and ran into the streets to be together, out of the factories, out of the shops, all flushed, excited, with sparkly eyes . . . They looked so alike, to his recollection. Like one big family. It was glorious. The way his own family had never quite managed. Why did things never work out as planned?)

VE day, now, that was really an event. We were all together. All part of it.

But these new events were something quite different, something he couldn't understand, something that happened behind his back, as if life went on, but he was left out.

Darren's voice stabbed him as he tried to doze. *You wrecked my life.* Alfred winced and fretted. *You terrorized us.* The boy was upset.

Put it out of your mind.

But he couldn't, just yet.

Chatting to Thomas had been very pleasant. A nice young man, a decent sort. Bit of a perpetual student, maybe, bit of a dreamer, but a good heart. Pity the wife had run out on him. That was women, though. They liked men to be men. If you were too soft, they would trample on you. (Not May, of course. His lovely wife. May was a very feminine woman. He was still in love with her, forty-odd years on.)

I hope we make it to our golden wedding.

It had been agreeable, talking to Thomas. For an hour or so, he had forgotten it, the thing the doctors had told him today, the thing that was waiting at the bottom of the bed, the thing that was lurking inside his head . . . I was feeling pretty chipper, talking to Thomas.

Then Darren barged in and lost his rag.

Please let me sleep.

I need to sleep.

I took the bloody pills, I deserve to sleep.

They clanked so much, the bloomin' trolleys. And the swing-doors swinging and whooshing closed. And the low thunder of the air-conditioning, he'd never held with air-conditioning, or was it the heating, it was always too hot – It was never quiet, on the ward. And the voices of the nurses. *Sweet and low*. There had been a song once, *Sweet and low*, sweet and low when he was young . . . They were sometimes quite loud, to tell the truth, but he admired the nurses. Always patient. Always smiling. Even the coloured ones. Lots of them were coloured. That gave him a surprise, to see so many brown faces. But he had to be fair. They were as good as the white. Not that he'd tell the white girls that, he wouldn't dream of hurting their feelings . . . They were all good girls. A decent lot.

It was just that at night, he didn't want strangers.

His own bed, his own dear wife.

His eyes wandered restlessly across his blankets. That statue thing that Shirley had given him. A great disappointment, once unwrapped, which he'd finally done when they all went away. It looked marvellous in its packing. Shining, gleaming. A bottle of really special spirits, he'd guessed. Very nice at Christmas, or on his birthday. Cherry brandy, maybe, to which May was partial. It would glow like wealth on the front-room sideboard. But when he got the paper off, he saw the little figure.

Ugly little bugger, to his eyes, at least. What did she want to buy a thing like that for? A nonsense, really. Expensive rubbish. There never was a John Bull, that he knew of.

And I know my history. Most of it.

'Land of Hope and Glory.' Stuff and nonsense. We had it once. Hope, and glory. Now the British Empire doesn't exist. I never thought that day would come. In my own life-time, the end of the empire.

He reached out fretfully to push the thing away, but his arm was tired, his hand was heavy. He closed his eyes so he wouldn't see it. Just go to sleep and leave it be . . .

Then he jerked awake, and it was looking at him. False little smile, like a wicked little demon, a devil that had got inside his bed. Or inside his head. He had to get it out. He gathered his strength and lunged out towards it, to turn it round so he couldn't see its face, but without his glasses in the dim light he caught it clumsily, it span on its side, tottered, nearly fell, and he tried to steady it but only succeeded in pulling it towards him – it fell against the metal bedstead and then on the floor, with a sickening crash.

He thought of the woman next door's bare feet. Wandering around in the middle of the night.

Guilty, ashamed, he rang his bell, and the nurse came at once, tall, leaning forward as if she had lived her life in a hurry, a young coloured nurse who had bathed him this morning, though he'd told her he could manage alone –

But now he needed her again.

'I'm sorry to be a trouble,' he said. 'Got myself in a pickle, here.'

She had washed his back where he couldn't reach. Oddly enough, he hadn't felt ashamed. But now he did. That stupid toy . . . And he shouldn't have been fiddling around with it.

Now she would be doing his dirty work. May would have done it, if they'd been at home.

'What a shame,' the nurse said, in her low night voice, her low sweet voice, as she swept it up. 'Did the family bring it? Never mind, Mr White.'

But Alfred did mind being old, and clumsy, and the tall young woman crawling round at his feet . . .

He must have slept for an hour or two, for when he looked at his watch, it was three a.m. He would never wake at that time, at home. The bars of light that criss-crossed the ceiling were turned down for the night, to a kind of dead salmon, dead fish stretching from side to side.

His stomach was suddenly gripped with anxiety. Dread, dread, fear and dread. A horrible time to be awake.

His head felt funny. He didn't like to move in case he set it off, whatever might be coming, whatever horror was waiting for him. Blockages. Spreading. Pressure in his brain. There were funny feelings in his neck, his temples.

What he'd talked about to Thomas. Not a word of it was true. In Alfred's mind the Park had gone dark. As he saw it now, everything was black. All he could remember was horror. Horror.

They had burned down the bandstand. A smoking wreck. With thatch like that, it would have gone like a torch. Just the iron was left. Black, buckled.

Then the children's train. They'd poured petrol on it. The police worked it out after it was all over. When he was right over the other side of the Park, at lock-up time, closing the small gate on Leeson Road, they'd thrown lighted rags over the cemetery wall. He'd smelled something, then he'd heard the crackling, and come back at the double over the crown of the hill and saw it blazing, like a scene from a Western, the little train blazing orange and black. Soon there was only the black, and the mess, and the flecks of dark smut all over the Park.

The bigger lake, at the back of the café, which the council could never decide what to do with. It was a bit off the beaten track, but always a favourite spot, with Alfred. Once there had been irises, flags they used to call them, yellow or purple or a beautiful blue. And the grass kept short, and picnic tables. But it was a lot for the gardeners to look after, and then they cut down the number of gardeners, and if they had to skimp on anything, it made sense to do it in a part that didn't show.

When the grass got long, and the weeds well-established, and the seats and tables were half-rotted through, some clever bugger down at the council decided it could be a Nature Reserve.

Nature Reserve! They made him laugh!

But it suited him to have it overgrown. That way he could slip away on his own and have a quiet thought, when things weren't busy, a quiet sit on the rickety seat. There were always birds. Butterflies, lots of them, thick in the air once the nettles grew.

And frogs. He never took much notice of them. There had always been frogs, all over the Park, hopping like the snapping of a rubber band out from under his feet in odd damp places. They spawned in the lake, late February, March, and a few weeks later there'd be millions of tadders, flitting about like shooting-stars. People came and took spawn from the lake for their ponds, and there was so much of it, he turned a blind eye, though one day he'd had a horrible turn when he saw a plastic carrier hanging from the fence, and as he got closer it moved, it shook, and he thought *Dear God it must be a baby,* but when he brought himself to look inside, it was a bag of spawn and panicking frogs.

Then a few years ago – five, six? – something went funny with the spawn. They laid all right, mountains of it. It lay there glistening, and the frogs, worn out. But it never developed from full-stops to commas. The tadpoles never wriggled away. It lay in the water, and then it sank, and the eggs went white, and the water went milky, and then it darkened, it was black as black, and after a bit it started to stink. The next spring, the same thing happened. And the next.

He rang London Zoo, who were very nice, always very nice to a fellow professional. They told him it might be the ultra-violet. The ultra-violet in the sunlight. There was too much of it now, they said, and it was killing spawn all over the planet. 'They're like the canaries down the mine,' the man said, having a bit of a laugh with Alfred. 'They fall off the perch, and we'll be next.'

Then Darren wrote that article, months later, about human sperm counts going down. (Darren needn't worry; he had four children.) Thirty per cent since the war, he said. And sperm, after all, were very like tadpoles.

Are we dying, then? Shall we all die out?

Although *he* had to die, Alfred didn't want that. He wanted a world for his grandchildren. (Not that he knew them. They wouldn't remember him. That was a sadness, that they wouldn't remember him. And now it was supposed to be all his fault. His fault that Darren never brought them to see him.)

And what kind of world would be there for them? At three in the morning, everything felt poisoned.

Outside the hospital, vandals abroad. Every summer, usually twice a year, he'd find the café in the Park broken into. Smashed glass, splintered wood, ice-cream smeared everywhere. It was kids who shinned over the fence at night, and Alfred would find it on his morning round. The cheery despair of his mate in the café.

As if we couldn't stop them. Not any more. As if everything had gone too far.

(Dirk is a thug, and Darren hates me. *You wrecked my life.* Unfair, unfair.)

The things Alfred found. The things no one knew. The children would never understand, but the job was stressful, the job was hard. Was it surprising he sometimes let rip at home? –

Things he could no longer put out of his mind, as he lay awake under the queasy fluorescent.

A mass of blood and flesh in the bushes. He never decided what it was. Some poor girl, he thought, some poor girl – And they say there's never been a death in the Park.

He was proud of Shirley. She never did that.

But her child was lost, and that was their fault, lost to the family, Alfred's grandchild. And Shirley was different; she didn't bear a grudge. Surely she at least didn't bear a grudge. She would have brought the little one to see them . . .

He'd never told Shirley that he was sorry. Could never manage to get it out.

She wanted to keep it. We should have helped. I tried to talk to May, but she wouldn't have it. She said the neighbours would never let it drop, but I said to her 'May, stuff the neighbours.' I gave it up though. May knew best.

Sorry, Shirley. I'm sorry, my duck.

Once Alfred had dreamed that the child came back. He could see she was theirs. She looked just like Shirley.

42 · Dirk

Ran for it. Legged it. If I were caught . . . Once we heard the sirens, I ran like crazy.

If they told my dad, I knew it would kill him. Or he'd kill me. That was my only thought.

We all split, in different directions. Well, none of the others came with me. I ran off up the hill where I could see better, up the hill where the moon was very bright, dipping and weaving between the trees, but I didn't feel right, I was still bumping into things – Then down over the other side. I thought I'd shin over the gate on Leeson Road which isn't as high as the other one. But then I thought the police might come that way. Sounded like two or three cars, to me, the fucking racket they were making, I don't know what's gone wrong with the police, waking up decent people in their beds –

I remembered the graveyard. It's fucking enormous. No one would find me, if I hid in there.

I'd never go in there, not normally. I must have been well pissed to do it. I've always had a nasty feeling about dead people, as if they might come back to get me. Like wriggling up from their graves, half-rotten. Like in an old movie, only real –

(Maybe I'll be frightened of my dad for ever. Even when he's dead, I'll still be frightened – Not *frightened,* of course. He's a great dad. It said it on the card Mum gave him on Father's Day; *Thank you for being a Great Dad.* I don't think any of us kids remembered. I dunno why not, there were cards in the shop. I don't mean *scared,* but sort of – in his shadow. As if he might give me a piece of his mind. As if he might give me a slap on the head –

I couldn't wait to get out of that Park.)

It was damp and brambly and chilly, in the graveyard. A cat shot out and half-scared me to death. Fat black moggy, screeching and yowling as if I'd stuck a fag up its arse.

I will do, one day, 'cos it gave me a fright.

The sirens stopped dead. They had parked, somewhere. I heard them, shouting, over the hill, and a short-wave radio, blaring and crackling.

There was a low flat grave between two other ones as big as houses, Victorian jobs. This one was modern, it felt like marble, ice-cold, sort of shiny, slippery. If I lay right along it on my belly and poked my head a bit to the left I got a not-bad view of the Park. The voices went on, but no one came. After a bit, my neck got tired. I rested it on my arms for a moment . . .

Next thing I knew, it was already light. The birds were singing, it was deafening, like thousands of them on different notes, maybe millions of them in a fucking great choir, all singing down on me, endlessly, they were hiding in the trees, their little bird eyes, little glass eyes all staring and flickering, sharp little heads pecking out of the leaves, and the leaves were sharp too, pricking and shaking, so many points even I could never count them, and I was all on my own, in pain.

I was practically frozen to the fucking gravestone. My head felt as if it had been split with an axe. Whenever I moved, the pain rolled back. My eyes were golfballs, sticking out of their sockets. My tongue had glued itself to my mouth. Sort of furry glue. Gasping. Desperate.

I didn't want to live. I felt like death.

I got up like a fucking geriatric, sort of unbending myself bit by bit.

And I was cold, but the morning was warm. The sun was, like, blinding. The grass was shiny. The Park looked perfect, as if Dad had tidied it.

Dad's got cancer, was my first real thought.

Dad's got cancer. Dad's going to die.

And then I remembered about my job.

Then I remembered the football match.

Then I remembered how I got the brush-off from Darren and Shirley at the hospital.

Then I remembered the barney in the pub.

Then I remembered the fight in the Park.

It was like bombs bursting, one by one, one after another, inside my head. I was twitching and wincing. Every time I winced, the pain in my head got twice as bad. As if my brain was connected to my feelings. Which can't be true. Or maybe it is.

I wanted to cry. Then I didn't any more. I wasn't a wimp. I wasn't weak.

I looked across the Park. It was green and sort of – yes. Green as a table-tennis table. Greener. More like a snooker table. Blank and shining in the sunlight.

My dad's whole life had been spent in that Park . . .The hairs on my arms all stood on end. (Mind you, I was chilly, but that wasn't the reason.)

It was beautiful, yes, that was the word. It was beautiful, and it belonged to us. Like the pubs, and the shops, and the streets, and the graveyard. Our people built them, and – fought the war for them. The sun was so bright, I could hardly bear to look at it. Blurry and flashing, my eyes were watering –

If so it was fucking tears of courage. Tears of fucking courage, you snotty bastards, all of you bastards, laughing at me, Shirley and Darren and Mum and the teachers. I stood there, making a fucking vow (but I wanted to sit down, I needed my breakfast, I had to get Mum to wash my clothes, there was a long yellow tongue of sick down my jacket) –

I stood there and made a fucking vow.

No more running. No more retreats.

Stand and fight, now. Stand and die.

Crouched on top of the wall between the graveyard and the Park, Dirk looked at his watch. It was nine fifteen. Nine fifteen on Sunday morning. The sun was out; it felt warm as summer. The grass was wet, as if the world had been washed. It made him feel dirtier. Thirstier.

Normally Dad would have been doing his rounds.

Dirk wished he could see him. Walking at the double across the hill, in his flat cap, waving. Or waving at someone who was doing something wrong. He was fearless, Dad. He would tackle anybody. If Dad was there, everything would be all right.

Everything might have been all right.

But Dad wasn't there, and Dirk had a sudden horrible feeling he would never come back.

And at the very same moment he realized that he was perched on the wall like a thief or a mugger, and if Dad was there he would have blown his whistle, so Dirk dropped to the ground, the soft green ground, the English ground of Albion Park.

This morning, no one would have opened up.

And then he saw a little figure in the distance, a small dark figure in the very far distance, at the foot of the hill, walking between the trees. Dirk turned on his heel and began to make off towards Leeson Road, guiltily, hurriedly.

And then he thought, no, I've done nothing wrong. I made a vow not to run away. It was probably just a temporary Park Keeper, and Dirk could have a chat with him about his father. Dirk walked towards him, straightening his jacket and scratching at the long scab of sick as he went.

No, it definitely wasn't a policeman.

Was it one of the animals they'd chased last night? *They come here and try and walk on our faces. And that Paki, yesterday, laughing at me –*

How he hated them. How he hated himself. His filthy clothes, his disgusting mouth, tasting of sick and beer and decay.

I'll die if I have to go down the Job Shop. Queueing with all the losers and coloureds.

They took my job. They took my future.

'Fuck you, fuck you,' he said under his breath, then louder, angrier, 'Fuck you all!', aiming a sudden kick at a tree, kicking the tree and hurting his foot.

When he looked up again, the man wasn't there, and then he was there, but at a different angle, walking away from Dirk, past the playground, and then Dirk was sure that he wasn't white. *Fuck you, fuck you.* His heart began to beat. He stopped behind a tree and watched for a moment.

Dirk saw that the man was looking at him. He had stopped as well, and was looking at Dirk. It was too far away to see his expression. In the bright sun, his face looked blank and curiously pale, but he wasn't white, he couldn't be white, he was certainly a nigger or else a Paki, Dirk stared at him and saw Dinesh Patel, he saw his tormentor, he burned, he swelled, he shook with excitement, trembled with anger.

Fuck you, fuck you. I'll fuck you for this.

He followed the man between the trees. He kept on staring; Dirk stared back. Dirk saw he was making for the toilets.

I'll kill him, he thought. He was almost calm. I'll use my knife. My bayonet. Dad's knife, yes. The thing he gave me. The thing I took, because I'm his son. I'll stick it in him. Into the heart. I'll get rid of them all. I'll clean the Park. I'll show them they can't come barging in here, taking over everything, going where they feel like. Looking at me as if I was dirt –

Yet he still hadn't got a good view of his face.

Stopping and starting, they walked into the shade of the deeper cover around the toilets.

Then the man disappeared into the dark of the doorway. A pitch-black slit. You could see nothing inside. There was a smell of urine, strong, choking. The usual notice about Police Surveillance propped across the same smashed pane of glass. The place his dad could never sort out. The place Dad said was a disgrace, an eyesore –

Dirk stopped for a second. He caressed the knife. He had carried it since he was eighteen years old. It was part of his father's army kit. He had borrowed it – stolen it. Five years ago. There had been a row when Dad found it was missing. Dirk didn't give in. He had lied in Dad's face. And Dad lost his rag and got him by the throat and shook him till he could hardly stand, 'I'll get the truth out of you, you little bastard –' 'I never saw it. Mum must have had it – She probably chucked it in the bin.' And Dad's face fell, and he let him go.

He ran his finger over the blade.

Then pressed until the pain kissed him.

His heart was fast, thumping, tightening, jumping in his chest like a living thing.

The nigger had gone into the place Dirk hated.

Time to be brave. *Time to be a man.*

One hand on his jacket, Dirk followed him in, into the sharp foul stink of the dark.

Dirk could hear him somewhere, but he was blind. He stood there, choking, peering round him, terrified of what was to happen. What had to happen. Pumping, pumping. The dreadful pumping of his heart.

But something soft brushed against his shoulder and he leapt round, swearing, knife in hand, and saw him clearly; he was black, pitch-black, African black, as black as the toilets, and his face had a horrible soft sort of look, like he was a girl, like he was in love, and fucking hell, he was touching his cock, I don't believe it, his great black cock –

And Dirk felt a terrible excitement, something he wanted, something he needed, and '*Fuck* you, *fuck* you,' he panted, he moaned, and he felt his cock swell inside his trousers, and he slipped the knife gently out of his jacket and hit the bastard in the middle of his chest, the blade sliding in surprisingly easily, sticking it, jerking it, forcing it in, holding it there, screaming with panic, '*Fuck you, fuck you,*' for the body was too heavy, too big for him, he would bring Dirk down, and Dirk only let go when the blood pumped out, drenching, spurting, so much, so hot, was he human, then, must they both fucking drown –?

The man slid down the wall. He looked at Dirk. His mouth was half-open. His eyes were very white. He reached out a hand. The palm was pale.

Sobbing, vomiting, Dirk turned and ran.

It was nine forty-five on Sunday morning.

THE CHURCH

43 · Shirley and Elroy

The two bodies lay there together.

It was nine forty-five when Shirley woke up. For a little while she lay almost still, side by side with Elroy, staring up at the ceiling, then moved very slightly to feel his warmth, stretching luxuriously, silently. One of his arms was on top of the blanket; she slid hers against it. Smooth warm skin. White on black. But she didn't want to wake him. She got up quietly, pulled on a wrap.

The events of the day before were dream-like. She needed time on her own to think.

They were going to St John's at eleven o'clock. That meant leaving around ten thirty. Plenty of time. Shirley felt happy. She wandered downstairs and poured herself some milk, a large beaker, and sat down to drink it. She could see herself in a mirror on the wall. Pink and cream. Flushed with contentment. Her pupils very large and black.

She wriggled in her chair. *Two in one night.*

She hadn't heard Elroy come downstairs, barefoot, so she jumped slightly as he touched her shoulder, caressed her neck and the base of her skull underneath the curls which he liked so much.

'Hi Beautiful,' he said. 'Hi Curly-head.' Because of his one white grandmother, her curls weren't such a lot looser than his, but he liked their blondness against her pale skin.

She felt caught out with her secret thoughts. 'Elroy, love. I was going to bring you coffee –'

'And I was going to bring you breakfast in bed.'

'You've never brought me breakfast in bed!'

'Well a lot of things round here never happen before.'

A few more than you know about, she thought, but she kissed him lovingly, enjoyed his soft lips.

And in the middle of the kiss, as their mouths opened, as she felt the damp heat, she suddenly remembered her father was dying.

A stone. A cold stone. A heavy little stone.

'Sit on my lap,' he said to her, and she got up, docile, and the pain melted, at least for the moment, she sat on his lap, lowered her head and kissed his chest, naked under his open robe, firm and black and beautiful. 'You made me come,' she whispered. 'I loved the way you made me come.'

'Can't say I didn't try before,' he said, but he was smiling, blowing in her hair, nibbling a curl between his teeth. 'Time for another go this morning? Maybe not – we have to get to church –'

'There's plenty of time,' she said, smiling. 'I'm going back upstairs. I'll be waiting for you. And all I need is a cup of tea.'

'Shirley, love. I been thinking. The Temple give me a hard time about marrying, and you give me a hard time by not agreeing. But you know, I don't feel sinful with you. Because our souls join. Our souls join already. It says in the Bible, 'My soul hunger for you; my body long for you.''

She smiled at him. 'Too much Bible, Elroy.'

Sometimes she felt he kept the Bible for her, because they'd met in church, on her first visit to the Temple, and perhaps he thought she was better than she was . . . Idealized her. Which was nice, but tiring.

Certainly he thought she was better than she was, Shirley reflected, thinking of last night. And she almost ran upstairs to the bedroom, springing like a girl from step to step, feeling the joy of her breasts pulling, their weight bouncing slightly as she moved.

Perhaps it's because I nearly died . . .

Maybe I've become a different person.

She'd thought that nothing would ever change. Especially the family. The White family. Dad was so proud of their name: the Whites. It was the Whites this, and the Whites that – 'The Whites don't have debts . . . The Whites never beg . . . The Whites don't lie . . . The Whites have their pride . . . The White family sticks together . . .' (But we didn't, did we? I lost my daughter.)

And later Dad was always pushing me away because he couldn't stand Kojo or Elroy. That force of hatred like a wall. You could never break it down, you could never climb over –

Then suddenly Dad is at death's door and all the family are back together and Darren comes flying in from New York and Thomas Lovell appears from nowhere –

And here I lie, a scarlet woman, with sperm from two different men inside me.

But the stone came back, falling through her body. Hardest to bear was simple pity. Dad looked so small, so weak, so – human. Would they let her mother be with him, in the hospital? Or – would he come home? Her heart began to hammer. Would she have to help Mum look after him?

I ought, she thought. He looked after us. He came home every night. He paid the bills . . . He did his duty, by his lights.

Rubbish, she told herself, don't be so soft. Look at the harm that man has done. Mum is his slave, but I don't have to be. Look at his sons. What good are they?

She remembered Darren at Kojo's funeral. He'd had a few drinks and talked too much. 'Isn't it frightful, I have no black friends. I wish I had. You're very lucky.'

But most white people had no black friends.

Elroy, Elroy. Why can't Dad see? He should be glad his daughter's got a man like Elroy. Doesn't smoke, hardly drinks, has a job, is faithful – Shirley thought he was faithful. Though sometimes there were things

– a telephone number with a female name written beside it in his jacket pocket. A woman who rang, then rang off, suddenly. Certain jokes his two sisters made, though Shirley suspected them of wanting to hurt her. A passing look of concern in her direction from Winston when Elroy disappeared with a friend.

But Elroy was so serious about the Temple. Wasn't he? He couldn't be leading a double life, could he?

Was each of them idealizing the other? It had to be harder to know a person when it wasn't easy to know their family.

Hard to know Elroy's friends, as well. She felt they saw her as Elroy's white woman. They were nice to her, but there was some kind of distance that was only partly bridged by her sex.

But she did know Elroy was a caring man. His job was caring for other people. Patient Care Officers fixed things for patients that they were too ill to do themselves. He put up with their tantrums and complaints. How many men could do that job? She made jokes about it. 'Patient Care . . . that's what you give me, patient care.' And he did; he was almost too nice to her. Kojo was different, very confident, a joker. She and Kojo talked all the time. Whereas Elroy was often strong and silent.

It comes from how Elroy was at home. He had to look after his mother and sisters and little brother when his father vanished. He's had to be the responsible one. Only twenty-nine, but seems older than his years –

Lovely Elroy. He's still my toy-boy. I love the smell of him, the feel of him – I've always liked the maleness of men. Talking to my women friends I sometimes wonder – They talk about men as if they hate them, their breath, their wind, their penises. But hating people gives them no choice – what can they do, except be hateful?

Waiting for Elroy. Wet for him. Wanting him as I never have. Touching myself and thinking of Thomas, touching myself and thinking of Elroy . . .

He brought up the tray, but seeing her lying there, he put it down, came over and kissed her.

'Is this the land of milk and honey? What you doing to me, girl, you look so sexy –'

'I feel so sexy. Ooh, and you're hard.'

She had lain like that on purpose to arouse him, posed so the duvet pushed up her breasts, and she pulled him down, she held him fast, she held his warm springy head in her hands, she burrowed down and sucked his dark penis, enjoying its blackness against her pale fingers, she kissed and licked it till it bucked in her hand like a living thing, like a force of life, she weighed his heavy balls in her fingers, she told him she loved him, she worshipped him, and as she pulled him inside her she was almost coming, already coming from deep deep inside, and his slow firm thrusting made her come up, up, coming to him, coming to meet him, coming like honey from a dense dark comb, coming gold and white and wet and moaning as doves come thrumming from their warm dark dovecote, trembling, flurrying, flying into sunlight.

And then the two bodies lay together, slowly breathing in the warmth of the morning. The brown and the cream, the black and the rose, each curl of dark hair, each shining iris, each curve of the lid, each moving eyelash, intertwined in their living beauty.

They arrived at St John's at the last moment, took their hymn sheets from the matron on the door who recognized them and smiled automatically, a sweet smile but tired and thin. Very few black people used this church. Kojo had liked it partly because, as he said, it was so much quieter than black churches; 'I've had too much of the shouting and jerking.' They had attended quite regularly over the years, and lots of people knew Kojo by name, though she realized how imperfect the friendships were when so many of them greeted Elroy as Kojo. He put his arm lightly around her shoulders, accidentally winning a radiant smile from a middle-aged woman with a large red face and a knotted rope of long grey hair who sat on the end of the pew they chose.

Walking up the aisle, she had felt without pleasure heads turning, as they did everywhere except the poorer parts of London where mixed relationships were common, the parts of London where black people lived. In Hillesden, so many of the families were mixed. But in other places, people still noticed. One of the cruder responses had been yelled at them from a passing car only last week: 'Oi darling, why do you like doing it with black men?' There were three young white men straining at the windows, crewcut, thickset, leering and making disgusting gestures. Just too late, she thought of a response. 'Because black men aren't mannerless yobs,' she said. Whereas here in St John's – where all was acceptance, where communion was taken for 'Our brothers and sisters in Islam and in the Jewish faith', where the vicar always asked at the end of the service if there were any newcomers or foreign visitors, so all the congregation could applaud them – people were more likely to romanticize them.

On some occasions the glances were from women, envying her both men for their good looks. She knew that women who had never had a black man believed they might be better, sexier. As did white men. And it made them afraid.

Fear and envy of the black penis. That was at the bottom of it all. (Indeed Kojo joked that all white men were gay, they didn't really envy it, they wanted it.)

Maybe in heaven there would be no colour –

But on earth, since Kojo, love had been black. She was drawn to Elroy because of Kojo, although she always had to deny that to him, for he didn't want to be in Kojo's shadow, Kojo who was older, cleverer, richer – She reached out gently, touched Elroy's arm, and mouthed 'I love you. I do, you know,' and he whispered back, 'Skeen, it's *blatant*' which made her laugh aloud into a sudden silence, for the procession was just coming in.

The priest and his retinue of deacons and cantors and other Latin names she could never remember, but some of them women, long-haired white women, floated down the aisle in a cloud of white surplices.

Then the priest asked everyone to greet their neighbours, and a wave of shaking hands, of embraces, kisses, of smiles and touches and chatter and laughter swept through the church like a flock of bright birds, light-feathered birds sweeping in from the south, and everyone was lifted, they hovered in the light, everyone was part of the flock, flying, and it only died down reluctantly, slowly, when the priest raised his hands and called them to prayer, as if they didn't want to cease and be still, to sink back into their single wooden spaces, as if once people moved, once they moved together, the tide of good feeling would rise to the rafters and float the great church straight down Piccadilly and over Charing Cross to the golden Thames, as if the life in people was unstoppable –

But no: they were middle-class, they were docile. Shirley and Elroy settled down with the rest.

The hymns began. They were always long, and the choir were the only people who knew them, their thin clear voices sprinting ahead with the congregation trailing after. The tunes were modern, to be honest rather tuneless, and each hymn seemed to have at least a dozen verses. The church felt cold; she moved closer to Elroy. She was wishing they had gone to Elroy's church, somewhere where they could move and dance . . . But St John's had its points, she reminded herself.

It tried hard to be democratic; so everyone did something, one a prayer, one a reading. Though it did make the service a little long. The Order of Service was a printed sheet, and the questions and responses went dutifully on. Liturgy, thought Shirley, this is liturgy. The word was unpromising, like something legal, and yet the repetitions were comforting . . . She knew it wasn't right to sit and criticize.

I suppose this was written to hold us all together. Which is why we come here; to be together. We could pray, after all, on our own at home. But heaven could never be lots of separate houses.

Shirley had always liked the priest. The Reverend Stewart had a sense of humour. He was passionate and honest, he was big and handsome with thick silver hair, and Kojo had liked him. He was kind to her when Kojo died.

Today, though, her mind wandered during the sermon. He was talking about the City of God. She was stroking Elroy's hand, tracing the veins, the tree of blood underneath the skin.

Suddenly she felt from the tension in Elroy that he was listening in a different way. The Reverend Stewart was leaning forward, raising his voice, thundering: ' . . . recent bloody acts . . . disgraceful blot upon our city . . . These poor young people, pointlessly murdered . . . White and black is just a matter of skin . . . Remember the speech that Shakespeare gave to Shylock, the Jew, addressing Christians. "If you prick me, do I not bleed?"'

Shirley grimaced at Elroy, helpless. There had been a lot of killings in the last six months. The guilt she felt was always wretched and total: *My people are killing your people.*

Now she longed for this church service to be over, so the two of them could leave with their arms around each other, so she could be close to him, show him she cared.

She tried to concentrate on the sermon again. 'My image today is the Heavenly City. The image of a sacred place on a hill. This longing runs through so much religious writing. Sometimes it seems to be a paradise lost, a place to which we shall one day return. Sometimes it's the Garden of Eden . . . and the English love their gardens, don't they? I often feel it's our most attractive trait . . . The way towards the city is a pilgrimage, for Christians. We see it as a light in the future, stopping us from getting lost, drawing us onwards. Perhaps we are only meant to find that city after we die, but I don't believe so, do you? I think that Christians should be building it here. I think we can build the good place in our lives. I think we can build the city for others. I hope we are trying to build heaven on earth . . .' His voice was clear, carrying, triumphant, lifting his people, lifting them up – 'But when I read about this senseless violence. When I read about white killing black, I know how many miles we still have to go . . . I ask you to join with me in prayers today for all black people living in Britain.'

What a shame, Shirley thought, nearly all of us are white.

The church was very quiet after he stopped speaking. Now there was a time for silent prayer.

Shirley didn't kneel because her knees were unforgiving, she always sat with her head in her hands, and as she sat there staring at the cage of her fingers, the dark pink bars of her crossed fingers, Elroy reached out and took her right hand, peeled it away from the face it was protecting, pressed it to his lips, then held it tight, saying to her as clearly as he could, I love you, Shirley, it doesn't matter. Nothing can stop us being together. She looked across and smiled at him, then covered her face with the remaining hand.

The words came into her head, unchosen, slipped into her head like a patch of bright silk – *Bring us all to the golden city.*

At the end of the service, there were always announcements, and as person after person came up to the front and (with varying skill at the microphone) told the congregation about a workshop on 'God and autogenic training', or a seminar on Creation Chanting, or a Circle for Christian Cookery, Shirley's attention began to wander. The Reverend Stewart had bouts of coughing that Shirley suspected were not accidental.

It was after one o'clock when they finally spilled out of the church into the bright Sunday sunlight. The Reverend Stewart stood at the door, smiling at people and shaking hands. He greeted them particularly warmly. He seemed about to talk to Elroy, but a middle-aged woman with two straight plaits and a semi-transparent cheesecloth dress came bustling up and began to pour out a torrent of impassioned speech, before which he visibly flinched for a second, then returned to vertical, smiling staunchly, trying to keep his flock on the road, trying to keep their eyes on essentials.

It was dazzling after the dark of the church. The sky was the heavenly new blue of spring. It soared above the black vale of Piccadilly, to the bottom of which the sun could not reach, though people's heads and shoulders were up in the sunlight. The bright glass and metal of the passing cars pushing on down the deep straight gully made her think, suddenly, of knives.

'It's good that he talked about the killings,' she said.

'Maybe. Yes. I don't want to dwell on it.'

So Shirley walked along, worrying her worries, and Elroy withdrew into himself. And the congregation, the three hundred or so souls who had stood so close and embraced each other and prayed together for the City of God, trickled away into the crowds of Piccadilly, leaked away through the veins of the city, the real city, grey and dirty, thinning out, becoming lonely, threes and twos and single people, losing touch for another week, fading away into dryness, numbness, the never-ending chatter of electronic noise, the dust and heat of the underground. Because the embraces, the handshakes, the greetings, were never quite long enough to stick, never quite deep enough to bind them together. For the British were shy, and solitary, and did not want to embarrass each other –

The two of them wandered on down Piccadilly. They had five hours before the service at Elroy's church in the afternoon. Outside the great arches of the Royal Academy where crossed red flags saluted the day, little cliques of greyhound-legged women in hats and cheery-looking men in dark suits and ties hallooed above the traffic in fluting voices.

Elroy said, 'I went to an art gallery one time. I was curious, right. The Tate, I think it is, the one by the river –'

'That's nice. I don't think I've ever been there. Did you like it?'

'Nice pictures. And you don't have to pay. But – I never see any of the brethren all day. Except a few in uniform, working as attendants, and one or two women in the canteen.'

'Oh,' said Shirley. She wished she hadn't asked.

'And the British Library,' Elroy mused. 'One time I do some research on nineteenth-century hospitals. Beautiful place. Very quiet, very peaceful. But most of them sitting there studying is white.'

'I'm sorry, Elroy. But I've never been there – I don't suppose they'd let me in.'

'When we raise kids, it will be different for them. God does not despise His captive people. He rebuild the cities of Judah, Shirley, and the children of His servants will inherit it all.'

'Are you still so sure that we shall have kids?' Shirley stared at a bus, ploughing forward through the traffic towards them.

'Of course we raise kids. Long as we have faith. What if I make you pregnant last night?'

Briefly, Shirley's heart lifted with hope. Then they were plunged into the shadow of the bus, and the sound of the engine drowned their voices.

When it passed, Elroy was talking about his brother. 'I got to have another talk to Winston. Time that boy is settling down. Mum's only got one grandchild from us four kids.'

'He's busy studying,' said Shirley. 'Not a good time to have a baby. When I was studying –' Then she pulled up. She had never told Elroy about her daughter.

'Winston's nearly twenty, and he don't have a girlfriend.'

'Doesn't,' said Shirley automatically.

'No good for a man not to have no woman.'

'Well maybe that's not what he's looking for.' Yesterday's film had made Shirley even more certain of the thing that she had half-guessed at before – Why were the family so blind about it? His mother always talked about Winston getting married.

'A man's never too busy to be interested in women. The girls at that college aren't real women.'

'Oh come on, Elroy –' He could be impossible.

'A good woman settle Winston down. Maybe you can fix him up with someone. Do you know any good Christian women round his age?'

'He could meet them at the church, any time. If he wanted to, that is –'

'He don't even come to church regular. I don't know what it is with him.' Elroy had begun to sound fretful. 'Sometimes I think I'm a stranger to my brother.'

'But you two are so close,' she protested. They hugged and joked and fought a lot, a play-fighting Elroy always won, being nine years older and twenty pounds heavier. Elroy's kind of closeness was not about words.

'Skeen, Shirley, he's my little brother. I always look after him, since he is a baby. I'd kill anyone who hurt my brother. But he need a good woman to care for him.'

They had passed the Ritz, which was still asleep, and came to the air and light of Green Park, the leaves unfolding on the trees to their left, two children suddenly cutting across them in the middle of some chasing game, a deck-chair attendant rubbing his nose. He spat on the pavement. It lay in the sun. One of the boys was panicking, screaming –

Further down was the Sunday Art Market. Paintings hung in packed rows on the railings. The crowds thickened up, became a forest, and Shirley and Elroy's talk fragmented.

'What would you think –' Shirley began, as Elroy stared up at a painting of deer, hung slightly too high for them to see clearly, dun dappled bodies leaping, free (could she and Elroy ever live in the country?) 'What if, you know, Winston didn't like women?'

But Elroy couldn't, or wouldn't, understand her. 'We see him in church this afternoon. Now you start thinking of a woman for him.'

It wasn't her business, in any case. But what was it, she wondered, about black people and homosexuality? It was as if they thought only white men did it. Even Kojo, who was liberal about most things, had been very uneasy around gay men. She remembered Elroy's grimace of distaste as they walked down Regent Street one day and a flamboyantly handsome black man erupted out of Liberty's, laughing, his arm round the shoulders of a fat older white man with streaked blond hair and tiny dark glasses that made him look slightly piggish, admittedly. Elroy had winced with distaste as they passed, then said, when they were still within earshot, '*Cha*, look at that battyman! How much do you think Piggy's paying him?'

Did everyone have to despise someone?

'He's too young to be married,' she said, making peace. 'Let him get his degree. Then you'll all be proud.'

'First one in the family to go to university,' said Elroy. 'My mother going to be dancing with joy.'

They could hardly move in the press of people milling forward to see the paintings. Here she and Elroy were happily invisible. Some black-hooded Arab women pushed and exclaimed, three African girls in reds and oranges swooped and skittered like graceful flamingos, an American couple in small cotton sun-hats twanged and complained and stuck close to each other . . .

'There must be thousands of people here,' she said over her shoulder to Elroy.

'Lotta people like paintings,' he replied, 'long as they not shut away in museums.'

'If only all this lot would come to church. Imagine Piccadilly jammed solid like this, with people coming to the morning service.' She was joking, really, but Elroy lit up.

'One day they will. His Kingdom come. The revival's coming, Shirley. Must be. The Lord's not slow in keeping His promise . . .'

'I hope you're right.' She looked away.

'You people have little faith.' He said it with sudden bitterness.

'What's the matter, Elroy? You know I believe.'

'You people don't need to, though, not like we do . . . is just a luxury for you.'

'It isn't true. Jesus saved my life.'

There was a long silence; she could see he was sorry. When he spoke again, he had changed the subject. 'I just get vex when I think about Winston.'

She knew what he'd said was partly true. It was black people who read the Bible on the tube, black people, mostly, who drove the cars with 'Jesus Saves' stickers on the windows.

They need the Kingdom more, she thought, because they don't have enough on this earth.

She turned to Elroy without thinking about it, looked at the sun on his handsome face, severe and sculpted, not an ounce of soft flesh, and rested her head against his shoulder. 'You're a king to me, Elroy.'

'And you're my baby.'

And when they got home they made love again, with a blind concentration and hurry, then, as if death were stalking them, and time was short, but after they were finished they fell asleep, and woke an hour later in a panic race to fling their clothes on and drive to the Temple.

Two churches in one day. Can't do better than that. Perhaps I'll be forgiven for two men in one night –

They always met Elroy's family. at the Temple. They glanced quickly into the nave of the church, packed with people, as it was every Sunday, but no one was looking round for them, and Elroy's mother always did, glasses glinting, a deep frown in her forehead under tight grey-black coils of plaits, not relaxing until all her offspring were there.

'Must be upstairs, then,' Elroy said. On the stairs she felt his hand patting her buttocks.

The gallery was like the circle of a theatre. The warmth hit you first, a surprising warmth when the Temple itself was high and stone-built. It was the warmth of hundreds of bodies, the majority black, but a true mixture, brown, pink, olive, yellow, old and young, Chinese, Japanese, even a few Indian faces. The whites who were there did not look rich, wearing anoraks or faded coats, the women with gleaming un-made-up faces, a striking contrast to the chic and gloss of the young black women in the congregation. More women than men. Always more women. Perhaps they came to pray for the men. Or to pray for deliverance from the men?

Electric organ played softly in the background, sweet, faintly mournful, modern. And the sadness rose in Shirley again, she saw her father's small face on the pillow . . . Shaking herself free, she looked round for Elroy's family. Beside two empty spaces she suddenly saw Sophie, waving her arms, beaming, mouthing, her arms and legs always remarkably thin besides her bulky, comfortable body, Elroy's mother who had come over in the fifties to be a nurse, but ended up a cleaner. Almost from the start she had welcomed Shirley.

'Elroy! Come on! We waitin' for you.'

Winston wasn't there; that's what Shirley noticed first. The sisters were there, Viola and Delorice, Delorice clamped to her exquisitely dressed baby, a little girl in layers of ribboned peach frills, and Viola who managed the boutique in Kilburn, in a tight, waisted black suit and high lacquered hair glued flat to her head in sharp strands and kiss-curls. Delorice, the youngest, was rather shy, jobless since she had a screaming row with Viola because she brought the baby to work with her. Sophie had told the whole story to Elroy, gasping with laughter – 'Your sistas killin' me, Elroy! Viola get so miserable sometime, she done shout at Delorice dat she no havin' no stinky doo-doo in she shop . . .' Now the two sisters were devoted again but Viola wouldn't have her back in the shop. And Viola, as Shirley knew only too well, was in the process of divorcing a white man, a college lecturer. He had seemed adoring until they were married, 'the perfect man', as Viola said, but soon became unfaithful, then abusive, and finally horribly violent. 'He just a little dog,' Viola had told Shirley, rubbing her face in all the details, making her suffer because she was white too.

She still wasn't used to Viola and Delorice, their edge of resentment, their sass, their chill, the suspicion in their eyes when they looked at her, so different from the warmth of her African friends.

But Africans *were* different, as Kojo had explained in the long-ago days when Shirley knew nothing. Africa was very big and very old, and in some ways white people had barely touched it. Things were very different for Caribbeans, all of them descendants of slavery. Was it surprising if they hadn't forgotten?

'Shirley, darlin',' said Sophie, hugging her briskly with one thin black arm. 'We miss you las week, dear. Come sit by me. Go *way*, Elroy, you too big to be kissin' your mummy that way,' laughing, showing two gold teeth, one of which Elroy had recently paid for.

On the stage below, spot-lit, smiling, looking round the church with a contented air, were the usual group, the Reverend Lack in his 'casual smart' blue foam-backed blazer and knife-creased flannels, and on the chairs behind him, two other white men of around the same age, in safari suits worn over careful shirt and tie, plus Leah, a handsome middle-aged black woman, whose role in the service was mostly smiling, and praying, arms upraised, with statuesque dignity. On her right were the singers and musicians with their mikes, the sax glinting like a golden treble clef.

And then the Reverend Lack welcomed them, and the music came up, and the singing rose, and the half-dozen television monitors dotted around the church flickered into life, deep indigo, and upon them the words of the gospel songs began to lift them and move them together, as people started swaying, as people started clapping and smiling at each other, as a young mixed-race woman to one side started dancing, rhythmically, sensually, without the self-absorption of sex, her head held high, her face shining, smiling, her hands held up in celebration, and then at least half the congregation were dancing, and Shirley began to move as well, her hips loosening, slowly, and her stiff white shoulders, and Sophie's hand was tucked through her arm, she was at least five inches smaller than Shirley but when Sophie danced she bobbed up to her nose, singing in a pure, slightly cracked soprano, smiling and looking round in approval at what was happening elsewhere in the church, perhaps also to receive the approval of others, for church, Elroy said, was where she was happiest, where she felt accepted in this country at last. (But the Church of England hadn't made her welcome, the church she had hoped would be her home. A hurt from fifty years ago, never forgotten).

This singing, this dancing always touched Shirley deeply, the feeling that they were all together in a perfectly simple, bodily way, all of them equal in God and the music, jackets and coats coming off as they moved – *Let them praise His name with dancing, for the Lord takes delight in His people.*

Hard to believe, in that ringing temple, that black and white people feared each other.

They sang the refrains again and again, but they weren't like the

SHIRLEY AND ELROY 305

choruses they sang at St John's, a rigid tag after every verse. Here they sang words again because they were moved to, they sang them again to go with the feeling, *Let His grace . . . fall . . . here, Let His grace . . . fall . . . here,* and as they sang, she could feel grace falling, she felt grace fall upon her heart, upon her hands, which she lifted to the sky, upon her hopes, upon all their futures. Death would pass; it would pass away, and hatred, and prejudice, all pass away, for those who hated must surely get tired, lay down their heavy burden and rest, *For today . . . is the day . . . of the Latter Rain . . .*

Viola's hands were lifted as she danced, such elegant hands with glossy red nails and the rings her departing husband had given her, leaning towards the platform below, and she flashed a sudden smile across at Shirley, as if she saw what they were doing was absurd but wasn't it also something fine?

Shirley didn't like the Reverend Lack, for all his thick hair and easy smile. He was British, born in Kenya, as he often reminded them, probably the son of missionaries, but his inflections were American, and his style of preaching seemed learned, not natural. He won their attention with rhetorical tricks, with sudden dramatic raisings of his voice, with appeals to the congregation for assent and approval – 'Amen, brothers?' (though most of them were sisters) 'Amen, brothers?' until they gave him back an 'Amen', appeals that sometimes seemed unconfident but sometimes almost bullying, especially as he primed them for the offertory song, telling them God would bless the givers tenfold, practically promising their money back. It didn't seem right to pressure them so much, when so many of the congregation were poor, but the bag came round, a capacious bag, and Shirley slipped in a note, and tried not to think how much Elroy was giving.

Then the Reverend Lack continued. He had been given a word. 'Brothers, I have been given a word . . .' He was often given words, and would shout his words at the congregation, suddenly, emphatically, yelling them into the microphone, disconnected words he used like bullets, 'Order,' was one, 'Order, ORDER,' and 'Revival' was another, 'Revival, REVIVAL,' and he was saying Britain was ripe for revival, that revivals were beginning everywhere, that together they could carry the word across the land, but the words fell like shotgun pellets on her ears, she was still very tired from the night before, and her mind strayed away to Thomas and Elroy, *Order,* ORDER, *revival,* REVIVAL . . .

Then a police siren howling in the street outside brought her up with a start, completely awake, cold sweat on her forehead and her palms.

It was death she thought of then, and disorder. Sudden, brutal. The thief in the night. What if her father had died last night? (Was it right between them? Had they made it right? His last words were 'You're a good girl, Shirley.' Dad, she thought. I wish I had said – 'It's all right, Dad. It's all right, now. I know you tried. The rest doesn't matter.' *When it gets to the end, the rest doesn't matter.* She hadn't said it; she said it now, her lips moving slightly, talking to him, sending a message to her earthly father, because time seemed short, everything felt fragile.) What if that screaming police car had killed her? – Where were the police cars rushing off to?

Sophie was sitting, deaf to the sermon, writing requests for prayers on the green cards supplied for the purpose. She always completed at least a dozen cards, which sometimes seemed faintly comic to Shirley, as Sophie sat through the sermon oblivious, frowning with concentration as she wrote, putting on and then removing her glasses. It was as if she was determined to get value from the church, and the value, to her, was the prayers and the singing and the feeling that here at least she was at home. She had left her old home so long ago, and Britain hadn't given her what it had promised, but she kept on writing in her spidery hand; here she was at home again, here she was happy. Every Sunday she was welcomed, respected.

Now Elroy was whispering to his mother. 'Why Winston not here again?'

'I jus callin' Winston name to the Lord. He not come home again las night. I tink he got himself a girlfriend at las, now we have to pray she a good gyal, Elroy . . .'

'That boy deserve some licks for not letting you know.'

'You watch your mouth in church, Elroy King.'

The sermon continued, now louder, now softer, its peaks as deafening as Shirley's memories of Alfred shouting when she was little. The Reverend Lack leaned forward and thundered, 'For we have to be ready to fight, brothers and sisters. We shall have to fight for the souls of the people. Great times are coming, wonderful times, times of renewal, times of revival . . . We shall see again the glory days of the Welsh Revival of the 1920s. All of us will have to stand up and be counted. Then it will not be enough to drink, to come and drink of the waters of life. Every one of us will have to go forth. There will be a new Battle of Britain, brothers and sisters. A Battle of Britain. And we are His Army. This is the word I am given today. Amen? Amen . . . I give you a new Battle of Britain . . .'

He was flying at last, no longer awkward, alight with the fire of divine anger, eyes blazing, waving his hand, pointing his finger in a way she didn't like, reminding her of something from history – was it a picture of God the Father, pointing? An old-fashioned picture from her childhood Bible? On all the six monitors his image flashed, flaming down on them, arm raised, shouting, and everyone stared at him, transfixed, more than a thousand people listening, gripped – suddenly she realized why she didn't like it. It was from the past, but long before her childhood, something from history, unspeakable, and she felt ashamed for even thinking it, but his arm on the monitors rose and fell, his voice roared on, hypnotic, dramatic – He wasn't a priest, he was the German Führer, and they were the crowd at one of his rallies, she had seen a film of it only last week. Then she shook herself out of the illusion, blinked, and he was just a man again, the Reverend Lack in his foam-backed jacket, trying too hard to lift his audience.

She looked sideways at Elroy, but Elroy was listening with puzzled respect, nodding his head.

Did people really want battles, and wars? Shirley had had enough of them. Who would we be fighting? Atheists? Muslims? Men believed in battle, women did not (but a glimpse of Viola leaning forward in her seat, eyes gleaming, fists clenched, nodding and smiling, told Shirley she was wrong. Viola couldn't wait.)

The Reverend Lack was drawing to a close. Now there would be prayers, with the organ playing softly, everyone standing, hands raised to God, and the church officials would come among them and pray with those whom the spirit moved.

Shirley still found the behaviour of the congregation during the closing prayers astonishing. Some laughed hysterically, raising their eyes, clutching themselves, others were weeping, some sitting on the floor, some half-supported in the arms of officials, some shaking uncontrollably and moaning, but down at the front they were falling, crumpling, toppling as if they had been struck by lightning at the instant the hands of the ministers touched them.

Now the Reverend Lack asked the whole second row of the congregation to come on stage and receive a blessing. They came, and he touched them, one by one, and they fell like playing cards, falling in order, and lay there pole-axed while prayers and music continued around them.

(On one of Shirley's first visits to the Temple, a Malaysian official, ugly and kind with big brown eyes and the Pentecostal badge upon her shoulder, had come and offered to pray with her, and looking in her eyes Shirley saw similar suffering, felt a kindness that came from pain, and she fell, she yielded, she sank down before her, 'Thank Jesus, thank Jesus, for He is good,' fell, in truth, partly as a gift to the woman, but once she was down on the ground she felt puzzled – it was hard and uncomfortable; she couldn't get up.)

And yet it was a wonder, in its way, this scene of transformation, of ecstasy, it was what St John's could never quite manage, with everyone in fluid, passionate motion as the spirit rippled round the building like wind, blowing some over, raising some up, shivering the outstretched arms like corn, the organ still stirring softly underneath them.

Then Shirley's eyes fell on the back of the stage where the two church worthies had sat throughout, the middle-aged white men in their spruce light suits, beaming approvingly on Reverend Lack. Their smiles, their posture seemed suddenly wrong, as if they had set themselves apart. She looked again at the praying priest, and his prayer, to her, became false, grotesque, maybe because he was being filmed in close-up and the image flashed all over the church, repeated six times on the TV monitors which hung above them, powerful as crucifixes, surely too big, too loud, too many – she focused again on the two watching white men, leaning back in their chairs, relaxed, smiling, though the stage at their feet was covered with the fallen, a battlefield covered with helpless bodies, nearly all of them black, lying dead still –

So many dead bodies. Why were those two smiling? How could they sit there, comfortable?

It was only a moment, then the image faded, the Temple around her returned to itself, she knew, she believed it was a good place, if they had a fault it was only being greedy, and even their greed, she supposed, was for God – Sophie was happy, they made people happy –

Why should it seem any different today?

But what she had seen was a vision of hell, and she shivered convulsively, and turned to Elroy. 'Time to go.'

'You in a hurry?'

'I don't feel well.'

Then he was all concern, whispering something to his mother and shepherding her through the crowd and down the stairs.

In the air he held her and stared into her face. She felt as though he might read her secret, so intent were his pupils, cold and small in the daylight.

'You're shaking, woman. Is it the spirit?'

'I think I'm just tired,' Shirley said. 'I think I should go home to bed. Going to church twice – it is tiring.'

(Having two men, being full of them.

Seeing such visions of life and death. The bodies lying there, the white men watching.)

44 · Thomas

Melissa, Melissa! She likes my novel! She loved my novel! She couldn't put it down! A woman of such taste, such discernment –

He was very glad it was the novel she'd read. For some reason he went hot and cold all over at the thought of her seeing *Postmodernism*. Melissa was brisk, Melissa was busy – a busy young woman might think he was mad. But the novel, the novel! His first-born child!) She's only had it for forty-eight hours, and she's nearly finished it. Nearly finished! Melissa, my love!

But she's not my love. She's – a young professional, a working woman, a – flat-dweller, a householder, a tax-payer.

Oh breasts and lashes and lips and booties and scents of vanilla and musk and sweat – tenderness, slenderness, huskiness, oh, soon, soon, Melissa, please –

Oh hell.

I have to be calm and sensible. I have to be a responsible adult. Melissa trusts me. She's counting on me. She wants me to come into the classroom today. Wednesday morning. At twelve hours' notice.

A little knock on the door last night, I knew it was her, I could hardly speak –

'Yes?'

'It's Melissa. Are you very busy?'

I remembered the loutish boyfriend, in the hall, and tried not to smile too adoringly. But in only a second, all was resolved – 'Thank you for saving me, the other night. I was just getting rid of this dreadful man who turns up every so often and tries to borrow money –'

'Delighted to be of assistance,' I said.

'He used to be a boyfriend. I've picked some losers . . . And now, please, you've got to save my life –'

One of her colleagues had just phoned to say she was going down with flu. (Melissa used the word 'colleague' – so delightful. Two college girls in stripy scarves –)

Professional, professional.

I must be entirely professional. Her sick colleague taught the other Year 3 Class, or the other Year 4 Class, I wasn't listening. In any case, Melissa wondered –

If I could possibly –

If I would consider –

She didn't want to trouble me –

Yes, just ask me and I'll agree! Robbing a bank, arson, murder –

(Better not make any jokes about murder. George was looking solemn in the paper-shop this morning. The oik wasn't there, Shirley's little brother, maybe everyone round here's got flu – so he served me himself. Puffing and wheezing. And he said there'd been a murder. Didn't know the details. Very near here. 'Probably some mugger.'

'They haven't caught anyone?'

'Don't know. But the way they dress, all hoods and woolly hats, their own mothers couldn't tell them apart.'

Naturally George assumed the killer was black. I didn't have the energy to take it up – In any case, he was probably right.)

Melissa's request, when it came, was easy. Would I come into school and talk to the children? Her own class and the ill woman's. She wants me to talk about the history of writing. 'I know you could make it exciting for them. Some of them just don't see the point. They'd love to meet a real writer.'

A real writer. Yes, I am! Not a journalist like Darren. Not an advertising hack. Not just a librarian. *I actually write books.*

They've been working on Egypt. Ancient Egypt. She's told them I'm like an Egyptian scribe –

But I mustn't look out of date to these children. Don't want them to be bored before I even start.

Jeans? Orange shirt? Leather jacket?

But five minutes later Thomas caught a glimpse of himself in the harshly-lit bedroom mirror. He tried a smile. It wasn't any better. The orange shirt-collar made his teeth look gruesome. They were usually fairly white, he thought. (But Shirley hadn't complained, had she? When he smiled again, he looked all right.)

He poured milk on his cereal, for calcium, and drowned his tea with more of the same. As he ate, he flicked through the *History of Egypt* he'd hastily picked off the library shelves.

I'll tell them, writers are time-travellers. Sending messages from six thousand years ago –

There was a picture there of Thoth, god of writers. He looked physical, and active, with strong legs and body below the profile of a curious bird – physical, yes. Thomas wanted to be physical. If he did more fucking, would he write better books?

Ring Ring!

He jumped, and ran to the door.

It was Melissa, letting in a gust of fresh air.

'Hi,' she said, smiling, laughing. 'Are you ready to go?

'One moment,' he said, and ran off to clean his teeth.

He returned to see, with a jolt of horror, that she'd picked up a page of *Postmodernism*. She waved it at him cheerfully.

'I got all excited for a moment – thought it must be your new book. But it's someone else's, isn't it?' She read out a bit before he could stop her. 'This is so phony, it's about The Simpsons. "Hyper-irony, and the meaning of life . . . Simpsonian hyper-ironism is not a mask for an underlying moral commitment." Who wrote this stuff? He's so *up* himself.'

'Not me,' Thomas gabbled, and thank God, it wasn't. 'It's just, you know, a silly quote . . . you see, I got interested in, er . . . I got interested in the death of, uhn, meaning . . .'

But she had lost interest: she was smiling at him. 'You look terrific.'

'Not too scruffy?'

'Extremely smart.'

'I thought I'd better not embarrass you.'

And they stood and smiled, a mile of smiles, till they were embarrassed, in a pleasant way, and Thomas shocked himself by thinking, I shall drop that manuscript in the bin.

The school was a pile of blackened red brick, four storeys high. 'Hillesden Green Church of England School' was carved in relief in bold Victorian lettering. The building was solid, rectangular, capacious, with a stalwart look, as if it would survive. (It would probably have to; no money to replace it.) The decorative panels over the front door looked familiar.

'That's rather attractive,' he said, pointing.

'Yes, isn't it? Local builder. He did the hospital around the same time . . . and the Park Keeper's lodge in the Park, as well. Late nineteenth century. They took pride in these things.'

'Civic pride. Not any more.'

She shook her head. 'It's whatever's cheapest.'

And inside, the school did look badly run down, full of makeshift materials that hadn't aged well, yellowing plastic, buckled aluminium, paint in layers like peeling skin.

The children, however, looked in tip-top condition. They were leaving the playground in jostling lines. He was surprised by how many of the children were black, a mixture of Afro-Caribbean and Asian. Surely there were more black than white. 'You have a lot of children from the ethnic minorities,' he whispered to Melissa, who looked away. (What was wrong with 'ethnic'? He thought it was OK. But then, the words were always changing. Was it 'minorities' that annoyed her?) 'Such pretty girls,' he tried again, and this time she nodded at him, and smiled. There were tiny Asian girls with thick waterfalls of hair, West Indian girls with heads like flowers, covered with bobbing stamens of beads, all crowding in through the door from the playground, bright-eyed, bright-skinned, arms around each other.

Though most of the teachers he saw were white. Nearly all women; it must be the pay . . . None of them, of course, was as lovely as Melissa. He followed her reverently into the hall where her own giggling troupe was assembled, waiting.

'Thirty-three children,' she said to Thomas. 'That's three too many. Even thirty is big. And the classes keep growing.'

'Really?' he said. He wasn't listening. He was thinking to himself, if I'm a hit with her class, she'll think I'm good with children – Women love men who are good with children.

Melissa was starting to sound heated. 'Rich people send their kids to private schools, with ten or a dozen in a class, max –'

A new Melissa. Flushed, scornful.

'That's awful,' he said. (She was beautiful.) 'That colour really suits you,' he whispered. They were walking upstairs, following the dancing heads of the children, who kept turning round, staring at him.

'I'm trying to tell you something,' she said.

'Oh. Yes. Sorry,' he gabbled.

'Most of the teachers do their best. But everyone hates us. The government, the papers –'

He looked at her amazed, trotting beside him, sweet Melissa become fiery and forceful, green eyes staring straight ahead of her. 'I don't hate you,' he said, truthfully.

'Hillesden is a poor area. It matters what we do. Schools matter.'

'I know you're right,' he mumbled, embarrassed. 'Of course you're right. Schools, hospitals'. He knew he had to do better than that. If she wanted indignant, he'd give her indignant –

But Melissa had to brush her anger aside, to walk into the classroom and take another lesson, to think of the children's immediate needs. 'Sorry to go on about it,' she said suddenly, 'It's just that our school is so desperate for money,' then, 'Quietly, children,' as she opened the door, and to Thomas, in a last private aside, 'I get so *frustrated*.'

And then she blushed. And the children poured through, and pushed them apart.

'It's beautiful,' he said, coming into her classroom, *beautiful, beautiful*, yes, and *frustrated* . . .

She'd made a palace from a room like a jail. A shoal of coloured fish swung from the roof, all shapes and sizes, catching the sunlight, and the walls were a mosaic of brilliant paintings that all but obliterated their dull yellow. Close up, he saw they were strips of hieroglyphics, long fish-shaped eyes, crouched figures, bird-heads, and a gallery of half-human gods. By the long narrow window, larger than the others, Thoth, god of writers presided serenely, the head of an ibis on a muscular torso.

'Settle down,' she called. 'Settle down, children. This is Mr Lovell. He's a published writer –'

'Is he famous?' a girl asked.

She hesitated. 'Yes.'

He began to demur; Melissa quelled him with a look.

(This way they'll listen. Of course I'm famous.)

'When we've done the register, children, 4P are going to join us, and Mr Lovell will talk about writing.'

It was very impressive, her control over the class. She strode about her classroom like a captain on deck, cheerful, confident, not missing anything, straightening a tie, removing some sweets, comforting a little girl who was crying because she'd forgotten to bring back her homework.

He tried to look modestly down at the floor and not watch the curves of her slender back, bent over her register to make a mark. But she was so good at this, and he was so proud. The children's eyes followed her as if she was God.

'Samuel. Are you listening?'

'Yes, Miss Simons.'

'Adil?'

'Yes, miss.'

'Beena?'

'Yes, miss . . .'

And so it went on; thirty-three names, thirty-three children welcomed, calmed, and then the other class came in, and it was Thomas's turn to take the baton.

'Hello,' he said. 'I'm Thomas Lovell. Some of you will know me from the library. Do you write stories? Who would like to be a writer?'

And so they were away, and the time began to fly, the eager little faces turned up towards him, their hands growing up like mushroom stalks, nearly all thirsty, curious. It seemed they had never met a writer before. They stared at him as if he were an alien life form, especially once he told them he had been on TV.

He took them back to the beginning of writing. The first marks on the first surfaces, feeling his own mind reel a little, watching their faces, so new in time, alive for nine or ten years at most, gazing through him into pre-history, following him back to the first human settlements big enough to need to write things down.

'Please, sir.'

'Yes.' It was a tall black boy, who had been listening carefully, chewing a pink pencil.

'Where do words come from?'

Thomas was silenced. That was the mystery, where language came from. It was part of us. Born in us.

'I know! I know!' A girl shouted out, her hand so far up she was almost climbing up it.

'All right, Philippa,' Melissa said, resigned. 'Do you want to tell us where you think words come from?'

'Do they come from God?' the blond child asked, shining, shining with faith and enthusiasm. 'Cos God made the world.'

Melissa looked bemused, but Thomas nodded. 'You might be right,' he said, smiling. 'Writers don't know where their stories come from. They come like magic, in the middle of the night. I say magic, but you say God.'

Somewhat thrown off his stroke, but also encouraged, he took some chalk and wrote 'TIME TRAVEL', huge, squeaking and sliding across the chalk-board. 'Writing is a way of bringing people together,' he told them, feeling like a missionary, now. 'You can speak to people even after you're dead. Writing is a kind of time-travel.'

(But would it still work for the twenty-first century?)

'Do you know who Thoth is?' he asked them.

'Please, sir! Please, sir!' Nearly all the hands shot up at once.

'He's up on the wall.'

'Yes' – They all looked, as Thomas pointed. In the picture on the wall, Thoth's body turned towards them, but his proud bird's head gazed out across the world.

Everyone had something to say about Thoth.

'He's like half a bird.'

'Sometimes he's a monkey.'

'Sometimes he makes jokes, like a monkey.'

They offered so many things, but not quite the one he wanted, till a tall Asian girl said, 'The god of writing?'

'Yes,' he said. 'Very good. Well done. And he was a peace-maker, did you know? After Seth killed his brother Osiris, Thoth made peace between Seth and Osiris's son.'

'Please, sir!'

'Yes?'

It was a tall, round-faced Asian boy with multi-coloured glasses and a cheeky smile. 'When I kicked Christopher in the goolies, I had to write him a letter saying sorry.'

Everyone laughed, but Melissa nodded. 'It's school policy,' she said to Thomas. 'When they've upset someone, they write letters of apology.'

'There you are,' said Thomas, pleased. 'And did it make Christopher feel better?'

'No!' shouted Christopher from the back. 'It smelled of Shiram's pooey lunch.'

But a small fat red-headed boy had his hand up. He spoke very slowly, and everyone listened. 'I liked it when Praveena wrote me a letter because she always said I was fat.'

'Why did you like it?' Thomas led the witness.

'Because she had to miss her play-time.'

Praveena, a grave-looking girl by the window, saved him: 'I felt better too,' she said.

'Why?' Thomas smiled at her encouragingly.

Her answering smile was flushed and smug. 'Because Miss said my letter was good. I did a picture of Patrick on it.'

'It made me look fat though!' Patrick complained.

'Did *not*.'

He stuck his tongue out at her, and grinned round at the class. 'In any case, I frew her letter in the bin.'

'Praveena, Patrick, please,' said Melissa, but Thomas could see she was trying not to laugh.

He decided to quit while he was ahead. 'So remember: Thoth is a writer, disguised as a monkey, or a holy bird. And he's very pleased when you children write things, here in the classroom, under his picture.' And it did look to Thomas as though Thoth was smiling, his proud beak dipped in the edge of the sunlight.

'Every one of you can tell stories,' he told them, lifted by his own eloquence, especially now Melissa was smiling at him, approving of him, surely, her head on one side. 'Miss Simons tells me you're good at writing stories. Every one of you was born with that gift. Human beings live by telling stories.' But now he was losing them, their faces clouding over. Too abstract, he told himself, and tried again. 'It's how we make sense of things, telling stories.' A boy put up his hand.

'Please, sir, we aren't all good at stories. Me and Shiram are hopeless at stories.' More laughter. Melissa looked at Thomas, inviting him to deal with it.

'I bet you tell stories in the playground. I bet you tell stories to your friends. It's just that some people are shy of writing.'

'It's because Shiram can't spell,' said a voice from the back.

'No calling out,' said Melissa, swiftly. 'Put your hand up, Christopher.'

'Well that doesn't matter,' Thomas said. 'A lot of professional writers can't spell. There are people called editors who check your spelling.'

'So could I write a book?' the first boy said, a radiant smile transforming his face.

'I don't see why not,' said Thomas, cautiously. 'If you were prepared to sit still a lot and be very patient, and not give up.'

He had been talking long enough, he sensed, but at least half the class had their hands up with questions. The giant plastic clock on the wall ticked on. He was sweating profusely, with half an hour to go . . . *How does she manage to do this all day?*

'If we send you our stories that we write, will you publish them?' an Asian girl asked, self-possessed, pretty, serious.

'He isn't a publisher,' Melissa smiled, trying to protect him. But Thomas saw an opportunity.

'Have you got a computer in this classroom?'

'It's broken, sir,' several of them said.

'Please, sir, it did the spacing all wrong.'

'All right,' said Thomas, Father Christmas, 'if each of you would like to write a story, or choose the best story you ever wrote, and give it to Miss Simons, she can pass it to me and I'll –'

Suddenly he wasn't sure. How much was he letting himself in for here? He was used to working on his own, most evenings. But maybe, he thought, I've been too much alone. If I give up *Postmodernism*, I'll have more time –

Besides, Melissa was listening. 'Yes,' he said. 'I'll print them out. We can make a book. Miss Simons might help me.'

'Delighted,' she said, smiling, smiling.

He looked at his watch. 'Just one more question.'

'Please, sir –'

Then there was a lot of giggling.

'I can't hear you,' said Thomas. 'Go on.'

'Please, sir, please, sir. Praveena said to arks, are you Miss Simons's boyfriend?'

'Carly,' said Melissa, blushing deep red. 'And Praveena. Really. What a silly question.'

They clapped him with great enthusiasm, and she was ecstatic, outside on the stairs. He was almost sure that she wanted to kiss him. And absolutely sure that they would kiss, later, when three hundred children weren't streaming past on their way to eat popcorn in the playground.

'Come and have a cup of tea in the staff room.'

It was stuffy and small and smelled of stale biscuits, but he entered it like a homecoming hero. Not many people were in there yet. The *Hillesden Trumpeter* was lying on the table.

'This is Thomas Lovell, folks. From the library. And a famous writer, as I told my kids.'

After such a success, Thomas did feel quite famous. But only one person looked up from her marking, a harassed nod, a tired smile. They were only just keeping from going under. Writers weren't going to save them, here.

He picked up the *Trumpeter* while Melissa made tea. Perhaps there was a good film on at the local. Perhaps the two of them would go –

But the headline story stopped him in his tracks. This must be the murder George had mentioned. He sat and read, his high spirits disappearing.

MAN FOUND DEAD IN BRENT PRIZE PARK

45 · Alfred and May

'Read it to me, woman. I'm not stupid.'

'It will only upset you –'

'He'd be interested,' Pamela insisted, from the next bed. 'It shows him in a most flattering light.'

'He's not supposed to be upset,' May told her. 'He's *my* husband. Mind your own business.' She was never openly rude to people, but now she was cornered, defending her own.

Alfred pulled himself up from the pillow, red-faced. 'If it's about the Park, of course I must read it.'

May had come in to find him sleeping. That bloody Pamela was reading the paper. May touched his cheek; his eyes opened. He gazed at her, short-sighted, fond, coming back slowly from wherever he had been.

Then the parrot started squawking in the next bed. 'I say,' she called. 'Alfred, dear. You're famous. This is all about you.'

And quick as a flash, without conscious thought, May had reached out and palmed Alfred's glasses which were lying on the bedside table, slipping them safe in the pocket of her coat.

She had meant to keep it secret until he was better. When he was stronger, he would have to know. But now, thanks to Pamela, she couldn't protect him. He was all het up. Red-faced. Furious. He might have an event, right in front of her eyes, if she refused to do as he told her.

Pamela pushed the thing under her nose. Stumbling, nervous, May began to read.

MAN FOUND DEAD IN BRENT PRIZE PARK

A murder hunt is underway after a youth was found dead on Sunday morning following a suspected affray in Brent's prize-winning Albion Park . . .

She heard his sudden intake of breath. She saw his colour draining away. But she had to continue. What else could she do?

The man was named as Winston Franklin King, twenty, a Humanities student at London University.

Police are appealing for anyone with any information to come forward. Police spokesmen last night said they had 'no reason to believe' the crime had a racial motive.

Winston King's family were said to be 'distraught'. 'He was a good boy who worked hard and never got into trouble,' said his mother Mrs Sophie King, sixty-nine. 'We were hoping he was going to get married.'

'The next bit's not very nice,' said May. 'Then there's a nice bit about you.'

'Read it all, woman,' he gasped, impatient.

The lavatories at Victoria Park have for some time been under police surveillance because of suspected homosexual activity there. Alfred White, who had been Park Keeper for fifty-four years, suffered a stroke last month, and his post was vacant at the time of the murder.

'If Alf had been here this would never have happened,' commented local trader Mr Ash Khalik. 'Some of these kids get out of hand, but Alf knew how to handle them.'

A council spokesman refusing to comment on reports that Brent is about to abolish the post of Park Keeper in its latest cost-cutting exercise, pointed out this was the first major crime in the Park since it was opened a hundred years ago. 'Of course we all deeply regret this tragic event, but we are very proud of our stewardship of the Park. Last summer we won the Steve Biko Bowl in the All-London Floral Displays Competition.'

She laid down the paper on the bed and looked at him, full of apprehension. 'I'm sorry, love,' she said. 'I didn't want to read it.'

'You read it too fast,' said Pamela. 'You have to learn about pace, and diction.'

May ignored her; hardly heard her. The last few weeks had been the worst in her life. A great lump of dread had settled in her throat. Since Dirk came home on Sunday morning she could not think, or sleep, or swallow.

'Murder,' said Alfred, slowly, hoarse. 'Murder in the Park. I don't believe it.'

'It had to happen one day,' said May. She had no idea what to say to him. He wasn't listening, in any case. Pamela was, though, blue-lidded, avid. May got up abruptly and drew the curtains round the bed, whipping the green stripes across the old woman's face, rattling the curtain rings in rapid fury.

'It's my fault, isn't it?' Alfred said. 'If I hadn't got sick, this would never have happened. If I'd stayed at my post. But I got sick.'

'Of course it's not your fault,' said May. 'The council should have got someone temporary.' She held his hand. It felt small and cold. He didn't see her. He looked shocked, wounded.

'I've got to have my glasses. I must read it myself.'

'There they are,' said May, and by turning her body she managed to shuffle them back on to his table. He put them on. He looked very old. He took the paper, and began to read, moving his lips slightly, as he always did, and it usually annoyed her, but today it meant nothing, for her world was tearing, breaking apart.

Dirk, she thought.

Fear; horror.

'So they're thinking of getting rid of my job.'

'It's just a rumour. You can't believe the papers . . .'

She tried to sound normal, but she sounded mad.

'It's all my fault. I should be back at work.'

'Course you shouldn't. Course you can't.'

But as she watched, he struggled out of the envelope of sheets and blankets, one leg, the other leg, and sat undecided on the edge of the bed. Then he looked at her. Her eyes were full of tears.

'Please don't, Alfred. Please don't. *Please*. You'll kill yourself. I knew it would upset you.'

'Trouble is, no one's told them I'm coming back,' he said. 'That must be it. It's a misunderstanding. I thought I would let them do a few more tests. But now I'd better get back straightaway.'

'Alfred,' she said. 'Get back in bed. I'll call Sister if you don't.' Then the tears began to flood; she could not stop them.

'You're crying, May. Don't take on.'

'It's worse than you think.' She was whispering. He held on to the blankets, swaying, uncertain.

'What do you mean? How could it be?'

'It's Dirk,' she said.

'What about him? George said there would still be a job for him. If he plays his cards right with the Asian chappy —' They looked at each other. He was making an effort.

'No,' she said. 'No, it's not that. Something worse. Something so dreadful . . . I can't tell you. I can't, Alfred.'

'You'll have to tell me.'

She sat a long time. He leant back on the pillow. Slowly, he swung his legs back up on the bed. She covered him, tenderly. Was he getting thinner? His shins felt sharp beneath the cotton. They both waited. Then she began.

'Are we in this together?' she asked him, very quietly. 'The family's what matters, isn't it, Alfred?'

'What do you mean? Of course it is.'

'Yes, but it matters more than anything? Anything at all?'

'Yes, yes.' He didn't understand. 'Get on with it.'

'Dirk . . . the child.' He had always been the child. 'He didn't come in on Saturday night.'

'What? I can't hear you –'

She could hardly get it out; she was sobbing with terror. '*He came in Sunday morning, at half eleven.*'

'Well that's happened before. He got drunk again.'

'He was covered with blood. *He was covered with blood.*' It was a whispered scream, a terrible sound, and she clutched at her own hair, as she said it, her thin white hair, she would tear it out –

'Fighting?'

'Alfred. His jacket was soaked. *His jacket was soaked with blood. And his shirt.*'

She saw understanding, then disbelief, then helpless horror cross his face. His jaw worked, but nothing came out. He cleared his throat, tearing, grinding.

'You think – it was him. You think – he did it.' He was shaking his head, as he spoke, refusing, shaking his head against the dark. 'Of course it wasn't. You stupid woman.'

'Alfred, Alfred –' She had nothing to say. He looked at her. They looked at each other. When he spoke again, his voice was stronger. 'Did you tell the lad to go to the police? So they could clear him . . . explain himself.'

'He's my son, Alfred. *He's our son.*'

'*May, this was days and days ago.*'

'He never said a word, Alfred. Just stripped off his clothes and went to bed. I was frightened, Alfred. I was afraid.'

(He would never understand how she was afraid.)

'But what did you do? What did you say?'

'He'd put them in a plastic bag. I soaked them all in salty water. It's the only way you get blood out –'

'You've a duty,' he said. 'You've a public duty.'

'I'm his mother,' she said, and she looked him in the eye. 'I gave birth to him. I'll never do it.'

Just then, the curtains were tentatively drawn, and the smiling black face of a nurse looked in. 'I've got to do your blood pressure and temperature, Alfred,' she said. 'Good afternoon, Mrs White. How are you today?'

'A bit upset.' May tried to smile. Would she guess something? But of course, tears were normal in their situation.

'Would you like to have another talk to Doctor?'

'Not just now. Thank you, dear.'

Once the blood pressure was done, the nurse automatically drew back the curtains, so they could no longer talk in private.

They didn't talk at all, in fact. They sat there, shaken, their glances sometimes meeting, mostly not, miles apart. Pamela, next door, had gone to sleep, head propped on a book, like a painted wax-work.

Or else she was dead. They were all dying, here.

Was it so terrible, then? One more dead person?

How could Alfred be so sure that it mattered?

'He was black,' May whispered, after a long while. 'Did you see. The man that died . . . He was black.'

'Doesn't make any difference.'

'He was black, Alfred. You could never stand them.' She knew what she was saying. She didn't care. It was family that mattered. 'You agreed, remember. Family comes first.' He looked at her remotely. 'Blood's thicker than water,' May insisted.

But he said nothing, no longer listening.

'He did it, didn't he. My fault,' he moaned. 'I am the Park Keeper. I am the Park Keeper. My fault, May. I left my post.'

They sat there quietly as it grew darker, as the shadows lengthened down the ward, as the lights flickered on and pinned them to their places, smaller than before, pale, stunned.

46 · Alfred and the Africans

That night was the longest of Alfred's life. He could not sleep: he had refused the tablets. He had to think. He had to plan. He remembered the night when he was demobbed, the night he came home to his mother's house and sat up on the sofa all night long, unable to believe he had gone off duty, unable to believe the long fight was over.

Now he was on active service again.

It wasn't hard getting off the ward. The agency nurse was talking on the phone, as she always did, nineteen to a dozen, but who could she be talking to, before six a.m.? Probably another continent, he thought. And the National Health would be paying for it. He slipped past her like a ghost, invisible, his old army greatcoat covering his pyjamas.

He was clear in his mind; completely clear. He knew he couldn't risk putting all his clothes on, standing there fussing and mucking about. Even that lazy cow would have noticed. But he had to wear something to inspire respect, so he'd knotted his tie, his old army tie which he'd found in the pocket of his army greatcoat, in the neck of his pyjama jacket.

It was nothing to him, being up at this hour. All his life, he had been up at this hour. Staying in bed was a penance, to him. But the greatcoat felt heavy, after light pyjamas, and his feet felt enormous, blockish, in boots. It wasn't a bad feeling, though. It felt – more real. Tied him to the ground, like a real living person, not floating about like a bloomin' water-lily.

He stared at his feet. He watched them go.

I need you, boys. Go for it.

He remembered the Arabs, in Palestine. At pilgrimage time, the time of the haj. You would see them coming in the distance, and the first thing you'd notice was the size of their feet, great huge feet like kangaroos, because they used to bind 'em up with blankets. They didn't have boots, or else they didn't believe in them . . . Weird beliefs. They weren't really human. They'd walk thousands of miles to worship God. You had to hand it to them, looking back, though it struck him as comic, at the time, these little figures with enormous plates-of-meat, plodding like donkeys across the desert. Never giving up, though some must have snuffed it, with the shooting and dirt and exhaustion and flies, and sometimes he'd heard their feet went septic. It didn't matter. They were – *pure spirit*. Spirit kept you going when the body failed.

For the past three weeks, the most exercise he'd got was the walk down the ward from his bed to the lav, but he'd walked all his life, and you didn't lose that. It would stand him in good stead, now he needed it.

Going downstairs he felt almost young, trotting neatly, swiftly, down, as usual, for he prided himself on never walking on stairs. There was no one about. It was a ghost hospital.

Turning into the immense modern foyer built at huge expense not so long ago, he found only a cardboard, hand-lettered notice: Reception Closed After Nine p.m.

So that was a bonus. He had made it to the door. Automatically, sweetly, it opened for him, and Alfred tramped out into the freezing air, but fresh, so fresh after the air inside, the air he loved, the air of London, with the faint green edge that spoke of the Park, not far away, his place, his home . . .

He tried to straighten up. He was on a mission. *Carrying essential information.*

He was walking through familiar country now, not enemy country, his own dear land, but he knew that he was in very great danger, perhaps the worst danger he had ever known. There were enemies everywhere, hiding, dodging, nurses, doctors, treacherous women.

Maybe he had enemies now at Brent council. Enemies, now, among his own men.

And then there was the enemy within. The queer changes within his own body. The false cells creeping, weakening him (but he would not weaken; he would never weaken. He'd keep going by willpower till his mission was done.)

In any case, he needn't believe the doctors. Perhaps they had said it to bring him down. Black propaganda, he told himself. Alfred wasn't born yesterday.

He went straight as a die down All Souls' Road. The street-lights were still on, but the sky was flecked with pink, the sky, he thought, he was back beneath the sky, the sky he had lived under most of his life, back outside, where a man should be, it was no kind of life, cooped up inside, he could never have worked all his life in an office –

So must I die in a hospital?

No, he thought, I'm going home.

I've had a good life. A life in the open. I have been lucky. I can't complain . . .

These streets hadn't changed since he was a boy, the little terraces, neat and tidy, six or eight of them joined together, sometimes a whole long street of houses, sleeping, now, dark, immobile, the line of the roofs like a long low backbone. We're tough, round here, he thought, we survive. We've lived through a lot, the people of Hillesden. Those of us who made it through the war. Those of us who stayed the course.

Here was the pub they always drank in. Always known it, since he was sixteen. He and George still went to the Admiral Nelson of an evening. And every Sunday while the lunch was cooking. It had been modernized badly, ten years ago, a box-like, ugly front added on and a glaring plastic sign, which had bust, only lasted three weeks or so before it bust, but the two of them kept on drinking there, it was people that mattered, not bloomin' designers. Wankers. Nancy-boys. What did they know? And underneath, you could see the old building, the old red brick of it wearing through.

He stood and watched, briefly, as the light increased. Remembering, remembering. He and George. So many good evenings. Would he ever walk in through the door again, cheerful, mouth watering for the cool of the beer, his week's work done, money in his pocket? Thank you, he thought, my friends, mine host. Thank you for standing at the bar with me. (For when all's said and done, a man needed friends, and however much he loved her, May was a woman.) *Goodnight, all. Toodle-oo, goodbye.*

But he mustn't hang about. He had to get on. It was harder than before, getting started again, as if his limbs had lost some essential information, as if the morning air had grown colder, as if part of his lungs was dead, frozen . . . But of course it was cold, out here in the desert, what did they expect, what was the point of moaning, had they forgotten the blaze of midday in Palestine, when the sun was highest, when they were young, in the bright blue heat, the lords of creation – had they forgotten the larks, the fun? If he paid for it now, he would never complain.

(Poor Dirk, he thought, poor boy, poor child, he never played sport, never fought, never travelled – never had a girlfriend, or a decent job . . . The young today, there was nothing for them. And the other lad, too. He was only twenty. And his name was Winston, like Winston Churchill. *My fault, my fault.* But he had to keep going.)

The houses he was passing were about as old as he was, 1920s, 1930s, the same three windows, the same front door, the little side window with modest stained glass – a bit fussy, he'd thought, when he and May bought theirs, a bit old-womanish, though May had liked it, and he had replaced the door with aluminium, and later regretted it, but never said so – never admitted as much to May.

I'm sorry, May, he thought, suddenly. For all the times I never said sorry. I am a proud man. It doesn't come easy.

I'm sorry, May. I shall cause you grief. All our life together, I've caused you grief, though sometimes I think I made you happy – Sometimes I know I made you happy. But now I have to cause you grief.

And a quiet voice, May's voice, spoke in his ear. Please, Alfred. If you love me at all. Don't be pig-headed. You were always pig-headed. You don't have to do this, Alfred, please.

But he brushed her aside; he kept on walking, though one of his feet had begun to drag, he was picking them up at the old steady pace but parts of his body weren't quite working. It didn't matter. Most of him was. He kept on going as the sun rose.

Because in the end, there's right and wrong. He argued with her; she had to understand. You and I don't matter (she mattered so much. Nothing mattered as much as his own dear wife. His own dear woman.) But you see, we're just little . . . We'll die, in the end, and the mess will be left. I must do my best.

It rose above the houses, glorious, a ball of fire, a ball of red. So bright, so strong, how do we bear it? All that glory over our heads. He kept a weather eye for enemy planes, but the ones that streaked over this morning hadn't seen him, they curved round steeply into the dawn, ploughing a track of fine pink foam.

I always meant to take May on a plane. Now I suppose I shan't manage it. May deserved to fly on a plane.

He'd been walking, for a bit, on automatic pilot, so it was with a surge of shock and sorrow that he realized he was limping down his own road, the long narrow road to his own dear home, and there it was, in the first rays of the sun, sleeping, still, but touched with gold, its rough white walls, the pale pebble-dash he'd put on to cover the faults in the brickwork, the curtains closed, and hidden behind them . . .

She would be sleeping. She would be there, curled on her left side, rosy, comfy. Not fifty yards away, now, not thirty . . .

And the boy. His boy. The child. His child. His youngest child, whose life had gone wrong. I'm sorry, Dirk, he thought, I'm sorry.

Ten yards. Five. The gate was half-open, why couldn't they shut it, the dogs would get in? He laid his hand on the iron of his gate, his own front gate, and he felt the cold, the cold came shuddering through to his bones, in the early light he was blue with cold, his old man's hand with the raised blue veins, and the whitewashed body of the house still beckoned, how warm it would be, how welcoming, how easy just to walk up the path and ring on the door and slip inside, and no harm would be done, he would have harmed no one –

Quick march, he told himself. At the double. He pushed the gate shut, to keep them safe.

Now every step had become an effort, every step was an effort of will. Not far now. At most, a mile. Around him, the world was waking up, curtains were twitching, the postman passed him, gave him a smile that he tried to return, if he'd had the strength Alfred would have saluted, both of them were servants of the people, both of them took pride in their uniform – and then he remembered, the uniform was gone, gone years ago. He stood there in pyjamas. It didn't matter. His greatcoat protected him. He wandered on, feeling his step become more ragged, one of his boots was bothering him, rubbing at his ankle, the rats gnawing, he kicked at them to scare them away and nearly fell, *Get on with it, man* –

He saw the building at the end of the road. It was a big modern station like an army barracks. The officers he had to reach were in there. *Carrying essential information* . . . They were good men, good men and true, they would come to the Park whenever he called them.

Then he saw the enemy come out into the daylight, three or four of them, between him and his goal. He knew better than to think he was in any state to fight them, so he'd have to use cunning. His mouth was dry. They would see at once where he was going – He was much too old. He'd been in civvies too long. But he wouldn't give up. They would have to kill him. And if they did, he was ready to die.

It took a very long time to get close to them. He realized they were moving much faster than him, but speed wasn't everything, staying-power counted.

Three of them. Young. African. Big! And he drew himself up, he tried to look jaunty, he even tried to whistle a bar of 'Colonel Bogey', but he didn't have any air in his chest – He suddenly felt he might fall on the floor, fall where he was and lie on the pavement, but it loomed behind them, the police station, huge, monumental, his goal, his rock, and he would not yield, he would stay on his feet –

He would stay on his feet. They would cut him down.

'Hey, man,' said one of them, 'wicked trousers!'

The enemy were looking at his pyjamas.

They were laughing, but it didn't seem unfriendly.

He saw something else; they were just children. They were giant teenagers, gleaming black. One of them had an enormous hat. One of them was smoking, with overdone gestures, blowing great clouds of it into the wind. She had bits of shining glass in her hair, like the beads May put in Shirley's Christmas stocking . . . How glad he had been to have a daughter. He hoped he had done right by her . . .

Sorry, Shirley. Sorry, love.

Then the boy who spoke first bent close to him. 'You all right, man? You don't look good.'

Alfred pointed, mutely, to the police station. This was all a dream, or perhaps a disguise, he was probably a fool to trust them, but he suddenly knew he couldn't do it on his own, his knees were buckling, and he let them help him, a wounded soldier, up the steps, never quite collapsing, in through the door, across to the counter, leaning on their arms (so they weren't the enemy, he'd just got confused), and he pressed the bell with the last of his strength, and his helpers disappeared like smoke.

The policemen were lurking behind a glass wall that protected them, he guessed, from loonies. Too many of them about, these days, wandering the streets, sitting on benches. He waved, authoritatively, at the policemen. They would recognize him straightaway, of course; he had often had to call them to the Park, in summer, when people got nasty.

But they couldn't seem to see him, now, in a different place, in different clothes. They were drinking mugs of coffee and smiling a lot, smiling at him, not particularly kindly. Then one of them waved back, rather a silly wave, and twirled his finger near his forehead.

After a very long time, someone came over. But when Alfred said, 'It's about the murder. About the murder in Victoria Park. Bringing information. I have information,' his silly smile died, he began to look grave, he helped Alfred into an interview room, and Alfred knew his last mission was accomplished.

'It's my fault,' he started, 'all my fault. I am the Park Keeper. I was the Park Keeper . . . What I have to tell you concerns my son.'

Now he must stand in the dock alone.

May, he thought. May. Forgive me.
And you, Mr King. The murdered man.
But Alfred could not imagine him.
Only his blood, flooding, darkening.

White, terrified, the face of his son.

Everything, now, would be put in motion, nothing could be stopped, nothing could be hidden –
Alfred took the stand alone.

47 · Elroy

No . . . Grave . . . Shall Hold His Body Down . . .

> *The message come, and summon me home*
> *Is the hand of the Devil*
> *Is Satan work*

> *Lord, I am saved, why do You forsake me?*
> *Awake, and rise to my defence . . .*

What have I done? What have we done? I go to church, I pay my tithe . . .
Ten per cent of my gross income . . .

Break the teeth in their mouths, O God . . . Let them go down alive to
the grave . . .

My baby brother. Winston, Winston. Does he break Your Law? What
happen? What happen?

*They murder Winston in the stinking darkness . . . They hate us, Lord.
They afraid of us. Anything we touch is black, to them. And they fear
anything with blackness in it. They right to be afraid, innit?*

*Lord Jesus, make them come to us. Come on their knees. Let them crawl
to us. Let them come and beg us not to destroy them, for Your wrath
destroy them, surely, Lord, Your wrath in us, Your holy anger . . . Surely
this anger come from You . . .*

Let them eat the flesh of their children, Lord

*Winston, Winston. My little brother. Everyone love him. Winston never
hurt no one . . .*

*Shirley, Shirley. She come to me. She beg forgiveness. Her big white
body . . .*
*Her face all wet, shining with tears, blotch red and white, she almost
ugly. Big mess of colours. But she still Shirley . . .*
I bloody hate her. Bloody hate her.
We bathe our feet in the blood of the wicked . . .

*I bloody hate her . . . Bloody love her. Shirley, Shirley. What happen,
what happen?*
How can I ever touch her again?

You are the Lord, there is no other . . .
You have created both darkness and light . . .

Jesus, Lord, shall we never come home?

No . . . Grave . . . Shall Hold His Body Down . . .

48 · May and Alfred

It was May who found him. Of course it was May. Who else could have guessed where Alfred would go? No one worried about him, once he'd done what he had to. A squad car was sent to take him back to hospital, but when May phoned the ward, Alfred hadn't arrived. At the station, no one recalled who was the driver. They hardly seemed to register Alfred's name, as though he had already slipped into the past, fading away as if he'd never been . . .

He'll have asked the policeman to drive him to the Park, she realized, suddenly, sitting there distractedly, pulling at her nails, frowsing her hair, listening to the clock in her empty house, her nest from which all the birds had flown, they had taken Dirk, her child was gone . . . The White family was finished, then.

But it was Alfred, finally, she minded about. Where had he gone, her duck, her dear one?

He'll have asked them to take him to the Park. Of course.

And she pulled on her coat, not her ordinary coat but her good blue coat, the one Alfred liked, for she had a feeling of dread, of occasion, and set off briskly into the wind, the wind that sharpened with the sun, it was a cold clear day, bright as a lemon, everything was seen, everything known . . . Their shame was known. The family shame.

Perhaps she had tried to hide too much.

Perhaps he was right, and she was wrong, but it didn't matter, as long as she found him –

> O that 'twere possible
> After long grief and pain
> To find the arms of my true love
> Round me once again . . .

Alfred Tennyson. *Alfred, Alfred.*

She saw him half lying at the foot of the hill, his hair a frail white flag in the sunshine, and started to run, for she saw he was down, but he rested on one elbow, on the green ground, it had been a clear night, he must be bitter cold . . .

'Alfred, Alfred.'

'Don't take me inside.' He could hardly speak, his teeth chattering, a bad yellow colour to the skin of his face, and the bone of his nose had begun to wear through, she saw it gleam beneath the skin, clear as death in the brilliant sunlight, but she also saw the look in his eyes as he recognized her, unsurprised, joyful, as if he had always known she was coming, as if he had been waiting for her, and his fingers twitched, his arm scarcely lifted but she knew he was reaching for her hand, and she slipped it into his grip of stone, trying to squeeze some warmth into it, he was turning into something else, he had always been a small man, modest, and now he was a statue, still, heroic. She didn't want it, she just wanted Alfred.

She wanted her Alfred. 'Alfred, dear. I'll leave you here and go for help.'

'No. Don't leave me. You said you'd never leave me . . .'

She cradled his shoulders, stroked his head. Still alive, still Alfred's. Her husband's, hers.

'Do you see . . . where we are?'

She looked. She saw they were by the edge of the oval of tarmac where the skate-boarders came, on summer days, at the foot of the hill, ringed with plane-trees. Above them, a single magpie circled. One for sorrow. Then another joined him.

'Yes?' For a moment, it meant nothing.

He meant everything to her.

'The band . . . The bandstand, after the war.' His breathing was bad, harsh as a saw-edge then quiet for a frightening length of time, but he wanted to tell her, wanted to speak, his eyes trying to tell her what he meant, still blue as the sky beneath his wild eyebrows, *Alfred, Alfred*, his eyes still bright.

'Do you remember?'

'Course. You asked me –' she was trying not to cry, not to let him down, 'you took me dancing, and you asked me –'

'We could be together.'

'We are together.'

Cheek to cheek . . . Around the dance-floor, cheek to cheek . . . Very gently, she placed her cheek against her dear one's, and was chafed by its chill, its surprising roughness, and she saw where the bristles were pushing through, perhaps he could no longer shave himself, and the nurses were too busy, May would do it –

No. It no longer mattered. No.

The long struggle could finally finish, the long attempt to keep mess at bay, to be dutiful, to fight against chaos.

Wind in the leaves. Among his people . . .

'I'm sorry, May . . .'

'Don't, Alfred . . .'

'May, dear . . .'

'So proud of you . . .'

His hand fluttered, faint, restless. 'Things to do.'

'No, Alfred . . . hush, dear . . . it's over, love.'

Here in the grass he was safe to sleep.

Cheek to cheek, in each other's arms, and the long war ended, and everything hopeful . . . Slipping away into the past, slipping away beneath the future, and through the dance-floor grew the roots, the great tree-roots pushed and flourished . . .

No Ending

No . . . Grave . . .   *No . . . Grave*

Shirley bore two boys, unidentical twins, two boys conceived on the same day, both olive-skinned, both curly-haired, but one much paler than the other.

Elroy, mercifully, has no doubts. They'll grow up together. They are blood brothers. Elroy, with luck, will be father to both, if his relationship to Shirley survives, for it's hard to bear such grief, such anger. But they lessen a little as time passes, time sweeping onwards, sweeping across . . . blurring the stains, patching the wounds. Babies, baby-clothes, bottles, nappies . . . Kindness, tiredness, ordinariness.

The whole King family loves the babies. They can never be separated from the past, and yet they are alive, and yelling . . . The first little boy was called Winston, of course. The other is Franklin. They're Shirley and Elroy's.

No . . . Grave . . . Shall Hold His Body Down . . .

Who's that walking behind Shirley and her double-buggy, with a puzzled face? She looks rather like a younger Shirley, but thinner, more thoughtful, little gold glasses . . .

The only thing she'd known about her adoption was the name of her family, which was all too common. Then, with the murder, there were pictures in the papers. She looked in the paper and saw her mother.

Nothing is easy. All new to her. But she had no siblings, and now she has two, and suddenly she catches up with Shirley, seizes the buggy, and runs down the road, making them laugh in the late sunshine . . . Shirley can follow her three children.

(Sophie's grief . . . Winston had no children.)

The two funerals had been on the same day, side by side, a triumph of mismanagement. Elroy was no longer speaking to Shirley, and she had been trying to comfort her mother, trying to make May eat and sleep. So Shirley didn't know they were burying Winston, three or four hundred black people come from all over London to protest the murder, to be together.

She turned up with all the White family and twenty or thirty local people, most of them ageing or elderly, to mourn their local Park Keeper. She arrived almost last, with Darren and Susie and May, three different masks of sorrow, in the limousine that followed the hearse, then a small delegation from the Parks Department, solemnly processing before George and Ruby.

What they saw was chaos. No one could park. The press was there, in banks, in droves, shoving cameras and microphones in the faces of weeping, shouting, reluctant people. Darren got out, blinking, miming, oddly fish-like as he took it in, as if he had never seen this before, though he must often have seen it before – but never before when it was his father.

Shirley saw Elroy. And a sea of black faces. Then she saw Dirk's friends. A little phalanx of them. Crewcut youths, pale, stupefied, scowling at the black people. Furious, frightened to see so many. 'White family funeral. Where's the White family funeral? Alfred White. What the fuck is this?'

Perhaps they had come out of respect for Alfred, perhaps they had come to catch a glimpse of Dirk, imagining him handcuffed between two policemen (though Dirk, in fact, had been returned to prison once the news of the mix-up was radioed across, for the police well knew he would never have survived – his small white face behind plate glass, lost, disappointed, shrinking in the distance) – but Shirley thought, what if they've come to make trouble? What if those louts start shouting rude names?

'I'm sorry, Mum,' she said, and she left her, she fought her way across through the crowd, she caught her lover by the arm, and he pushed her away, she touched him again, and he nearly struck her, and she dropped back, she fell into the line behind, the line of his people who were now her people, hers by choice, and Sophie saw her, Sophie couldn't look at her or kiss her but she let her walk by her, she took her hand –

No . . .   Grave . . .   No . . . Grave . . .

Shirley had crossed the river. She walked with his people. The song was deafening, they sang together and it burst from the graveyard, rolled through the Park, soared skyward, skyward, up the sunny hill –

No . . . Grave . . . Shall Hold His Body Down . . .

No . . . Grave . . . Shall Hold His Body Down . . .

Darren, meanwhile, was fighting the press, slugging it out with a man from the *Sun* –

A police helicopter over Hillesden Green Cemetery watched the crowd fan out among the gravestones, hundreds of ants at their invisible purpose.

'How are we supposed to make sense of this lot?'
'No effing idea which side is which.'

No ... Grave ...   *No ... Grave ...*

Close up, you see the two separate streams, the jostling, the little pockets of aggression, the angry looks, the different skins. Move back a little, and you see the river. It has two banks, but all of it mourns. A great tide of people stops in the graveyard, crying, poised on the edge between past and future.

Straight-backed, Sophie and Shirley walk, and Sophie mutters the Psalm of David. *The night will shine like the day. And darkness will be as light ... He has created both darkness and light ...*

Blindly gleaming, stubborn, warm, life in Shirley pushes, quickens.